Praise for one of America's
finest literary talents,
JOHN GARDNER

"One of the best writers in the country . . .
he has style, imagination and intelligence."
St. Louis Post-Dispatch

"An artist of rare imagination and power."
Saturday Review

"A major talent, as good as anyone writing in
America today and better than most."
The Wall Street Journal

"NICKEL MOUNTAIN . . . is shapely and
moving enough to make you believe, while
you are reading it, in ancient forms and
permanent truths."
The New York Times

Also by John Gardner
Published by Ballantine Books:

GRENDEL

THE SUNLIGHT DIALOGUES

OCTOBER LIGHT

THE WRECKAGE OF AGATHON

THE KING'S INDIAN

FREDDY'S BOOK

NICKEL MOUNTAIN

A Pastoral Novel

John Gardner

BALLANTINE BOOKS • NEW YORK

Library of Congress Catalog Card Number: 73-7293

ISBN 0-345-29294-4

This edition published by arrangement with
Alfred A. Knopf, Inc.

Manufactured in the United States of America

First Ballantine Books Edition: January 1975
Fifth Printing: February 1982

For Joan

I

NICKEL
MOUNTAIN

1

In December, 1954, Henry Soames would hardly have said his life was just beginning. His heart was bad, business at the Stop-Off had never been worse, he was close to a nervous breakdown.

Sometimes when he was not in a mood to read he would stand at the window and watch the snow. On windy nights the snow hurtled down through the mountain's darkness and into the blue-white glow of the diner and the pink glitter of the neon sign and away again into the farther darkness and the woods on the other side of the highway. Henry Soames would pull at his lip with his thumb and first finger, vaguely afraid of the storm and vaguely drawn by it. He would imagine shapes in the snow that shot past, mainly his own huge, lumbering shape, but sometimes that of some ominous stranger. Though he stood in the lean-to room behind the diner he could hear the hum of the diner clock, and sometimes he would see in his mind the red and blue hands and, unaware of what he was doing, would try to make out what time it was—twelve, one, quarter-to-three. . . . At last, he would sink down on the bed and would lie there solid as a mountain, moving only his nose and lips a little, troubled by dreams.

Even when they interrupted his sleep he was always glad when people came, that winter. The diner lights were always on, and people knew he didn't mind being roused. The Stop-Off was the last place until you got to the outskirts of Slater, and if the weather was bad, the Stop-Off could be a godsend. Henry would call out, "I'll be right with you," and he'd pull on his robe and hurry to the counter, blinking, and he'd yell, "Great

3

weather for polar bears," and he'd laugh, grim, not fully awake, and would slap the man on the shoulder. Generally it would be drunks that came after two— old men with bad teeth, or no teeth, and liver spots and hair that needed cutting. One old man came especially often, a heavy, dignified old Russian, or a Pole perhaps, named Kuzitski. A junk dealer. He drove an old blue Chevy truck with his name and phone number lettered on the door, and he always wore a suit and vest and in winter a great black coat he'd bought for a song, long ago, at the bus depot in New Carthage. His walk was slow and determined, seemingly not the walk of a drunk but that of a man engrossed. He would seat himself very solemnly and would meditate, then remove his hat and place in on the counter, and finally, politely, he would ask for coffee. There would be beads of ice on his moustache. Henry would serve the man his coffee and would serve himself a piece of apple pie and he'd stand behind the counter while the old man poured whiskey into his coffee and drank. Sometimes after Kuzitski's second cup, Henry would mention his heart.

"They give me a year to live, Mr. Kuzitski," Henry would say. "I had one heart attack already." His tone never quite went with the words, but the old man could no doubt see that Henry was a frightened man. "I get dizzy spells," Henry would say.

Kuzitski would nod sadly, and after a while he would say politely, "Sister of mine had that trouble."

Henry Soames would shake his head and look out the window at the snow and after a minute he would say, laughing shortly, "Well, we all go sometime."

Occasionally he would let it go at that. More often he would press further. He probably had no idea how often he'd said it, the very same words, the same high-pitched voice; certainly Mr. Kuzitski had no idea. "It's a hell of a thing. You just can't make yourself believe it, that's the worst of it. They told me, 'You just lose ninety pounds and you'll live for another twenty years'; but you think I can do it?" He would shake his head. "It's a funny damn world." He would turn and squint out the window a while, trying to think about it, sensing the profundity of it but unable to find the words to express it even to himself. Vague images would come: children, trees, dogs, red brick houses, people he knew. He felt nothing; a heaviness only, a numbness in the chest.

"Nobody ever would marry her," old Kuzitski would say. "I should have loaded her up in the truck and hauled her away to the dump. Ha ha."

Henry would eat, glum, and then he would lean on the counter, looking at his huge, hairy-backed hands, and to fill the silence he would say more. He always spoke calmly at first. He would tell about his father, how he'd had the same trouble, and he'd talk about all a man wanted to do that he never got done, never got around to—places he meant to go, things he promised himself he'd see. "Jesus." Shaking his head.

Henry would begin to pace then, still talking. It seemed to make Mr. Kuzitski uneasy, but Henry had to do it nevertheless. The sound of voices in the diner at three in the morning filled him with a kind of hunger. He would grow excited, gradually, and his words would come faster, and something that rarely showed in him at other times would show in him now: a streak of crazy violence. Like a drunken man, he would clutch his fists against his chest and his voice would get louder and higher in pitch, and sometimes he'd stop pacing to pound the counter or a tabletop, or he'd lift a sugar dispenser and hold it tight in his hand as if thinking of throwing it. Mr. Kuzitski would sit precariously balanced, his widened eyes fixed on the sugar dispenser. Henry must have seen the hopelessness of trying to put what he meant into words, whatever it was, if anything, that he meant. He would check himself, straining to face death bravely, gallantly. But he was a weak

5

man and childish, especially late at night, and all at once he would catch the old man's arm and would cling to him, not shouting now but hissing at him like a snake. His eyes would bulge, and tears would run down to the stubble on his fat jowl. Kuzitski would look down at the floor and, clinging to the counter, would recoil from Henry's grasp.

Though it happened again and again that winter, neither of them was ever ready for it. Henry would be shocked and humiliated, and would apologize and curse himself. He would cover his face with his hands, rubbing his eyes like a bear, and sometimes he would lean on the counter and sob and Kuzitski would rise and would back away toward the door. "I promise you, I'll mention this to no one," Kuzitski would say.

"Thank you, I know I can trust you," Henry would say, crying.

"Not a living soul, no one; I give you my word," Kuzitski would say, and slowly, ponderously, he would leave. Henry would see the wind snatch fiercely at the old man's black coat, and he would feel great compassion.

The old man's promise was sincere: In a general, somewhat foggy way he felt sorry for Henry, and when the taverns closed on a winter night there would be nowhere left to go but home if bad blood between himself and Henry Soames should rule out the Stop-Off. Nevertheless, he forgot to keep his promise, and it came to be understood that Henry Soames was not himself. People began to be unnaturally polite to him and to ask him too often about his health. Little by little, old Kuzitski's experience became a common one. People talked among themselves about the violent streak in Henry Soames (not that they lacked any trace of compassion: The fact remained that the thing was obscene), and they observed that, looking back, one could see that it hadn't come up miraculously out of nowhere. Many a time on a warm summer night he'd locked up his diner and got out his old Ford car and roared up Nickel Mountain like a man hell-bent on destroying himself and maybe collapsing the side of the mountain with him. As for Henry himself, he preferred not to think about it. He watched the snow, his car locked in the garage by drifts, and he waited. Then came spring.

2

The girl appeared as if by magic, like a crocus where yesterday there'd been snow.

He had known her mother and father for years and so of course he had known her too, had watched her grow up. When her father came by to prepare the way, saying that Callie might drop by in the morning to ask about a job, the image Henry had summoned up was of Callie at eleven, a horse-faced, gangling, long-footed girl who stood interminably at the counter, not certain what it was she wanted. But now she was sixteen, not a grown-up but not a child either, and she seemed to him, as all young people seemed to him, beautiful and sad. It was only the weather perhaps, the smell that had been in the air all week of wet, gray-brown hillsides coming to life, roots stirring, trees budding someplace to the south.

She was tall, like her father, and she had the same hand-whittled look, the squareness of nose, cheeks, and ears. But the softness of her skin, the slightly affected tilt of her head, and her eyes, all those she'd gotten from her mother. Especially the eyes, Henry thought. They were gray, friendly, and eager, and at the same time calculating; and like her mother's eyes they made Henry Soames self-conscious.

"What do you want to work in a diner for, Callie?" he said.

"I need experience," she said. The answer came at once, not as if she'd prepared it beforehand but as if it was something she'd known all her life. "She's got drive," he thought, a little uneasy in its presence, "yes, sir." He stared down at the counter, thinking suddenly of Callie's mother as she had been at sixteen, and of how his heart had been broken and how he'd been sure there was nothing left to live for.

"Someday I'm going to New York City," Callie said. Perhaps he looked puzzled. She added quickly, "You can't get a job in New York City unless you've already worked someplace before. A girl in our class at school found that out. I'd hate to tell you what happened to *her* in New York City."

"Mmmm," he said, rubbing his chin. He realized he'd forgotten to shave.

She wasn't as pretty as her mother had been. Her voice was like a boy's, so exactly like a boy's that he had to nod abruptly, puckering his lips to keep from smiling when he noticed it.

She said, suddenly embarrassed, "Actually, I don't *know* what happened to her, I only know what they say."

"Here, here," Henry said, "no harm done." He patted her arm, then drew back his hand immediately and chuckled. "You didn't even mention her name. I like that."

"It wasn't anything personal," she said, looking past him.

"Of course not," he said. "Of course not."

A semi went past and Henry watched it climb the long, steep hill, stand as if poised a moment at the top, then dip out of sight. "You're a fine girl, Callie," he said. "Your folks must be proud."

The words were very moving to him. Her mother had been prettier, but Callie was a girl you had to admire, a girl with a heart. He began to feel terribly sorry for her and, vaguely, for himself and all mankind. Her father worked over in Athensville, at the plow factory, a pretty fair job to judge by the car and the paint on the house; but Frank had always had his troubles. He drank, and according to young Willard Freund he sometimes did worse. It looked to be about up with Callie's parents, and no doubt that was one reason Callie was here. It must be a terrible thing for a girl, Henry thought. A crying shame. He looked at her hands folded on the counter and thought they were like a child's hands, frank, not cautious or self-conscious like a grown-up's. Her mother's hands had been like that once. And yet Callie was sixteen now, a woman. Terrible, he thought. Terrible.

"When you want to start, Callie?"

She lighted up. "Right now, if you can use me."

"Good," he said. "Come on in back, I'll get you one of my aprons."

He lumbered back into the closet off the lean-to room behind the diner and rummaged through the dresser there. When he turned back to his living room the girl was standing by the door to the diner, unwilling to come any farther in, checked perhaps by the clutter, the wrinkled clothes, and magazines, tools, the mateless sock left, strangely clear-cut, like a welt on a woman's arm, on the sunlit rug.

"Excuse—" he began.

She said quickly, "I didn't see where you'd went to," and laughed awkwardly, as if his disappearance had given her a turn. Once again Henry was touched. When she put on the apron she laughed again, a brief, self-conscious laugh aimed, as it seemed to him, at her own thinness rather than at his fat. The apron went around her twice and came clear down to the tops of her shoes, but Henry said, "You look good enough to eat."

She glanced at him with an uneasy smile. "I know that line," she said.

Blood stung his neck and cheeks and he looked away quickly, pulling at his upper lip, baffled.

3

"I'm an old friend of the family," Henry Soames said to Kuzitski that night. "I've known her folks for years."

"A friend in need is a friend indeed," Kuzitski said. He smiled vaguely, thinking back. "Old proverbial expression," he said.

"I went to school with her mother and father," Henry said. "As a matter of fact, Callie's mother's an old flame of mine." He chuckled. "Name's Eleanor. I guess she gave me my first broken heart. I was just about Callie's age at the time. I never really got over it." He shook his head. "Life's a funny thing."

Kuzitski waved his cup very slowly. "Hope springs eternal in the human breast, what oft was thought but ne'er so well expressed," he said. He set down the cup. "Pope." He sat carefully balanced, smiling sadly, deeply satisfied. After a moment he poured more whiskey into his cup.

"Well, it was a long, long time ago," Henry said.

The old man seemed to consider it, stirring his coffee. At last, having thought it out, he said, "We're all of us getting on."

Henry nodded. "That's the way it goes."

"Time comes to turn over the plow to a younger hand." Kuzitski said. He raised the cup solemnly, toasting the future.

"Nobody lasts forever," Henry said.

"Time waist for no man," Kuzitski said, nodding. "Ashes to ashes and duss to duss." He toasted the past.

It was after three, a night deep and still, as if all time and space hung motionless, waiting for a revelation. The old man sat with his cup aloft, miserably smiling, staring with glittering, red-fleshed eyes; then, slowly, he lowered his cup.

Henry laid his hand on the old man's shoulder.

"It's a sad, sad thing," Kuzitski said, blinking and nodding in slow-motion. He looked down into his cup. Empty. "All her life my poor sister Nadia wanted a man and a family. I watched her dry up like old grapes." He raised his fist and shook it slowly, thoughtfully, at invisible forces above the grill-hood. "A man doesn't need that sort of thing. Fact is, he doesn't need anything at all, except when he's young. When he's young a man wants something to die for—some war to fight, some kind of religion to burn at the stake for." He refilled his cup with whiskey, holding the bottle with both hands. "But a man gets over all that. A woman's different. Woman's got to have something to live for." He toasted womanhood, a toast even more grand than the last, on his face the same dazed, miserable smile, then drew the cup very carefully toward his fleshy lower lip. When the cup was empty he set it down and at last, very deliberately, stood up and started for the door.

"That's true," Henry said. He felt a mysterious excitement, as though the idea were something he'd drunk. He watched the old man move slowly to his truck, the truck clear and sharp in the starlight, the highway clear and sharp beyond, the woods so clear, dark as they were, that he almost could have counted every needle on the pine. The truck started with a jerk, came straight for the pumps, swerved off and scraped the RETREADS sign, then wandered onto the road.

He found himself scowling at what was left of the

pie on his plate, and at last it came to him that it wasn't what he wanted. He scraped it into the garbage can. A dizzy spell came, and he leaned on the sink, frightened, fumbling for his pills.

4

The girl wasn't afraid of him as other people were except for some of the drunks. She was quiet at first, her tongue caught between her lips, but quiet because she was concentrating on her work. As she mastered the grill, the menu, the prices, she began to talk a little. When they were cleaning up at the end of the third day she said, "Mr. Soames, do you know a boy named Willard Freund?"

He wiped his brow with the back of his damp arm, the counter rag clutched in his fist. "Sure," he said. "He stops by now and again. He built that car of his in my garage." Her hands moved smoothly from the towel-rack to the rinsed cups in the wire web beside the sink. He grinned.

She closed one eye as she wiped the cup in her hand. "He's sort of nice. In a way I feel really sorry for him because he's so nice."

Henry leaned on the counter, looking out at the darkness, thinking about it. For some reason his mind wandered to the time Callie's father had stolen the rounds from the schoolmaster's chair—Henry Soames' father's chair. Frank Wells had had that smell on his breath even then, but in those days Callie's mother hadn't noticed the smell, or had thought of it as something she'd get around to when the time came. She'd had all her mind on Frank's lean hips and the way he slouched through doors. When Henry Soames' father's chair gave out and the old man was weeping like an obscene old woman on the floor, Callie's mother had said, "Why, isn't Frank Wells the horridest person, Fats?" Frank had grinned, hearing it, but Henry Soames, sweet little Fats, hadn't understood, of course; he'd choked with disgust because his own father was flopping on the floor with his hairy belly showing, like a pregnant walrus, and couldn't get up. But Callie's mother had married Frank in the end. (And hunchbacked old Doc Cathey, diabolical, right in his judgment as usual, had said, "Henry, my boy, human beings are animals, just the same as a dog or a cow. You better accept it." And old Doc Cathey, old even then, had winked and laid his cold-fish hand on Henry's neck.)

After a minute Henry remembered himself and chuckled, "Yes, sir, Willard's a fine boy, Callie." He was vaguely conscious that his fingers were drumming on the counter-top as, chuckling uncomfortably again, he glanced about to see that the percolators were clean and the chili put away.

"He really is the kindest person," Callie said. "I've danced with him after the basketball games sometimes. I guess you know he wants to be a race-car driver. I think he could really do it, too. He's terrific with a car." Her hands stopped moving and she glanced at Henry's chest. "But his dad wants him to go to Cornell. To the Ag School."

Henry cleared his throat. "I think he's mentioned it."

He tried to picture methodical, sharp-boned Callie dancing with Willard Freund. Willard was a swan.

(Henry had sighed, helpless, sitting in the back room with Willard the night the boy had told him of his father's plans. He'd felt old. He hadn't stopped to think about it, the feeling of having outgrown time and space altogether, falling into the boundless, where all contradictions stood resolved. He had listened as if

13

from infinitely far away, and it had come down to this: That night he had given up hope for Willard, had quit denying the inevitable doom that swallows up all young men's schemes, and in the selfsame motion of the mind he had gone on hoping. For perhaps it was true that Willard Freund had everything it took to make a driver (Henry was not convinced of it, though even to himself he'd never pinned down his doubt with words; he knew only that the boy had a certain kind of nerve and a hunger to win and the notion—a notion that everyone on earth has, perhaps, at least for a while—that he was born unique, set apart from the rest), but even if it was true that he had what it took, there was no guarantee that he would keep it. Things happened as a boy got older. Speedy Cerota, the man who ran the jeep place down in Athensville, had been lightning once. He'd married a girl that drove in the ladies' and they'd had three kids as quick as that, and one day Speedy had come in second—bad car, he said —and then fourth, then fifth, and pretty soon, without his ever knowing what had happened, it was over, he couldn't pass a stoneboat. But as surely as Henry Soames knew that, he knew too that you never knew for sure until it happened. And even if you knew beforehand that what they wanted, the grandiose young, was stupid in the first place and impossible to get in the second, even then you had to back them. If it wasn't for young people's foolish hopes it would all have ended with Adam. Henry Soames thought: *What could I say?*

He was too old for such hopes. Nevertheless, he had rubbed his palms on his legs, that night, brooding. A vague idea of taking his mother's money out of the bank in Athensville for Willard had crossed his mind. It wasn't doing anything there—molding and drawing interest for him, Henry, who wouldn't pick it up with a gutter fork. It had never been his any more than it was his father's. Hers. Let her climb up over her big glassy headstone and spend it. "Remember you've got Thompson blood," she would say, and his father would laugh and say, "Yes, boy, look at the bright side." And he would feel threatened, nailed down. Sometimes even now he would bite his lip, giving way for a second to his queer old fantasy of some error by Doc Cathey or the midwife, for well as Henry Soames knew who he was, the idea that a man might be somebody else all his life and never be aware of it—live out the wrong doom, grow fat because a man he had nothing to do with by blood had died of fat—had a strange way of filling up his chest. In bed sometimes he would think about it, not making up some new life for himself as he'd done as a child, merely savoring the immense half-possibility.

But it wasn't money that Willard would need. It was hard to say what it was that Willard needed.)

"Well," Henry heard himself saying, "yes, sir, Willard's a fine boy, it's a fact."

But by now Callie was thinking of other things. Glancing around the room, she asked, "That everything that needs doing?"

He nodded. "I'll drive you up to your house," he said. "It's cold out."

"No thanks," she said, her tone so final it startled him. "If you do it tonight you'll end up doing it every night. It's only a few steps."

"Oh, shucks now," he said. "It's no trouble, Callie."

She shook her head, a sort of fierce old-womanish look around her eyes, and pulled on her leather jacket.

Henry studied her, puzzled, but it was clear she wouldn't change her mind. He shrugged, uneasy, and watched her cross to the door, then pass from the diner's blue-pink glow into darkness, heading up the hill. Two minutes after she'd disappeared from sight he went to his lean-to room in back. He pulled off his shirt, then stood for a long time looking at the rug, wondering what it all meant.

5

As always, it was hard to put himself to bed. It had become a ritual with him, this waiting between the peeling-away of the sweat-soaked shirt from chest, belly, arms, and the unbuckling of his wide leather belt. Doc Cathey had chortled, "You lose ninety pounds, Henry Soames, or you're a goner. Like your old man before you. You'll sit up in bed some one of these mornings and you'll turn white with the effort of it, and *click*." Doc had snapped his fingers, brown, bony fingers that wouldn't go fat if you fed 'em on mashed potatoes for a month. And his voice had been aloof, amused, as though he'd gotten his JP and MD jobs mixed up. Doc sometimes did that, people said, laughing about it while Henry dished up their orders. That had been before Henry went in for his checkup; otherwise maybe he mightn't have noticed Doc's manner. Doc would talk to an old offender, they said, in his kindly-family-doctor voice and to an expectant mother with his high and mighty sneer. And he, Henry Soames, had paid a dollar to be told what he'd known for most of his life, right down to the click, and ten for pills, and four dollars more for the little brown bottle that ruined his appetite all right but made his belly ache like he had the worms and his eyes go yellow in the mirror. A man didn't owe his flesh to his doctor; he could still choose his own way out. Three dollars' worth of pharmacist's bilge poured down the sink was maybe thirty bellyaches avoided. Old Man Soames had used whiskey for the pain, and whiskey—that and the little white pills—would be good enough for Henry.

He sat still on the edge of the bed, breathing deeply.

There was a little wind outside. On the hill just beyond the lean-to window the scraggly pines were swaying and creaking. Between the pines there were maples, lower than the pines, and below the maples, weeds. As always on windy nights, there was no sign of the low-crawling fog. He sometimes missed it a little when it didn't come. Because it brought customers, maybe. "A man gets to feeling weird," one of the truckers had told him once. "Ten miles of sharp turns stabbing out at you from the mist, cliffs as gray as the fog itself to tell you you're still on the road, and now and then a shadowy tree or a headlight, dead looking, everything in sight, dead. And lonely as hell. Brother." He'd shivered, hunching his shoulders in for warmth and sucking down the coffee Henry served him on the house. From the wide front window of the diner Henry would see the fog, just after sunset, sliding down the hill like an animal; and then again sometimes the fog would just appear out of nowhere, ruminating. It would lose itself here in this pocket between two hills, and then in the morning sun it would shrink up into itself and vanish, leaving the trees wet and the highway as hard and blue as the curved blade of a knife. The lines of the hills north and south of Henry's Stop-Off would be sharper then, and the barns that belonged to Callie's father would stand out like tombstones after thaw.

But tonight was a perfect night for truckers; it was foolishness to sit here hoping, if he was. Which he wasn't. He'd had one heart attack already, and he'd never known it at the time. It took all his effort to keep his mind off that. When a man's heart stopped, the whole machine ought to shudder, lights ought to flash in the head, the blood should roar: But his heart was scarred, and he hadn't the faintest idea when it had happened, as if some hand had flicked a switch off, then on again, letting the machine freewheel for an instant and then dig in as before. He might have

17

died without ever knowing he was dying—a year, a year-and-a-half ago maybe, and all that had happened since might have been nothing.

A truck was coming up 98 now, but he wouldn't pull in even though the neon was on, as it always was, and one of the three lights in the diner. He'd want to push on, no doubt, to please his boss or his union or the people at Morse Chain. But maybe a drunk would stop, seeing the light burning away in there like an altar lamp. The semi was speeding-up on the quarter-mile level run in front of the Stop-Off for the hill a little ways north—the hill that would rise and suddenly break, pushing your heart up out of your chest, to drive three miles down banked curves into New Carthage. The truck was rolling now, maybe up around fifty, depending on the load. The grind of gears came, meaning he was halfway up the hill, and the new engine scream pulling down to a low, pained roar; another shift, to low, to low-low, the pounding throb—far away, though—and then the purr at the peak of the hill and the purr rising, pulling back against the thrust, strangling itself on the downgrade. All a mile away now, from the sound of it; so faint that you couldn't know how much of it you heard and how much was only a tingle in your skin.

Maybe he should get out the Ford, he thought. But no. He was tired, and he was in no mood, these days, for rattle-assing over the hills, thanks to the tightness in his chest. A bad sign, no doubt. He'd have to draw up his will, as Doc Cathey had told him.

Outside it was quiet now, except for the light breeze. He could smell rain. It would be a good idea to check the cardboard in the window; easier than getting up after he was in bed, when the rain, if it should come, would be batting down and seeping over his dusty windowsill and onto his neatly stacked books—down over the pitiful leather-bound Bible that had belonged to his father and had *his* father's and his father's father's names penned into it under "Deaths," between the Old and New Testaments. No other names; no wives, no children. The Bible had ridges across its back like the ridges on one of his mother's people's lawbooks, which was funny, when you thought of it, because a lawbook was what it had been for his father. And that too was funny, because now it had a fermented, museum smell from the rain that always seeped onto the books no matter how careful you were with the window beforehand.

Beside the old Bible he could see his father's anemic-looking schoolbooks and, on the shelf below, *National Geographics*, Shakespeare, an old almanac with notes in the margin, written in his father's childish hand. These books, too, had the musty smell, and something more complicated: a burnt-out, un-lived-in smell like —he had to think a moment—a hotel room. A sudden, unexpected feeling of guilt bloomed inside him, pushing up through his neck. He knew what it was for an instant, but then he had lost it again. He concentrated his gaze on the books, but whatever it was that had come to him was gone.

"Damn rotten shame," he said aloud, vaguely.

His father had been a dairyman first, Henry remembered his mother's saying, and he'd failed at it, no doubt because of the pain of hauling his weight like a twelve-foot cross from cow to cow. After that the poor devil had sold apples from his orchard, and then, or perhaps before that, he'd raised sheep, painted road-signs, clerked in the feedstore in Athensville. Nothing had worked. In spite of his tonnage, he had been a sentimental dreamer, as Henry's mother had put it. "Should've been a monk."—Making sure her little Henry would not trudge in his father's footsteps. One job after another would cave in under his father, and she, who came from a fair-off family, lawyers mostly, would give him just barely enough of her money to set him up in the new project which, sure as day, would fail. He was as simple and harmless all his life as a great, fat girl. It was the floundering harmlessness, no doubt, that Henry's mother had hated in him. And so she'd driven him to schoolteaching at last. Because, she had said, he'd been through high school and couldn't do anything *but* read books. "You don't need capital for teaching school. Maybe it'll make a man of you," she'd said. And so Henry's father had suffered the final indignity, plopped sweating in front of people like Frank Wells, enduring their pranks as a woman would, with his own son in the classroom, and in between times teaching them multiplication and poetry and Scripture. Which explained why Henry's mother's name had not been put in the Bible under "Deaths." It was hard to say why his grandmother's name wasn't there. Maybe his father's womanishness had become, at last, a hatred of women in general, or at any rate a refusal to admit that they lived and died. His last delusion: that here at least, between the Old and New Testaments, a man stood on his own. (But Doc Cathey had said once, pushing his crooked knuckles down in his coat's side pockets and shaking his head, "Solid as stone your daddy was. Solid as stone.")

He fitted his hands down beside his legs on the edge of the bed, feeling the power in his fingers. He leaned forward over his knees and pushed up slowly. He made his way to the window above the books.

The cardboard windowpane was snug, this time. It wouldn't let the water in no matter how bad the storm. He ran two fingers over the spine of the Bible.

The ridges on the leather were dry and cracked, but queerly slippery like the petals of an old pressed flower. Inside, it was as though someone had ironed every page, scorching the paper a little and making it brittle. The two names, his grandfather's and his grandfather's father's, had been scribbled in hastily and were almost unreadable. Henry frowned, not so much thinking as waiting for a thought to come. He laid the Bible down gently and went up front again for the ballpoint pen.

When he'd written in the names, with all the dates he could remember, he half-closed the book, then paused and stood for perhaps two minutes staring at the gold on the edges of the pages. He racked his brains for what it was that had slipped his mind, that had come and vanished again in an instant as he wrote, but then, discovering nothing, he put the Bible back where it went and, after another pause, recrossed the room. Standing across the room from the bookshelf he could see the prints his hands left in the smooth skin of dust on the Bible's cover.

He lowered himself onto the bedside and closed his eyes for a moment. In his mind, or under his eyelids, he could still see the gold tooling on the Bible, and beyond it a pattern of crisscrossed distances. Slowly the lines seemed to form letters, a name in gold. He felt his forehead muscles tightening, and the nerves trembled in the back of his neck. But before he knew what it was he was dreaming, he was awake again, staring at the Bible as before, or almost as before: staring from a new point in time now, perhaps only minutes after the other, perhaps several hours.

(What would he have missed if he'd died, that first time? Had anything happened? Anything at all?)

While he slept, that night, old man Kuzitski's light blue junk-truck wandered off the road, nudged through the guard rail, and rolled down a sixty-foot embankment. Everything burned but the door, which fell free and lay in a blackberry thicket (the branches still gray and limp this early in the spring), the lettering clear and sharp in the moonlight: *S. J. Kuzitski . Fl 6–1191.*

6

George Loomis pulled in a little before noon, on his way back up from Athensville to his place on Crow Mountain. He left the pickup idling by the side of the diner as he always did—George's truck was a devil to start—and he came in whistling, cheerful as a finch. He slid off his old fatigue cap and slid himself onto the counter stool by the cash register in one single motion, and he banged on the counter-top with his gloved fist and said, "Hey, lady!"

Callie smiled when she saw who it was. "Why, George Loomis!" she said.

He was close to thirty, but he had the face of a boy. He'd had more troubles in his almost thirty years than any other ten men in all the Catskills—he'd gotten one ankle crushed in Korea so that he had to wear a steel brace around one of his iron-toed boots, and people said he'd broken his heart on a Japanese whore so that now he secretly hated women; and when he'd come home, as if that wasn't enough, he'd found his mother dying and the farm gone back to burdocks and Queen Anne's lace. But there wasn't a sign of his troubles on his face, at least not right now.

"You working here now, Callie?" he said.

"Couple three days," she said.

He shook his head. "You don't let that old fat bastard push you around, hear? And make sure he pays you cash. Tightest damn man in seven counties."

"George Loomis, you ought not talk that way," Callie said soberly. But then she laughed.

"How come you're out in broad daylight, George?" Henry said.

"Oh, every once in a while I like to remind myself how things look." Then: "Been to Athensville with a load of grist."

"Smash your hammermill, George?" Henry said.

"Not me," he said, very serious. "Damn shovel did it. You care to buy a good shovel, Henry? Assemble it yourself?"

Henry laughed and Callie looked puzzled, as if she got it all right but didn't see anything funny about it. George said, "You hear about old man Kuzitski?" still smiling.

Henry shook his head.

"Tried to make a new road, I guess. Killed himself all to hell."

"What are you talking about?" Henry said.

George shrugged. "That's what they say. Found the pieces down the foot of Putnam's cliff this morning. I drove by to look, but there's troopers climbing all over it, and they won't let you stop."

Callie stared out the window, perfectly still.

"Christ," Henry said. "Poor devil." He shook his head, his chest light.

George said, "Tally ho, junkman."

"George Loomis, you're *vile*," Callie said, whirling. He looked at his gloves. "Sorry," he said, suddenly withdrawn. "I didn't know you were related to him."

Henry squinted, one hand on the counter, seeing in his mind, as though it were all a part of one picture, the old man lifting his cup in a toast, George staring at his leather gloves, Callie standing with her jaw set, looking out the window. Beyond the drab hill and the deep blue mountains the sky was the color of old dry shale. He said, "What can I fix you, George?"

He seemed to think about it a moment. Then, slowly, studiously not looking at Callie, he stood up. "I guess I better move on, Henry." He smiled, but his eyes were still remote. "Hell of a lot to do this afternoon." He looked down at his gloves again.

When he'd left, Henry took a pill and went into the lean-to room in back and sat down. He could hear Callie fixing herself a hamburger, banging the scraper on the grill as if to smash it. He put his face in his hands, thinking, fighting his own urge to break things —starting, maybe, with her, and then maybe George Loomis. He could hear Jim Millet's John Deere popping and growling on a hillside a half-mile away, and Modracek's Farmall whining down on the flats, and the thought of good sensible grown men at their farm work, this year like last year and the year before— and a hundred thousand years before that—calmed him a little. You had to be patient with young people. It was natural for them to be pious, full of noise and sanctimonious gesture, sure of their creeds. The hell with it then. Nevertheless he clenched his fists, furious at their intrusion into the sanctuary of his tiredness, and if anything worthless had lain handy he would have smashed it. After a while he remembered he was out of cut potatoes for french fries and got up.

Callie said, "Maybe I was wrong to snap like that." It was an apology, not an admission, really, or so it seemed to Henry. The idea that she might actually have been wrong was the farthest thing from his mind.

He compressed his lips. "Not wrong, exactly," he said. He thought of a great deal he could tell her, a whole lifetime of words, in a way, and he began to get mad again. But beyond the woods the mountains stretched out tier on tier, farther than the eye could see, dark blue fading to lighter and lighter, merging with the sky, three hawks flying above the trees, getting smaller and smaller, and he couldn't think where to begin.

He said, "He lived alone. Why should anybody pretend to be sorry he's dead?" His eyes filled with tears all at once.

Callie patted his arm, passing him on her way to the sink. "Well, it's all for the best, I suppose."

It was then that he exploded. "Shit," he bellowed, and he hit the counter so hard the metal napkin dispensers tipped over and a mustard pot fell to the floor and splattered.

She stared, frightened. "All I meant—" she began. But Henry stormed out to his car.

7

Henry Soames' feelings about having a girl here working for him were mixed, to say the least. He'd run the Stop-Off alone for so long, summer and winter, never closing even on Christmas from one year to the next except when he went out for an hour or so for a drive or to pick up something in town, that the place had become an extension of himself. The work in the diner or out at the pumps was as natural to him as walking or breathing, and to hand over jobs to somebody else was like cutting off fingers. It might have been different if business were heavier now than it had been before; but business never changed much here—it picked up a little from July to September, when the tourists passed through (only a few of them ever came in: people too low on gas to make it to the bigger, shinier stations farther on)—but even when business hit its peak he could handle it himself. When he'd hired Callie it had never entered his mind to wonder if he needed her; but he thought about it constantly now. He wondered how long she'd be likely to stay, how much he'd let himself in for. Keeping her busy, hard worker that she was, meant that he himself had, really, nothing to do. And that was the least of it. He'd spent a good deal of his time, in the old days, sitting at the counter reading the paper or talking with some farmer about the weather. He couldn't have Callie doing that —not at ninety cents an hour. She wouldn't have wanted it anyway. So he made up jobs for her, jobs he'd put off year after year not only because they were unimportant but because in fact he didn't want them done: painting the gas pumps, tearing the yellowed old signs off the diner windows, oiling the floor, planting flowers. The character of the place began to change, and it made him uneasy: He felt like a man away from home—felt, in some way he could not quite pin down, false, like a man belligerently arguing for something he didn't believe in. Worse yet, he had to make up jobs for himself. He couldn't very well just sit there letting Callie do all the work. So he cleaned the garage that had looked like a dog's nest for fifteen years— sorted the bolts and put them in boxes, hung up his tools (he found seven Phillips screwdrivers he'd forgotten he had), replaced the cardboard in the windows, swept and washed the floor till you could have eaten off it. People began to comment on how nice the place looked, and business improved. That is, people he didn't know or liked began to come in and bother him with questions about the Indians or complaints about what he didn't have on the menu. Above all, Henry regretted the loss of solitude. All his life, or all his adult life anyway, he'd thought of himself as a lonely man; but he learned the truth about himself now. If it pleased him when people came by to talk—some farmer he'd known for twenty-five years, or old Kuzitski, or Willard Freund—it also pleased him to be able to be by himself sometimes, to stretch out for a nap in the middle of the day or take off his shoes in the back room and sit with a magazine. He did it sometimes even now, but it wasn't the same when you had to make an announcement about it and throw in some kind of excuse.

On the other hand, he liked her, and at times it was very good to have her around. She made him positively glow, now and then. She treated him like a kindly old uncle she'd known all her life, telling him about baby-sitting with the Dart kids or her work for Mrs. Gil-hooley when the thrashers came; talking about her parents, school, the time she'd gone to Albany with her cousin Bill, how much she'd saved so far for her escape to New York. In fact, sometimes he loved her like a daughter. Once when he was sitting on the cus-tomers' side of the counter reading *Scorchy Smith* she came up in front of him and picked off his steel-rimmed glasses and said, "You ought to get different glasses, Mr. Soames. You look like a Russian spy." "You can't teach an old dog new tricks," he said crossly. She smiled, and when she put the glasses back on him her touch was so gentle he felt for an instant as if time had stopped and all the sadness on earth was pure illusion.

But even the fondness he felt for her, when he wasn't resenting the changes she'd made in the Stop-Off and himself, was complicated. Henry Soames knew enough of life to know that, after the first warmth, Callie's friendliness would cool. People were like that, that was all. And though he dreaded the cooling off and halfheartedly fought it by keeping out of her way sometimes, he was resigned. Callie Wells surprised him, though. She talked more and more freely with him as the days passed. Sometimes the corners of her mouth would tuck in as though with disgust, but she laughed with him sometimes, too, and they—he and she—be-gan to understand little signs like the clearing of a throat or pursed lips intended to suppress a smile or, again, slight irritation. She seemed for the most part not to mind, or rather to forgive, the weak, sentimental Soames in his blood. It came to him full force one night when he was serving a trucker.

He was a little blond man with nervous eyes and a wide nose and a way of holding his cigarette between his thumb and middle finger. When Henry brought his coffee, the trucker said, "How's business, Slim?"

"Can't complain," Henry said rather loudly. "You?" With nothing to do but watch the man drink his coffee, Henry stood grinning behind the counter waiting for conversation.

"Can't complain," the man said, looking off down the counter.

Henry remembered what the man had said last time he'd come in, and, thinking vaguely of himself, George Loomis, old man Kuzitski, Henry leaned forward and asked, his voice low, "How's the wife?"

The man glanced at Callie bending over to restock the gum and candy counter. "Oh, not bad, not bad," he said. "About the same." He settled his teeth down over his tongue, grinning, still watching Callie.

Henry planted his elbows on the counter and shook his head. "I sure hope things'll work out for you." He reached out and touched the man's shoulder, then drew his hand back, shaking his head again.

"No, no, everything's dandy, thanks." The man rubbed his shoulder as if Henry had stung it, and he got up. He tilted his head in Callie's direction and said very softly, "Branching out, Slim?"

At first the question seemed to make no sense. But the trucker winked—Callie was standing now with one hand on her hip—and Henry understood. He blushed, then chuckled, angry. "Hell, no," he said, "Callie works here in front."

The trucker strolled over to the candy counter and smiled, his head cocked. "Buy you sumpm, honey?"

She liked it all right. Henry couldn't very well miss that. But she said, "No, I work here. Thanks kindly, though." There was a kind of grim loyalty in her tone that didn't go with the smile and the flush of pleasure in her cheeks. Henry was puzzled at first, then pleased.

The man went on staring at her, grinning; but she wasn't used to truckers yet, and much as she wanted to play his game—as it seemed to Henry, at any rate— she couldn't, and her pleasure changed to something else. A kind of tightening came around her eyes, and the smile became fake. "Did you want something?" she said.

He went on grinning, but now it was the trucker who was embarrassed. Henry went to him and said heartily, "Finest selection of candy bars in New York State. Everything fresh this week. Something for the kids?"

Hastily, a little clumsily, the man bought a pack of Camels, threw out one last grin, and left.

"Stop by again next time you're passing," Henry shouted, leaning over the counter. But the poor devil was hurrying toward his idling truck, turning up his collar against the shout. The cab door slammed and the truck clanked off up the hill, the stainless steel glinting in the moonlight.

Henry bit his lip. The man had been afraid of him —like all the others, except Callie, maybe, or some old, old friend, or a drunk. That was what had sent him into his big-man act and finally pushed him out the door. People shied from you when you tried to get to them, talk of a wife's sickness, a jackknifed truck, hoping to make them feel at home. And if they didn't shy away right off, it was worse. He thought of old Kuzitski, how he, Henry, had ranted and raved at the poor devil when it was all Kuzitski could do to keep upright, and then others, too, when Kuzitski hadn't proved enough. He would laugh too loudly and maybe even get really excited and pound the counter, and sweat would shine on his forearms where the sleeves were rolled tight, and all on account of the weather or the weight-limit laws, the general stupidity of things. And then by God they would shy!—would run like somebody'd tried to rape them, and maybe not come back. Or if they came, they came back to stare one more time at all that fat or now, maybe, to flirt with Callie. Hell of a place for a girl like that, here where all she saw was truckers or drunks.

("And what do you think he *does* sittin' up in his room all night?" Willard Freund had heard the man at the feedstore say. And the man had answered himself, "Why, he boozes, man! You ever seen him drive?"

And Willard had said, looking down and cracking his knuckles, "I know it's a stupid damn lie, Henry. I just thought you'd want to know what they're saying.")

Drunk. Maybe they were right. Not drunk from whiskey, but drunk from something else, maybe. Drunk from the huge, stupid Love of Man that moved through his mind on its heels, empty and meaningless as fog, a Love of Man that came down in the end to wanting the whole damn world to itself, an empty diner, sticky places on the counter stools, bolts and old wrenches, sheer pins, cotter-keys, baling wire up to your knees on the floor of the garage. Drunk with muscle and fat and padding around his circles in a grease-stinking lean-to behind a trucker's diner. So he pounded the counter about the weather or where he'd have gone if he'd ever lit out, or he rattle-assed through the mountains in his '39 Ford.

On a clear night you could make it to the top of Nickel Mountain and back, teetering in the square black Ford, the walls pinning you in like the sides of an upended coffin, bumping down gravel and macadam roads and over the warped planks of narrow bridges that rocked when you hit and echoed *brrrack!* through the hills and glens. The trees would slide into the headlight beams and the wind whipping through the open window made you feel like Jesus H. Christ charioting to heaven. Nickel Mountain! That was where the real hills were, even when you stayed on the highway. And when you came whamming down around a corner, letting her coast free as a hawk, you'd suddenly see the river hundreds of feet below, on your left. Even by daylight it was beautiful: flat, blue shale ledges, the black river, misty fields, and the cluttered, peeling brick houses of Putnam Settlement. But at night, with the ledges outlined in icy blue like glass, rippling panes of moonlight on the water—Christ! A trucker had gone off that spot once, poor devil. Bad brakes, probably. That was the funeral that had been up in Utica. It was a long time ago now. Ten years? Well, the man had chosen beautiful scenery for it. Beautiful. That was the big mistake in Henry Soames' father's life: to sit, waiting for it, in his bed. She'd done a job on him, all right.

He ran his hands over his chest and sides. He was still staring at the door as if to hurl angry apologies at the trucker's blackened tailpipe. Callie stood leaning on the cutting board, her hands on her hips, looking at him. When he glanced at her, she asked, "Did that man really have a wife, Mr. Soames?"

He nodded. "Diabetes. All she can eat is Jello." He turned heavily and put the dirty cup and spoon in the sink.

"He's got a nerve, then, *I'd* say."

Henry scowled, seeing her again with her hand on her cocked hip, smiling, playing with sex the way little boys play with flares along the railroad tracks—and seeing, too, the trucker, with a wife home dying, but for all that there he stood grinning at Callie like a sly old bull—and seeing himself, Henry Soames, reaching out like a fruit to pat the man's shoulder. "I'm getting to be a damned old woman," he said. He pulled at his upper lip.

She didn't dispute it. "Well, you're a nice old woman," she said, not smiling. She sounded tired. She turned to look out vacantly at the darkness. He found he couldn't make out her features distinctly. Eyes burning out like the rest of him, he thought. A sharp, brief pain came into his chest then vanished, a little like a mouse peeking out of his hole then ducking back. He heard her words again in his mind, a nice old woman, and he was touched. Touched and depressed.

He leaned on the front of the sink and waited for his breathing to calm. He was always waiting, these days. For customers, for the grill to heat, for night, for morning and the tuning-up of the blasted little gray and white speckled birds outside his window. How long? he wondered. Another tentative pain. He cleared his throat.

8

It was four nights after the trucker came that Henry found out exactly how touchy his situation was. A Saturday. George Loomis came in drunk as a lord and said, "Henry Soames, you old somvabitch, I come to take the place of the late Kuzitski."

Callie knew as well as Henry that that was merely George Loomis's way, that the speech was as much an apology as anything else, however ugly; the only kind of apology George Loomis knew how to make. Or if she didn't know, she was a fool. But she spun around when he said it and glared at him.

"What a horrible thing to say!" she said.

"Yes'm," he said.

She said, "You're drunk. You ought to get home to bed."

"Now, Callie," Henry said.

"Drink's very wicked," George said, nodding. " 'S the devil's helper. Ought to be ashamed. Come sit 'n my lap here tell me 'bout Demon Drink." He lunged over the counter suddenly, snatching at her hand, but Callie dodged him. Her face went white and she said in dead earnest, "I'll break your brains for you, George Loomis, that's what I'll do."

George sat down again, smiling as if sadly, leaning on his hand. "She's given her heart to another," he said, looking at Henry. He turned back to Callie, drawing himself erect. "He's a son of a whore, Miss Wells," he said. "I say it for your own good. He'll get drunk every night and he'll beat you with a stick."

She looked as though she really would hit him— her fists clenched, her cheek muscles taut—and Henry went over to get between them.

"George, let me get you some coffee," he said. He got out a cup and saucer.

"Don't mean no harm," George said. "Just trying to do the Christian thing."

Henry nodded solemnly, filling the cup.

"Callie's lovely girl," George said. "Girl with real spirit. Admire her very much."

Henry said, "Have some coffee."

"Deeply devoted to Callie Wells. Ser'ously considering marriage. But at the moment—" He paused, his face gray. "At the moment, sorry to say—very sick."

Henry's eyes widened and he waved at Callie. "Get a pan," he said.

She jumped, then ran to the sink for the chili pan and brought it over. George vomited. When he was through, they got him into the lean-to room in back and stretched him out on a blanket on the rug. He fell asleep at once. Henry kneeled beside him, patting his shoulder as he would a child's, shaking his head.

"Why do people *do* things like that?" Callie said. She stood in the doorway, her head leaning back on the frame and her eyes narrowed. The white of her blouse stood out sharply against the pale red neon glow on the diner window behind her.

"That's what love does to a man," Henry said, meaning it as a joke but getting the tone wrong. He got up. He knew well enough that love was not George's trouble. If somebody else had been there instead of Callie it would have been somebody else that George admired very much. Callie said, "Pah."

He seated himself on the edge of the bed feeling old as the world. George Loomis looked dead, lying on the floor with the steel brace on his boot sticking out below the bottom edge of the cover. He looked as if he'd fallen there from a great height. Callie's face was drawn to a half-wince as though she could barely stand the smell.

A kind of excitement began to rise in Henry Soames' stomach. It was important, all at once, that Callie understand the confused and complicated emotions he'd never been able to find words for even to himself. He pulled at his right hand with his left and rocked toward her a little. "George Loomis is a fine boy," he said. Then, in confusion, "And Willard's a fine boy, too. And you're a fine girl, Callie." She watched with her head drawn back a little, eyebrows lowered. And then suddenly he was babbling, telling her—and though it enraged him, he couldn't stop— about how his mother had hated his father, about old man Kuzitski's sister, about darkness and the sound of rain in his childhood. The words came out every which way, jumbled poetry that almost took wing but then pulled down into garble and grunt, and he got to his feet and went to her and closed his hands on her arms, hissing at her, his eyes full of tears, until, abruptly, her eyes wide, she pulled away. They stood still as two trees, hardly breathing.

"I'm sorry," he moaned, covering his face with his clenched fists.

She didn't move or speak for a long while. Then she said, keeping her distance, "You'd better get some sleep, Henry."

He went back to the bed, careful not to step on George, and sat down again, as miserable as he'd ever been in his life. "I meant," he said after a deep breath, "that people—" He let it trail off.

She stood silent, watching him as if from far away.

Then she said, "Here, I'll help you off with your shoes."

"Don't trouble," he said, grieved at having made her feel she was partly to blame, or grieved because he'd made a fool of himself and had left her no way to get free from him except by a gesture of charity, the kind of gift one gives to cripples. But she ignored him and came to kneel between him and the inert George Loomis. Her collar was low, open, and he could see the slight blue-white curve of her breasts. When she glanced up and saw that he was looking at her a paleness came to her cheeks and she raised one hand instinctively to her collar. He shifted his gaze to his own huge belly and said nothing, pushed to the final humiliation.

She sat on her heels and said, "Is that better?"

He nodded. "I'm sorry," he said. "You mustn't let me keep you this late again. I can't tell you—"

"It's all right," she said. Her lips formed an angry pout, but the anger seemed to have nothing much to do with him. It was as though she too, at sixteen, was growing old.

He seemed to stare at her for several minutes, meeting her eyes, but then he realized she was gone. For a moment he wasn't quite sure she'd been here at all. In his mind he saw, all at once, Mr. and Mrs. Frank Wells eyeing a nervous, stoop-shouldered trucker who wanted to marry their daughter. And he could see the glee of old man Cathey, when the service was over, kissing the bride—a dear-old-family-doctor, not a JP kiss. Henry pulled off his shirt, then sat in nothing but his trousers, trying to rearrange the words and gestures into something that would express his huge, jumbled thoughts. He clenched his fists, struggling to keep her from kneeling in front of him again in his memory. But the memory changed for the worse. In his dreams that night the Soames in his blood rose again and again like a gray-black monster out of a

midnight ocean: He dreamed of himself in bed with
her, misusing her again and again violently and in un-
godly ways. Then, disgusted with himself, his chest
burning, he found himself half-sitting on his bed with
sunlight in his room and the sound of birds. George
Loomis sat against the wall across from him, his eyes
tight shut, both his hands clinging to his head. He
opened his eyes for an instant, then snapped them
shut again.

"People are no damn good," George said.

Henry could hear the churchbell ringing very faintly, far away, at the New Carthage Salem Baptist
Church.

"Oh, well," he said, shrugging, sagging where he
stood. He thought about it, or thought about things in
general, then sighed and nodded. "Ah, well," he said.

9

Willard Freund had found out about some fool contest,
first prize a thousand dollars. By God he knew as
much as anybody, he said, about customizing cars. He
had to read Henry the contest rules in the magazine,
and he had to show him the drawings he'd done this
afternoon. They went to the lean-to room in back, and
Henry sat down on the side of his bed and closed his
eyes, listening to Willard read. Willard read slowly,
like a man reading nothing but headlines or a lawyer
stressing the importance of every phrase. When Henry
would look at him, frowning a little, trying not to
seem too skeptical, Willard would lean over the table
farther, reading more slowly and insistently than before. It went on and on, stipulation on stipulation, and
Henry's mind wandered to when he'd been Willard

Freund's age. Old hollyhocks and the yellow brick houses of Putnam Settlement, over by the mountain rose rectangular and dull in Henry's mind. People he'd known a long time ago came back to him, and people who'd been younger then, still full of life. There was his father, huge and motionless as a boulder down in the bottom of a gorge, and Doc Cathey, parchment-skinned, grinning, swinging his serpentine walking stick, squinting over his cheekbones. There was Callie's mother, soft and white and bosomy in those days, and Willard's father, sly and casual, drawing out the faults of a holstein while arithmetic clicked behind his fat-lidded eyes. They'd had great hopes in those days. There were important things to do.

"Damn it, Henry, it's a natural," Willard said. "Christ, they've ruled *out* all the real competition. No pros, no relatives of GM or Fisher or anybody that counts! And look!" He spread out his drawings and Henry got up and went over to the chair across from Willard. He adjusted his glasses and drew the nearest of the drawings to him. A needle-nosed, wing-fendered car, high in back, tortuously drawn on yellow paper.

"I thought you wanted to drive, Willard," Henry said.

"Hell's bells, I could drive to the moon and back on a thousand dollars." He jabbed at the paper with one squared, big-boned finger. "What do you think?"

"I don't know, Willard," he said. "God knows I don't know much about designing cars."

"What do you think, though?" He was squinting, his cheek muscles tensed, watching Henry's face.

Henry looked down at the paper again, first through his glasses, then over them, and Willard got out a cigarette and lit it.

Henry said, "It's a fine-looking car all right." Then: "There is one thing, maybe. It doesn't look—" He couldn't find the way to say it. He tried to shrug it off, back down and merely praise the car, but Willard pressed him and, finally, feeling like a fool, he let it come out: "It doesn't look like you."

"It what?" Willard said, half-standing up.

"I told you I—"

"Well what in hell is it supposed to mean?" He couldn't decide whether to be mad or puzzled. "Look, maybe it's really crap or something, and maybe I didn't draw it so pretty, but it *is* supposed to be a car, I wasn't trying to make a picture of my goddam face."

Henry pulled hard at his lip, trying to think, and his seriousness, if nothing else, made Willard calm himself and wait. "Put it this way," Henry said. "It doesn't look like anybody, it just looks like a picture of a car. Take old Kuzitski's truck. It looked like Kuzitski, you know what I mean?"

He shook his head, cross.

"Well, take Burk's secondhand Cadillac, then. Would *you* have a car like that?"

It was useless, of course. The more he argued the less Willard saw it. Henry flipped through the magazine, pointing to cars and their drivers—and the truth was, the more he pointed the less Henry Soames saw it himself. He sat with his chair close to Willard's now, his arm around Willard Freund's shoulders, and though smoking was sure to kill him, Doc Cathey said, he smoked his pipe, for Willard smoked cigarettes like a trucker, one after another.

He quit at last. "Maybe it's nonsense," he said. "I guess it is." And he tried to talk merely about how the air would flow, where the weight would sit—things he knew for sure he knew nothing about.

When they talked about Willard's father and farming and old Kuzitski's accident—all this later that night—Willard smoked less and Henry quit. The boy crossed his knees and leaned back in his chair across the room from Henry just as Willard's father always had, or had when Henry had known him. They seldom met now. And yet even at moments like this Willard Freund did not quite seem at ease.

"Sorry, Willard," Henry said as Willard left, a little after one-thirty.

Willard smiled, cocking his head, looking off over Henry's shoulder. "Don't matter," he said. "I guess the whole thing's a pretty dumb idea."

"I never said that," Henry said seriously.

"No. Well, we'll see." He winked, pulled down his sweatshirt a little, and went out.

Afterward Henry lay in his bed going over and over it in his mind. He was sure he was right, even if sometimes looking at pictures in magazines he couldn't seem to see it. The only real question was whether or not it was important, whether or not it had anything to do, really, with designing a car. As he lay thinking, or brooding rather, his mind all at once called up the image of George Loomis's house, and for some reason Henry was shocked. A gaunt old brick house among tamaracks, the round-topped windows always dark except for the eerie flicker thrown by the television he kept in the kitchen. There were maybe fifteen, sixteen rooms, and George Loomis hardly set foot in more than three or four. But maybe that was different, he thought. A hand-me-down might be something else again. Give George a choice of the kind of house he'd live in, and sure as day. . . . But then he knew it wasn't true. A man did things to the world but also the world did things to him, and that was the house all right. If something or somebody didn't interfere, that would be George Loomis.

He lay looking up at the ceiling for a long time, thinking.

10

Two nights later Willard came again. He came in around ten, while Callie and Henry were cleaning up.

"How's it going, boy?" Henry said, serving him coffee and the blueberry pie he always ordered when there was some.

Willard sipped the coffee, looking over the rim at Callie, and then he said, "Bad. But there's a reason now. I figured out what you meant."

Henry frowned, not getting it at first.

"Cars and people," Willard explained. "What you said. It's the craziest goddamn thing!"

In a flash the old excitement was pounding inside him, and nothing *he* could do to stop it. He held back, struggled hard against himself like a lion converted to Christianity, but, even as his mind held back, his body pushed toward Willard. In his clumsy excitement he bumped Willard's coffee and spilled it, and he didn't take time to wipe it up, he was telling the boy—in sentences and slow at first, then faster and faster—about the fire he, Willard, had inside him, how somehow he had to get hold of it—the fire of the artist. The words were making no real sense, Henry knew as he said them, but the pitch at least—the pitch, by now, of a Pentecostal sermon—that and the big hands slapping the counter might partly make sense crash through. Willard Freund was leaning toward him, squinting as if to see better into Henry's thoughts, but leaning wrong somehow—or so it seemed to Henry—maybe faking, or maybe partly faking, conscious of himself leaning forward. Callie was coming closer too, looking troubled. The muscles beside her mouth were tight. But Henry concentrated on the boy.

"Anything you make," he was saying, gripping Willard's arm, "anything you make at all has got to be finding out what you want to make. I mean, finding out what you are. Maybe you'll draw cars or maybe you'll drive them, either way it's the same thing, you do what you do because of everything you ever did, or in spite of all you ever did—I don't know. I mean, it's love, it's like every kind of love you ever felt and the sum total of every love you ever felt. It's what poor old Kuzitski used to say: It's finding something to be crucified for. That's what a man has to have. I mean it. Crucifixion." His voice cracked—stupid, sentimental, Soames voice—and Willard Freund jerked back and laughed. Callie too seemed repelled by it, but she reached out to touch their arms, Henry Soames' and Willard's. Then she drew her hands back, for Henry was blundering on.

But was he saying anything at all? he wondered. All so hopelessly confused. And yet he knew. He couldn't do it and maybe never could have, but he *knew*. He was a fat, blubbering Holy Jesus, or anyway one half of him was, loving hell out of truckers and drunks and Willards and Callies—ready to be nailed for them. Eager. More heart than he knew how to spend.

It came to him that he had to tell of the bitch in Utica.

Mess.

He'd met her in the hallway of that cracking brown-papered hotel. He'd gone to Utica for a funeral, a trucker had killed himself—Ron, or Don—he'd forgotten the name—a trucker anyway; truckers were truckers. His semi had slid off 98, down in the hills, and had somersaulted to the shale banks of the river, then into the water. Henry had liked the man and had been afraid there'd be no one at the funeral. He'd been wrong, of course. The pews of the tiny white

church were packed—old men, old women, children—
and below the altar with its glinting, gold-embroidered
cloth and fourteen candles and thin-necked statues
the closed casket was buried under flowers and wide
ribbons. Henry had sat in the last pew and had sobbed.
And then in the hall of the Irishman's hotel where
he was staying he had met this idiot woman—though
that wasn't true, quite; in spite of the eyelashes and
the lipstick that lied about the shape of her lips, she
hadn't laughed when he'd told her why he was in
town. They'd walked along down the hall without
speaking, earlier in the evening that was, going in the
same direction, and they'd ended up at the same little
tavern for supper. He'd been off his head, probably,
with the funeral, and she'd been drunk as a fish when
they went to her room, or she'd pretended to be. And
there, with only a candle burning, throwing huge
shadows on the heat-buckled brown-paper wall, they
had talked about loneliness and devotion and God
knew what, and he had held her in his fat arms trying
to tell her of the bursting piece of sentimental stupidity
inside him that had longed for something or other
all his life. Her hands playing on his back had been
warm, vaguely like the big drops of rain that came in
August. He'd told her by God he would marry her—
he didn't even know her name—and she'd laughed her
head off, not even drawing back, still rubbing against
him, working him up. And at last in a kind of terror
he had struck out at the damn drunken idiot, the
stupid animal love in her raw hands and lips. What
he had done, exactly, was hard to remember, or how
she'd taken it. He'd hit her in the face when the
climax came, that much he would never forget. That
and the dry summer heat and the fact that now sometimes sitting in just his trousers, waiting, he could hear
her moaning on his bed. The sound was distinct: so
clear that he sometimes thought, in a moment of panic, that he'd lost his mind.

Callie's hand was reaching once more toward Henry Soames' wrist, but he ranted on, trying to tell the story to Willard Freund, but trying to tell it without details, without particular people, a story somebody's father's father had told—a story that, stripped of details, was absolute pointlessness. He stopped himself and, once more, caught Willard's arm.

"I'm sorry, Willard," he whispered frantically. "I'm a blubbering old man. I'm sorry."

Callie cried, "Stop it, Henry. For God's sake, please shut up!"

The room went silent. Henry felt the corners of his mouth twitching. The girl blanched as if nauseated, then turned on her heel and ran into the lean-to room behind the grill. She slammed the door behind her.

After a long moment, Willard held out a cigarette to Henry. Henry took it, his fingers trembling, and lighted it from Willard's match. He listened to the hum of the electric clock. "I'm sorry," he said again, calmly this time, so ashamed he couldn't look at the boy.

Willard laughed—he-he-he—like a Negro. "Man, you do get carried away," he said.

Again there was a silence between them, longer this time. Willard seemed on the point of speaking once, then shook his head and turned away to walk over to the window in front and look out at the highway. No sound came from the room behind the grill. At last Willard said, "Old man, I came here to tell you something."

Henry waited, and Willard came over and leaned on the counter, his arms stiff, hands far apart. "I leave for school tomorrow," he said. Then: "Ag School."

Shame came again, mushrooming inside him as he realized that all his rant had been not only foolish but worse, unwanted. It surprised him that Willard had not told him sooner, and for a minute he was furious.

But that passed. It wasn't Willard's fault, God knew. He asked feebly, "It's settled, then?" He watched Willard's eyes, but he found himself listening for a sound from the lean-to room behind.

Willard stared at his cigarette, then shrugged. "Guess it is," he said. "I don't really start till the summer session, but my old man swung this job for me, if I can start right now . . ."

"You told Callie?" Henry said.

"I mean to tell her tonight."

"Will you need money?"

Willard blushed. Like father like son, Henry thought. A friend as close as Henry was ought to have a right, surely, to offer money. But he was more sorry for the boy than bitter. Like father like son, he thought again. A terrible shame. He jerked his head in the direction of the door into the lean-to room in back, and after a minute Willard went in.

Henry turned off the grill, though it was early, and gently scraped the grease into the trough, listening. He heard them talking quietly, and he could hardly stand the sadness of it, the doom of hope. It was a good thing to be old and past that, rolling steadily downward to the grave. In his mind he could see her clinging to him, crying maybe, and confused with the picture was another of her reaching, on tiptoe, for a plate on the top shelf, her head back and her breasts high. They might have done each other good, Callie and Willard. Good kids, he thought, half in sorrow, half in thanksgiving. Fine, fine kids. He laid the scraper down quietly on the tray beside the grill— his fingers were still trembling, he noticed—and he pulled on his brown wool sweater. His belly pinched behind the wheel, he drove out onto 98, heading south. In his rear-view mirror he saw the light in the back room go off. He felt a moment's unrest, like a parent. But he said to himself then, *Sensible*. Now drunks wouldn't interrupt their parting. Still, Henry was puzzled and a little frightened, though he could not admit what it was exactly that frightened him. He shifted to high.

By the time he reached Nickel Mountain he was calm. The air was clean here, with cool wisps of fog in the hollows. The brilliance of the night, the shocking perfection of the stars, the trees, the rocks, made dawn seem far away. As he curved above the river, he rode the brake gently, oppressed by an odd notion that he was somehow not on the usual road. Then came an even stranger idea, almost a conviction, the old fantasy with a new face. Somehow, emerging from a draught of winter wind, he found himself not little Fats and not Henry Soames but someone who had been cold and dead for a long time—his father, perhaps, or someone whose life Henry Soames had lived hundreds of years ago. He was making it up, of course, and he knew it; but he let himself believe it nevertheless, or let himself toy with it; and it grew on him. At the top of the mountain he parked the Ford and leaned back in his seat, waiting for the pleasure of the delusion to pass.

When he returned to the Stop-Off, Willard and Callie were gone. Henry undressed for bed and, without realizing he was doing it, snapped off the neon light. Catching himself an instant later, he turned the light on again, shaking his head. From his lean-to window he could see the fog wallowing down through the trees, stretching out thick, fleshless arms like the tentacles of some cavern beast, or like the white arms of a blind man. After a little more than an hour he pounded the dottle from his carved black pipe for the last time and lay down.

11

When Callie Wells came in, the following morning,
Henry saw almost at once that she was as cheerful as
ever—more cheerful than usual if anything. She talked
of Willard as she always had, of what a fine driver
he would be, of how clever he was, how kind, how
terribly thoughtful. And so Henry saw that Willard
had lied. He hadn't told her and hadn't intended to.

Henry said nothing.

The following day the cheerfulness was gone, and
all the rest of the week was a grim business. The
weather maybe. The wind had turned wintry, and for
two days it snowed. Still neither of them said a word.
On Monday she was in good spirits again, and it wasn't
long before she told him what he could easily have
guessed, that she'd gotten a letter from Willard. His
job was going fine. He'd be home toward the middle
of August. He sent his best to Henry. She worked him
out of things to do that week, finishing up every chore
he gave her in half the time it should have taken and
driving him pretty near to his wits' end. She would
hum to herself from morning to night, sometimes the
same song hour after hour, and he thanked God he'd
had the jukebox taken out three years ago.

And then, some while later—a month, maybe—
another change came: She worked harder than ever,
but not singing now, not laughing with truckers, never
speaking except when she was spoken to; and finally it
dawned on him that Callie was afraid she was pregnant. Her fear turned into near certainty—it was easy
to see, though she still said nothing about it to him.
She vacillated between stony silence and intense, ner-

46

vous chatter, and she began to ask pointed questions about the Freunds. As for Henry, the suspicion that Callie was pregnant touched him deeply and gave her in his eyes a kind of holiness. He began to worry constantly that she would overdo or that she would fall. He began to walk, himself, like a man on ice.

June ended; haywagons stopped rolling by, and the farmers up and down the road turned to cultivating corn. The pines took their richer summer color, and the maples and beeches were so full of leaves that the woods across from the Stop-Off were dark as an apple bin. July came, and farmers began to combine oats. The silence in which he and Callie worked had become a settled matter now, as if something they'd consciously agreed on. And yet, in spite of the silence, it seemed to Henry that he and the girl were closer than they had been before. Perhaps she guessed that he knew and shared her fear—surely she must have guessed—but if she did she did not tell him. He studied her eyes, her hands, her ankles, watching the signs, and at night he couldn't sleep for worry and the pain in his chest. Because sleep came later and later, he began to oversleep sometimes. When he awakened, in the middle of the morning, he would find the door of his room closed and he would hear the clatter of dishes and the small-boy banter of truckers in the diner. When he went in to help her, Callie would snap, "You need your rest, Henry," and would turn away, too busy to waste more words. Tears would smart in his eyes. He would insist—these days, it seemed to him, Callie ought hardly to lift a napkin—and she would give in without ever asking the obvious question, Why are you doing this? She'd begun to show a little now, and those who watched their comedy—his solicitude, her indignation—drew the obvious conclusions (but this neither one of them would know until later). At night, just before she left, she would come to his room to dust or straighten his chairs, irritably, then stand near the table in the middle of the room, sharing his dull, trivial thoughts, wondering with him, but wordlessly, whether or not the rain would come or, after it came, whether it would stop in time. Henry, alone with her in his room, learned to hug his arms to his sides as though the slightest movement might drive away a mist that protected them both, covered, on his side, sagging flesh, lumbering absurdities of soul, and covered, on her side—well, nothing, of course. Youth. Unhappiness. Her stony Baptist guilt and, maybe, terror.

One afternoon (it was the end of July; a hot, muggy day) Henry said, "I sure don't know what I'll do around here without you, Callie. When you go and get married this place here's gonna fall down around my ears."

She smiled, false, then covered her face and cried, and it hit him that Willard Freund was not coming back.

"Now here, here," he said, going to her, patting her shoulder. "Callie old girl, you been working too hard. You just take this afternoon off."

"Get away," she said, pushing at his arm. "Damn you, *please*. Just this once, leave me alone!"

Henry backed off, scratching the back of his hand. He went back into his room.

12

"All right, then," he said to himself. "All right, then."

He'd sent her home early, a little before eight, and had turned out the neon and the diner lights and closed the lean-to door behind him. The only suit he had was the black one his father had left, but it fit as though it had been made for him. (He *was* getting heavy, by Jesus. He'd never have believed he could fill the old man's suit.) He found the old brown fedora on the shelf, and that fit too, nearly. It rested on his ears. When he inspected himself in the mirror he found he looked very good. Big as the world, but good. Serious, anyway; imposing. That was what he was after. He locked the back-room door behind him, because of the dark formality in his chest—he hadn't locked that door for maybe fifteen years—and went out to his car. The night was as hot and muggy as the day had been; not a breath of air, not so much as a cricket stirring. He took one of the little white pills and started the motor.

Crow Mountain was dark as a tomb. All the way up to George Loomis's place there wasn't a car but Henry's on the road. He pulled up in the driveway and sat a moment to calm himself and go over what he meant to say one last time; then he got out. The house was dark and he felt an instant's panic: He hadn't been prepared for the possibility that George might be away. But then he saw he'd made a mistake. There was the usual blue-white flicker in the kitchen. He knocked.

"Well, Jesus please us," George said, stepping back from the door. "Who in hell died?"

Henry took off his hat. "Do you mind if I come in, George?"

George held his hand up. "Let me think a minute. Yes, I do. I do mind. You've taken up selling Bibles on the side."

"Now, George," Henry said.

"Well, shit," George said, "come on in, then. But don't tell me why you're dressed up like that. Either you been to church or you been courting, and whichever it is, I think I might get sick."

"Now, damn it, George," Henry said.

"Oh, hush up and sit down. It's good to see you.

I'll see if I still got some whiskey." He started past the television, paused a moment to watch one of the cowboys shoot the other one, then went on to the cupboard under the sink. "Just a little bourbon left," he called back.

"That's fine," Henry said. He could use it.

George talked about television programs while he fixed the drink and brought it over to the metal table. Henry was missing a great deal, George said, refusing to give in to the electronic revolution. He ran on for maybe five minutes or more, Henry merely nodding helplessly, playing with the hat on the table in front of him, missing half of what George said because of the noise from the machine. At last Henry said feebly (it was hardly going exactly as he'd planned), "Could we turn the television off, George, so we could hear?"

"What the hell? Sit in the dark?"

"Maybe the room lights still work," Henry said. He laughed.

George considered it, then got up and went over to the switch by the door. The lights went on, and George seemed surprised and pleased. He turned off the television. "OK," he said then, "what are you selling?"

"I want you to marry Callie Wells," Henry said. He had not meant to make it quite so blunt, and he felt himself reddening.

George stared, then looked over at the television as though maybe that had said it. He came over and sat down. "You're willing to pay me, I suppose?" he said, lifting his glass to drink.

It seemed to Henry a natural question, though he hadn't expected it would come up so quickly. He said, "I'll write you a check right now for a thousand dollars."

George choked, set down his glass, and got up to go to the sink. "You crazy old goat," he began, but another choking fit hit him. The cords of his neck pumped, and it looked as if he might retch. Henry watched, wide-eyed, the checkbook in his fist. "You crazy old goat," George Loomis roared, "you think I'd marry some girl I hardly know for a thousand dollars? Or ten thousand? Or a thousand million? Look, I don't love her. I don't even like her. She stinks. You know that? The word of God!"

"George, that's not true. You said yourself—"

"I said myself what?"

"You said you were thinking of marrying her."

His eyebrows lowered, and suddenly he wasn't partly joking any more. He looked scared. "Now, wait a minute," he said. He looked at his hands, saw they were empty, then came over quickly to the drink on the table. He said when he'd swallowed, "Since the day I was born, Henry Soames, I never said—"

"Yes, you did," Henry said. "That night when you came to my place drunk you said to her—to *her*, George—"

"Jesus God," George said.

"You did, George." He added, inspired. "There were witnesses, too."

George Loomis bit his lip, staring. Abruptly, he got up and went over to the cupboard below the sink. The bourbon bottle was empty now. He dropped it in the woodbox beside the stove and opened the cabinet to the left of the sink—full of antique china and real cut glass—then closed it again and went over to the cabinet on the right. At last he came back to the table and sat down. He leaned his forehead on his hands.

Henry said, "She's a fine girl, George. It's the truth. She'd make you a good wife. Inside a month she'd have this place of yours—" He caught himself too late.

"Christ, don't I know it," he said. He shook his head like a man driving out a nightmare. Then he said, "What else happened that night, Henry?"

Henry frowned, puzzled.

"I mean, what did I say exactly? And did I—" He waved vaguely.

"You said you admired her and you were thinking of marriage."

"I remember that, yeah. But did I—?" He wet his lips, then said quickly, "Well, I noticed that Callie these last few weeks—that is, there are signs—you know what I mean."

Henry's heart ticked rapidly, and for an instant the temptation seemed irresistible. But he said, knowing the moment he said it that he was beaten now, "No, not that. That was somebody else."

George let out his breath as though he'd been holding it half-an-hour.

Henry said, "It's not true that she stinks, George. It's a lie and you know it."

George smiled, watching him, sly.

"I'll give you fifteen hundred dollars," Henry said. "That's as high as I'll go."

"I don't love her, Henry," George said. "And Callie don't love me either, near as I can tell. I seen on television, how they act when they love you."

"Well, you can *learn* to love her. She's a good, hard-working, honest girl, and she's a sweet girl, too. When she touches you she can be gentler than—I don't know what."

George still sat watching him, more sly than ever. "Why don't *you* marry her, Henry?"

"Listen, a man that can't learn to love Callie Wells can't learn to love anybody. You ready to admit you can't love any woman at all? You ready to admit you want to die all alone in this godforsaken museum and be found sometime two years later?"

George said, "Why not you, Henry?"

He clenched his fist. "I'm twenty-five years older than she is, that's why. And fat and ugly to boot."

"But you love her," George said, grinning like a cat.

"Love her, hell! I'll be dead inside a year. Doc Cathey said so."

"But you love her," George said, dead serious all at once.

It suddenly came to Henry that that was true. "Maybe so," he said. He drank. The next instant Henry felt faint, then violently sick, some sudden incredible explosion of, maybe, indigestion, and George jumped up and came around to him.

When he woke up he was in George Loomis's bed and Doc Cathey was over by the window. When Henry moved his hand Doc Cathey whirled and pointed at him. "Lie still, you damn fool," he shouted. "You stay like you are or I'll cave in the side of your head."

13

He didn't know and didn't ask whose idea it was that Callie move in to look after him. She hung a curtain across the corner of his room behind the diner and put a cot there for herself, and she fed him and looked after him as if she were his slave, or maybe his mother. If he moaned in the middle of the night, bothered by dreams, or if he woke up suddenly and stirred in his bed, she'd be there in a minute with one of six different pill bottles. He did whatever she told him to do, not because Doc Cathey had told him to on pain of death but because he liked to, at least for now. During the day she'd come in to see him from time to time, to bring him the paper or see how he was or make sure he didn't try crossing to the toilet by himself. He felt strong as an ox, and secretly he suspected it was all some kind of plot; but he had no objections. At the end of two weeks he was doing as much as he'd ever done, except at mealtimes. He had to lose weight, Doc Cathey said, and Callie could see through walls. Then one day Callie took down the curtain and folded up the cot, and that night, when the diner was straightened up, she went home.

Henry Soames felt more lonely that he could remember ever having felt in his life. He sat in his room sunk in despair, and then, wanting no intrusions on his grief, he turned out every light in the place, then sat for a full two hours on the side of his bed, dressed in the old black suit, brooding. Though the room was dark he could make out the lines of the chairs, the tables, the books distinctly. Outside the room he could hear the faint creaking of the pines. Misty rain was muttering on the gravel driveway and the lean-to roof. He breathed slowly.

"I'm sorry," he thought, thinking of his father and mother, the injustice he'd done them, his presumption that he knew anything at all about their life.

A truck was roaring past, building up speed for the hill. Henry listened, feeling his muscles tighten, then grow limp once more. Useless, he thought. He wouldn't sleep tonight, not unless he knocked himself out, which perhaps he could do by sitting out in the diner with the fluorescent glaring on the page of some dull old book from his father's shelf. He slid one foot along the side of the bed, hunting for his slippers, but he didn't get up. There was a sound then, the rattle of a sudden gust, or perhaps a knock. When the knock came again he recognized it, pushed himself up from the bed, and called, "Come on in. I'll be right with you."

"Don't get up," Callie said. She was wet, and she was breathing hard; she'd been running. When she reached the door of his room she stopped and leaned on the doorpost. She said nothing for a moment, catching her wind. Then: "I'm sorry to bother you. I saw your lights were all off, and I thought—"

Henry looked down.

She came into the room and stood by the window. She rubbed the back of a book with her thumb, making the binding gleam, but her eyes did not seem focused on the book. Henry watched the self-conscious movements of her hands. He would hurry her home before her parents woke to worry, he thought.

"You want to sit down, Callie?"

She'd left the door of the diner open, and he could feel cool air sweeping across his chest and back. The rain had stopped now. She went on rubbing the book, looking at nothing.

"What is it, Callie?" he said.

Then suddenly she came to him and pressed her wet head against his chest, her fingers digging into his fat. Her back under his hands shook with her sobbing. As always, only his hands could communicate. "He's a good boy, Callie, and you love him," he was whispering hurriedly, senselessly now, as though the weighted heat in his chest could be pushed off by words. He'd said these words before with her wet hair against his shirt; but no, that was wrong. Never. And yet she was looking up now as he'd known she would, saying, "No, I don't. I didn't. Stop talking, Mr. Soames. Please. I hate you when you talk. I can't help it, I truly hate you. I'm sorry." Her face was close, and she hissed it at him, every word increasing the heat in his chest. He thought, if only she could get away someplace, to rest and straighten things out in her mind. He had money, after all; all the money she would need.

She said, "When I saw your light was off I was certain something had happened to you. I couldn't stand it, you've been like a father to me, almost like—" She broke off. His hands stopped moving on her back. After a long time she said, "Mr. Soames, have I led you to believe—?" She drew back, looking at him, frightened.

"It's all right, Callie," he said. "It's nothing, nothing."

His lips were trembling, stretching out like a sad clown's, and he remembered that with his glasses on he looked like a Russian spy. She pressed close to him again, clinging to him as if in horror. "Oh, boy," she whispered. And then, as if on second thought, "Oh, Holy God." The burning in his chest was like fingernails cutting into his skin, blocking out the light and the candle flame and the blistered, dirty, brown-paper shine of the old hotel room walls. Her hands had gone limp with the pain, he remembered all at once, and yet even while she sobbed she had reached for his hand. It came to him now why she'd laughed.

"I love you, Callie."

"I shouldn't have come," she said. "I was out of my mind."

"I know how you feel, Callie. I only wanted—"

"You don't know how I feel at all. Let me think."

14

The fog had pounced suddenly, from nowhere. Henry sat for five or six minutes at the end of his driveway, just off the macadam, his arms resting over the steering wheel. The girl, wrapped in an old army blanket, sat hugging her knees, breathing deeply, like a child. Her face, framed by the window, was gray as lead. The Ford's headlights seemed to bore only a few inches into the fog. Gray, airy arms moved over the hood and seemed, sometimes, to be lifting the car, turning it so that Henry wouldn't know where the highway lay. A drunk was knocking at the front door of the Stop-Off, shouting, "Henry, hey, Henry, git up!" Henry kept from turning his head. Somewhere off in the hills to his right a semi whined. Someone he knew, probably, driving against a deadline. A yellow glow appeared on the hill, moved closer, then changed abruptly to a gray-black shadow shooting past to vanish, swallowed up by the fog. The trucker would kill himself, letting her roll that way. Poor bastard. Poor, stupid, vicious, fat bastard. Breathing shallowly to cut down the burning, Henry nudged the Ford out onto 98, heading south —but not for the hills and Nickel Mountain this time —driving into the fog. He'd have to raise Frank Wells and his wife, and get Doc Cathey after that—or no, get Doc in the morning, perhaps; not as a medic for once, thank God. All quickly, before the click.

There would be time, though. Might have years left yet. A whole new life. No sense driving with the window open, all the same. Made breathing harder. Be realistic.

He was tired, soaked with sweat inside the great black suit.

(Nickel Mountain. That was where the real hills were, and the river, cool, deep with echoes of spring water dripping into it and sliding from its banks!)

Callie's head came to rest against his shoulder, and her hair had a young clean smell. (He must have been teasing me, he thought. *Surely* he was.) Her head on his shoulder was pleasantly heavy; heavy enough, almost, to crush bone.

II

THE
WEDDING

1

Callie Wells stood in what was normally the sewing room, just off the parlor. Both doors were closed behind her. She was wearing the old Welsh wedding gown, but she seemed hardly to know it, standing with her hands folded, looking out the window. The room, the weather, the round blue mountains in the distance all seemed to defer to her stillness. The house around her hummed like a hive, but Callie scarcely noticed that either.

It seemed to her the first chance she'd had to be alone in weeks. Every time she turned around there was something to be fitted for, some decision to make —where to put Uncle Russel and Aunt Kate (who were coming from Cleveland after all), what to do if the rings didn't come from the place up in Utica in time for the wedding, how to get Aunt Anna to the rehearsal since she flatly refused to ride in Uncle Gordon's truck. But it couldn't be weeks, or anyway it couldn't be more than two, because it was just two weeks and three days ago now that they'd decided.

Her father had come into the kitchen blinking like an owl, holding up his flannel pajama bottoms with one hand, scowling, cross enough to eat roofing nails, and Henry had said formally, holding her hand, "Mr. Wells, I'd like your permission to marry your daughter." Callie had glanced up at him sideways and had seen again, as if it were a new discovery, how much she truly admired him, comical as he might seem to some, and she'd felt awe that he should be going through all this for her. He was painfully embarrassed, and scared as well, though he was older than her father. He was feeling, no doubt, as ridiculous as he looked—a great fat creature in steel-rimmed glasses, his ears pressed flat to his head as though he'd spent his whole life in a tight-fitting cap.

Her father said, "At two A.M. in the morning? You crazy?"

"I'm serious, Frank," Henry said. All the house and the surrounding night seemed to echo his earnestness. *He's serious.*

She'd broken in quickly, holding Henry's hand more tightly, "Daddy, I'm going to have a child."

His face went white, then red. He was angrier than she'd ever seen him, angry enough to murder Henry (but Henry could break her father in half as easily as Prince snapped hambones between his teeth). Her father began swearing but she broke in again, "Not by Henry, Daddy. By somebody else." He just stared at her then, and then at Henry. Then he pulled out the chair from the kitchen table and sat down. His stubbly cheeks were hollow and there were shadows between his ribs. He chewed his lip and wrung his hands, tears washing down his nose and whiskers. After a minute he called her mother, and she came in at once—she'd been standing just behind the door—her plump white hands catching the bathrobe together.

She said, "Mother, we're going to be married."

Her mother's face squeezed into a grimace and she started crying with a great whoop, splashing up her hands and running to her, falling on her, hugging her tightly and sobbing. "Oh, Callie! My poor baby! We've *failed* you!" Immediately Callie was crying too, sobbing her heart out. It must have been two minutes they cried like that. Then it came to her that Henry was there, and that they didn't understand at all.

"Mother," she said, "I *love* Henry. I'm *happy*."

"Child. My child!" her mother said, and a new burst of sobbing overwhelmed her.

She felt a strange sensation: as if the floor were

moving, shifting gently, carrying her somewhere, as in the old story, and telling her something. She accepted her mother's tight embrace but felt unresponsive, separated in a way that in a moment there would be no repairing. Her mother felt it too, or realized that Callie was not crying now, that something had changed.

"Mother," she said again, "I love him."

After a moment her mother drew back to look at her, trying to read her face like a word left by Indians. She said, "Love, Callie! You're only seventeen years old."

Callie said nothing.

Her mother was baffled; grieved and frightened, but more than that, filled with an emotion too deep for separation into grief and fear: as though Callie had gone down to a small boat at night, and her mother stood on a towering ship that was drawing away and could never turn back. Without words, Callie knew—with a sinking feeling—that her mother could never know for sure—anymore than she could know of her mother—that she was happy. For the first time now, her eyes still baffled, Callie's mother turned to look at Henry. She stared as if she'd never really noticed, in all her years, that he was grotesque. He endured the look in patience like an elephant's, an enormous hulk of misery, his hands folded behind his back, huge belly thrown forward, his head slightly tipped and drawn back a little. (Could she see that, inside that suit like a mortician's, he was a gentle man, and a good man besides?)

Her father said, "This calls for a drink!"

Everything called for a drink, to her father. Her mother said, "I'll put some coffee on."

"Hell," her father said, "it don't call for coffee. Damn coffee, that's what *I* say. Is that what you say, Henry?"

Henry smiled, showing his overbite. "Mmm," he said, noncommittal.

"Don't curse, Frank," her mother said.

"Right," her father said. "Fuck cursing!" He got out the Jim Beam and two of the painted glasses from the gas station and some ice. He was so nervous he could hardly get the cubes from the metal tray. He waved Henry to a chair and opened the bottle.

Her mother went over to the stove. When she'd turned on the butane under the pot she looked around, horrified, weeping again. "I forgot to say congratulations!" She came back to Callie and hugged her as tightly as before, and now once more both of them were sobbing, but happily this time, Callie anyway, her mother still undecided.

"Congratulations, you two!" her father said, exactly like someone on television. He stood up and reached over to shake Henry's hand, his other hand clutching the pajama bottoms.

They'd sat up all night after that, talking, her father and Henry drinking whiskey, she telling her mother how happy she was, and looking fondly at Henry (growing more and more erect and dignified as the drinking wore on, smiling more and more foolishly, his speech increasingly labored and solemn—her father's, too). She had wanted to shout, *Oh Mother, look at him, look at him!* And every glinting glass and dish in the cupboards understood. But how could her parents understand it? What was important was unspeakable, both on her side and on her mother's. And so instead they had talked about plans, and she had wondered, Is that what everybody does, in every marriage. She and Henry had meant to be married by a justice of the peace, but her mother insisted on a wedding in church. You only get married once, she said; a church wedding was a sacred thing; the relatives would be hurt. Aunt Anna would be the organist, because it wouldn't do for her own mother to be organist at her own daughter's wedding. Callie would wear white. "Mother, I'm *pregnant*," Callie said, "I'm already beginning to show." "People expect it," her mother said. She'd given in to everything. It didn't matter. In fact, she was secretly glad she'd be married in church. She'd said, "Henry, what do you think?" "Ver-y good," he said, nodding, judgmental. "A ver-y solomon cajun." When dawn came and the robins started singing, Henry and her father were fast asleep, her father lying on his arms on the table, Henry sitting erect and placid, mouth open, like a sleeping child.

From that day to this she'd been running every minute. When they'd told Aunt Anna it was to be in two weeks, she'd looked instantly at Callie's belly, her old eyes as sharp as when she threaded a needle, and she'd said, "Well, well, well, well." Callie's mother had cried as though the sin were her own. (Sin was the only word for it in Aunt Anna's house, pictures of Jesus on every wall, sequin and purple velvet signs reading *Jesus Saves* and *I Am the Way*.) Then, to Callie's astonishment, Aunt Anna's wrinkled-up leathery face broke into a witchly grin.

But all the preparations were over, finally—the rushed-out wedding invitations, the fittings, the telephone calls, the far-into-the-night planning of housing arrangements for relatives and transportation to the church. All the relatives were assembled, mostly from her mother's side, more Joneses and Thomases and Griffiths than she'd seen in one place in all her life. It was like an Eisteddfodd or a Gymanfa Ganu. Her father said you couldn't spit without knocking down fourteen Welshmen. (Great-uncle Hugh had liked that. He'd slapped his knee and rolled it over and over on his tongue, getting it wronger every time he said it. Her father would be quoting it for the next fifteen years, the way he'd been quoting for the last twenty-five, "Fool Ahpril, Bill Jones! Fly-horse on door-barn! Fool Ahpril!)

And so at last she could be alone. In half an hour Uncle John would drive her to the church, and there would be the last-minute bustle, the anxious fuss, the fear that every minute detail might not go perfectly, according to proper ritual. She thought: We should have gone to a JP and told them afterward.

In the old Welsh wedding gown she felt unnatural—false. It would be different if you were pretty, she thought. She'd been shocked when she'd seen herself in the mirror the first time, trying it on. The gown was scratchy and tighter than she'd expected. It was yellowed by time, yet, in spite of that, mysteriously pure, she thought; serene. But at the lace cuffs her wrists were bony, and her hands were like a man's. With the veil lifted up her face showed angular and grim: She looked neither innocent nor gentle and wise, merely callow. She had said, "It doesn't fit."

"Don't be silly, Callie," her mother had said. "We just need to alter it a little, that's all."

She'd said frantically, "I mean, it isn't *right* for me."

Aunt Anna said, "Breathe in."

When they had it pinned up, her mother stepped back to study her, and she smiled, teary, blind to how terrible Callie looked. And now her own tears came gushing. "Mother," she said, "my *feet* are too big."

"One wedding I played at, the girl tripped and broke her wrist," Aunt Anna said.

"Mother, *listen* to me," Callie said. "*Look* at me once."

"Hush," her mother said. "Callie, you look lovely."

She had clenched her teeth. But she had given in, to the gown as to the rest. Soon it would be over.

It was a beautiful day. She stood as still as the glass of the window, with her hands folded, the veil drawn over her face. Across the road lay golden stubble where Mr. Cook's wheat had been, a few weeks ago. Off to her right the land dropped sharply, falling away toward Mr. Soames' diner and the lower valley, at the end of the valley gray-blue mountains rounding up into blue-white sky. It was pleasantly warm, a light breeze moving the leaves of the maples on the lawn. She watched the bakery truck slow down at the mailbox and turn in. *A beautiful day for a wedding,* she thought. She meant it to be a happy thought, but she couldn't tell whether she was happy or not. Children were singing, around the corner of the house, out of sight.

> *Karen is her first name,*
> *First name, first name,*
> *Karen is her first name,*
> *Among the little white daisies.*

The song made her remember something. She had whispered to her friend that her boyfriend's name was David Parks—knowing perfectly well the rules of the game, that all of them would now find out that Callie Wells liked David Parks—but when her friend turned and told the others, and when the whole ring of children began to sing it, their voices gleeful and merciless, she felt sick with shame and believed she would never dare look at him again. The memory brought a sudden, fierce nostalgia, a hunger to be once again and forever the child she could now see with fond detachment, loving and pitying her, laughing at her sorrow as once her mother must have laughed. For some reason the memory triggered another, one that was intimately related with the first, but she couldn't think how:

> *Poor Howard's dead and gone,*
> *Left me here to sing his song. . . .*

Panic filled her chest. *It's a mistake,* she thought. *I don't love him.* He was ugly.

2

All around the room—everywhere but in front of the closed doors and the window where Callie stood—the wedding presents were laid out for show on borrowed card tables covered with linen cloths. With the sunlight streaming in (burning in the great, red, antique bowl from Cousin-Aunt Mary, gleaming on all the silver plate, the silver candlesticks, the cut-glass napkin holders, lacework, china salt and pepper shakers, glass and china bowls, mugs, painted vases, popcorn poppers, TV trays, steak knives, wooden salad forks), the presents seemed too beautiful to be real. Like the gown, they had, to Callie's mind, a serenity and elegance she could not match. They overwhelmed her—the hours that had gone into the crocheted antimacassars from Aunt Mae, the expense of the candlesticks from Uncle Earle, who had bought them, she knew, without an instant's hesitation or so much as a fleeting thought of the expense: In all her life she would never crochet as Aunt Mae could, not if she worked at it week in, week out, and she'd never be as rich as Uncle Earle, or as calmly, beamingly confident of all she did. Why had they done it all? Over and over that question had come to her; not a question, really, an exclamation of despair, because she knew the answer, no answer at all: They had sent the presents—hardly knowing her, hardly even knowing her parents any more—because it was her wedding. She thought: *Because brides are beautiful, and marriage is holy.* Again and again she had watched them come down the aisle, transfigured, radiating beauty like Christ on the mountain, lifted out of mere humanness into their perfect eternal instant, the flowers they carried mere feeble decoration, the needless gilding of a lily too beautiful for Nature; and again and again she had seen them later, making their first formal visits as wives, the lines of their faces softened, their eyes grown shrewish or merry. How she had envied them, she the poor virgin, novice, barred from their mystery! She knew well enough what it was, though not in words. She knew it was not the marriage bed, was only feebly symbolized by the bed. They went up the aisle white forms, insubstantial as air, poised in the instant of total freedom like the freedom of angels, between child and adult, between daughter and wife, and they came down transformed to reality, married: in one split second, in a way, grown-up. It was that that the relatives lifted up their offerings to: the common holy ground in all their lives. But that common beauty would not be for her. Her marrying Henry Soames was almost vicious, an act of pure selfishness: she was pregnant, and he—obese and weak, flaccid in his vast, sentimental compassion—he had merely been available.

I'll run away, she thought, standing motionless, knowing she would not run away. Tears filled her eyes. *I'll run away somewhere—to New York City, yes— and I'll write to Henry later and explain. It's the only honest thing to do.* She closed her eyes, hurriedly composing.

Dear, Good Henry:
Forgive me for leaving you and causing you so much embarrassment and expense. Please ask all my friends and relatives to forgive me too. I hope I have not hurt anyone, and I know how disappointed. . . .

Dear Mr. Soames:
Miss Calliope Wells has asked me to tell you (since she is unwell. . . .

Because of the presents she couldn't run away. And because Uncle Russel and Aunt Kate had come from Ohio, and Aunt Anna had altered the dress and was going to play the church organ, which she loved doing more than anything (and had once done beautifully, so people said), and Robert Wilkes had come all the way from the Eastern School of Music to sing "Because." She slipped her hands up inside the veil and covered her face. In fifteen minutes Uncle John would be here.

She remembered sitting in the grass as a child, watching Uncle John at work. He was a carpenter, and the tools were like extensions of himself: He was one with the plane that glided down the pineboard, lifting a long, light curl of white; one with the quick, steady saw, the hammer that sent nails in cleanly at two blows, the wooden rule, the chalk, the brace and bit. When she tried, the nails would bend over cruelly, and Uncle John would smile. She'd fly into a temper, and he would laugh as though he and the old claw hammer knew a secret, and then he'd say kindly, "Be calm. Be patient." She thought: *Uncle John.* He was old now, retired. His hands were twisted with arthritis. It was Uncle John who had brought her Prince when she was eleven. He was still just a puppy. He didn't look at all like a police dog then. Furry as a bear that had not yet been licked.

She thought, fiercely, *Of course I'm going to marry him.* But Willard Freund was her own age, handsome and graceful: She saw him again in his white suitcoat at the senior dance, smiling at her with his head lowered a little, shy. Somewhere, surely, there was a man who was young and handsome and good as well, someone who would love her as completely as Henry did, and would make her heart race the way Willard did, by nothing but a smile. If she only waited. . . . The thought made her want to laugh bitterly, or, better yet, die. She would hate the child inside her. How could she help it?

But the maples on the lawn in front said, *Be calm*. In their heavy shade where the tables were, it would be cool. Always when there were family reunions, funerals, weddings, they would set up the tables there, as they had today, and cover them with bright colored cloths, and all the older women and some of the girls would work in the kitchen, and the men would play softball on the level space at the foot of the steeply sloping back yard, tromping down the clover, using burlap bags full of straw for bases. When Prince was young he would bark and chase them as they ran, or he'd steal the ball. (Uncle John had taught him to sit and stay.) Some of the women would play softball too, the girls and some of the younger wives. Uncle Grant was always the pitcher for both sides (smoking his pipe, wearing calf-manure-colored loafers and white slacks and a light blue cardigan sweater with leather buttons); Uncle Harris would be at third base, his suitcoat off, the striped suspenders tight-looking, and when nothing came his way he would stand there grinning, just like Bill, his jaw thrown forward as if crossly, stiff hair curling out from in front of his ears as her grandfather's had done. Each time, some of the younger wives who'd played softball last time would not play this time but would sit on the porch with the older women, watching the children in the grass below and talking, laughing or complaining. When she'd hit her first homer, Uncle Grant had pretended to be indignant at her having connected with his pitch, and her handsome cousin Duncan had smiled as though he were proud that she was his cousin. Duncan was always the best of the players. If he missed a catch it was because he wanted to give you the run, or because one of the smaller children had grabbed hold of his legs. They made him bat one-handed, to be fair, but that was a joke; he would pop out a fly—so gentle that it seemed to float down to you on dove's wings—to whichever of the younger kids hadn't caught one yet, and if you missed the catch he would be out at the first base he came to that wasn't being covered by a grown-up. They called him "the loser," because every time he came to bat he would get himself put out, one way or another, and when he was at field he'd put nobody out except—he pretended—by accident. They razzed him and hooted at him and loved him: Useless as he was if you wanted to win, he was always the first one chosen. He was beautiful and good—he didn't even smoke—and juggling three bats, gently and precisely popping up flies, standing on one hand, coins dripping from his trousers—and grinning, always grinning—he seemed to shine like an angel . . . or a bride. (When he'd brought the present by last night, he'd smiled again exactly as he'd smiled all those years ago when she'd hit that first homer, as though he was proud to be related to her. "Do I get to kiss the bride now?" he'd said, "—in case I come down with a cold sore?" She'd give him her cheek, blushing, and he'd kissed her lips and said, "Missed!" She'd pretended to slap him.) She thought of Henry Soames trying to play softball.

But, after all, her cousin Bill was no ballplayer, and she loved him as much as Duncan. They would sit in the room that had once been her grandfather's study —this up at Pear Hill, the old family place—playing chess. He'd sit with his horn-rimmed glasses in one hand and would talk about books she would really like, he was sure. (She would promise herself faithfully to get them from the city library in Slater, but always she would forget the titles.) Bill was going to be a lawyer and maybe go into politics, like Uncle Earle. He was only twenty-two, but already he was a member of the steering committee for some organization that had something to do with Indians. He and Duncan were like brothers, and always it had been sad to her that she was younger. Even grown up they were as splendid

as ever, "professionals," her father said—the two prides
of the family. (Her father, the family failure, in a way
—he'd left off farming to work in a factory—was even
prouder of Duncan and Bill than the rest of the
family.) Bill had given her a subscription to the
Columbia Record Club. When Cousin Mary Lou had
said, "Who's the cheap one?" fingering it, Callie had
bristled with anger. Bill gave away money to every
charity there was and probably some that had gone
out of business fifty years ago, and one time he'd given
Callie a book worth fourteen dollars, pictures of famous
places. He gave presents because they seemed to him
right, just like Uncle Earle. He would have given her
the same present whether it cost him fifteen cents or
a thousand dollars, practically. "That just shows how
little *you* know," Callie had snapped. Cousin Mary Lou
had been hurt. And immediately Callie had seen that
Mary Lou was right, everyone who didn't know him
well would think the same thing Mary Lou had thought:
so that even the wedding presents weren't hers, it
turned out, but everybody else's; she decided to put
his present out of sight.

"You don't really like me," Mary Lou said, tears
in her eyes.

"Don't be stupid," Callie said. "If I didn't like you
would I choose you for maid of honor?"

"Your mother made you do it," she said. One of
the tears rolled down her fat cheek toward the fold
between her chins.

"Oh, *really*, Mary Lou!" She took her hand, feeling
guilty (it was true, Mary Lou had been her mother's
idea), and she said, "Mary Lou, I feel closer to you
than to anybody else in the world." She was amazed,
hearing herself say it; but Mary Lou believed it. If she
didn't like Mary Lou, she ought to. Mary Lou had
hardly eaten a bite since the morning Callie had asked
her to be maid of honor, dieting ferociously to look

pretty for it. She hadn't lost weight; she'd gotten circles under her eyes.

Mary Lou wiped her eyes and blew her nose and said, "I really was proud that you chose me, Callie. I always loved you more than anything, and I didn't think you knew I was alive. Do you remember the time the Griffith boys threw stones at me and you came and caught my hand and we ran home?"

Callie gave her hand a gentle squeeze. She didn't remember.

Mary Lou said, "I was four-and-a-half and you were six." Suddenly she was weeping rivers. "Oh, Callie, I *do* love you."

"*Dear* Mary Lou," Callie said softly, standing thousands of miles away, shaky at the revelation. How had she not realized? And how was it that her mother had known? How was it possible that one could be so incredibly, selfishly blind? And so that night, busy as they were, they had talked for hours, or rather Mary Lou had talked, Callie listening intently—in secret feeling trapped and bored—as if the two of them had just got engaged, or as if she was catching up on the life of a friend after years of separation.

A long, low truck carrying a big orange machine that looked vaguely military passed on the highway in front of the house. It was time now, but still no sign of Uncle John. She heard her mother shouting into Aunt Mae's good ear, in the front parlor, and then she heard Cousin Rachel calling in the children from outdoors.

She smiled to keep from crying. It was supposed to be the groom that ran out at the last minute, not the bride. (She saw herself slipping quietly out the cellar door—she could reach the cellar from the pantry without anyone's seeing her—and she saw herself lowering the cellar door again gently behind her, then going down swiftly toward the haylot and the woods beyond, carefully holding up the train and raising the skirts of the wedding dress.) Henry Soames would not run out, of course. He would be there in the church coatroom now, sweating in his tight collar, pulling nervously at his upper lip, wiping his forehead again and again, nodding and smiling whenever anyone spoke to him, no matter what it was they said. Aunt Anna was perhaps at the organ already, playing the favorite old hymns very softly, dragging her feet a little on the pedals, playing slowly, slowly, scowling at the page with her mouth bit shut as though she had pins in it. The ushers would be taking people in, the friends of the groom on one side, the friends of the bride on the other. Robert Wilkes would be fitting himself to a choir robe. The Griffith boys and John Jones and Ben Williams—maybe even Cousin Bill and Cousin Dunc— would be behind the church tying tin cans and shoes onto Henry's car, and putting signs on it, or worse. Again Callie smiled. Henry loved that car, beat up and old-fashioned as it was. He loved it as much as Uncle Grant loved his cream-colored hardtop. When they came out of the church and all the people were throwing rice and confetti and she was getting ready to throw her bouquet, there would be the car, poor Henry's pride, at the foot of the walk, pushed around from where he'd parked it so that it would be the first thing he saw when he came out. It would be fixed shamefully, all its square antique dignity mocked by streamers and vulgar signs (they wrote on one car, "Hot Springs by sunset"), and Henry would gape, having known all along it was going to happen, for all George's caution, but still not prepared, deeply shocked, feeling as though a whole part of his life had been torn from him and trampled. He'd stand frozen, staring in disbelief and sorrow. *And then what?* she thought. *And then he will smile.*

The bakery truck was still outside, and around the corner, out of sight, the man was saying, "Lady, I don't care who signs it, I don't care if a two-days-old

baby signs it, but when I check in all the slips are supposed to be signed." Aunt Joan's voice said, "Don't
you sign it, Priscilla. Never sign for merchandise till
you've checked it." The man said, "So check it. I'm
stopping you?" Aunt Joan said, "There might be nothing inside, only rocks. He might be a thief that came
here to steal the jewels."

When Uncle John's green Buick appeared (all at
once, as if out of thin air, nosing tortuously into the
driveway), she felt dizzy. The same instant there came
a soft knock on the door and a child's voice—Linda's
—calling her name. "Callie," she said, "your mom
says to tell you it's time."

3

When she opened the door, her mother and the bridesmaids and all the aunts who hadn't left for the church
were standing with their faces turned toward her, beam-
ing. Prince got up slowly, with an old-dog sigh, and
came over to stand at her feet. Uncle John was standing at the front door, watching too. When he saw her
her he took off his hat. No one moved or spoke for
an instant (except the children, as indifferent to what
was happening as Callie was unaware of their indifference) and Callie was overwhelmed by her sense of their
mutual helplessness: They had done everything they
could, had swarmed to her side as they might in a
time of tragedy, some of them hardly knowing her,
from Cobleskill and Rochester and Cleveland, Ohio,
and even, one of them, California, bearing gifts that
would make her house beautiful and give it its solid
anchor in tradition, and they would join her celebration
of the ancient forms—the ride to the church with her

mother's oldest brother, the lighting of the symbolic candles, the pure white runner now walked on, stained, her father's words, signifying to all the world (she understood now for the first time, in alarm) that she had lost forever what she'd never realized she had. There would come the magical exchange of rings, the lifting of the veil, the kiss, and then Aunt Anna would play that organ maniacally, tromping the pedals, not caring how many of the notes she missed, for Callie (poor Callie whom we all knew well) had died before her time and had been lifted to Glory—and the rice would rain down (Uncle Gordon ducking, trying to snap pictures, shielding the expensive camera he'd bought for taking pictures of the flowers in his garden and the prize turkeys he raised for the Fair)—rice and confetti raining down like seeds out of heaven, numberless as stars or the sands of the seashore, shining like the coins that dropped from Duncan's pockets—and then the symbolic biting of the cake, the emptying of the fragile glass (Uncle Gordon taking more pictures, frenetic, even George Loomis the eternal bachelor smiling, joyful, quoting scraps of what he said was Latin verse). They would join her in all this, yet could no more help her, support her, defend her than if they were standing on the stern of a ship drawing steadily away from her, and she (in the fine old beaded and embroidered white gown, the veil falling softly from the circlet on her forehead), she, Callie, on a small boat solemn as a catafalque of silver, failing away toward night.

I will love him, she thought. *I don't know whether I love him or not, but I will.*

It was suspicious, now that she thought of it, that they'd left her there alone for half-an-hour, knowing where she was, surely having things to say to her but not saying them, waiting, gathered at the door: Not even one of the children had violated the room. Not even Prince. But now they were all of them talking at once, saying, "Callie, you're beautiful, beautiful, an't-it?" Saying, "Hurry, hurry! Just fifteen minutes," and "Children, out to the cars! Quick about it!" And now Uncle John was beside her, giving her his arm.

Neither of them spoke on the way to the church. She sat very still, hands folded in her lap, looking out at brilliant yellow wheat stubble on hills pitched or slanting away into tree-filled glens where spring water ran and brightly dappled guernsey cows could go to drink or lie down in the heavy shade. They came to the maples and beeches of the slope, the nearer mountains bright with twenty shades of green (in a month it would all be gold and red), the higher mountains in the distance clean blue. They passed the little store—Llewellyn's American Eagle Market—with its sharply pitched roof and long wooden porch where in her grade school days she'd played jacks or sat with her lunchpail eating sandwiches and black bean salad, sometimes going in to buy an Orange Crush with a dime she'd earned picking up sticks from the yard or with a handful of pennies that had spilled out of one of the thrashing men's overalls. They passed the cottage-like house where David Parks lived once, the house crudely snow-fenced, set back from the road, shaded by pine trees and jutting out from the mountain's bank like a granite boulder, and she remembered sitting in the swing in her yellow dress the day of his birthday party, shyly watching his older sister Mary holding hands with her boyfriend from Slater. Uncle John slowed down, pointing up into the woods with his bent first finger, and she saw a deer. She smiled. It was a lucky omen. And then the church steeple came in sight, and then the whole church, white and old-fashioned, the paint peeling, the shingled roof newly patched with yellow-red cedar, and all around the church and all along the highway more cars than she could remember having seen in one place in all her life. (They'd be hustling Henry away from the window, because he mustn't see her until the moment all of them saw her at the end of the aisle. George Loomis would be there beside him, looking him over, telling him he looked like Good King Jesus (for the Preacher's benefit), and keeping one eye on where the car was hidden, actually believing he'd be able to protect it.) Everywhere she looked there were birds—orioles, robins, blue jays, waxwings, nuthatches, sparrows—bright as the red and yellow roses climbing the bank at the foot of the lawn. The sky was bright blue, the bluest sky in the world, with just one white cloud, so precisely outlined it looked like a picture in a child's book of fairy tales.

Uncle John nosed the car up the drive and right to the steps. There were dozens of people there, mostly friends and relations who bowed and waved when they saw her, a few conspicuously strange to her, queerly stiff and peculiar, friends or relatives of Henry's. Uncle John said, "Here we are, Callie." He smiled, and the smile summoned memories, so many in an instant that she couldn't single one out, no more than she could have separated the rays of the sun; as if all her past happiness were poured together into one silver cup and the cup was overflowing. She said, "Uncle John," all the meaning of her life flowing into a name, and he reached for her hand, formally. *"Gras fyddo gyd â chwi,"* he said. Grace be with you. Mary Lou and Susan Cooper came running to the car, Dorothy Carrico a little behind them, shining like all summer in their bridesmaids' dresses, and Mary Lou reached through the window to hug her. She said, "Quick, quick!" then backed away while someone—one of the Griffith boys (how tall he'd grown!)—opened the car door and helped her out.

Inside, downstairs in the third grade Sunday school room, fiery with memories and sunlight from the casement windows, she stood patiently while they fussed with the dress and admired the bouquet, every few

minutes shushing Tommy and Linda, who were to
carry the cushions with the rings. She answered them
all when they spoke to her, politely admired their
dresses, but she felt as though she were not there. She
felt weightless, mysteriously separate from the cream-
colored walls and the dark oak doors, the windows
with sunlight streaming in, the faded wine-colored
plush chairs in front, the wooden folding chairs all
around, the pictures of Jesus and Lazarus, Jesus and
the children, Jesus praying. Beams creaked over her
head and she could hear feet shuffling, voices talking,
a rush of indistinguishable sounds, the music of the
organ playing hymns, a steady murmur of sound that
seemed to come from all directions like the sound of
a waterfall heard from up close, but not loud, gentle,
almost comforting, saying. . . . The feeling of weight-
lessness grew on her. She gave her mother her cheek
to kiss and heard her whisper strange syllables, saw
her wiping her eyes (all far away, far, far away, the
kiss, the whispered words); she saw Linda and Tommy being led to the stairs, Mary Lou and Susan and
Dorothy Carrico tripping away, blowing kisses to her;
she felt Cousin-Aunt Tisiphone taking her hand. The
hum around her began to die out. Then silence, complete and terrible as a silence in a busy dream. She
heard the organ, suddenly loud as thunder in her ears,
and her mind sang wildly, hurled back to childhood:

> *Here comes the bride,*
> *All fat and wide!*

And then she was standing at the rear of the church,
her father beside her, taking her arm, and Dorothy
Carrico was walking toward the candles and flowers
and the blazing music and the bright reds and blues of
the round church window; and now, without feeling,
as weightless as the cloud passing over the mountain
(out the window to her right, beyond the maples),

she, Callie, was walking slowly, her father hopping twice on one foot to get in step. She thought, oblivious to the roar of the organ:

> *Soames is her second name,*
> *Second name, second name. . . .*

Henry Soames was watching her, dignified and comically beautiful, as all her own family was beautiful, and she walked slowly, having all eternity to taste the strange new sensation of freedom, knowing that she too was beautiful now, yes, more beautiful than the wedding gown, lighter, purer, immutable as the gown was not, as even the ceremony was not. Their faces surrounded her, looking up, shining as if reflecting the secret radiance thinly veiled, her total and untouchable, virginal freedom. In a moment, she would feel her weight again, her mere humanness, the child inside, but not yet. The church window said, *All will be well.* The white of the cloth on the pulpit said, *Go slow.* She watched Henry, more solemn and splendid even than her Uncle Earle when he won the election for Mayor, more beautiful than Duncan, looking up, tossing a child in his arms, or Bill with his hand poised over the chessboard, or Aunt Anna paring apples with speckled, swift fingers. Then suddenly the room was real again, full of organ music, the lead mullions of the stained glass window as solid as earth, the rich colors deep and heavy as stone, even the professional simper of the Preacher solidly real, as heavy and solid as iron chains and as heavy as the golden burning bodies and faces of the people around her—the people she knew and those she didn't. Only she herself was weightless, and in a moment she too would be real again. *Go slow,* said the room. *Be patient,* said the trees. She could feel weight coming, a murderous solidity, hunting her.

III

THE
EDGE OF
THE
WOODS

1

At 5:00 A.M. when his wife woke him up Henry Soames opened his eyes at once, and he kept them open, unblinking, as he moved to the telephone table in the living room. He let himself down into the over-stuffed chair, his long, thick upper lip lifted slightly from his teeth, and picked up the receiver. The wire hummed. Old Prince appeared in the bedroom door-way, ears raised, head cocked, seeing what he was doing. Then he turned and went back to his place on the floor beside the bed, next to Callie.

It was neither dark nor light in the room. The bloom of snow outside dimly lighted the wallpaper, bringing out silver glints and blue-gray lines—a man and a woman in old-fashioned dress standing on a path under a willow tree near a bridge, their two children, a boy and a girl, running up the path toward a man and a woman in old-fashioned dress, a willow tree, a bridge, two children, a man and a woman. Snowlight sharpened the angles and curves of the fur-niture so that each piece stood distinct and detached. In the entry room where there were no windows the wallpaper design blurred to shadows and then dark-ness. He sat looking straight into it, but he felt the entry room more than saw it. There was the old roller piano they never used except for putting photographs on—it had belonged to his mother once—and the oval rug, the nicked old shelf table with hymnbooks and magazines underneath and a limp runner over the top, and on the runner, waiting to be hung up again, the wall lamp. In the entry room things seemed settled in, permanent, but not here. The furniture here was like furniture that had just been moved into a new house or is just about to be moved out of a house where nobody lives. In the half-light, the carved oval frame high on the wall above the davenport—it was an old picture of Henry Soames' father holding a book— seemed to have nothing in it.

"Number, please," the operator said. He gave the number and waited again while she rang it.

Over the phone the doctor sounded half-asleep. He said, "Well, sometimes it's two or three hours after the sac breaks before contractions begin. When they do, you run her in to the hospital and have them phone me."

"Yes, sir," Henry said. He started to say more, but the doctor said goodbye and hung up. Henry sat in the darkness pulling at his left hand with his right. The skin was loose. He'd been getting his weight down lately.

It had snowed some more during the night, and the snow was sharp blue under the neon sign up front. This was the new part of the house, and he thought again how it was good they'd put the house where they had after all, with the Stop-Off right handy. It was Callie that had decided it, not Henry. He'd have thought she'd want something nicer, more like a home, a place with a lawn and trees and a view of the mountains. So had her folks. ("Now wouldn't you rather have the old Kelsey place, or maybe a new house up on the hill next to our place?" her father had asked, and she'd said "No." Henry had said, "The Kelsey place'd be real pretty with a coat of paint and some fixing up, and—" but she hadn't let him finish. "Henry, be practical," she'd said. She'd snapped it out. George Loomis and Lou and Jim Millet and Nick Blue the Indian and neighbors from here to Athensville and New Carthage had pitched in and helped him lay up the cinderblock house behind the diner and right next to the lean-to room where he,

Henry, had lived all those years by himself—and they'd done it all by fall, had just finished up in time for them to pull down the scaffolding and sweep up the yard and go take over the work at George Loomis's place when George had his arm torn off in his corn binder. Callie'd been six months pregnant by then, but she still ran the diner alone while he painted outside and inside, wheezing, oozing sweat, knocking together windowboxes and planting zinnias and laying yellow-painted rocks out along the driveway. When it was done they'd stood at this same window looking out at the neon sign where it jutted out from the corner of the diner, watching the semis roll by on the dark highway past the diner—and now house—and Callie had said, "It's real nice." She had stood with her elbows close to her sides and hadn't looked at him, or not until he'd put one finger under her chin and turned her face around. She'd looked past him even then.) The snow lay smooth, sharp blue right out to the highway. Beyond the highway more snow, luminous white in the darkness, stretched away to the trees. The edge of the woods was vague, ghostly this early in the morning. The woods were over a mile deep—they came out over by Freund's place—and though they never had in the old days, they made Henry uneasy now. It was as if there was somebody in there moving around. He dreamed about him sometimes, and sometimes when he was wide awake he wondered how it would be if Willard came back. They never talked about him.

He looked at the crack of yellow light under the bedroom door.

Jim Millet had said three days ago when he'd pulled in for gas, "You be sure and call the doctor yourself. There's a night nurse down there gets a real charge out of delivering babies herself." Dr. Costard, the obstetrician, had told Callie almost the same thing. He'd patted her arm with his white, soft hand and said,

"When the time comes, be sure to call me, Mrs. Soames. Don't leave it to the hospital. They get rushed sometimes, and you know how it is." But that had been in mid-afternoon, when Dr. Costard was wide awake.

The chores lights were on up in Frank Wells' barns on the hill, but no lights in the house. They'd driven to Cobleskill for a family reunion. It was too bad, for Callie's sake. But then, they'd never been close. Frank Wells drank most of the time, these days, and though he was never much trouble himself—sometimes on his way home from town he'd pull off the road and down into the creek to sleep it off—it made things troublesome, in the end, because Callie's mother was religious. She played the organ at the New Carthage Salem Baptist Church. That was partly why Callie'd come to work at the Stop-Off in the first place, she said. To get away.

He squeezed his upper lip between his finger and thumb and blinked slowly. He got up, shoved his hands down into his limp bathrobe pockets, and moved to the bedroom door.

"Looks like you're gonna have that watermelon after all," he said.

Callie smiled back. Neither of them ever called it a baby.

It looked as if she had pillows inside her nightgown. Her legs and arms and neck were thin, gray, and her head, turned toward the yellow plastic bedlamp, was flushed and too large.

"If it didn't come soon I was going to call it off," she said.

Henry went to her, smiling, sliding his slippers on the hardwood. He stood for a moment with his hands in his pockets, then touched her shoulder with the tips of his fingers. She didn't move her hand to his.

Under the light her hair looked dry. He stood for a long time looking at her and smiling, thinking, Well I'll be damned, it's really come time. And in his mind he saw Willard Freund leaning over the diner counter, sharp-elbowed, tiny-eyed, smiling and talking to Callie. In his mind he could see it as if it were yesterday, Willard's wide mouth, his cocked eyebrow, his face lighted under the lamp, the cluttered room behind him dark. Sometimes the three of them had talked. And then he'd found out what Willard was doing, had done already by that time because by that time he was gone, had run out on her as a man would run out on some common country whore. And now he would catch himself watching the woods, though it wouldn't be from the woods he'd come; he'd come by the highway if he came. He'd come in with his hands in his pockets and his collar turned up, his eyes shy, and maybe Henry would feel sorry for him because he'd been a damn fool, and then again maybe he'd kill him, he didn't know. Sometimes before he knew what it was he was thinking he would look at his wide, short hands and would close them slowly.

She said, "Let's go to bed, Henry. It may be hours yet." She looked past him; she hadn't even turned her head.

He nodded. It was the truth that he needed his sleep. He wasn't a kid any more. Twenty-five years older than she was, old enough to be her father. A fat old man with a weak heart, as Doc Cathey, their regular doctor, had said. "You get your beauty sleep, boy. You keep on settin' up half the night and one of these days Callie'll be a widow." Doc had chuckled, hunched up and watching him sideways as if the idea of it pleased him all to hell, and maybe it did.

(Out by the gas pumps Doc had sat in his dented-up car fidgeting with his plastic hearing aid, his head brown and wrinkled as an old baldwin, and then he'd grinned, embarrassed maybe, and he'd said, "I s'pose you don't want to talk about it, eh? . . . about Willard?"

Henry had half-turned as if he'd heard a footstep crunch the gravel behind him, but there was only the long, flat diner, the new white-painted house, and, beyond the roof, mountains and white clouds, and birds flying, starlings. He turned back to the car and put his hand on the cold metal of the gas pump, and Doc leaned farther out the car window, his eyes squinted almost shut behind the thick glasses. "You know I ain't one to noise things around. Don't bring on no coronary for nothin'. I never said she ain't happy with you and this place here, I never inferred it." He looked down at Henry's hands.

"I don't know what you're talking about," Henry said. His voice was quiet, so quiet it surprised him. It was like a woman's voice. The old man looked at him, and Henry could hear the noise of the starlings half-a-mile up the mountain.

The corners of Doc's mouth twitched back. "Now, you listen here. Somebody was gonna bring it up sooner or later, whether it's the truth or not, and there's people could be a lot meaner about it than me. You get use to hearing it, boy, get use to it. It's for your own good; you take my advice."

"I don't know what you're talking about," Henry said again, a whisper this time. He leaned toward the car and touched the door handle. He felt sweat prickling. The dog appeared beside the diner, ears lifted, watching.

Doc Cathey counted out his money with his thumb clamped down so hard on the bills that they almost tore as he pulled each dollar free. Henry took the money and didn't count it. The old man switched on the ignition and ground on the starter button. A muscle in his jaw jumped. "I'm just trying to help out," he said. "You know that. Don't be a damn mule." Henry didn't say a word, and after a minute the old man rammed the car into gear and out onto the highway, spattering gravel. The dust he stirred up hung in the air, mixing with the smells of gasoline and exhaust fumes; then, very slowly, it settled.

Henry went in, moving automatically, looking up the highway toward the hill. In the sticky heat of the diner he rang up the price of the old man's gas, not looking at the register, bent over it but not looking at it, and then, knowing what he was going to do and knowing he would have to fix it, he closed his two hands around the age-dry sides of the cash drawer and bent the wood outward until it split and broke away. Change fell out and hit the floor and rolled, ringing. His chest burned white hot. After a minute Callie came up and stood beside him, not speaking at first. He pulled at his lip. She said, "Have you gone crazy or something?" She waited. "Henry, go take a nap or something. You act like you've gone crazy." She spoke slowly and evenly, keeping back from him.

"Callie," he said. His voice cracked. He thought for a split-second of his father's voice.

They looked at each other, and then she looked out at the pumps, or past them. Her lips were puffy from the dryness of August. "I can manage out here. Go on." She didn't come any nearer. That afternoon Henry went hunting. He shot three crows, and it took him till after dark.)

He pulled out of his bathrobe and slippers and crawled into bed and snapped off the bedlamp. He lay there awake, or lay there believing he was awake, breathing shallowly. Two hours later, at seven, the labor pains started, and Callie said, "Henry!" She shook him, and when he opened his eyes he saw that she had been up for some time. She was dressed up as if for church, even wearing her hat.

It was the twenty-ninth of December and the road to Slater was ice-packed and banked by gray drifts. The sky over the mountains was as gray as the snow, and there wasn't so much as a sparrow moving on a telephone wire, and not a trace of wind. Black telephone poles stood out sharply against the gray all around them, pole after pole, a series winding downward as if forever. He was conscious of them as he passed them; even when he thought about other things, his body registered the rhythm of the telephone poles going by.

Callie looked at her watch once or twice on the way, timing the pains. She sat too close to the rattling door.

"Holding up all right?" he said.

" 'Course I am, Henry. You?"

His right hand let go of the steering wheel as he shrugged. "I'm fine. Jim dandy." He laughed. It was so cold in the car that their breath made steam. He pulled at the toggled wire heater control and the heater fan clanked into motion.

The tamaracks up on the mountains were bare, like dead pines. This year—every year—the bareness looked final. He let his hand fall to the seat between them, and after a minute, as if she'd thought it over first, Callie touched his fingers. Her hand was warm. The warmth surprised him, seemed out of place, mysterious.

The road curved sharply and they reached the bridge into town.

2

The waiting room at the hospital was small and cluttered—coffee cups, floor ash trays, magazines. It was like the lobby of a cheap hotel. The wall paint was dark with age, and up on the wall over the magazine table a stuffed owl stood staring on a hickory limb.

The woman at the desk said, "I'm sorry, but, just as I've told you, we have to collect when the patient enters." She looked them over.

Henry pulled at the fingers of one hand. He leaned forward and said, "I'll have to go home for the damn money then. But you've got to let my wife in right now. She's in labor."

"Don't cuss, Henry," Callie said. She smiled at the woman.

The woman at the desk said, "It's a hospital rule. I'm sorry." She was big-jawed and had colorless, close-set eyes.

"Write them a check, Henry," Callie said.

Henry wet his lips. He looked at the woman and hunted through his pockets for the checkbook he never carried with him, then took the blank check the woman slid across the desktop and filled it out. She held it up to look at it. She was suspicious, but she said: "Through the double doors and turn right and straight down the hall to the end. Mr. Soames, you wait here if you like."

Callie smiled at her again, politely, looking through her.

For fifteen minutes Henry sat with his hands clasped together, leaning forward under the stuffed owl, and every now and then he turned his head to look for the doctor, but he didn't come. A young nurse came up, with her square head slung forward and down like a bull's but her mouth was gentle, and led him to the labor room and opened the door for him. Henry went in. It was a drab green room with two beds, one of them empty, and shelves along one side of the room, with bedpans, washpans, colored bottles, towels, sealed gray bags. At the far end of the room there was a window, and he could look out and see dirty snow and a street and old houses and a dark, thick pine.

"You all right?" he asked.

She nodded. "Has the doctor come?"

"Not yet." He pulled a chair up to the bed and sat down.

"It's all right," she said. "He'll come." Henry slid his hand under hers and she patted it and looked out the window.

He held her fingers, feeling the warmth, and after an hour he got up and got the dominoes out of her suitcase and dumped them on the bedside table. Henry still held her hand as they played. Every five or six minutes she looked away and shut her eyes, and Henry stared at the dominoes, feeling out as if with his hands their gray, cracked surfaces and yellowing dots. They'd belonged to his mother and father. A car started up on the street right outside the window and then another one farther down, and a boy carrying a box moved past on the sidewalk, running four steps, sliding, running four steps, sliding; then two men passed in long coats. Directly across the street an old woman backed out of her front door dragging a faded Christmas tree with bits of tinsel still clinging to the branches. The doctor didn't come. A nurse came and took Callie's pulse and put her hand on Callie's stomach, then left. The pains were sharper now but not closer together. Henry stacked the dominoes neatly and put them away in their battered white tiebox and fastened the rubber band. Sweat prickled under his arms.

"You all right?" he said.

She nodded.

At eleven o'clock the doctor came in and examined her.

When he came out to the hallway where Henry stood waiting he didn't say how she was. He put his hand on Henry's arm, smiling, looking at Henry's forehead, and said, still holding onto the arm: "You had your breakfast yet?"

Henry nodded without thinking. "How long will it be?"

The man tipped his head down, the smile still there, and he looked as if he were thinking it over. But he was studying the pattern in the floor, moving his gaze tile by tile down the hall. "No telling," he said. "It's a beautiful day for it." He waved toward the windows at the end of the hall. Sunlight streamed through the diamond-shaped panes and gleamed on the brown and white tiles and on the leaves of wilting plants in the planter by the desk.

Henry kept from moving, because of the hand on his arm. He said, "Will it be today, then, you think?"

"It'll come," the doctor said. "Don't worry yourself. It's all right, I've been through it too." He winked slowly, the way a woman would, and gripped Henry's arm more tightly, then left, walking with his toes pointing outward, his head tilted to one side and back. Henry went in again. He stood heavily, balanced on his heels, his fingertips in his tight hip pockets, watching a pain take her. Then he sat down by the bed. "Poor Callie," he said. She frowned and met his eyes as though he were a stranger, then turned her face away.

He looked for a long time at the side of her face, the line of her jaw, and he felt somehow uneasy, guilty, the way he felt on the long afternoons when he sat in the diner watching cars and trucks and buses pass on the highway, glittering in the sunlight, not stopping. He would feel uneasy, for some reason guilty, as though it were his fault they didn't pull in, but then evening would come, suppertime, and somebody would come—truckers, or somebody like George Loomis, who would talk about things he'd seen in the Service —he had spells when he came sometimes four, five times a week, maybe because he lived all alone in that big old house—or Lou Millet would come, with gossip —or sometimes Willard Freund. But not Willard any more. Henry locked his fingers together and looked at the floor. Callie pretended to sleep.

At seven that night Doc Cathey came in with coffee and sandwiches. "Henry, you look worse'n her," he said. He opened his eyes wider, as if it helped him focus, and the loose red netting on the whites made Henry look down. "I bet you ain't eaten a bite all day long."

"I'm all right," Henry said.

Doc Cathey ignored him, holding Callie's wrist, ignoring her, too, taking her pulse and watching the door as if he were afraid they'd run him out if they caught him. Callie compressed her lips and Doc Cathey glanced at her, then slid his hand under the bedclothes and onto her stomach. "She ain't moved it down much," he said to the room in general. "Looks like what they call primary inertia, maybe stiff cervix." He looked at Henry. "You told Costard she's a bleeder?"

Henry nodded. "He said he'd give her some kind of vitamin."

Doc Cathey scowled and looked at the door again. "He will if he remembers. They don't know one damn patient from another. Eat your sandwiches, Henry." He looked back at Callie and grunted. "You lie here and keep at it a while, girl. See Henry gets some sleep."

He went to the door and stood there, hunchbacked, looking at the doorknob. "She's Rh negative too, ain't she? What's—" he paused "—the daddy?"

Callie said, "Henry's negative."

Nobody spoke for a minute. Henry sucked in his loose upper lip and felt the quick light ticking of his heart. The old man didn't move. Henry said, "That's right."

Callie leaned up on one elbow and said, "Anyway, it doesn't matter on the first one. The doctor said so."

Doc Cathey peeked at her over the rims of his glasses, then at Henry. "May be," he said. "That may be. They know everything, these fancy city doctors." He shook his head. "You've thought up every complication I know of, you two."

Callie asked, "How much longer you think it will be?"

"Lord knows. If your insides are froze up like I think, it'll take a good long while yet, maybe two days."

Callie lay back again. She closed her eyes, and Henry leaned toward her, groping with one hand for the foot of the bed, watching her face. Her mouth was closed and her nostrils were narrow, as if she'd stopped breathing. After a minute she said, almost in a whisper: "It's the waiting that's so awful." She opened her eyes and looked at Henry, then closed them again and moved her head from side to side on the pillow. Her lips tightened, then relaxed. Henry touched her foot.

Out in the hall Henry asked, "Will it pain her much?"

"Maybe a little," the old man said. "Maybe a good deal." He fiddled with his hearing aid and watched Henry out of the corner of his eye, with a smile like a grimace. "She'll get tired, and her insides'll likely rip all to hell." Then he said, "Worried about her, ain't you?" He went on smiling and watching him. Henry closed his right hand and the nails bit into the palm.

" 'Course I am. Anybody'd worry," he said. "She's my wife."

Doc Cathey pushed one hand down into his coat pocket and closed the other over Henry's arm. " 'Course they would." The queer smile was still there.

When Henry went back, Callie lay facing away from the door. She didn't say a word as he came in.

3

Callie slept and Henry stood at the window watching darkness settle in. Lights went on in the front room of the house across the street, and down at the end of the block the supermarket neon blazed pink and blue, *Miller's*. It began to snow again as he watched—big, light flakes that dropped onto branches and hung there as more flakes fell, mounding up. A boy passed on the sidewalk, pushing a bicycle, and four women got off the bus at the corner and came up the street slowly, carrying packages. None of them looked toward the hospital as they passed. Down on the supermarket parking lot there were cars and farm trucks parked, some of them with their taillights on, glowing like a few last scattered coals in a furnace. People moved around on the lot and inside the supermarket, on the other side of the full-length windows, and on the sidewalks beyond the lot—children, grown-ups, old people—a hundred or more in all. He pursed his lips. It was queer, now that he thought of it, how many people there were in the world, moving around, hurrying—in Slater, in Athensville, Utica, Albany, down in New York City—millions of 'em moving around, bent forward a little against the snow. He sipped the coffee Doc Cathey had brought and then he stood looking again, holding the cup in his two hands, feeling its warmth under his curled fingers. Millions and millions of people, he thought. Billions. His mind couldn't seem to get hold of it. Callie groaned and half-wakened, and he set down the cup and went to her and fitted his two hands around the small of her back and pressed in as Lou Millet had told him he'd done with his wife to ease the pain. She breathed deeply again; her breathing was the only sound in the room.

He sat down by the bed and stared at the fuzzy shadows thrown by the nightlamp—a long shadow curving away and two thinner straight lines running into it, the head of the bed. When he shut his eyes he saw the highway in front of the Stop-Off, and trucks moving along it, dark, speeding up for the second of the two hills that rose one on each side of his place, and then the road leading down to Nickel Mountain where the bends got dangerous and where the up-grades got steeper, leading through bare-branched beeches and maples and into the firs and tamaracks and then into open space where if it wasn't bad weather a man could see stars and, far below, the river. Callie groaned again and he pressed in on her back. It was hours since they'd checked her.

The door opened behind him and light flattened across the bed. The nurse said, "Somebody to see you, Mr. Soames. Out in the waiting room."

He hesitated. When she didn't come in he said, "It's been hours since they checked my wife."

"I'll tell them at the desk. I'm off duty now." She turned away, and he eased himself up out of the chair and moved into the hall. Callie groaned behind him and he stopped. She was quiet again.

In the dimly lighted corner of the waiting room George Loomis sat in his too-big sheepskin jacket, with an unlighted cigarette in his mouth, turning the pages of a magazine with his left hand, his head bent down to see. His right jacket sleeve hung empty. He was thirty—there was gray in his hair—but he looked no more than a boy. He glanced up and grinned as Henry came near.

"Any news?" George asked, getting to his feet.

Henry shook his head. "She's been in labor for

sixteen hours. The labor room next door they've had three women in and out."

George went on grinning, watching him, and Henry wondered all at once if it was pride that had made him say sixteen hours right away. Maybe he was hoping Callie would be in labor for a week.

George patted his jacket pockets, hunting. "It takes a while sometimes," he said. "Cigarette?" He found the package, fumbled with it, tapped it against his leg to shake a cigarette out to where Henry could get hold of it, and held it up. Henry took it though he never smoked now, on account of his health, and put it between his lips. George held the matchbook and struck a match, all with his one hand—the wall beside him brightened for a moment—and lit Henry's cigarette, then his own. They sat down. "You look tired," George said.

Henry waved it away. "You're out pretty late, aren't you?" There were dark green shadows under George's eyes and his cheekbones jutted out. His mouth was pale, like the mouth of a dead man. He hadn't gotten his strength back since the accident.

"Chores," George said. He held the cigarette out sideways, as if to see if it was straight, and Henry knew well enough what he meant. Chores with one arm—three hours for a one-hour job—because neighbors could come, a hundred of them, to milk while you lay in the hospital, and fill your yard with stove wood, and grind your grist and chop your corn and water your chickens and plow for you, but after a while you had to come home, and they had to go cut wood for themselves and grind grist and plow and plant, and if you were young yet, like George Loomis, you still had years of wood yet to cut. Even with two arms it wasn't easy.

"How's she doing?" George asked, turning away as he spoke, looking up at the owl on the wall.

"Fine so far. Doc Cathey thinks it might be rough."

George nodded as if Doc had told him already. "Callie's one hell of a gal." He looked back at Henry. "What can I get you?"

Right over their heads an old man shouted something, or groaned, and George's eyebrows drew inward. Henry looked at the ash on his cigarette, moved it carefully toward the ash tray, and scraped off all but the red cone. He remembered then and said, "We don't need a thing."

"I'll bring you some breakfast," George said. "Doc says you didn't eat all day till he brought in some supper. He says to tell you be sure and get your rest."

Henry nodded. "I sure appreciate this."

"Forget it. I guess I'd better get a move on. It's a long, long trail a-winding." He grinned again, then stood up. "Say, I ran into—" He stopped, confused, then concentrated on his jacket zipper; but Henry understood.

"Who?" he said, sitting balanced, squinting.

George went on tugging at the zipper. He freed it finally, then looked up, pretending to smile. "He was bound to come back sooner or later. You know that."

Henry watched him. "How long's he been in?"

"I don't know, maybe a day or two, maybe a week. I didn't ask."

"You talked to him?"

"I ran into him and I said hello; that was it. He's got a job over at Purina. That's where I saw him."

"He means to stay, then?"

"No way of knowing." He came a step toward Henry. "I'd really better get going, though. . . ."

Henry leaned forward, folding his hands, squinting more. He said—and in the half-dark room it did not seem a surprising thing to say—"I'm going to kill him."

George blanched. He said quietly, looking at him, "You're out of your fucking head."

"I mean it."

Abruptly, George got out his pack of cigarettes,

shook one into his hand and lit the new cigarette from the one he had going. "I never heard such a thing," he said. His hand trembled. "You sit there cool as a cucumber and—"

"I'll tell you why."

"I don't want to hear. I don't want to hear a thing about it. You're crazy to even think it."

"I'll tell you what he did."

George pivoted away, then back, determined. "Look, I've got to get started home. It'll take me half-an-hour through this snow." He came toward Henry again. "And listen, remember what I told you, get some rest."

Henry reached out to block his way and George paused, but then Henry let it go. "I'll try," he said.

"Do it, now."

He nodded. He sat perfectly still, his fists closed tight, watching George move past him and toward the door. George waved, and after a moment Henry returned the wave. He thought, So he's come back. It made him feel light, as though the ground had dropped away and he hung in empty space.

He got up at last, slowly, looking at the doorway where a minute ago George Loomis had stood, where now there were only reflected lights and, beyond the reflections, snow. He turned it over in his mind: So Willard's come back home.

Callie was still asleep when he went in. He sat down beside her and put his left hand on her back and closed his eyes. With his right hand he pulled at his upper lip. For two hours she didn't make a sound, and then it started again, worse. Her back was tender now and, gently, she pushed his hand away.

4

The night nurse was a spindly country woman, an old maid with a squeezed-shut face and brittle gray hair like steel wool. "This room's a mess," she said. "Clean up this room and in half-an-hour you got it looking like a hogpen." She moved past the chair where Henry sat, sniffing at him as if he smelled, and straightened the unmessed second bed and the shelves on the wall. "Dominoes," she said, disgusted, lifting the box from the bedside table with three fingers. "What'll you people think of next." And then she went out, not looking once at Callie.

He got no sleep, or no sleep that counted. He dreamed of the woods and thousands of birds turning and turning, a vortex above the trees, black against the gray of the sky. The next morning at seven, when Callie had been in labor for twenty-four hours, Dr. Costard came in again and sent Henry away while he made his examination. After five minutes the doctor came out and stood at the door pulling off his rubber glove.

"How is she?" Henry asked. His voice was like an old woman's, or like his father's—exactly like his father's.

"She's coming along," the doctor said. "We'll just have to be patient a while yet." He walked over toward the desk and Henry followed him. The doctor said when the nurse looked up, "She's dilated to three cm's. Have her examined again in four hours."

"Is that good?" Henry asked. "Three cm's?"

"It's a start." The doctor smiled, plump-faced, like

103

a hotel keeper. He had curly hair turned silver around the front.

"How much farther does she have to go?"

"Quite a ways yet." He looked at Henry, then put his hand on his arm. "Ten cm's," he said. He smiled.

"Will it be today, you think?"

"Could be. There are a lot of things we're not sure of yet in this business." He started down the hall, toeing outward.

"She's been in labor for twenty-four hours," Henry said, following him. He said it quickly, his middle fingers interlocked and pulling at each other.

"They'll do that sometimes." The doctor waved at him vaguely, with his back turned, and walked on. Henry watched him go.

An hour later they called him to the waiting room and he found the breakfast George Loomis had left—cheese, crackers, two apples, coffee. George hadn't been able to wait. It was eight miles each way from his place, but that wasn't it, Henry knew.

He started back for the labor room to eat, and as he passed the cigarette machine he stopped and bought a pack of Old Golds with filters. He stood for a minute looking down at the package and then he remembered: Willard Freund leaning into the lamplight in the lean-to room behind the diner, rain drumming on the roof, full of the smell of burning wood, and Willard reaching toward the table for the cigarettes he'd laid there, the pack glossy under the lamplight, yellow and red. Old Golds were what Willard Freund smoked. He saw the woods again in his mind, the gray, dead tamaracks, the darkness farther in, the birds. He stood for a long while looking down at the package.

It went on, hour after hour. Doc Cathey came and went and nurses came on duty and went off again, and nothing happened. Once they gave her a shot to stop the labor and give her a rest. Henry smoked and just held Callie's hand now. Delivery carts rolled by in the hall outside the door, and sometimes he heard the cries of newborn babies. When he looked out he saw new fathers talking, smoking cigarettes and looking in through the windows along the hall at the rows of baby beds—two squat, red-necked men with water-combed hair that needed cutting. Later there was another man, an Italian in an expensive suit. Callie lay still, white, with beads of sweat on her forehead. Outside the window the snow was still blowing, too thick to see through. At 6:00 P.M. Dr. Costard came in and examined her and gave her a shot. He smiled, as if sociably, then patted her arm. "I'll drop back later to see how you're doing."

Callie ignored him.

Outside the door Henry said, "Still the same?"

The doctor puckered his lips, then smiled again. "No change to speak of." He waved, then paused, turning back. "If things haven't improved by morning maybe we'll section her."

Henry waited, balanced on the balls of his feet.

"Caesarian," Dr. Costard explained. He winked, smiling. "But no use rushing Mother Nature. We'll see how she does tonight."

"She's a bleeder," Henry said. "When she cuts herself she keeps on bleeding."

The doctor nodded, still smiling. "We'll see."

Henry went back, touching the wall as he walked.

It was dark. He stared at the shadows thrown by the nightlight, then turned his head to stare at the dominoes in the box. His father's. They would sit up nights, his mother and father—his huge shirt would be open, showing spongy skin like wet clay and gray, curling hairs—and they'd stare at the oil-cloth-covered table where the dominoes lay, the winding paths, the boneyard, the fourteen in play up-ended like tombstones, and after a long time his father would place one and would smile, almost giggle, old-womanish, and his mother would place one right away, and then there would be the waiting again, like a wait in a game of chess, and then, as if kingdoms depended on it, his father would place another. He almost always won. There would be specks of dust on the burbon in his glass, and once in a while his hand would move to the glass mechanically, and the corners of Henry's mother's mouth would tighten. He would sit with his eyebrows drawn outward for a moment after he'd drunk, his thick lips wet, his forehead white, and then he'd say, Ah! as if drunk for pleasure.

("Fat's what got him," Doc Cathey had said. "The same thing that's gonna get you. I just hope you got your will made out." That was before Henry had married Callie. Nowdays Doc would say: "You lose ninety pounds, boy, or Callie'll be a widow." He would leer when he said it and touch Henry's arm, as if he were one of the family.)

The wind pushed past the window and blurred the outlines of the pine close to the street, bent in the churning snow. Except for the blooms of brightness in the snowy air, you wouldn't know there were lighted windows across the street. The snow had covered up everything now. The short space of lawn that you could still see was drifted high, and where there had been bushes before, right under the window, there were only mounds. Up in the mountains the roads would be closed, and truckers would be pulled up into farmers' yards, and maybe pulled up in front of the Stop-Off, too, because the place was never shut down, the neon sign burned night and day, week in week out, or had until now anyway, and it was worth a little bad driving to get to where people knew you. There would have been accidents by now, maybe. There sometimes were in blizzard time. Trucks jackknifed across the road or turned upside down at the foot of a cliff, half-sunk in the river, the icy water running through the cab, the bearded trucker dead a hundred, two hundred miles from home. It didn't happen often, but it happened. When you ran a diner for fifteen, twenty years maybe it seemed oftener than it was. You saw them, you dished up chili to them, and coffee and pie and cigarettes, and they waved and left, and you told their jokes to somebody else, and two weeks, two months, two years later you saw their clean-shaved faces staring out at you, dead, from the paper. That's how it seemed. He thought of George Loomis. His picture had been there too, and he'd been as good as dead; it had been touch-and-go for a week. That day too there'd been snow falling—an October snow, thin, icy, almost rain.

("Jesus Christ," Lou Millet had said. He never talked much, Jim was the talker. Jim Millet was there too, drinking coffee, his nose still wrinkled from what he'd seen. "George Loomis," Lou said. "Poor bastard must be hexed. You'd think he'd be just about ready to change his name and start all over."

Callie had stood with her back to them, wiping cups. Her hand moved, but the rest of her was motionless, the way she'd stood a long time ago when they talked about Willard Freund, before she'd found out about him, before he ran away and left her in trouble with nobody on earth but fat Henry Soames to turn to, a father to her in Frank Wells' place, or so he'd thought until that night in the lean-to when she'd said to him, "What can I do?" She was wearing a man's white shirt, and rain had pasted it to her.

Jim Millet talked and she listened with her mouth pressed shut.

"It was bloody," Jim said. He shook his head and took another gulp of coffee. "The damn corn binder was still running."

Henry had seen the place—this was later, though— a rocky strip of land four rods wide and a half-mile long that angled along beside the woods, up above the swampland. It looked like a place where something like that would happen, and what was strange, it wasn't three rods from the place where fifteen years ago Ba-Ba Covert had rolled over his spike-wheeled tractor and crippled himself for life and would have killed himself if he'd been sober. White stumps jutted up out of the water, and around the edge of the swamp there were half-dead willows and then locusts and then two tamaracks so tall that in late afternoon their skeleton shadows stretched the length of the cornlot.

"Ok," Lou said, not looking at Jim, watching Callie.

"The goddamn cylinder was going around and around—" He made a circling motion with his right hand, touching his left bicep and circling away, touching the bicep again, circling away. "You could see slivers of bone—I never see nothin' like it—red with blood and then redder in half-a-second, and the blade chewing away like a fuckin' rasp."

Lou stood up. "Ok," he said.

Jim had nodded, looking into his coffee again. He said. "Christ in a crock."

And Callie had said afterwards, "You forget things like that can happen."

Henry had nodded. "Poor devil. He's had one hell of a life."

She said, "If only he'd find some nice girl, after that other one, I mean." Her eyes were half-closed, thinking. "It's not right for a man like George to live up there in that big old house all alone that way. He must have loved her something awful—or hated her."

"Well, it's none of our business," Henry said.

"Whose is it, then?" she asked. She was like an old woman sometimes. He put his arm around her. The next morning Henry had gone to see him, and he'd stayed at the hospital all day.)

He looked at the snow. There would be trucks parked by the Stop-Off, banked in, hub-deep by now, and maybe Willard Freund would be there in his dented-up sawed-down Dodge, with the motor on, and the heater. But, no. He was back, but he'd be at his father's place. Sitting in the kitchen drinking coffee and reading *Scorchy Smith* and *Out Our Way* in the paper, or up in his bedroom playing his banjo or lying with his eyes open, staring at nothing, like a blind man, the way he always did, and grinning, shy. Maybe he even grinned when he slept.

5

Henry stayed awake. He sat with his hand on Callie's, his eyes staring at the shadows at the head of the bed, his mind wandering up and down roads that would be drifted in now, where truckers would sit shivering in their cabs. Suddenly he remembered his father sitting gigantic in the chair by the fringed lamp on a winter night, reading a book. He hadn't remembered his father so vividly for a long time. He could almost count the liver spots on the side of the old man's head. Then he remembered his father as he'd been toward the end, sitting asleep like a boulder with his hands folded over the head of his cane, his unlaced shoes toeing inward. Chippies could walk on his shoulders without waking him. He'd looked dead.

The night nurse came on, the cross one, and cleaned up the room and muttered and left.

At 1:00 A.M. the pains all at once got sharper, and he saw Callie's eyes open. She whispered, "No," and he leaned closer, holding her hand more tightly. Her eyes closed again and she whispered, the corners of her mouth trembling, "Surely it can't last much longer."

He sat still, waiting. He could smell the plants in the hall. She groaned again, and the groan was different

109

now, there was fear in it, and Henry's chest tightened so hard he had to brace himself against the pain. She moved her head from side to side on the pillow, tears running down her cheeks, and then she lay still again for a minute. Another one came and she whimpered, "Oh, please, please, God." It passed. She whispered, "Henry, get the doctor here, get a nurse."

He got up and went to the door and out to the desk but there was nobody there, and he stood biting down on his lip, panicky, tears in his eyes too now, his palms wet. The night nurse came out of a room down the hall and glided toward him with a water pitcher. She stopped suddenly when Callie screamed.

"My wife." He caught himself breaking a leaf from the big poinsettia and tearing the leaf between his fingers.

She glared at him and moved on again and put the pitcher on the desk, then went back to the room where Callie lay and closed the door behind her. Another nurse came up from behind him—the quiet nurse with the square face—and touched his arm and said, "Poor kid."

"I've never seen her like this," Henry said.

She nodded. "It's like that sometimes."

"Couldn't you call the doctor?"

"I can't. Miss Childres will, when the time comes." She winced, because Callie was screaming again, piercing. "Cheer up," she said then. "Six months she'll never remember a thing."

The night nurse, Miss Childres, came out, pulling off her rubber glove. There was blood on it. She nodded, smiling, passing Henry. She said, "We're coming nicely."

"She's bleeding," Henry whispered. "For God's sake, call the doctor."

"All in good time," Miss Childres said. "The perineum is tearing. Perfectly normal."

Heat leaped through his chest and he clenched his

fists. "Wait," he said, his upper lip lifted. "Other women don't go through all that. I been sitting here two days."

"It happens sometimes," Miss Childres said. But she went to the desk phone and lifted the receiver. Henry hurried back to the room.

She wasn't white now. Her face was flushed, as if she were burning up. She was breathing hard. She lay with her teeth clenched, tears squeezing out of her closed eyes.

"They're calling Dr. Costard," Henry said. "You're getting there. The nurse says you're coming fine." He gave her his hand and she clutched it.

Callie shook her head. "I can't stand it. Henry, I *can't.*"

And then she screamed again. Henry bent over her and pressed her hand to his stomach, and tears ran down his cheeks. The nurse came in with a hypo and Henry hung onto Callie's hand, and, when it was over and the nurse had left, Callie screamed again. Henry tensed against the scream, and then all at once he was sobbing. It made him feel free, as though he'd burst out of a tight, solid box.

In ten minutes Callie was out of her head. She screamed at the sound of a cart passing by in the hall, and screamed again when the overhead light went on and the doctor came in, and screamed when the doctor touched her wrist. She gripped Henry's hand as if to crush it.

"I've never seen her like this," Henry said, shouting at them. "It's not that she isn't brave. It's killing her."

The doctor nodded. He said to the nurse, "Get another hypo ready." The nurse left. "You'd better leave, Mr. Soames."

Henry didn't move.

"You'd better leave," he repeated. He smiled, grim.

The younger nurse came in, and Costard said, "Bring in a wagon, we'll move her into Delivery."

The girl nodded and glanced at Henry, then left. Calmly, the doctor pried Callie's hand away from Henry's. Callie screamed again, half-sitting up in bed, her mouth a flat, black rectangle, screaming, *Goddamn you, Goddamn you! Henry why don't you help me!* She twisted, and it moved the sheet. The sheet underneath was bloodstained.

The doctor turned to Henry. "You'd better leave."

Henry backed toward the door. Callie screeched after him, *I hate you. It doesn't matter. I hate you. I love somebody else.*

6

He sat for five hours in the waiting room out front. He held a magazine in his lap, on the cover the lower branches of a Christmas tree and under them the same magazine, the same cover, the same Christmas tree, magazine, tree, magazine, falling away like a shaft. For four hours he heard her screams and sat motionless, his hands closed over his face. Between her screams he heard voices mumbling, but there was no one near. It grew light outside and the wind dropped off and the nurses changed shifts. A day nurse touched his arm and said, "Coffee?" He looked up and nodded, not understanding. He said, "My wife—" She came back with coffee and he sipped it and his mind cleared a little. "She's stopped," he said. For an instant he felt light, giddy; then a vague possibility came to him, and after a moment, staring at the magazine without seeing, he was sure of it: She was dead. It made his heart trip. "She's dead," he whispered. The nurse said, amused, "Nonsense."

Doc Cathey and George came in, talking and laughing. George hesitated at the door. Henry called out, getting up, "They phoned you?"

George shook his head, still holding back. "Not me. Baby born yet?"

"She's dead. I think Callie's dead."

Doc Cathey stood still for a second. "Chickenmanure. They ain't that stupid."

Henry shook his head, pulling at his hand so hard it hurt. "She was in labor for forty-eight hours, and then the bleeding. I don't know. I think—"

"Faddle," Doc Cathey said. He leered, but he pivoted away and went through the double doors. He didn't come back.

George said abruptly, "You and I are going to have some breakfast. Come on."

Henry stood there unsteadily, his seat and the backs of his legs numb, and then went for his coat. George closed his hand over Henry's elbow as they moved to the door and out into the cold and down the steps. The brilliance of snow on the lawn, on trees, on rooftops, stabbed at Henry's eyes. For an instant the ring of mountains around them seemed to be moving; then they were utterly still, blue-white.

George slid in behind the wheel and ground on the starter a minute before the truck motor caught and roared. The truck cab shook, and through a gap in the floor boards Henry saw the motionless, soft snow on the road. George slipped his hand around the wheel to the gearshift and pulled it to low, then shifted to high and caught at the wheel.

"You're tired, Henry," he said. "If this business kills anybody it's gonna be you." And then he said, "Or maybe it's me it'll kill." He laughed.

It might have been a boy, Henry thought. A boy like George, maybe born unlucky, who'd grow up to be orphaned and go off to the army and half-kill him-

self for a Japanese girl sixteen years old and a prosti-
tute, or that was what Lou Millet said, and would come
back home after that and crawl back to farming, a
worn-out farm with worn-out equipment that would
eat him alive, limb by limb, and maybe after that his
heart if there was anything left of it. They'd have
named him James.

Henry said, "If Callie was to die—" It came to him
that he didn't believe any more that she would die.
He'd stopped thinking it the minute he'd seen George
and Doc Cathey. He felt better, then worse. He should
never have left. They might call for him any time.

George said, "The hell with you. You're gonna have
a little boy with a big wide slit of a mouth like Callie's
and a three-foot span across the shoulders and he'll
love up the country cunts till a guy like Freund looks
like a eunuch."

Henry breathed in shallowly and held it, and after
a second he saw that George was shocked too, afraid
even to explain what he meant, if he could, because
Henry might have missed it. Henry tried to think what
to say. He watched the brown snow on the street flash
by under the floorboards.

George stopped the truck at Leroy's place, and they
got out and went down the ice-coated steps and in.
The air was too warm, greasy. The place was crowded,
a few women but mostly the old men who came in every
morning from houses and attics and furnished rooms
to get breakfast. At both ends of Leroy's place there
were mirrors; they made the room go on forever. Henry
thought again of how many people there were in the
world—fifteen, twenty here, ten thousand in town, another six thousand in Athensville, still more in Albany,
Utica—it was hard to believe: "All these people sitting
here without a worry," he said, "and my poor Callie—"

George slid into the booth, looking down, then
grinned and said, "It's a funny damn thing . . . human
beings, horses, cats. . . ."

Henry nodded, uncertain what he meant. He remembered the blood on the sheet.

George watched him, then held a cigarette toward him. He said, as if thinking of something else, "They look like they've had a hell of a time of it, don't they."

Henry looked, frowning. There was an old man with whiskers and a wrinkled neck, a large blue lump on his temple. At the table beside him there was a younger man reading a paper, leaning close to it.

Henry said, "I guess you don't remember my father."

"Vaguely," George said. "I was just a kid then."

Henry leaned forward and folded his hands and looked at the boy with the newspaper. "He could talk to birds, all kinds of them. They'd walk on his shoulders like he was a stump. Fattest man you ever saw in your life. Three hundred and seventy pounds. It finally killed him."

George waited.

"He was an elephant. He walked with a cane two-inches thick. I remember he use to read poetry nights. It would make him cry."

"They say he was a fine man," George said.

Henry nodded, then shook his head slowly. "He was an elephant. Christ, you should've seen the coffin. Biggest damn coffin you ever saw, big as the world. With him in it it must've weighed six hundred pounds."

George was watching the old man with the lump on his temple. Behind the old man there was a woman with penciled eyebrows and a powdered face and lumpy hands. A boy was with her, thirteen maybe, weak-jawed and weak-eyed and grinning. He looked like his mother, trapped already in what his mother was. Maybe it was like that with everybody, Henry thought. The spindly, crochety night nurse who liked to deliver babies herself, dead or alive, she was somebody's daughter. And Costard, narrow-shouldered, toeing out, pot-bellied under the vest, he had children, he said. Henry shook his head. "It's funny," he said. "Jesus."

George drew in on his cigarette, then let smoke come out with his words. "It's funny as hell. You know what every one of these people's got? A mirror. Put a man on a desert island and the first thing he'll set out to find is a clear pool where he can see how he looks."

It sounded bitter, and Henry laughed uncomfortably. Then he covered his face with his hand.

"Matter, boy?"

"Nothing," he said.

He'd forgotten completely. He'd been sitting here for ten minutes, and he'd never thought about her once, not even to wonder if she'd meant it when she'd shouted, "I love somebody else." It had seemed a long way between where he'd stood and the bed where Callie lay. He'd stood there helpless, his head pulled in, old, as if past all human use. Maybe she had meant it, too. Because there was, even now, Willard Freund. You never had a chance. Maybe you'd find something you thought a lot of, but it didn't matter, all you could ever count on for sure was someday your heart would quit. His hands clenched.

George said, watching him, maybe reading his thoughts, "You look tired as hell."

He relaxed. The waitress came. She had a long, pocked face, and she had on pink lipstick. She smiled at George, a come-on, and when she left, Henry said, not looking up, "She likes you. You ought to marry her."

George grinned. "Once burned, twice shy."

"You ought to marry somebody," Henry said. "I mean it. Callie says so too."

He wasn't prepared for what it set off. George sat still and didn't speak, then abruptly crushed out his cigarette and stood up. "We better get back." He grinned then, but on the way to the hospital he didn't talk.

The woman at the desk said, "Mr. Soames, you can go down to Maternity now. Dr. Costard's been looking all over for you."

Henry wet his lips, then went to the double door. When he glanced back, George winked. He was sitting down now, over in the shadowed corner of the room, by the magazine table. His eyes, looking into the light, were shiny like the eyes of the owl. His face was the color of ashes.

At the Maternity desk Henry almost asked if either of them had lived, but he stopped himself, simply stood leaning forward, one hand clinging to the other, waiting.

"You may see your wife," the nurse said. And so he knew that it was the baby that had died if one of them had, not Callie; but he held himself back. She hadn't said that. And then they were leading him into a room and somehow he knew at once—though she lay still, as if unconscious—that she was alive. The guard rails were up on the bed. When you were dead you didn't need any guarding. He touched her hand. The nurse said, "It wasn't Caesarean. They cut from below and used Kjelland forceps."

"Did the baby live?" he asked.

The nurse smiled, cat-like. "They're cleaning up now."

He started to ask it again, but she left him.

Callie opened her eyes a little, looking at him. He leaned toward her. "Doctor," she said, her voice light, drugged, "isn't Henry here yet?"

He stood perfectly still, puzzled, his back going cold.

Her fingers moved as if to grasp his hand, but she was too weak. She said, "You been good to us, Henry and me. Everybody's been. I want you to tell

Henry. . . ." She smiled, far away, as though she really had died, withdrawn to where none of them could reach her, and she whispered, "Doctor, my husband is a good kind man. Tell him I said so. Tell him I said it in my sleep." She smiled again, mysterious, suddenly foxy, and her eyes closed. Henry blinked.

And then it was Doc Cathey beside him, leading him through blinding sunlight past wilting, burnt-up plants to the wall of windows that looked in at the cribs.

"Doc," Henry whimpered, shaking now, off his bearings; his right hand pulled at his left.

"Don't blubber," Doc snapped. "You'd think it was the first brat born on earth. Cain maybe. You make me sick."

The nurse said, "It's a boy, Mr. Soames. A big, big boy. Nine pounds, one ounce." It lay with its hands folded up like a monk's, its mouth angular, like Callie's. There were forceps scars across the cheeks and one ear was black and cauliflowered. The head was browless and misshapen. The mouth quivered, crying.

"Well?" Doc Cathey barked. He cupped his hand under Henry's elbow.

Henry leaned his forehead against the glass, his chest flaming. He could hear the baby's voice through the glass. Then he couldn't see anymore, he was crying now, and things were in motion all around him, reeling. "He's beautiful," he said. Tears ran down and he could taste them. "He's beautiful. Holy Jesus."

7

And so, it seemed to Henry, it was different now. Out
of his hands. He looked around as he passed through
the waiting room, but there was nobody there. Sick
people, some plants, a doctor leaning over a chair and
speaking in a whisper, George Loomis looking up,
startled, from a magazine; that was all. He walked out
to his square, black Ford and started it up. Doc Cathey
came through the hospital door and started toward him,
shouting. But Henry pulled out into the street as if he
hadn't seen him. He watched the sidewalk, and then
he was outside town and he still hadn't seen the slightest sign. At the Stop-Off there were trucks parked,
four of them, long, dark, mounded in snow, and he
opened up and invited the truckers in and perked
coffee. The dog lay by the door and watched every
move he made, wondering what he'd done with Callie.
He told them about James, the baby—he used the
word now—and gave out White Owl cigars, laughing,
waving his hands, but all the time he spoke there was
another excitement too, and he kept one eye on the
door and the wide window that looked out over the
highway toward the trees. There was nobody.

There was still nobody when dusk came. The lights
still away. More customers came, and they kept him
busy at the grill. The next thing he knew it was dark,
and still no sign. At midnight he cleaned the grill and
the chili pans and dishes and locked up and turned out
the lights.

He went into the living room—Prince coming sor-
rowfully at his heels—and sat down facing the window
in the dark. The snow lay blue-white under the moon,

119

and the walls of the room around him were blue-white silver glints, the man and woman, the bridge, the tree, the children. The woods were quiet. Up on Crow Mountain, in the fourteen-room brick house where George Loomis rattled around alone like a ghost, there were no lights on; nothing moved. There would be no light on down at Freund's place either, beyond the woods; the family would be asleep; there were chores to do in the morning. Willard Freund would be awake though, sitting smiling to himself, or would be flitting around somewhere outside.

Voices mumbled around him, unintelligible, and he leaned forward in his chair. He saw without surprise that there were birds flying above the woods, thousands of them, gliding silently like owls, but talking, mumbling words like human beings. They flew through steam from the trees, or fog, or smoke maybe. Sometimes he could see only the smoke and the birds, as though the woods had disappeared or slipped from his mind, and then he could see the woods again, gray, moving closer. A sound of wind or fire blurred the voices and stirred the smoke into slow torsion, obliterating the birds, the bridge and the willow tree, the pines. When he saw the man coming across the yard, Henry jumped up.

The snow lay blue-white, crisp, and the trees were far away again, distinct in the sharp night air. The dog was watching him, ears raised.

And at last it all came clear to him. There never would be anybody there. Willard Freund wouldn't show himself again as long as he lived. Callie wouldn't see him either, or if she did it wouldn't matter, because it was too late now. It was as if it was him, Willard Freund, that was killed by it. You had to be there, and Willard Freund hadn't been, and now there was no place left for him, no love, no hate—not in his father's house, even. Willard would see. No place but the woods—bare trees and snow and the low-moving shadows of dogs gone wild and birds and, maybe, if stories were true, bobcats.

He moved toward the window a little, not knowing he was doing it, and stood bent forward, looking out, not aware anymore of the room behind him. There was a game, a child's game, where you stood the dominoes in a row and touched the end one and made them fall one after another, clattering. If one of the dominoes wasn't in line it would still be standing there after the others had fallen down, would still be standing there erect, like a narrow, old-fashioned tombstone, all by itself on a windy hill, till doomsday.

Henry stood at the window looking out for a long time; then, breathing shallowly to cut down the pain, he turned and moved into the bedroom.

IV

THE
THINGS

1

Henry and Callie came out on the porch to watch him down the driveway. Callie was holding the baby, wrapped up in its yellow blanket, she herself in one of her own tricolor afghans, three shades of green, waving with her free hand, and Henry was close beside her, a little behind her, like a balding upright bear with one paw on her shoulder, waving too. The dog was at her other side. The porch light was on—cheap imitation of a carriage lamp—and beyond that there was the light in the living room windows, giving the figures on the porch a kind of aura, their faces not as light as their outlines. On the yard, in the dewy, new-mown grass to their left and in front of them, there were rectangular splays of light from the windows and the open door, and there was a faint light on the sharp little crocuses below the window and still fainter light on the carious trunks and lower boughs of the tamaracks at the edge of the driveway, beyond the painted rocks. The tops of the trees were dark silhouettes, as black as the mountain or the gable of the house; on the other side of the silhouettes was the abyss of sky dotted with stars. It was all like a picture for a life insurance ad in *The Saturday Evening Post*. He could envy them.

When he came to the highway he stopped and waited, the only hand he had leaving the steering wheel to shift down to low, his foot on the brake, the truck nosing sharply downward. There were headlights coming from the south. He looked back and saw Henry and Callie going into the house, the dog standing up now, neither friendly nor unfriendly, merely official, the way shepherds were supposed to be, watching. The porch lights flicked on and off—Callie saying one more goodbye—then stayed off. Almost the same instant, the headlights on the highway veered toward him crazily, then teetered away again, the last possible second. The car's inside lights were on, and he had a fleeting glimpse of drunken kids leering out at him as their car burned past. "Crazy sons of bitches!" he thought, his heart pounding, and he was still hearing, as though time had snagged, the sudden howl of the motor and the rushing wind and the scream of bad tappets. They shot away down the level space in front of Henry's, then up the farther hill. In a matter of seconds they were over the hill and gone, and the night was empty. He pulled out onto the highway, his right leg shaky on the accelerator. And now—the whole beautiful night gone sour—he was thinking again of the murder.

Henry had told him about it. He'd heard it on the radio. "It was up on Nickel Mountain, not ten miles from here," he said. "Some old man. They said his name was—I forget. I guess when he come home they were already inside the house. They hit him on the head with some kind of a pipe. The way they had it on the radio, he was a mess."

Callie was sitting with the baby on her lap. The light from the lamp over her head gave her hair a sheen. The baby was asleep, its fingers curled around one of hers, but she was still singing to it.

George had said, "They know yet who did it?" The picture in his mind was of his own house, as isolated as any to be found and one that would no doubt be attractive to vandals or thieves—a high, old brick house with balustered porches, round-arched windows, lightning rods, cupolas, and facing the road a Victorian tower like a square, old-fashioned silo. "They don't know yet," he said. "Could've been anybody. Those lonely old houses, it's a wonder things like that don't happen more often."

("Sit," Callie said. The dog lowered himself again slowly, like a gray-black lion at her feet, and laid his wide head on his front paws, ears raised, mournful eyes looking up at her. He sighed.)

George Loomis turned the spoon over idly in his hand while they talked. It was silver plate, one of their wedding presents. He was sorry they hadn't chosen something real—because they were his friends, and it disturbed him that friends of his should have junk in their house. She'd chosen it because it was "practical," no doubt, forgetting that plate would scratch and wear away and that anyhow when you married a man who'd been a bachelor all those years you didn't need to squeeze your pennies till Lincoln squeaked. But above all what was wrong was that it was light: In your hand it felt like nothing. With good things, you knew you had them when you had them. That was how it was with all their things—except the solid old sterling candlesticks (up on top of the player piano where they didn't belong, no candles in them) and maybe the antimacassars from Callie's Aunt Mae, and Callie's afghans. But if it didn't matter to you then it didn't, that was it. Except that he knew it did matter to Henry. Why did he let her do it? He said abruptly, "Maybe it was thieves."

Henry shrugged. "They don't know yet. Could be thieves. Then again could be kids, or some tramp."

"Jesus," George said. He'd thought often of the possibility of thieves breaking in. He was not a worrier by nature, but it was a fact that he had a lot of good things in his house, some of them things that had been in the family for two hundred years—God only knew how much those might be worth—and some of them things he'd picked up himself from time to time, in junk shops up in Utica, at auctions here and there, in used book shops. Bill Kelsey had told him he should open a store.

("You got more old stuff than any twenty people,"
he'd said.

"There's a lot of it, all right," George had admitted,
"and more in the other rooms; even some in the woodshed. I walled it up with insulation, so it's dry." He
opened the door to what had been his mother's bedroom and stepped back so Bill could look in.

"Christ in a crock," Bill Kelsey said, "what's all
that?"

"National Geographics," he said, grinning. "Whole
file of them. The rolls in the corner are maps. Thirty-
seven in all. Engraved." There were various other
magazines too—*Linn's Weekly Stamp News, Texas
Gun Collector, American Rifleman.*

"What in hell do you use them for?" Kelsey was
amazed. Impressed, too, but mostly amazed. He stood
tipped forward, looking, his thumbs hooked inside the
bib of his overalls.

George had said ironically, closing the door again,
"Use them for? Sometimes I go in and touch them,"
and he winked. But it was true. It was the richest
pleasure in his life, just picking them up, knowing they
were his, safe from the destroyers who cut the wood-
cuts from great old editions like his illustrated Goethe,
or saw down hand-crafted Kentucky pistols and weld
on modern sights. In the pearwood breakfront he'd
found at the Goodwill at Oneonta he had nine original
Hohner mouth harps, in wooden cases as solemn and
elegant as coffins. They'd cost plenty, once. Every
stroke of the infinitely elaborate design was cut in by
hand by some nearsighted old German silversmith, dead
now for more than a century.

"Man, you'll collect anything!" Bill Kelsey said.

George nodded, serious.

Bill Kelsey cocked his head, looking down at the
newel post, saying, "I wonder if a person could get
anything for that junk in my attic."

"Could be," George had said, excitement in his chest. "Why don't we take a look sometime?")

He set down the spoon with finality. "It must have been kids," he said.

Henry opened his hands. Nobody knew.

It was a warm night, for May. He drove slowly, as always, his left foot riding the slack in the clutch, the ankle stiff in its metal brace. Fog lay white as snow in the valley bottom, the trees at the sides of the valley dark and gloomy. Here away from the lights of Henry's house, no lights in sight but the stars and the moon and the flickering headlights of his own truck, the night seemed less dim than it had before. If he wanted to, he could drive with his headlights turned off. Might have to if that wire was to jiggle any looser. He ought to have fixed it weeks ago, but he'd put it off. He put off more and more, these days. The accident was eight, nine months ago now; according to Doc Cathey he was as fit as he was ever going to be, the remaining left arm grown unnaturally muscular, the wrist conspicuously larger now that it took the whole beating of stripping out the cows. He could do pretty much what he'd done before, if he wanted to. It just took him longer. But he'd lost his drive, the whole thing had made him older. He'd skipped the cultipacking this year—the disking had left the ground level enough, and the rain was pretty good, the ground would likely hold in enough moisture to get by. Lou Millet was putting in the soybeans for him—labor Lou owed him from two years ago—that would take care of seven acres, and the soil bank would take care of ten more. The alfalfa took care of itself. If the sky fell in he could live all right on the disability pension from the army. So he let things slide. He'd get up in the morning and milk the cows and clean up the barn, and after that he'd work for a couple of hours at the plowing, already so far behind schedule it didn't much matter.

(*Corn knee high by the Fourth of July.* He'd be lucky if he had the stuff planted.) Around noon he'd come in and quit till five-o'clock chore-time, spend his time pasting stamps in, or silver-polishing the two ceremonial Scottish swords (he'd gotten them both for seventy dollars), or just sitting in front of the television, half-asleep. Plowing had been a pleasure once—the smell of new-turned sillion, the blue-black sheen of the cut earth rolling off straight as an arrow, dark under the pines at the top of the hill, the ginger-water jug showing dull silver in the burdocks under the trees, the plowed ground richer and warmer where the sunlight struck. He'd be conscious of both the past and the future riding sidesaddle on the tractor seat, one hand on the steering wheel, the other on the plow: He would remember intensely, as if still inside them, other springs, plowing with that same F-20 or riding the gas tank while his father plowed, rear end growling as if running on chains and the air sad-sweet with the scent of new buds and pinesap running and new-turned ground, and in the same flow of intense sensation he would see his crop growing and ripening, field corn towering over your head, the stalks oozing sweeter than honey when the blade bit through. Even after he'd come back from Korea, one foot smashed and his breathing bad from the mess-up in his chest, the plowing was good, he could handle it. But now it was changed. He plowed one-handed now, fighting the steering wheel left-handed, jerked off balance whenever the front wheels climbed over a rock, his right hand no longer there to anchor him; and when he saw a big rock coming at him he could no longer raise the plow on the run but had to throw in the clutch with his gimpy foot, reach back for the lever, and drive no-handed for a minute. More often than not, it seemed to him, he saw the rock coming in under too late, and before he could shove in the clutch he was hearing the crack of steel like a rifle shot and the point was gone, half the moldboard with it, and the plow was skidding along, one wheel in the air, like a crippled duck. One of these days, as sure as anything, he'd break the one fist he had left, hitting the tractor tire in his rage. The accident had left him hard-up as hell (let alone the way his picking things up was beginning to cost him), yet he'd seen no choice but to get a new plow, a trip-spring rubber-tired son-of-a-bitch the F-20 wasn't horse enough to pull, which meant getting the big DC. They'd pretty near laughed in his face at the bank. But they'd loaned him the money, finally. Because the house was worth plenty, never mind the land. ("Business is business," the man had said. He poked his moustache with with his pen, feeling guilty. George Loomis had said, "Sometimes," sarcastically, meaning that sometimes it was more, a way of staying alive; but he hadn't bothered to explain what he meant, had merely signed where the man made the X with his ball-point pen.) If he ever did get the corn in the ground he'd need a new outfit to get it up into the silo. It was the fucking antique corn binder that had taken off his arm. (A long time ago, it seemed by now. A different life.)

It would be something, he thought then, walking into your house one night and finding a couple of nuts there, standing in the kitchen with big lead pipes, or pistols.

He turned up the dirt road that wound up Crow Mountain to his house. The lights were all off at the Shaffer place. Walt's jeep was parked by the mailbox as usual, under the limbs of the beech tree, in case it should rain. The green and white plastic lawn furniture sat as always in the bare dirt yard among metal toy trucks and plastic blocks and pieces of dolls. The thought of their oldest girl, Mary Jean, passed briefly through his mind. He would see her bringing in eggs in a wire basket sometimes as he was driving past. She would wave, and he would wave back. She looked Polish, like her mother. Light brown hair, thick ankles.

Somebody'd told him she had a cedar chest full of things for her marriage. Be too late pretty soon. She was getting close to her thirties now.

At Sylvester's there were no lights in front but the flicker of the television. Sylvester would be sitting with his shoes off and no shirt on, his wife ironing in the barren back room. The kids would be sitting around more or less naked, invisible as the overstuffed chairs they sat in in the darkened room, or invisible except for their eyes and their dirty underwear. That was the last house for more than two miles, as the road went— the last house on this side of the mountain except for his own and the Ritchie place, abandoned now for ten years and gone to ruin.

The headlights jiggled out and he leaned forward. They came on again.

Then he remembered the man he'd met down in Slater, at Bittner's. He couldn't say at first why the trifling memory made him uneasy, or why he should happen to remember it at all—except, maybe, that the man's disappearing somehow fit with the general uneasiness he'd been feeling ever since that car full of kids had come barreling straight at him.

Bittner had been sitting ritched back on two legs of his red wooden chair, squarely facing his open front door, a little ways back from it, where he could look out into the street. George had been in town for a couple of errands at Salway's, and he'd decided to drop by the old man's shop on the chance he had stumbled onto something he didn't know the worth of. When he went in the old man said, "Odd do," as usual, lifting his eyebrows, looking over his glasses, and George nodded, standing in the doorway a moment, getting his eyes adusted to the darkness and clutter—rickety tables, fairgrounds-glass vases, clocks, feather dusters, crocks, baskets, chairs, firedogs, scuttles, bird cages, pictures in ornately machine-carved broken frames, maple spindles, chests of drawers, hundreds of dusty, disintegrating books (*The Ladies' Respository*—Volume 24, *Ideal Suggestion, Elsie Venner*). He started along the nearer wall of bookshelves, not reading the titles or even looking at particular books, gazing vaguely, like a hunter taking in acres at once, waiting for a good binding to separate itself from the surrounding trash. When he was halfway down the aisle, Bittner said, "Here's the man you should talk to. He must have a spinning wheel or two." He turned and saw that the old man was not talking to him but to another man, standing in the darkest part of the room, reaching down into one of the bins of odds and ends. The man looked around, not slowly, but somehow too cautiously, and George knew the man was blind. "How do you do?" the man said. He had dark glasses on and a touring cap. In one hand he held a pair of carved ivory chopsticks, in the other, his cane. George nodded, realizing only later that a nod did no good.

Bittner said, "George is a collector. I don't know what-all he's got."

"You don't say," the man said. He wasn't from the Catskills. Vermont, maybe.

"He's got old records, magazines, stamps, I don't know what-all."

"I'm not really much of a collector," George said.

Bittner said, waving, "Boot-jacks, arrowheads, antique furniture, picture frames, china, paperweights—"

Again, thoughtfully, the blind man said, "You don't say." He came toward him down the aisle, smiling vaguely, moving the cane almost casually back and forth across the aisle like a witching rod. When he was within three feet of George he knew it, and held out his hand. "My name's Glore," he said. They shook hands. "George Loomis," George said. The man's skin was pale and flaccid, as if he'd spent years in the darkest corners of junk stores. "Do you really collect antique paperweights?" he said.

George said, "I've got a few. Nothing valuable."

After a moment he added, "A couple of them were family things, and I happened to run across some more that looked good with them. I don't really collect."

Bittner laughed scornfully, behind him. "What he means is, he ain't letting anything go. Regular miser. He-he-he!"

The blind man's interest was sharper now. He inclined his head very slightly, his left hand groping out toward the bookshelf. He said, "I'd be interested to *see* your things some time."

"Anytime you say," George said, not as heartily as he might have. He liked nothing better than showing off his things, but Bittner was right, he was a miser.

The blind man said, "Where do you live?"

George told him, and the man listened carefully, as if taking it down in his mind. When he had it, he said, "You expect to be home this afternoon?"

"I expect so," George said.

That was the last he'd seen of the man. When he'd asked Bittner about him, later, Bittner said he didn't know who the man was. "Glore," George said, and Bittner remembered that that was the name he'd said, yes, but that was all he knew. He'd come into town in an old Lincoln, Bittner remembered then. A young black-headed fellow driving for him. They'd come and they'd gone. "That's business," Bittner said. George had nodded, thinking.

He wondered now, for the first time, if Glore had really been blind. He put the thought out of his mind at once, sensibly, but he still felt jumpy. He carried the idea of the murder on Nickel Mountain like a weight on his chest, that and the teasing contrast of Callie and Henry waving in the warmth of the yellow porchlight, behind him, ahead of him a carload of teen-agers burning toward him, brainless and deadly.

He'd come to his own driveway now. He could look down to his left and see the whole valley, the willows and the creek cutting through the middle, and directly below him the gleaming rails of the New York Central tracks curving onto the trestle. He let go of the wheel to grab the gearshift and shift down to second, then caught hold of the wheel again. He pulled up past the overgrown lawn in front—his headlights sweeping across the weeds and treetrunks—and turned sharply at the fence and backed into the shed. When he switched the ignition off the stillness dropped around him like a trap. He'd noticed the same thing once before, tonight, when he'd first come out of the Soames' house onto the porch. Callie had noticed it too and had said, "It's quiet tonight. Must be rain coming."

The headlights—staring ahead and a little upward, because of the pitch of the shed's dirt floor—made the weeds around the hand-crank gas pump look pocked-gray as old bone. Every line of the American-wire fence stood out, unnaturally distinct, like the chipping sign on the pump: *Warning. Contains Lead.* Far beyond the fence the headlights eerily lighted just the top of the gambrel peak of the haybarn roof.

He turned out the lights, got out of the truck, and slammed the door behind him. It was then he knew, with a certainty that made him go cold as ice, that somebody was watching from the house.

He knew that very possibly it was nothing but nerves. Even probably. The story of the murder, the car swerving at him, the odd encounter (as it seemed to him now) two weeks ago at Bittner's—all that together might naturally give you the jitters. But he didn't for one minute believe it to be nerves. There was somebody there. He knew it as surely as he'd known it that night when they started up the quiet-looking valley in Korea: It was as though a sense keener than the ordinary five had caught some unmistakable signal. He'd kept on walking, that night, cautious, but not giving in to the feeling that there were rifles trained on him; and then suddenly, crazily, he was staring into lights, and McBrearty was falling back against him, dead already, and

135

he felt the hit, and the next minute he was coughing blood and couldn't breathe and knew for certain he was dying, thinking (he would never forget): *Now I'll find out if this horseshit about heaven's really true.* But he'd lived, and now he was no kid anymore, he knew what he couldn't have imagined then: If they wanted to kill him, they could do it—he was mortal. Everything on earth was destructible, old books, guns, clocks, even bookholders of bronze.

He stood out of sight against the wall of the shed and tried to make his mind work. The truck smelled of gas and heated belts and alcohol in the radiator. The motor was clicking. He could smell the dirt floor of the shed and the lighter, delicately acrid scent of molding burlap. *I meant to patch the bags,* he thought. *It must've slipped my mind.* He had to get calm. The obvious thing to do, he knew the next instant, was climb into the truck again and get out of there; go get help. It would take him ten minutes to get to Sylvester's and call up the sheriff, ten minutes more for the sheriff and his men to get to Sylvester's, another ten minutes to get back. And then *they* could go in; it was what they were paid for. By that time maybe whoever was there might be gone.—Gone, if they were thieves, with maybe fifteen thousand dollars' worth of his things.—And if they were kids?

He saw them again, far more sharply than he'd seen them at the time, leering out at him as the car roared past. What if they were to set fire to the house? His heart was beating so hard it ached, and he pressed his fist to his chest, unable to breathe. He could no more get rid of the ache than the image in his head, fire churning behind the round-arched windows of all three stories, the burning furniture not even visible in all that hell, flames licking the balustered porch, crawling out the eaves to the great carved dentils, then walls falling down like a landslide inside the brick shell, the fire going suddenly white. He'd seen ordinary houses burn. It would be something.

He got hold of himself. The house stood silent and severe as ever; inside, no sign of movement. For an instant he was certain there was a figure at the middle living room window, but the next instant he no longer knew for sure. Then he remembered the rifle in the woodshed.

He'd left it there—on the cloth-draped cherry dresser he was storing there—months ago, at the time of the bobcat scare. Somebody had found tracks by his cow-barn door, and he'd called the troopers and the troopers had said they were bobcat. The word got around quickly, and pretty soon bobcats were showing up everywhere—flitting across a mountain road just in front of a car, prowling in the bushes beside some outhouse, standing stock-still on a moonlit, snowy lawn. Sylvester's wife had been scared, and when George Loomis had seen she couldn't be kidded out of it he'd told her he'd bring her the rifle. He'd gotten it out and cleaned it up and loaded some bullets and thrown them in a paper sack, and he'd taken it out to the woodshed to loan Sylvester when he came for the milk. When Sylvester got there, the cat had been shot already, the other side of Athensville, so he didn't take it. ("There may be more," George had said. Sylvester had grinned. " 'Ere's always more," he said. " 'Ose old woods is somethin' else.")

The driveway was white in the moonlight, but he hopped across it fast, foot swinging, and dived into the weeds on the far side. Nothing happened. He lay perfectly still with his forearm pushing into the soft, gritty earth, the damp weeds touching his face rotten-smelling and sappy-smelling at the same time, and he waited. Then he started crawling, circling three-quarters of the way around the house to get to the wood-shed without crossing an open space. When he got to the walnut tree at the edge of where the garden had been last year—grown up in weeds now, the same as the rest—he stopped again and raised his head to look up at the house. Still no sign. He thought: *What if it really is all just nerves?* The minute he allowed himself to ask the question, he knew, secretly, the truth: There was no one there. If he weren't crazy he'd stand up right now and walk on into the house. But he was. Or he was gutless, more like: The very thought of standing up made his legs go weak.

The ground was mucky, this side of the house. It squeezed between his fingers when he leaned on his hand, and it clogged the brace on his ankle, making his foot as heavy as it would be in a cast. His sweater was damp and redolent of wood from the dew he'd come through, and his pantlegs were as soaked as if he'd fallen in the pasture brook. He reached the brick wall and got up, pressing close to it, and in five seconds he was in the woodshed, leaning against the tool-bench, getting his breath.

When he jerked the door open ("Ridiculous? Jesus!" he would tell them all later), plunging in with the rifle leveled, the kitchen was empty. The door to the living room stood open, as always, and he knew before he reached it that there was no one there. There was no one in the dining room, the library, the pantry, or the downstairs bedroom—he went through each room, turning on the lights—and no one on either the front or back stairs, no one on either the second floor or the third. There was nothing, no one in the house but himself and his things.

And now, rational at last, he recognized with terrible clarity the hollowness of his life. He saw, as if it had burned itself into his mind, the image of Callie, Henry, the baby, and the dog, grouped in the warm yellow light of the porch. If Henry Soames had crept through wet grass and mud that way to protect what was his, it would have meant something. Even if it had been all delusion, the mock heroics of a helmeted clown, it would have counted.

"Fool!" he whispered, humiliated and hot from head to foot with anger, meeting his eyes in the mirror, ready to cry.

The rifle crooked in his arm was heavy, and he glanced down at it. It was old as the hills—a .45–70 Springfield from 1873, an officer's model, according to the chart in *Shotgun News*—yet there was still blue on the barrel, beautiful and cool against the mellow brown of the walnut-stock. It was a rare thing to find one that old that still had the blue. Most people wouldn't notice or think it was important, but, just the same, it was a rare find; a thing that should be preserved. And then he thought, feeling a flurry of excitement, as though he were about to discover something: *I was never more scared in my life. My God. Right from the first minute, I thought I'd had it.* He went back into the kitchen to hunt up a polishing rag and some whiskey. He figured he'd earned it.

V

THE
DEVIL

1

Simon Bale was a Jehovah's Witness. He would appear one Sunday morning in the dead of winter, early, standing on your porch, smiling foolishly and breathing out steam, his head tipped and drawn back a little, like a cowardly dog's, even his knees slightly bent, his Bible carefully out of sight inside his ragged winter coat, and his son Bradley would be standing behind him, as timid as his father but subtly different from his father—not so perfectly hiding his readiness to shift from fawning to the kind of unholy fury that was going to be his whole character later—and neither Simon Bale nor his son would seem a particularly serious threat—especially on a bright December morning with a smell of January thaw in the wind and churchbells ringing far in the distance, the blue-white mountains falling away like Time. All it took to get rid of the two was the closing of a door.

Until his fifty-fourth year, Simon Bale worked as a night clerk at the Grant Hotel in Slater. It was a four-storey, blackish red-brick building as square as a box, flat, stale, manifestly unprofitable, stained with rust from the eaves that hadn't held in their water for longer than anyone in Slater could remember. The lobby was the size of an ordinary country parlor, a faded and threadbare rug on the floor like the rugs you find in the Sunday school rooms of country churches, the pattern no longer distinguishable, vaguely floral. On the rug stood an old, sprung davenport, a couple of squarish armchairs from the forties, a rickety checker table over against the wall, piled high now with magazines, a television in the corner. Old men lived there, and a couple of women whose business Simon quietly and patiently endured. It was not a proof of remarkable broad-mindedness in Simon, that quiet endurance of what he himself called harlotry, and no proof that he was a hypocrite, either. Their wickedness was one with the general corruption of the times, one of many signs that the end was at hand. They would burn for eternity, it went without saying, but so would most of the rest of mankind—for pride, for covetousness, for forgetting the Sabbath, for believing the devil to be dead. Confronted by evils so overwhelming, a man could only look to the state of his own soul and, on Sunday mornings, go out on his futile, stubbornly persistent rounds, giving the warning—to whole families, if possible, to the husband alone, if only the husband would listen; or to only the wife; or to the child alone in the yard.

He kept leaflets on his desk, tucked inconspicuously beside the register. No one ever took one. Sometimes when the spirit moved him—when he glimpsed in the eyes of some guest a flicker of humanity answerable to his own—Simon would timidly press one of the leaflets into the hand reaching out for keys. He would even sometimes venture a joke, though humor was perilous: "Here are your keys," he would say, smiling horribly, like a man with some disease of the nervous system. When there was no work to do he would read, never any book but one. He would run his square, black fingertip along under the words and would move his lips, not merely because he was an ignorant man or only half-literate but also because he read with intense concentration. He read the *Daily News* in the same way, systematically, beginning with the front page and moving to the back, column by column, skipping nothing, even when he came to the advertisements or the comics the *Daily News* carried, *Major Hoople* and *Scorchy Smith*. How much he understood of what he read, and in what queer mystical fashion he understood, God only knows. Since he never read the page four continuation of a front-page story until he happened to come to it in his methodical, column-by-column way, it seems unlikely that he read with intense curiosity. Nevertheless, he read his paper every day for some forty years, which is proof, at least, of the regularity of his habits, no mean virtue. His mouth would sometimes snap shut or twitch as he read—his obsequious smile had by this time become a nervous tic—and it seems very likely it twitched because Simon was angry, or, anyway, impatient. (One thinks of the way George Loomis used to read, twenty years younger than Simon was but more like Simon than either of them would have cared to admit. He too—late at night, in his big, lonely house—read column by column, except that he never bothered about the continuations or the advertisements or, above all, the comics—except for Scorchy Smith's half-naked women—and all the time he read (his left leg balanced on his right knee, the paper on the leg, the thumb of his left and only hand flickering nervously at his cigarette) he would wince, outraged by all that hit his eye from the machinations of Democrats and Russians to the stupidity of typesetters. Compare, on the other hand, Henry Soames, reading when he had no customers to talk to at the Stop-Off. He would lay his paper out on a table—a cup of black coffee on the top left corner of the paper, tacking it down because of the breeze from the fan on the shelf in the corner—and he would spread his arms out to left and right to lean on the table as he bent his huge bulk toward the news, and he would glance over all the headlines, moving his uptilted head like a man hunting for the piece he needed for a jigsaw puzzle, and he'd work out in his mind what he wanted to look into first. Then he'd start, and he'd go straight to the continuation, and sometimes he'd smile or he'd murmur "Hmm," and sometimes he'd call, "Callie, listen to this!" and would read to her aloud (which Callie Soames hated). If world events were upsetting or baffling, he'd mention the trouble to every man that came into the diner or stopped for gas, and his premise, deeper than judgment, something in his blood by now, was that somehow even the most outrageous behavior of Russians or Democrats or the Farm Bureau must make some kind of reasonable, human sense. He'd work that sense out, eventually, finding good even in the most unthinkable points of view (very often by logic that only Henry and God could fathom, and frequently only God), and from then on Henry would be nearly as moved by pronouncements made from that point of view, however Henry might disagree, as a country woman would be by her "Search for Tomorrow" on TV. "You're a damn fool," George Loomis would say. "You forget the whole secret of human progress, pure meanness." "I don't believe there is such a thing as pure meanness," Henry would say, "or pure anything else." "Well you got to have faith in something," George would say. As for old Doc Cathey (hunchbacked, sly, infernally testy), he never read the papers at all. He never read anything, in fact, and profoundly distrusted any man who did.)

When he finished at the Grant Hotel, at seven in the morning, Simon Bale would put on his old brownish coat and nod goodbye to Bill Hough, who clerked days, and go out to his old gray Chevy and drive himself the half-mile home to his black-shingle house just beyond the city limits. His wife would have his toast and eggs ready, and he'd eat his breakfast without a word, leaning far down over his plate and sliding in the food with his fork turned upside down, and then he'd shave himself with his electric razor and take off all but his underwear (loose jockey shorts and an undershirt with straps which he changed not more than once a month) and go to bed. He'd sleep five hours, then get up and go out on the porch with his Bible, and he'd sit there reading or meditating or dozing, or maybe watching crows making circles high above him, bringing to mind the circle in the fire, or he'd look at the mountain that rose up, awesome as Judgment Day, at the end of the valley, or at the oak tree in his yard. In August he would watch Ed Dart and his boys across the road combing wheat, which reminded Simon Bale of Christ, as did they, who were in a sense Plowmen, or Harvesters of the First Fruit, and he would smell the sweetness of the air, which bespoke in Simon's hairy nostrils the boundless mercy of God. Around his yard there was a weathered snow fence and there were chickens in the yard, and in these too there were lessons. It was this way of seeing, above all, that made his mission hopeless. Going out on his calls on Sunday morning (his son, before the time of this story, sitting humble and surly in the car beside him, Simon himself a little on edge for lack of sleep), Simon might as well have talked ancient Hebrew to the people he called on. In a sense, he did.

One night, long after his daughter Sarah had run off (had married a Trailways bus driver who'd gotten her pregnant, not without coaxing on her part, a girl of fifteen with the figure of a full-grown woman and a mind arrested at seven or eight, a face as long and blank as a cannister, given to hallucinations, pursued by demons, fond to the point of lunacy of charm bracelets, pins, brooches, anklets, dime-store rings) and a short while after his son Bradley had moved out to run, with monstrous tyranny, a household of his own Simon Bale (his thin, brownish hair now beginning to turn gray around his ears) got a phone call at the Grant Hotel. Old Chester Kittle was there and saw it all. Simon stood very still, the Bible open on the counter, the dirty red ribbon dangling out over the edge, and the tic-smile came and went again and again, in shadow now, because the dim lamp over the desk stood diagonally behind him. He looked like a man being scolded harshly—for the leaflets on the counter, perhaps, or for a pious message left by some prankster on one of the old iron beds. No one would have thought it could be anything more; nothing of much significance could be expected to happen in the life of Simon Bale. But apparances fail us. Simon Bale's house was on fire (someone had set it, but the troopers didn't know that yet), and his wife was in the hospital probably dying. Simon hung up the telephone and turned to the Bible and hung onto it with both hands as if it was the only thing steady in the whole dark room. Still smiling—on, off, like a face in the funhouse at the county fair—Simon started to cry, a kind of howling noise that didn't sound like crying or laughing either but was the kind of noise a hound might make, and old Chester jumped up and went over to him, his heart and brains in a turmoil.

2

Simon Bale had no friends. He was not only an idealist but an ascetic as well, both by conviction and by temperament, and the death of his wife (she died early the following morning) meant the end of all ordinary contact with humanity—or would have except for Henry Soames.

Simon was at her bedside when she died. He'd gone there at once (abandoning his desk to old Chester Kittle, who after ten minutes' wine-befogged consideration locked the door and went to bed) and he'd sat there all night long wringing his hands and praying and weeping, in his heart knowing her lost already be-

cause of the bandages covering most of her head and
because of, worse, the tubes taped to her body and
rising, at the foot of the bed, to a glass bottle hanging
upside down. When the doctor told him she was dead,
Simon was through for now with his weeping, though
not through with his grief, and he merely nodded and
stood up and went out, none of them knew where. He
stood on the front steps of the hospital for a long time,
his hat dangling from the end of his right arm (it was
spring, and the trees were green with new leaves) and
then like a man in a daze he wandered across the lawn
in the general direction of where his car was parked.
He wandered up and down the sidewalk, still quiet and
empty at six in the morning, passing and repassing the
car, maybe unwilling to leave the place, maybe simply
in a mental fog, unable to recognize his car when he
saw it. He stopped right beside the car, at last, and
stared at it for a long time, his face as white and soft
as bread dough, his mouth collapsed like the mouth
of a dime-store goldfish, and finally he went over to it
and got in and drove back to the hotel. He let himself
in by the door at the side and went to the first empty
room he found and stretched out on the bed and slept.
For hours he slept like a dead man. Then he dreamed
his wife was alive, sewed up from one end to the other
with green thread, and tranquilly glad to see him, and
he woke up. It was late afternoon.

He didn't notice he was hungry and unshaven. He
drove to the remains of his house, where everything
he owned was now smoke and ashes, including his
money, since Simon had never trusted banks, and he
stood beside what was left of the snow fence as he'd
stood this morning in front of the hospital, looking at
the place as the others did—curiosity seekers, neighbors, farmers who'd happened along on their way into town to the movies or the Silver Slipper. Finally
somebody recognized him and they all gathered around
him to console him and ask him questions and, in

general, torment him, all of which he met with a luna-
tic, apologetic-looking smile that made people wonder
(not for the first time) if he'd set it himself. Now and
then he'd bring out a stammered word that only those
nearest to him caught ("Forgive," he was saying,
"Lord forgive") and then, suddenly, he sank to his
knees and fainted. They called the police. But it was
not there that the troopers found him; they found him
at Henry Soames'.

It was still early, a little after eight. Henry's little
boy Jimmy was in bed; Henry's wife was in the diner
taking care of the last of the supper customers, and
Henry stood in the living room in the house jutting
out behind the diner, the room almost dark, only the
floorlamp in the corner turned on, Simon Bale in the
armchair below it, staring at the carpet as if in a daze.
Standing enormous and solemn at the living room
window, Henry looked out past the end of the diner
at the highway and the woods beyond. He could see,
past where the woods dropped away, the crests of the
mountains on the far side of the valley. It was a time
of day he especially liked. The mountains looked closer
when the light was dimming from the sky and the
clouds were red, and sounds were clearer now than
they were at other times—milking machine compressors
in the valley, cows mooing, a rooster's call, a semi
coming down the hill to the right with its lights on. It
was as if one had slipped back into the comfortable
world picture in old engravings—in old geography
books, say, or old books of maps in a law office. (The
world would seem small and close when dark came,
too—sounds would seem to come from closer at hand
and the mountains ten miles away seemed almost on
top of you—but in the dark he would not feel himself
a part of it; the trees and hills were like something
alive, not threatening, exactly, because Henry had
known them all his life, but not friendly, either: hos-
tile, but not in any hurry, conscious that time was on

their side: they would bury him, for all his size and for all his undeniable harmlessness, and even his own troublesome, alien kind would soon forget him, and the mountains would bury them too.) In his present mood, watching sunset come on, he felt at one with the blue-treed mountains, and at one, equally, with the man in the dimness behind him. He saw again in his mind the charred boards, ashes, dirty bubbles of melted glass, and he recalled the intense acrid smell that had filled the air for a mile around. *Poor devil,* he thought. He had never known Simon Bale, had hardly seen him before, but at a time like this that was hardly important. A man did what he could.

Perhaps it was the way the light slanted in, or the way the long silver truck rolled past and went out of hearing: Something came to him. He knew as if by inspiration how it was that a man like Bale saw the world. For an instant he too saw it: dark trees, a luminous sky, three swallows flying, all portentous. Henry half-turned, covering his mouth with his hand, and studied the man. The brown shoelace on Simon's black right shoe (directly in the floorlamp's beam) had been broken and knotted together again in twenty places.

Then the troopers came. Henry wouldn't hear of their talking to Simon until the following day, after he'd rested a little and pulled himself together. They might have insisted, but Doc Cathey came in while they were talking and took one look at Simon Bale and said, "This man's in shock," and, soon after, the troopers left. Henry put Simon in the bedroom off the kitchen, and Doc Cathey stayed with him awhile, fussing and muttering to himself, and then Doc came out and closed the door and they sat at the kitchen table drinking coffee. Callie was with them by now.

"What in hell do they want to be pestering him for, in his condition?" Henry said. Putting the question in words made him feel an indignation he hadn't felt until this moment.

"Because they think somebody set the fire on purpose," Doc said, "and most likely they're right."

"But what would Simon know about it?" Callie said. She asked it a little too calmly, with too much detachment. Henry didn't notice it, but Doc Cathey did.

"He'd know if he set it himself," Doc said, and he laughed, as sharp as acid.

"That's crazy," Henry said. His hands started shaking. He said, "His *wife* died in that fire. It's right in the paper."

"You don't know these people," Doc Cathey said. "I do. You watch."

Henry leaned over the table toward him, and his face went dark red. "You're a vicious old fool," he said. "I could—" But he couldn't think what it was he could do, or rather he knew all too well what he could do—he could knock Doc Cathey through a wall—and his realization of how angry he was checked him.

Doc Cathey clamped his mouth shut and got hold of himself. "We'll see," he said. "Don't you go havin' a heart attack over *him*."

It was then that Callie Soames stood up, and both of them looked at her. "I don't want him in my house," she said. "I want him out, tonight."

Henry went as red as before. He fumbled for the pills in the bottle in his shirt pocket, and he took one out and went over to the sink for water. He stood motionless for a long time after he'd drunk, leaning on the sink, and his wife and old Doc Cathey were as quiet as rocks. Henry said, "He's staying."

She said very quietly, "Then I'm leaving."

"Go on," he said.

Her look clouded a little, and she didn't move.

3

Henry Soames was up at dawn. It was like Easter morning: The sun hit the late May dew like music, and the trees across the road were all silver and gold, still and breathless. He stood at the open kitchen window breathing in the cool, clean air, and all his body seemed more awake than it had ever felt before. He could hear farmers' milkers running, infinitely far away in the valley, and he heard a truck start up, the milk truck, probably, down around Lou or Jim Millet's. The thought of Simon came into his mind and partly saddened him, partly made him nervous. Callie hadn't said another word last night, and, even though he knew he was right, Henry had felt and still felt guilty. He thought of putting breakfast on, but there was no way of knowing when the others would wake up, so he let it go. He put on his wool-lined frock, frowning, and went out in back to look at the garden. He saw at once that more of the lettuce shoots had been nibbled off even with the ground. Then he saw there were three young rabbits on the grass to the left of the garden, lying with their legs out behind them like dogs. "Shoo!" he said, waving but keeping his voice down, letting the house behind him sleep on. The rabbits jumped up and bounded off like deer. Henry stood again, slipping his hands into the pockets in the sides of his frock. It was colder than he'd thought. The ground was soft under his feet and clung to his shoes. He ought to shoot those rabbits probably; but he probably wouldn't do it, because of Jimmy. There was a good deal a man with a family couldn't do—Jimmy,

Callie, Callie's folks. It was lucky it was more or less worth it.

It was a good little garden. He'd put in most of the vegetables only this past two weeks, three-foot rows of amazingly delicate-looking radishes and beets and garden lettuce and onions. To the right of those, toward the mountainside and the trees, was the rectangular patch where he planned to put in tomatoes and pumpkins and corn. Beyond the rows and curving out to the left a little lay the square he'd put in, mostly last year, mainly flowers, the crocuses and the tulips around the birdbath already in bloom—yellow, red, blue. He had three rose bushes and, around the border, honeysuckle, already in leaf, and to the right, where the mountain began to climb, a lilac bush. They would sit there on the white-painted bench, evenings last summer, he and sometimes Callie too, when Callie's mother ran the diner for them, and they'd watch little Jimmy crawl around in the dirt, drooling and laughing and talking to himself. It was heaven out there on a cool summer evening. Sometimes they wouldn't go in till long after dark.

He straightened up and, after a moment, went over to the salt and iron bench to sit down. In two minutes he was asleep, sitting with his head tipped down and his hands over his belly like a bear in clothes.

He didn't wake up when Jimmy called to be gotten out of bed. Callie went to him, throwing on her bathrobe first, remembering from the first instant she opened her eyes that something unpleasant was in the house, and she seated Jimmy backwards on the toilet (it would take him forever to be sure he was through) and went down to put on breakfast. The bacon hadn't been sizzling two minutes before sounds began to come from the room off the kitchen. She stood still, glaring at the top of the stove, listening; then she went to look out where she knew her husband would be sitting asleep and called, "Henry, come in here." He looked up with that stupid, lambish look he always had when he wasn't quite awake, and with all the venom she could muster she said, "Come see to your friend."

She slammed the door and went back to her bacon. Jimmy came into the room, naked as a needle, and she pointed at him and sent him back for his clothes.

"No clothes," he said.

She said, "Jimmy Soames, you get your clothes or I'll give you a whipping you'll never forget." The two-year-old turned vaguely toward the stairs, not obeying, merely baffled, working up tears, and she said, "Stop it!" She laid out paper towels to dry the bacon on, and she heard him going up, very slowly, crying. She knew he wouldn't get them, of course. He'd forget what he was after in about three seconds, or he'd come across a doll or a fire truck, or—most likely—he'd go to bed and sob. She'd have to go get him and make up to him, and she'd have to hunt up the clothes herself and dress him. She wished to hell Henry would get in here, and at that moment Henry came in. She said fiercely, "I'm sorry to be so crabby. I don't feel good."

"It's all right," he said. "Let me help you." He took the spatula.

"Henry, you smell," she said. "When did you last take a bath?"

Just then from the bedroom off the kitchen there came a crash, and both of them jumped. Henry stood staring at the floor, pulling at his mouth. Callie took a deep breath. "Your mother's old water pitcher," she said. He nodded. Callie said wearily. "Well, see if he wants to eat."

Jimmy, for one, had no intention of eating. He sat in his high chair stirring the yolk of his egg with his spoon and watching Simon Bale. Henry sat solemn and uncomfortable, erect, so expressionless in his steel-rimmed glasses you might have thought him lost in troubled thought; but he couldn't help seeing how

Simon ate, and couldn't help knowing why Callie suddenly put down her fork and got up to fuss needlessly with the coffee. Simon sat bent almost double, unshaven, his mouth almost level with the plate, scooping his egg in with his fork turned over, trapping it when he needed to against the side of his cracked finger. Sometimes, as if he knew there was something wrong but had no idea what, he would roll his eyes up toward Henry or Jimmy and would smile as if in panic, but he said not a word, and for minutes at a time he would seem to forget they were there. Henry hovered between pity and revulsion. Tears would come suddenly to Simon Bale's eyes, and he would draw out his stiffly wrinkled, unbelievably filthy handkerchief and blow his nose with a sound so like that of a man unashamedly breaking wind that, each time he did it, Callie would turn, behind him, and stare. When she slid his coffee across to him, keeping back from him as from anthrax, Callie said, "Would you want some more eggs?"

None of them was prepared for what it set off. He looked up with grotesque anguish and said, "Forgive—" and then, abruptly, began to cry. Callie's eyebrows lifted, and she stood balanced a minute, then came around the corner of the table to his side and stretched out her hand as if to touch him, but on second thought drew it back. "Here now," she said, almost gently.

Jimmy said, "Man is crying."

"Hush," Henry said.

"My wife," Simon Bale sobbed, "God grant—"

She put her hand on his back and said, "Shh, shh!" as she would to a child, but her touch opened all the rivers of Simon's heart, and he began to whoop. Quite suddenly Jimmy began to cry too, as if his heart would break; and as if hardly knowing he was doing it, Simon reached over blindly and patted at the high chair tray, mumbling "Bless . . . no importance . . . ," getting

156

his fingertips in egg yolk, and at that Henry too began to cry.

"It's all right," Callie said as if indignantly, tears running down her cheeks, the look of surprise still there on her face, "we'll take care of you, Simon, it's all right; now stop."

The room was full of sunlight and the smell of coffee like heaven's love, and Simon blew his nose. Henry pulled off his glasses and thought of asking for the handkerchief but changed his mind and got up for a Kleenex and used it and offered the unused part to Callie, who reached out, then hesitated, and decided to get one of her own.

"Simon," Callie said, "you *must* see Henry's garden!"

"Me too!" Jimmy said. He prepared his face for outrage in case they shouldn't let him.

They laughed, even Simon (but horribly, Callie thought—forgiving him, though with some reservations, even as she thought it), and Henry got up and said, "Jimmy, you show Simon our rabbit tracks."

Henry got Jimmy down out of his chair, and Callie helped Simon up and led him, as though he were an old, old man, toward the door. "Thank you," Simon said. "Forgive—" He blew his nose, then straightened a little, flashing his idiotic smile, and looked out at the green morning. He nodded. "Praise," he said. The cracks in the back of his neck were grimy, and his hair needed cutting.

"You want to take Simon's hand, Jimmy?" Callie said.

Jimmy thought about it, looking at the man, and Simon leered at the little boy and held out his hand, a limp, raised claw, and waited as if in terror. Abruptly, Jimmy reached up for the hand. Henry laughed, and Callie, after a moment's hesitation, laughed too.

4

Callie's mother came down that afternoon to help out at the diner. She was a heavyish, determined little woman with iron-gray hair, a pretty face, dimpled elbows; "artistic," she liked to say: She played the piano and organ at the church. She enjoyed working at the diner, which she tended to think of as Callie's, not Henry's. Certainly the place was greatly changed since Henry Soames had married Callie: new paint, clean linoleum, bright artificial flowers on the tables. Callie too had an artistic streak; no doubt she was a throwback to Uncle Al—Callie's mother's Uncle Al who'd done oil paintings of imaginary country scenes . . . among others, the picture in Callie's dining room, called "Summer Evening." Eleanor Wells had never thought highly of waitresses, but it was different now, in her own daughter's place, her own grandchild running about, solemn-faced, his right arm sawing across the front of him as he ran. It was a *family* diner, as she liked to say, a place people brought their whole families to, and one of these days, who knew?, they might expand it and make it a truly first-class restaurant, like the Chicken Pot, down in Slater. She'd gone so far as to mention it once or twice to Callie, and though Callie hadn't said one word back, she'd listened, and she would think about it, you could see. After that Ellie Wells had taken to wearing her black hostess's dress when she came to help out at the Stop-Off, with a little white apron she'd bought especially, and all she did she did with elegance. Her Frank would say (with a half-dozen curse-words she wouldn't repeat), "No wonder men hate their mother-in-laws," but he didn't know a thing about it. Frank couldn't understand Henry Soames like she could. Henry appreciated her help, and he respected her, he truly did. He would listen to anything she had to say with all the patience in the world (he was a *good* man, he truly was), and almost always, when he'd thought about it, he would come around to her way of thinking (something *her* Frank never did). That, as a matter of fact, was why she'd come here today.

She said nothing, however. She could tell from the minute she came in that there was something in the air, the way they pussyfooted, her daughter and Henry, but for the life of her she couldn't make out if they were mad at each other or what. Jimmy was out in the garden with that man, and it was all Ellie Wells could do to shut her teeth and ignore it. She peeked out at them from time to time, when Henry and Callie were out of the room, and as far as she could see it was still all right. Just the same, it made her heart beat fast that he was there. Callie was just too innocent. "Just like a baby," she thought. (It was just like that time at church camp, when she'd let that town man, a perfect stranger, comb out her hair, down by the lake. Or like the time she'd left her purse with that lady at the bus depot.) But Ellie polished the napkin holders and pursed her lips and waited.

The man just sat on the bench like a tramp. He had stubble on his chin and filthy-dirty clothes and a queer way of sitting with his knees and toes together and his heels thrown out to the sides. He had his hands on his knees and his calf-eyes riveted to the ground. Jimmy would talk to him sometimes, and the man would tip his head and smile and maybe pat him on the back and say a few words (she'd have given a half-dollar to hear what they were saying), and then he'd fall back into his staring fit, and, to Ellie Wells' enormous relief, Jimmy would wander away.

Toward mid-afternoon, when she and Callie were alone in the diner, she said, "Where does Henry know him from, Callie?" As if it had just now happened to come into her mind.

"Know who, Mother?" Callie said. (Callie had always been like that, never letting on when things were bothering her. It had always made it hard, even when Callie was a little girl. It put you in the wrong when all you intended was truly her own good.)

"Why, your company," she said, not quite as lightly as she'd intended.

("Now damn you, Ellie, you leave them alone," her Frank would say. "You keep away from there and mind your own business," and he would bang his fist on his leg like a little boy having a tantrum. And, oh yes, that was fine to say, "mind your own business." He'd minded his own business for fifty years, even when Callie was in trouble and no place to turn but Henry Soames. "They're like children," she'd said— that was this morning, before she'd come down. "They don't know about people like that." "Like what?" he'd said. Well she didn't know, she would admit it, and maybe she was being a worry-wart, she'd admit that too, but what was she supposed to do, Henry Soames being the kind of man he was, and Callie even worse? It was so hard, trying to do the right thing. Why was that? Why couldn't they be grateful?)

"Oh, you mean Simon Bale," Callie said. "Simon's an old, old friend of ours. He stops in all the time."

Ellie Wells tipped her head and pretended to be satisfied. She rearranged the pies in the rack and dusted her hands and went over to see how the sugar dispensers were. She'd bet fifteen dollars that man had never been here in all his life. She made a clucking sound.

"It's a terrible time for him," Callie said. There was a hint of reproach in her voice. "His house burned down, you know, and he lost his wife in the fire. It's really just terrible."

"The poor thing," Ellie said. There she was, put in the wrong as usual. She'd never *said* it wasn't terrible.

"Didn't you know?" Callie said. She looked straight at her, as if daring her to lie.

"Why, no," Ellie said, "I hadn't heard." She did feel sorry for him, she truly did, but she didn't have to like it that he was here. A man like that might do something crazy at a time like this. It was just one of those things. She said, "How long is he staying?"

"Oh, just a day or so, I think," Callie said. She bit her lip as if she'd like to be able to take back that "I think."

Ellie met her daughter's eyes just long enough to let her know she had her own opinions. Then she said, "Poor man." Then: "And poor Henry. He's so *good* to people." She dropped it casually, as if it meant nothing whatever (what it did mean, as a matter of fact, was vague in her mind). She had all the sugar dispenser tops off now. She went back to the kitchen for the sugar jar, and again, in misery, she began to cluck.

Doc Cathey came in a little after that and asked where Simon Bale was (straight to the point, as usual; no "How do you do" or "Nice weather we're having"— nothing), and when she pointed to the bench in the garden Doc Cathey nodded, scowling, and went out to him. The next time she looked out the window Doc Cathey and Simon and Jimmy were all gone from sight. They'd gone on into the house, most likely. She wondered what Doc Cathey was doing here—up to no good, she was pretty sure—and it so puzzled her she forgot to smile at the customers for maybe five full minutes. She forgot, too, to listen to what the customers were saying among themselves, until finally it came to her that all they could seem to talk about, at least the people who lived around here, was the fire. Someone said, "They say he set it himself," and she was so startled she nearly dropped her tray of salt shakers. *It's possible,* she thought, and it was as if it had been in her mind all the while: It truly is *possible.* All at once she was so frightened that she had to sit down a minute till she'd caught her breath.

5

It was Doc Cathey who brought up the question of funeral arrangements. When he'd finished looking Simon over he sat with his hands on his knees, opposite his patient, looking at the floor between their two chairs as if crossly, his glasses far down his gray beak of a nose (Callie over by the window, with her hands folded; Henry standing against the refrigerator; little Jimmy playing, oblivious to it all, on the floor). Doc said: "You thought at all about the funeral, Simon?"

Simon went pale, and his hands, busy buttoning his shirt, stopped moving. He had a wart on the knuckle of his middle finger, and Callie couldn't help but wonder if it came from his never getting clean. He smiled, just a flicker, as if in fright, and said, "The Lord will provide."

"The hell he will," Doc Cathey said.

"Now, Doc," Henry said.

"Well she can't stay there in the hospital morgue," Doc said. "One way or another she'll have to be buried. What kind of fun'ral do you people normally put on?"

Simon looked as if his mind had stopped. "The Lord—" he said. Then he said, suddenly awake for an instant, "Every nickel we had—" He looked at Callie, as if in panic, then over at Henry.

"You mean to say you let it burn?" Doc said. His face squeezed shut with fury and he shook his head. He fumbled with the hearing-aid button on his vest.

"Simon, don't you have any friends you can turn to?" Callie said.

He looked smaller than ever, as it seemed to Henry. Like a woodchuck beset by dogs. He folded his hands and sat thinking, or daydreaming, perhaps, the frightened smile playing on his face, on and off. At last he said, and this time he knew what he was saying—there was no question of it now—"The Lord will provide."

"Faddle," Doc Cathey said. He reached for the bag by his foot.

But Simon looked up sharply, his mouth open, raising his clasped hands a little, like a man with handcuffs on, the muscles of his face tense, and the brightness that had come into Simon's eyes made even Doc Cathey stop and wince and listen.

"Or ever the silver cord be loosed," Simon said, "or the golden bowl be broken, or the pitcher be broken at the fountain, or the wheel broken at the cistern, then shall the dust return to the earth as it was; and the spirit shall return unto God who gave it."

Doc Cathey leered as if with some sort of vicious triumph. "Much study is a weariness of the flesh," he said. "Who pays the mortician?"

"It's of no importance," Simon said. "Dust to dust."

"What?" Doc said. He leaned closer, turning his hearing aid toward Simon.

"Of no importance," Simon said again.

They were like a couple of old witches, the two little men sitting knee to knee, bright-eyed as a couple of hawks. Doc Cathey said, "I believe you'd just roll her in a ditch and leave her lay!"

"Stop it," Callie said, startled.

But Doc Cathey had understood.

"A living dog is better than a dead lion," Simon

said, "for the living know that they shall die: but the dead know not any thing, neither have they any more a reward; for the memory of them is forgotten."

"Now Simon, you don't know what you're saying," Henry said, and Callie felt a flush of pleasure, as if he'd defended her.

But Doc Cathey lifted his hand to hush him. "Yes, he does," he said, looking at Simon for the first time as though he were in some sense human, not actually human, maybe, but related. "He's saying the body in the morgue has nothing to do with his wife, let the County take it. And maybe he's right, at that."

"That wouldn't be decent," Henry said, but Callie Simon said, "I will reoice. I will divide Shechem, said, "If that's what Simon wants—" and mete out the valley of Succoth." Then, abruptly, as though it had been coming for a long time, waiting for the magic word *Succoth,* Simon began to cry as he'd cried this morning, but not so violently now. Jimmy had paid no attention to their talk, but he turned quickly, when Simon started crying, and looked up.

"Well somebody better see to *some* kind of arrangement," Doc Cathey said. He stood up.

Henry looked at the floor, upset. "I'll drive down tonight and see what needs to be done," he said.

Simon continued to cry, but without a sound, wiping his eyes with his knuckles.

Jimmy said, forgetting all about him, "Go to the store with Daddy!"

"Hush," Henry said. "Nobody's going to the store."

Callie said, "Simon, why don't you come into the diner and have some supper." He didn't answer, made only a confused sign with his head, something between a headshake and a nod. She came over and stood beside him, but she made no move to touch him. When she saw that he was about to reach in his pocket for his handkerchief, she crossed over to the cupboard

above the sink and brought back the Kleenex. Simon
blew his nose.

Henry walked out on the front-door steps with Doc
Cathey and closed the door behind him. There Doc
Cathey paused and got out his vestpocket watch and
opened it and looked longer than he needed to at the
time. He said at last, "They're funny damn people."
He shook his head.

Henry looked past him at the diner and the valley
and the hills beyond, but he was seeing none of it. He
saw, instead, Simon Bale as he'd sat nearly all day on
the bench in the garden, like a man in a daze, with
Jimmy at his feet. He walked down the steps with Doc
Cathey and slowly along the gravel walk that led
around the diner to the front, where Doc had his car.
He said at last: "You don't still think he set that fire
himself?"

"I dunno," Doc Cathey said. "I suppose I don't."

"You wouldn't if you'd seen him this morning,"
Henry said. He opened the car door and Doc Cathey
got in, very slowly, pulling himself up in with one hand
on the steering wheel, the other on the seat back, and
drew the door shut behind him and hunted in his coat
pocket for his key ring.

"Likely not," Doc Cathey said at last. Then for a
minute he stopped hunting for his keys and sat perfectly
still, thinking. He tilted his head and looked over his
glasses at Henry. "You be careful," he said. It wasn't
as if he knew something more than he cared to say
or even as if he had an uneasy hunch. It was some
kind of half-pitiful, half-revolting plea, an old man
pretending the years brought wisdom they hadn't
brought, wanting to be first to have given the warning
if anything bad should come of all this, but wanting
it without the faintest notion of whether what was coming would be bad or good.

"Oh, don't worry, Doc," Henry said. He slapped the old man's shoulder.

Doc Cathey went back to hunting for his keys and found them at last and started up the car. Oil smoke bloomed up from underneath as if the car had caught fire. Henry stood with his arms folded, watching the old man pull away. Then, taking his time, brooding, he went back to the diner. He'd no sooner closed the door than the bell rang, calling him back to the pumps.

It was after six when Henry drove down to the hospital in Slater. He drove slowly, ponderously erect in the seat, as always, the steering wheel rubbing against his belly, and all the way down the winding road he wondered what the devil he was going to do. It wasn't right that the woman should be shoveled away into a pauper's grave and forgotten: Sooner throw her on a manure spreader like the carcass of a calf and haul her away to some gully. He'd said to Callie's mother, "What do you think? Would the Church have money for that sort of thing?" and she'd said, "The *Baptist* Church?" He'd pursed his lips and drummed on the tabletop. "No, I guess they wouldn't," he'd said. "The County handles hundreds of cases like that," Callie's mother had said. "It's no shame, these days. Since buryings have gotten to be so expensive, some people get the County to do it even when they truly don't need to. Some people think it's a shame to spend money on the dead instead of the living. You should hear Frank talk about that!" Henry had nodded. He'd heard. There wasn't anybody in this half of the state that hadn't heard Frank Wells on funerals. But you could bet your bottom dollar old Frank would go in style: She'd see to it for spite.

The white guard posts curved down and down, on his right, and he could look off and see the whole valley like a painting, the river smooth and silent as mercury, reflecting the trees. This side of the trees there were flat acres of winter wheat and peas and hay and stretches of new-plowed ground. It was like a garden, in the gold light of late afternoon; it was exactly what Paradise ought to be like: a tractor humming along, far below him, small, on the seat a boy with a wide straw hat; to the right of the tractor, red and white cows moving slowly down the lane to a big gray barn with clean white trim. With a little imagination a man could put angels in the sky, the kind in Bible illustrations, and great golden clouds like those. Except of course that eternity wasn't going to be like that. No tractors, in any case, or trees, or fields. Whatever good you might say of the spirit, you had to give the things of earth their due—silver cords and golden bowls and whatever else it was. He thought all at once of the old country cemetery up on the hillside behind his house, where his father and mother were buried. There'd been a road through there twenty, twenty-five years ago, but they'd moved the highway now and the place was isolated, you couldn't reach it in a car except by driving down a two-rut lane like a cowpath through overgrown meadow. He would see it sometimes when he went up onto the ridge to hunt, and each time—especially in late afternoon, when the light was queerly changed, the way it was now—it would be as if he were discovering the place for the first time: a natural garden that had been the same for a thousand thousand years. All at once he said to himself, startled, "Why not?" The reasons why not rushed over him like August rain, and he put the thought out of his head and kept it out until he stepped into the long, tiled hall in the basement of the Enloe Memorial Hospital, where the smell of formaldehyde made his stomach turn, and the girl in white and blue beside him—she couldn't be more than seventeen, no more than a baby—said, "You think *this* is bad, you should watch them do an autopsy! Glaagh!" He looked at her in alarm. "Dozens of times. They take this saw—" she drew a line around her forehead from ear to ear "—and they lift off the top of the head like a bottlecap."

They showed him the body. Henry Soames stood huge and sagging, his skin gray, and stared in disbelief at the woman's indignity. Her burnt flesh smelled like hoof rot. The doctor or attendant (he couldn't tell which) at the desk said, "Who'll be handling the funeral?"

"Wiegerts' Funeral Home," he said. The words came out calm and flat, but his heart was racing and the skin of his neck tingled.

"You a relative?" the man asked.

"No, a friend," Henry said. "But I'm to take charge of it."

The man got out papers, and Henry thought again of Callie and, worse, of Callie's mother, and he shut his eyes for a quick, dead serious prayer to whatever might be up there to watch over fools and children.

It wasn't until he faced his wife, two hours later—he'd stopped at Wiegerts' before coming home—that he fully realized the magnitude of what he'd done. "Callie," he said at once, bravely, but his knees went weak underneath him, and he said only, "how is he by now?"

"All right, I guess," she said. "I really can't tell."

She was in the dining room, sewing. Scraps were spread from one end of the room to the other. "He surely is good with Jimmy, I'll have to hand it to him." She pressed on the sewing machine pedal, and Henry waited for the noise to finish.

"What do you mean?"

"Oh, you know," she said, "just the way Jimmy's taken to him. You never have to wonder where Jimmy is at all. It's like having a full-time baby-sitter."

Henry laughed, but hollowly, his heart sinking with

the returning thought of the money Callie believed they still had sitting in the bank. He swallowed.

She said, "But I can't say Mom's very happy about it."

He thought with a sudden leap of excitement that he still might stop the check. At least he could have paid on "time." He was sweating. "Well, good," he said. He smiled, white.

"Good?" She looked up. "—That Mom's not happy?"

He was rubbing his sweating hand on the front of his pantlegs. "I meant something else," he said.

She squinted at him, but after a minute she let it go. She was used to his seeing things in queer ways, and maybe it didn't seem worth the trouble of straightening out. "Well, anyways—"

At that moment, upstairs in his bedroom, Jimmy screamed. Henry ran for the stairs, off the kitchen, and Jimmy screamed again.

When Henry reached the bedroom door, Jimmy was sitting bolt upright in bed, shaking like a leaf. Henry scooped him up in his arms, and the child clung to him. "Hurt," he cried, "hurt!"

"What was it?" Callie cried, behind him.

But Jimmy was relaxed now. It couldn't be that he was sick.

"Nothing," Henry said, "a dream. It's all right now, eh, Jimmy?" Henry's heart was thudding.

Callie leaned close. "What did you dream, Jimmy?"

Already Jimmy was halfway back to sleep.

"You see, it really was nothing," Henry said softly. "Kids always start having nightmares around his age. He's over it already."

Callie kissed Jimmy's cheek and patted his back, her eyes troubled, and gently Henry laid him in his crib. Callie stood with her hands on the crib rail, looking down. After a long time she turned to look at Henry, her face white and indistinct in the darkness. She said, "Henry, I'm scared."

"Of what?" he said, exasperated.

"How do *I* know?" she said. "I'm just scared, that's all. Really. Aren't *you?*"

He looked past her, out the window at the silhouettes of the pines where they rose out of fog. It was still now, as it always was when the fog came in, as if nothing were left alive. The fog hadn't gotten to the garden yet. The moon was bright, and if there had been rabbits there he would have seen them.

Well, yes, he thought, *yes.* He tried to think what it was George Loomis had said. It wasn't here, it was up outside Utica; they'd driven up to the stock car races. He'd mentioned Jimmy, how he'd felt the time Jimmy had had the convulsions, and George Loomis had said—who lived alone, who kept intact his isolation despite all pressures, finally, and would someday die, in his barn, maybe, and not be discovered for two, three weeks—"You take on a responsibility like that, and you say to yourself you'll move heaven and earth to protect the kid you love, or the woman, or whoever it happens to be, but the minute you say it you're forgetting something."

"What's that?" Henry had said.

George Loomis stared down into the night, leaning forward over the steering wheel, and he said, "You can't."

"It's what drives you to God," Henry said with a little laugh.

George too had laughed, like a murderer.

6

That same night, two hours after Jimmy's cry, Henry sat at his kitchen table, catching up his books. It was long past his bedtime. Normally he was careful to get to bed by ten, doctor's orders, but he knew it would be no use tonight. By now he felt downright panicky at what he'd done down in Slater. Even without any trimmings whatever, everything plain as plain could be (a thing old Wiegert seemed to find distressing), his bank account would be lighter by six hundred dollars. He couldn't believe he'd done it, now. Sweat ran down his chest, and the more he tried to think why he'd done it, the wilder it seemed. It would be one thing if he were all alone, no family to think about. He'd often acted on crazy whims before he'd married Callie. Maybe he'd gone unmarried too long. It was hard as the devil to change the whole pattern of your life when you got to your forties.

The fog lay all around the house now, sealing it up like a box. At every window he saw his own reflection, but when he let his mind wander he was aware of the others; it was as if he could hear them breathing: Simon just on the other side of that door straight in front of him, Callie and Jimmy just up the stairs that opened onto the kitchen to his right. Outside, nothing moving. A hundred thousand birds would start singing when the sun came up, and in the valley cows would move in from their pastures toward lighted barns. In the fields, mice, woodchucks, rabbits, dogs would run, when dawn came, and the mountainsides would be rife with wild things, from squirrels to foxes—but just now, nothing. But no, that was wrong of course. Fog or no fog, everything was the same as always, animals stalking animals stalking animals in deadly procession, quiet as dreams.

She'd had plans for that money. He'd never agreed to Callie's plans, but it was settled between them that one of these days they would have it out; he'd had no right to spend six hundred dollars on something insane. Unless maybe that was why he'd done it: not for Simon's wife but against his own.

(He remembered vividly the way cows would push at the fences on his grandfather's farm. Even if you pastured them in clover and the other side was barely stubble, still they'd push to get out. He and his father and grandfather would go out in the middle of the night —two fat old men and a fat little boy—and they'd shout at the cows and turn them around with pitchfork handles, and the cows would go anywhere on earth but where you wanted them. When you finally got them to the open gate or the hole in the fence, you had to twist their tails to run them through.)

But that wasn't all of it. He remembered the way Callie had reached out, finally, and touched Simon Bale when he was crying.

The thought was comforting for a minute, but the next minute he wondered if he would have brought Simon here at all if it weren't for the others who'd stood above him doing nothing. There was a story about two old brothers named Sprague—a true story, Jim Millet said. They'd lived together in Slater all their lives, and when they were eighty they'd sold their house and moved down to Florida. Nobody knew them there, and the second day one of them killed the other with an axe, just like that, nobody ever learned why. It would never have happened if they'd stayed where they belonged, Jim Millet said. The man had never done a thing to cover up his crime. He'd carried the body to

the garage and shut it up, and as soon as it started to
smell, the neighbors found it.

The story was puzzling, and Henry leaned on his
fists, frowning. He was still thinking about it when he
dozed off. When he woke up again—he couldn't tell
how much later—Simon Bale was standing over by
the stove, blinking. He had on only his suitcoat and
trousers, no shirt or undershirt, no shoes.

"Trouble sleeping?" Henry said.

Simon waved as if to say it was unimportant.

Henry squinted at him, wide awake now, and it was
as if, seeing him here in his own kitchen where every
pot and pan had its precise meaning, he was seeing
Simon clear for the first time. It was like something
that came to you early in the morning when you'd
first gotten up: Compared to Callie's light blue apron,
not a brute object but the sum of its associations, Simon
Bale was old and sallow-faced and strangely bitter,
maybe devious. Against the yellow of the walls he was
tortuously old-fashioned, grim, as rigid as an angle
iron. It made Henry's skin creep.

Simon stood with his big-knuckled hands at his sides,
his belly out, chest caved in, head forward, looking at
the coffeepot on the stove. He lifted the lid, saw that
the pot was empty, and replaced the lid as if that too
were of no importance. He came over and stood with
his hands in his side pockets, looking disapprovingly
at Henry's ledger. After a moment he drew out a chair,
smiled apologetically, then looked grim again, and sat
down.

"The house gets cold, these foggy nights," Henry
said.

Simon nodded and smiled.

For a long time after that neither of them spoke.
Henry thought of mentioning the funeral, then thought
better of it. Not mentioning it was pure cowardice, he
knew: To tell Simon would be, in effect, to tell Callie.
But Simon was completely uninterested in her burial,

or so he said; as likely as not, he wouldn't even bother to go when Henry did tell him.

The muscles of Simon's face were working, and he had his eyes fixed on Henry's forehead. After a moment, with a darting motion, he drew a stack of small, white leaflets from his inside coatpocket. He leered and slid them across the table toward Henry. WATCH AND WAIT! the top one said. The next said, WHO SHALL BE SAVED? Under the title there were words in italics: *But why dost thou judge thy brother? or why dost thou set at nought thy brother? for we shall all stand before the judgment seat of Christ. (Rom. 14:10)* It was not what Henry would have expected; he would have expected, well, something about God's wrath, say, or the seven angels of doom. "Is this what Jehovah's Witnesses believe?" Henry said.

However mild the text, there was a spark of anger in Simon's eyes. "Not what we *believe*," he said, "the *truth!*"

"Yes, of course," Henry said, looking down.

"Do you dare to deny the Judgment of the Lord?" Simon said. He was leaning forward now, his lower lip trembling. His fury seemed to Henry inexplicable, unwarranted by anything Henry had said.

"I don't deny anything," Henry said.

"But there *is evil*," Simon said. "Woe to the man—"

"Perhaps so," Henry said sharply, cutting him off.

Simon looked at him for a long time, then at last bowed his head. "You have been kind to me, within the bounds of your understanding." After another moment: "I am deeply grateful. May the Lord keep you, Mr.—" He seemed to cast about for Henry's name.

Henry winced, watching him closely, at once repelled and fascinated, like a man watching a rattlesnake behind glass.

"I accept your hospitality," Simon said, suddenly smiling grotesquely, tears in his eyes. "God's will be done."

7

The troopers came in the next afternoon and casually asked to speak with Simon. Behind the counter, Henry Soames stood thinking a moment, the lenses of his glasses blanking out his eyes. "I'll see if I can locate him," he said. He rubbed the side of his nose, still thinking, and then, reluctantly, he left the diner to look.

He was a little on edge to start with, as he frequently was when Callie's mother decided to come down and help out. She'd been here most of the day again, busying herself when there was nothing to do, mopping the floor when it was perfectly all right, bending the old gray spoons back into shape, criticizing the electric potato peeler for eating up three-fourths of every potato. He wished she'd get down to what she'd come here to say, but she didn't, and gradually Henry was beginning to believe she had no intention of getting down to it. Maybe she figured she would drive out Simon Bale by just hanging around. Well, she figured wrong. When Henry asked her, "You seen Simon, Ellie?" she had looked surprised, as if she hadn't heard what the troopers had said, five feet from where she'd been careful to be standing, and she'd said "Why, no. Henry, I been too busy. Does somebody want him?" Henry had nodded and hurried on by her.

Simon wasn't in the garden, this time, and when Henry called into the house he found he wasn't there either. "Why do you want him?" Callie called back, but Henry ignored her too. He started for the garage.

He didn't know what to think by now. Not just about the money, about the whole damn business, from the minute he'd first seen Simon Bale slumped down on the ground by his snow fence, and the people around him not moving a muscle. There was something he'd read, about a week ago: Some old man had been stabbed in New York City, it said in the paper, and there were fifteen people standing around and even when he asked them to, they never even called the police. It was hard to believe they'd all just stand there, fifteen of them, and not even one of them lift one finger, and he'd thought and thought about it. It didn't seem natural, and he'd tried to see it from their side, because if there was any way on earth to explain it, the secret had to be in those people's feelings. He could understand their not helping: afraid of the fellow with the knife. But to merely stand there like a herd of cows—it was past all comprehending. A man could turn into an animal, then. It was something about living in the city, that was all he could figure. And he *could* understand that, it came to him. He'd felt it himself one time in Utica. He'd never have believed there were that many people in all this world, especially that many poor people, burnt-out-looking; and walking in that crowd, looking at faces that stared right through him (no two faces in all that city exactly alike, each one marked by its own single lifetime of weathers, suppers, accidents, opinions), he'd felt a sudden disgust—or not even that, a calm disinterest, as though he were seeing it all with the eyes of a thinking stone to whom all human life was nothing, to whom even his own life was nothing. If there were millions and millions of people in the world, they were nothing compared with the billions and billions already dead. But then he'd seen a man he knew, and he could hardly recapture, when he'd thought back to it later, that vision of people as meaningless motion, a stream of humanity down through time, no more significant than the rocks in a mountain slide. It was different in the country, where a man's life or a family's past was not so quickly swallowed up, where the ordinariness of thinking creatures was obvious only when you thought a minute, not an inescapable conclusion that crushed the soul the way pavement shattered men's arches. And so they had stopped being human. It was outrageous that it could happen, but maybe it did, and, worse, maybe it was the people in New York City that were right. What was pleasant to believe was not necessarily true. Elves, for instance, or Santa Claus, or what he'd never have doubted once, the idea that Henry Soames would live practically forever. He thought: Or angels. He could remember—it seemed like centuries ago, when he was four or five—lying in bed with his grandmother, looking at pictures in the *Christian Herald*. It was in an upstairs room in the big old house where his parents had lived, and outside the window there were pines moaning and creaking in the summer wind. She had told him about angels, and there had seemed no possible question of its not being true. Once, standing on a hillside watching the northern lights, he had seen an angel with absolute clarity—as clearly as, another time, he'd seen a great, round frying pan in the sky when he was looking for the Big Dipper. But then the evidence against them came in, piece by piece, fact after fact, until by sheer bulk the facts overwhelmed them, and what was good to believe—for the world was vastly more beautiful with angels than it was without—was incredible. He'd been right, then, at least in this: He wasn't acting *for* but *against*—Callie, Callie's mother, the people who said on no earthly grounds but animal distrust that Simon had burned his own house. And maybe he had, who knew? How far would Henry Soames go on what George Loomis would call pure meanness? He thought of the money and the sinking feeling returned. He was sweating again.

He found them behind the garage. He stopped when he saw them, and neither Simon nor Jimmy looked up. Simon was sitting on a tipped-over oil drum, writing something with a pencil on a piece of wood, and Jimmy was standing at his elbow watching. Henry stopped and it came to him that, close he was, they didn't realize yet that he was there. Jimmy was saying, "Why?" and Simon said, "Because he loves all little children, if they repent." Jimmy said, "Who *is* God?" Henry said sharply, "Simon!"

The man jumped a foot, then instantly went into his obsequious cowering. He said, "H'lo."

Henry said nothing. A muscle was jumping in his jaw, and his chest was churning so badly he could hardly get his wind. Jimmy looked up as if caught at something. At last Henry said, "The troopers would like to talk to you, Simon. In the diner."

For a moment Simon seemed unable to make sense of the words, but then their meaning came through, and he stood up.

Henry waited with his hands behind his back, keeping his fury inside, and when Simon reached him, he turned and walked with him toward the diner. Jimmy started to follow, and Henry said, "You go back to the house." The child opened his mouth to protest, but Henry pointed toward the house angrily and Jimmy started across the grass. By the time he reached the door he was crying.

"What were you making?" Henry asked abruptly.

Simon blushed like a child and held out the piece of wood. The letters were cut deep, like the writing on a schoolroom desk: GOD IS LOVE. Around the writing there were curlicues.

Henry said nothing. They reached the back door of the diner and Henry reached ahead of Simon to push the door open. Simon hesitated a moment, looking up at him as if in fright, and the tic played on his face; then he went in. Callie's mother stood fussing with the mustard pots at the end of the counter.

The younger trooper had a clean-cut, Italian look. The other one was maybe fifty, a large belly but a small, lean face. They had their hats off. Simon went over to stand beside them, leaning on the counter, his suitcoat hanging down limp, the crotch of his baggy trousers low, and he waited. He looked very small, to Henry, and he stood like an old man, bent forward a little, his knees turned slightly inward. The trooper closest to him, the younger one, said, "Sit down, Simon." Simon got up on the stool.

Henry went to the near end of the counter and stood with his arms folded, looking at the floor. His anger began to cool a little now. He'd been unfair, in a way; there was no doubt of it. It was ridiculous to fly into a rage at an old man's teaching a child that God was Love. It was the word "repent," maybe, that had set him off. But if so, that was more ridiculous yet. What did "repent" mean to a boy two years old? Or maybe what had done it was his finding them out there behind the garage. But he couldn't blame Simon for that, after all. Jimmy followed him everywhere, and in fact they themselves, he and Callie, had encouraged it. Even now he felt angry, but he felt, at the same time, ashamed. Then what the trooper was saying caught his attention:

"What happened before you went to work the night of the fire?"

"Why?" Simon said. It was as if he wanted assurance that the question was important before he would trouble to remember.

"Just tell us what happened," the other trooper said.

Simon touched his forehead with the back of his hand. "I had supper," he said.

The younger trooper said impatiently, "We understand you had a disagreement with your wife."

Simon looked at the man in surprise, then over at Henry. "Why, no," he said, "no." His smile came. Callie's mother was standing motionless, looking out the window, and Henry felt a clutch of fear.

"Did you ever have arguments with your wife?"

Simon seemed baffled, and the older trooper said, "How did you and your wife get along, Simon?"

Simon said, "We never had any trouble."

"We've talked to your son Bradley," the younger trooper said. Then, casually: "We understand you used to beat him some, with your fists."

Simon flushed and said nothing. He leaned his elbows on the counter and began folding and unfolding his hands.

"Is it true?" the trooper asked.

Henry's hands were sweating. He began to doubt things he'd have sworn to five minutes before. Why were they questioning him here, in front of strangers?

"He'd sinned," Simon said. It was almost too soft to hear, and he cleared his throat and said it louder.

"Sinned?" It was as if it were the first time the trooper had heard the expression.

Simon said nothing, and the trooper said with distaste, "Let's talk about your daughter, Simon. Your son tells us you used to lock her in the shed for days." He waited. "Is *that* true?"

"Not days," Simon said in a whisper. He went on folding and unfolding his hands.

"But you locked her in the shed."

He said nothing.

"Did she cry, Simon?" It was faintly ironic. After a moment: "Did she scream sometimes—for hours?"

"God forgive—" he began vaguely. No one spoke for a minute.

The younger trooper sat watching Simon's hands. "What was the argument with your wife that night?"

He shook his head. "We didn't argue."

"Your neighbors say—"

"False witnesses!" For an instant anger flared up in his look, but he stopped it.

The older one said, "What was her sin, Simon?"

Again he shook his head. He was pale, and he was wringing his hands as if in anguish, but his jaw was set.

"Why would they lie—your son, your neighbors?" the younger one said. "What difference would it make to them?"

Henry pulled at his lip. He kept from breaking in, but he knew he wouldn't keep still much longer. His anger was confused now, aimed at all of them. Strange to say, he was angriest of all at Callie's mother, who had nothing to do with it. Her face was turned away and he couldn't read her expression. But he could see the eavesdropping tilt of her head, the tense, righteous indignation in every muscle and bone.

"Mr. Bale," the trooper said, "the fire at your house was arson, set with burlap and gas from your own shed. Who had any reason to set it? Who knew you had the makings right there?" And after a second: "Besides you."

And at that Henry did break in, no more knowing now than he would know later why he did it. "That's not fair, officer." He went over to stand bent toward them, in front of them, the blood stinging in his face, and Callie's mother, behind them, looked up at him, wide-eyed. "Any tramp could have come onto the gas and rags. And the neighbors—anybody in the county, for that matter—maybe they took it into their heads to hate him. It would be natural. No, let me finish. He does what he believes in, he even sneaks around trying to convert your children behind your back. It's natural it would make people mad—maybe so mad they tell lies about him, or imagine things. You can't take a man to jail because people don't like him." In his excitement Henry didn't see George Loomis's pickup truck pull in in front of the diner, and, though he saw the door open, he paid no attention. "People don't believe in Simon's God, the end of the world anyday now, things like that. They think a man that believes such things has to be crazy, and crazy people burn houses, so Simon must have burned his own house down. Pretty soon they remember a fight they never heard, and it fits in with everything they know and pretty soon it's not even remembered any more, it's predestined fact. People think—"

"Simon," the younger trooper said, getting the floor from Henry without ever raising his voice, "have you ever seen the devil?"

Henry waited, checked, not sure what the man was driving at but thrown off balance, frightened again.

Simon nodded.

"Many times?" the trooper said, as if innocently, as if strictly from curiosity.

Simon nodded again.

The trooper looked at Henry, and there was no triumph in the look; a kind of helplessness. "How can you know if he's sane, a man like that?"

George Loomis was leaning against the doorpost. He said heartily, "What the hell! Of course he's sane. Lots of people see the devil. Happens all the time. You ever see the Watkins Man? I do. I believe in him. The Watkins Man is good."

"Don't clown, George," Henry said.

George came over to the counter, the brace on his boot clumping on the linoleum, the empty sleeve dangling. To Simon Bale he might have been, even then, the devil himself: triangle-faced, maimed, a cynic, waspish in his irony; but Simon was grinning apologetically, his mouth trembling, ducking his head away from George Loomis as if afraid George might strike at him.

George said, "What's going on around here, Ellie?"

Ellie said, tight-lipped, "They think Simon—" All at once she was in tears, and George looked startled. Henry hurried around to her, furious, and furious at Simon Bale and himself as well. "It's all right," he said. "Here now, after all—"

The two troopers sat relaxed and patient, watching, looking vaguely interfered-with but mainly just patient.

"Look, you guys leave Henry alone," George said.

Henry said, "They're just doing their job." He felt furious at the troopers now, too. "I'm sorry I lost my temper," he said. He went on awkwardly patting Callie's mother's shoulder. She cried into her apron as well as she could; it was too short to get up to her eyes. A little peeping noise came out as she cried, and she said, "I'm sorry, I'm truly sorry."

The troopers looked at each other, and at last the younger one shook his head. "Well, thanks for your time," he said. He looked over at the older one again, and they both stood up. The older one put two dimes on the counter, and then they walked over to the door. The older one said, nodding toward Simon but looking at Henry, "He'll be here if we need him?"

After a second, Henry nodded.

Simon said all at once, earnestly, "I'm sorry."

They looked at him as one might look at a sideshow freak—mildly curious, mildly embarrassed. The younger one smiled at Henry and shook his head; then they went out to their car. Henry and George watched them pull away. When they were out of sight, over the crest of the hill to the south, Henry wiped his forehead on his sleeve. Callie's mother blew her nose on a paper napkin and went over, sniffing, to refill the matchbook box by the cash register. "I don't know what came over me," she said.

"Now, just don't you think about it," Henry said.

George Loomis slid onto the stool beside Simon and bent down to look into his eyes. "What does the devil look like, exactly, Simon?" he asked.

"Now that's enough, George," Henry said.

8

Henry had not defended Simon Bale in order to win his love or praise; nothing of the kind. But he was shocked to find how little it meant to Simon. When he said, as he was getting George Loomis his coffee, "Don't you worry, Simon, we won't let them go after you that way again," Simon merely waved, his face falling into that idiot's smile, and said, "Oh, no importance." His hands were folded and quiet now. Henry said, "No importance if they put you in jail?" "Ah, well," Simon said. He looked up at the ceiling.

George Loomis said, "If you think it's God's will that you're sitting here, mister, you're mistaken. God and the devil are out watching the sparrow, and all you got to look to is that man right there." He pointed at Henry.

Simon studied George exactly as the troopers had looked, a few minutes ago, at Simon.

George ignored him at first. He got out his cigarettes and shook one out on the counter, put the crumpled pack away in his jeans again, and got out his matches. When Simon continued to stare, George turned irritably and said, "Come on off it now, Simon. We're all friends here. No point you sitting there spreading the crap about God and all his legions." He lit the cigarette.

"Now I mean it, leave him alone, George," Henry said.

"Why? Does Simon Bale leave people alone? Simon Bale, I bring you Good News." He drew on the cigarette and blew a huge cloud of smoke at the ceiling. Simon looked up at it. "Simon—" He leaned toward him. "There is no God. You got that? Absolute truth,

184

and people that say there's a God only do it for one
of two reasons—because they're fools or because they're
vicious. Clap your hands twice if you understand."

Callie's mother was looking outraged again. It was
as if she'd explode any minute. It might have seemed
funny to Henry another time, but right now he was
sorry for her; she was in the right. He said, "George,
shut up. Have a little consideration."

"Why?" He looked up, and he saw Henry nod toward Callie's mother, and he looked down again in
disgust and swung around toward the counter and
scowled at his coffee. "Hell," he said, "Ellie knows I'm
kidding."

"God forgive you for your blaspheming," Simon
said softly, as if absentmindedly, watching the smoke
go up from George's cigarette.

Suddenly, after thinking about it first, George Loomis
hit the counter with his fist and said, "Shit! If you don't
have to listen to the truth from me, I don't have to
listen to your crackpot drivel. Now shut your goddamn
teeth."

Henry caught his breath.

Callie's mother said, "He's *kidding,* he says. You're
truly a card, George."

Two men came in behind George and Simon. They
were laughing as they came through the door, and they
seemed not to notice that anything was wrong as they
glanced at the four of them and walked past them to
the booth at the end. Ellie went over to them, her lips
drawn taut. "Just like summer out," one of them said.
She smiled grimly.

"What I want to know," George said quietly, "is
how come you put up with all this crap from him."
He looked up at Henry, then down again. "I'll tell you
why you do. It's because you think he's a moron. If you
thought he had the same brains as anybody else you'd
try to talk sense into him, but you don't. Or her," he
said still more softly, jerking his thumb toward Ellie,

over by the customers. He dropped almost to a whisper. "She's as cracked as Simon, and you know it damn well, with all her hymn singing an' carrying on. And if she's better than Simon it's only because she's worse. He goes around trying to save people in his crackpot way; she believes they're all damned, and she figures, 'Ah, screw 'em.'" She came around to the grill and he shut up.

"What's the matter with you, George," Henry said. "I never saw you like this. You must've been mad already before you get here. There's nothing here could get you as worked-up as that."

"The hell," he said. "Nobody ever says anything because he believes it, is that it? If I come out against burning Jews it's because I've got gallstones."

"Simon's no Nazi," Henry said.

George thought about it, his shoulders hunched, head slung forward. He said, not turning toward Simon, "You know what the Jews say about Jesus, Simon? They say he was a fraud. There's a word for him, they say. Megalomaniac. He may have said lots of good things, I don't know, but when a plain ordinary human being thinks he's God, the fact is he's a nut. That's what the Jews say. Or do you think maybe he was just pretending—for the good of mankind, because philosophy goes over better if you salt it with superstition?"

Simon said nothing, watching the smoke.

"*You* say he was a human being, George," Henry said.

"Sure. And Simon would burn me too. But were you there? Do you really know?" He remembered his coffee and drank it down at once, hot as it was.

"That's nothing to do with it. Nobody knows." He was going to say more, but George said:

"That's right. And yet a man that'll burn you over something nobody in all this world knows and most people think is a whole lot of crap—"

"Yet you'd do the same on the opposite side! What's the difference?"

"You're right, yes I would." He pushed his cup away. "I'd burn up all the holy bigots on earth, all the death-wishers that ever lived, if you can call it living. There's not one in a million of 'em that's honest. Not one! You think anybody in this world's so stupid he can honestly believe in the man with the beard in the sky? What does it mean? Heretic fires and Jew fires and scientist fires, noble wars against conveniently rich pagans. Pah!"

Simon Bale said, "The desire of the wicked shall perish. Thus saith the Lord."

"And I say, 'Pah,' " George said.

Callie came in the back door with Jimmy and started over to the booth to the right of the door with him, to give him his supper. She looked over at George, then kept on walking, holding Jimmy's hand. Her mother went over to her and they started to talk in low voices, never looking in the direction of the counter. Jimmy peeked around behind his grandmother's back. George went on ranting, his voice low and brimming with disgust, but Henry could listen with only half his mind. He wanted to concentrate on the argument—there was something important that wasn't getting said, he couldn't just yet say what, though he knew it was there—but more customers had come in now: a family, people on a trip of some kind, the man stocky and tired-looking, wearing sunglasses, a blue short-sleeved shirt; the woman fat and blonde, a light green dress with white circles on it, brown and white shoes; the little boy (seven or eight) in jeans and a T-shirt and a New York Yankees baseball cap. Henry filled water glasses and went over to them. "Evening," he said. (George was saying behind him: "Religion's strictly a gimmick people use to get power over other people. You want to know who says 'God' more often than a minister? A politician. Fact.")

"Beautiful country you got here," the man said. He had reddish hair, almost all of it gone from the top of his head, and where he was bald he had freckles.

"Yes, sir," Henry said. "Best country *I* ever saw." They laughed, even if the joke was not very clear. *"Only* country I ever saw. Ha, ha," he added, too late. They laughed again.

"Hope you've got cooking like your scenery," the woman said, "I'm famished."

Henry said, wide-eyed, faintly excited as he always was when he became the spokesman for all the region, "I never heard of anybody leaving the Catskills hungry!"

They laughed joyfully; he could have reached out for their hands. The boy said: "You got hamburgers?"

"House specialty," Henry said. They laughed.

George Loomis was saying: "If I was your kid and I took up smoking, would you whip me for it, Simon? Is it a sin, smoking? It gives you cancer, yes, everybody knows that—though on the other hand it can sometimes save you a nervous breakdown—but is it a sin?"

Simon said, "I will praise the Lord with my whole heart, in the assembly of the upright, and in the congregation."

"Fuck the congregation's bloody cunt," George Loomis said. He stuck out his lower lip and chin, like a child gone insane.

Henry left the tourists looking over the menu, because the woman was one that would take a long time, he knew the type. When he got back to the counter the truckers were ready to pay up. Callie's mother was sitting across from Callie and Jimmy, and they were leaning toward each other like gossips. Jimmy was watching George, paying no attention to his supper. One of the truckers said, "Boy they really go at it, eh, Slim?"

Henry shook his head, smiling (but he felt frustrated,

cross. There were things that weren't getting said. He wanted to make them shut up and think a minute, talk sense). He rang up the truckers' checks.

"Henry," George shouted over to him, "I ask you man to man if it's not a fact that there isn't any devil and there isn't any God, and even if there is, a man who doesn't believe in God lives a better life than a man who does. Now I want you to tell me the truth." Henry started to answer, but George said: "A man that thinks he's righteous is deadly, you know it. He takes credit for things he's got nothing to do with—accidents like his living where he happens to live and knowing exactly the people he knows. He thinks he's Jesus H. Christ and it makes him arrogant."

But the family in the booth was ready now. "Some other time," Henry said. He went over to the family in the booth.

The man said, "I guess I'll try that beef sandwich, Slim."

Henry got out his checkpad.

By the time Henry had their orders ready, more people had come. It was the busy time, and he saw there was no hope now of his getting back to the argument. Callie and Jimmy had finished eating, and Callie left Jimmy sitting in the corner with a couple of toy trucks while she and her mother helped Henry keep up. George and Simon, the next time Henry got back to them, were gulping down food, still arguing—or rather, George still arguing, Simon still sitting tense and silent for long stretches, then suddenly breaking in angrily with some long quotation from the Bible. Then Doc Cathey was there, standing with his hands in his suit-coat pockets and his glasses down his nose, picking his teeth with his tongue and looking mad as the devil. He said, "You sound like a Commie, George." "Damn right I do," George said. "Fine, that's the spirit," Doc Cathey said. "You turn over half your farm to Simon Bale and I'll believe you. But till then I'll tell you right out it's nothing but lies." They were shouting, all three of them now, Simon saying, "Woe unto them that call evil good and good evil." But nobody especially noticed the shouting. The diner was full now—four truckers laughing loud about a story of another trucker in Pennsylvania who'd fixed a cop that was tailing him too close, Jim Millet telling about a fellow he'd fixed a tire for last night on 99, Nick Blue and Walt Forrest's hired man talking about the new houses going up this side of New Carthage, two men in business suits, salesmen maybe, talking about how some Chevy place gave away free flowers every time a lady bought a new Corvette. It was a time of day Henry normally liked, the supper hour when the whole room began to hum and the walls when you put your fingertips on them shivered like the top of the piano when somebody was playing it. He would sink down into that bustle the way he would sink down into warm river water, and he would be sorry for people who weren't caught up, as he was, in the buzzing, blooming confusion. But tonight he was eager for the time to be over. There were a hundred things he wanted to say, and every few minutes he would glance over where George and Simon and Doc Cathey were, to see if they were still there. (Doc Cathey was saying: "*All* Reds are liars. That's not a matter of opinion, it's a matter of fact. You take a man that's spent years breeding coonhounds. You tell that man he's got to pass his hounds around among people that don't know a hound from a cow, and that man will cave your head in, and rightly so.")

Callie said, "Henry, why don't you break them up?"

"How can I?" Henry said.

She said, "They're bothering the others. I mean it. They're yelling like a bunch of drunkards."

But then Callie's mother came and told him the dishwasher had quit, and he had to hand over his counter checks to Callie and go fix it. It was the usual trouble, the belt underneath, and as usual it took him half an hour to get it fixed. When he got back, Doc Cathey was gone. Most of the others were gone, too; there were only six people left, four of them people who'd been there before he went in to the dishwasher, two of them truckers who'd come in. George was saying, letting smoke out with the words, "I can't talk to you. You're cracked." Simon sat with his shoulders pulled in like a man wrapped tightly in rope, his fists under his chin. It was dusk outside, almost dark. George got up and paid his check, and Henry walked over to the door with him.

George said, "What in hell did you bring him *here* for? Boy, I just can't make you out."

"He didn't have anywheres to go," Henry said.

"Crap." He pushed open the screen a crack and spat. "You bring home every rattler you find in the weeds?"

"I don't shoot at everything that moves on the theory it *might* be a rattler."

George Loomis looked out at the road. "I guess that makes you Jesus, don't it."

"Oh, for Christ's sake, George," Henry said.

George nodded, then shook his head.

"Don't go away mad, George," Henry said. He gave a little laugh.

"Let me ask you just one thing," he said. "Does it make you feel righteous, taking him in out of the cold like that?"

"I don't know."

"The hell you don't."

Henry held fire a second, then he let go. "It's a question nobody in his right mind would bother to answer," he said. *"You,* now, *you* can feel righteous all right, but anybody else it's a dirty word. If I feel righteous for taking him in I'm a bastard, and if I don't I'm a fool, because there's no reason for taking him in except to give myself the thrill of righteousness, according to you."

George said, smiling but hissing it at him, "And why *did* you take him in?"

"Get out," Henry said. "I mean it. Get out of here."

George put his hat on.

"He's the devil," Simon Bale said, right at Henry's elbow. "The devil is in him." Bale's eyes were fire. Henry looked furiously past him. "May the devil have no power in this house," Simon said. He was in deadly earnest.

Henry said, "Damn you, Simon, shut up before—"

"You tell 'im, Lord," George said. He left.

9

Henry Soames was less and less sure, as the days passed, why it was he'd taken on the role of friend and protector to Simon Bale. His mother-in-law appeared day after day, saying nothing, butting in on his affairs and condemning him for his own mismanagement only by her presence. Because of the way he'd let the thing drag on, Callie scarcely spoke to him now from morning to night. Once when Doc Cathey came in and made some stupid remark (Henry could no longer remember it) and Henry had blown up at him, Callie had said with quiet rage, "Are you satisfied? Henry, when are you going to have had enough?" On Sunday morning, the second week of his stay, Simon Bale went out on his calls, and Henry was so angry he felt sick—angry at something he couldn't even name: not the people who would be thinking, *He comes from Henry's place, glides down from his cool tranquility to our poor ordinary mortal domain where you earn your keep by the sweat of your fucking brow;* not angry at Simon, exactly, either, whose materialization on some country porch carried, inevitably, the sanction Henry had never given and whose preaching was, insidiously, the word from Henry Soames; not angry, even, at himself, because what he had done was beyond stupidity or wisdom, it was what it was, pure and simple, old clothes on a clothesline, neither bad nor good, merely there, the inevitable and inexorable law of Henry's constitution. Seeing Simon slumped down again, accused and no more able to answer than a fat, stupid sheep could answer his butcher, Henry would do it all again, this time knowing even as he did it the complete absurdity of what he did; and seeing the woman's blistered, naked body in the morgue, in the gloom and the inexhaustible stench of the hospital's bowels, he'd react to even that as he'd done before, would raise her up at his own incredibly excessive expense, and would feel the same useless irrelevant remorse at having done what it was impossible for him not to do, and, as before, he'd no doubt by the very necessity of his nature keep the thing as secret as he could, revealing it only in the form of cryptic red entries in his books.

So that if Henry had no reasons for having taken Simon in, he nevertheless accepted the fact that he'd done it and couldn't get out of it now, come hell or high water—and they would. George Loomis and Doc Cathey still came in from time to time, but between them and Henry there was a coolness now that none of them could dispel. Ironically—as Henry saw—George Loomis's anger was partly at what Henry was doing to himself, letting Simon Bale take over his house, pervert his natural feeling for justice to a sick kind of pity, turn his diner into a beggar's banquet, rob him of all he had ever saved, all he had every right to call his own. And partly, of course, George's anger was the effect of just and reasonable envy. The two of them had been close once, and it was unforgivable that Simon should have Henry's ear, should be free to talk nonsense without fear of contradiction or reproach, and George Loomis not. What right had Simon Bale to dawdle in Henry Soames' garden or dispossess him of his bench? But he was there, apparently settled there more or less permanently; he showed no sign of going down again to the Grant Hotel. Thinking about that gulf yawning wider and wider between himself and George, Henry Soames would clench his fists in anger. He would rather have George to talk to, late at night; there was no question about that. George was brighter, even if he was sometimes irascible and overbearing; and he'd been around longer—though by now Simon Bale seemed to have been here, not only inside Henry's house but inside his skin, forever. And George was not, like Simon, a bore. They would fight far into the night, in the old days, battling over nothing at all with splendid thrusts and sallies and glorious alarums, never knowing for sure who was winning or who was losing and not caring much, since nobody ever really lost in those airy wars. But it was different now. Though they still talked, they talked as if from opposite ends of an expanding universe: because one of them no longer talked with his own voice or defended what he could honestly consider his own kingdom.

As for Doc Cathey, he came and went like a shadow no longer of any great significance. Sometimes in the past he had been for Henry an older and wiser spirit, someone to lean on, likely to come up with outrageous opinions but nevertheless sure to come up with opinions that, one way or another, would be of use. But he had nothing whatever to say, now. If he approved Henry's course he gave no sign. He would laugh sometimes, as if at nothing, but he left in his wake nothing solid to catch hold of, only the nameless turbulence of his indefinite, violent moods.

Most of the time Simon Bale would sit there in the sun, watching Jimmy play, telling him stories, or sleep-

ing. At other times they would find Simon crying in
his room. Both the sitting and the familiar grief, by
now an old friend to Simon, were disgusting to Henry,
and he would be tempted to lash out at the man with
all the thunder of his indignation. He didn't, though,
and in fact couldn't, because the fact was that Simon
had every right to his grief, and it was his grief that lay
both behind his dawdling, day after day, and his mourn-
ing alone in his room.

But idleness and crying weren't enough for him. He
went further: He began to appear in the diner with his
pamphlets (he was shaving again now; that much could
be said; but on the other hand he'd given up taking off
his suit when he went to sleep). He would get into conversation with the customers, smiling his idiotic smile
or standing there with his mouth hanging open, rolling
his eyes, craning his dirty, wrinkled neck.

Callie said, "Henry, *do* something!"

And so Henry said, "Simon, this is a diner. You go
do your preaching somewheres else."

"The Lord's work—" Simon said, lifting his eyebrows.

"Not while they eat," Henry said. "Go someplace
else."

Simon did not like it. He had no natural feeling for
ordinary requirements of Nature. But he accepted it.
After that Simon would meet them at the door as they
were leaving, and he would press his pamphlets on
them and writhe along with them as they went to their
cars, Simon smiling and hissing about Kingdom Come.
Callie compressed her lips and said nothing, and Henry,
despairing, pretended not to see. George Loomis said
once, coming into the diner jerking his thumb toward
the gas pumps where Simon ministered, "You know
what that bastard's telling them? He's telling them
they're going to hell. You ought to trade him in on a
goat or something." Henry clenched his jaw and tried

195

to think, then at last went over to the door and pushed it open and stuck his head out. "Simon!" he said.

Simon looked up, his head far forward, like a buzzard's, his tie hanging outside the front of his suitcoat. At last he came over.

"I don't mean just the diner," he said, "I mean no place in my sight. Leave the customers alone. You hear?"

"God forgive you," Simon Bale said.

Henry clenched his jaw tighter yet and pulled his head in and let the door slam shut behind him. He started back toward the counter, then on second thought turned and ducked down to peer darkly through the glass. Simon was heading straight back to the people he'd been talking to, but he didn't disobey—at least not yet. The car started up and swerved out onto the highway and escaped.

"Damn it, Henry," George Loomis said, "that man's crazy."

"Maybe so," Henry said. "How can I say?"

But he was thinking: Those fifteen people in New York City might be right in the end, but you had to act, and beyond that you had to assert that they were wrong, wrong for all time, whatever the truth might be. And it was the same even if you only *thought* you saw an old man being stabbed: You ran to the center of the illusion and you jumped the illusory man with the knife, and if it was empty, sunlit sidewalk you hit, too bad, you had to put up with the laughter, and nevertheless do it again the next time and again and again. So Simon. It wasn't true that the world was about to end or that sinners were going to torment, but all the same he was right to go out with his crackpot pamphlets: Henry Soames would try to persuade him, but he wasn't going to stop him—except in the diner, because the diner, at least, was still his own.

And yet he felt no quiet. The truth was that there was something Henry was afraid of, something as un-

defined in his mind as the substance of his child's
nightmares, but real, for all its ghostliness: some possibility that became increasingly troublesome. He thought
of the money he still hadn't said one word about to
Callie or to Simon either, though the woman was buried
now, with no one at the graveside at all, and he felt
sick for a minute, but that fear was different, because
Callie's finding out was inevitable, the only question
was whether he could somehow cover the loss, make it
back again or anyway make some of it back so the
shock to her wouldn't be so great when it came. What
troubled him was something else. He remembered
something very strange, though this wasn't what was
the matter either, though somehow it seemed related:

One night almost a year ago he'd been sleeping on
the floor in Jimmy's room (he couldn't remember why
anymore; maybe he'd just fallen asleep there, or maybe
they'd had company that night and the beds were in
use; it didn't matter). Jimmy was asleep on the floor
beside him. Jimmy had moved, or had said something,
and Henry had sat up and opened his eyes without
quite waking up. He'd thought there was some kind
of animal in the room, and, thinking of Jimmy (vaguely
identifying the voice, perhaps), he'd lunged at the animal, and it had run, the legs moving fast—a kind of
blur, very much the way a rabbit would run—out into
the hallway where the light was on, and Henry had
caught it and lifted it up with a shout and then he'd
come wide awake and he was holding Jimmy by the
waist and Jimmy was screaming. Henry had calmed
him almost at once, and Jimmy had seemed never to
remember it, but for Henry the memory of that night
was like a wound that would never heal. He would
wonder, again and again, later, at odd moments when
it all rose up in his mind more real than the diner or
the dim-lit kitchen around him, what would have happened if he hadn't awakened just that instant. And he

couldn't answer it. Then something else: He began to wonder if it had ever happened at all. There was no way of finding out.

Then one afternoon the troopers called. Callie answered the phone. She came running into the diner, carrying Jimmy (he had to be with someone constantly, these days; Simon's attentions had spoiled him). As soon as she was inside the door, she called, "Henry, that was the troopers. They think they may have found who set the fire."

Henry went cold. He hadn't realized until this moment how far his trust was removed from his rational judgment. "Who did it?" he said.

"They think it was a couple of kids," she said. She hiked Jimmy up a little, getting a better hold on him. "They don't know, you understand, they just *think*. Two teen-agers. The troopers are on their way up here with them now. They want them to see Simon face to face."

Henry thought: *Thank God he didn't do it!* But carefully he cut God from what he said. "Then he didn't do it."

"It's not sure, but they think not."

Then: "Where is he? I'll go tell him the news."

"I don't know," Henry said. "In back, I guess."

She left, still carrying Jimmy.

Henry's legs went weak. He went over to the corner booth and sat down. He leaned his forehead on his fists and breathed deeply, and it was as if all his stomach had turned to jelly. He was still there when Callie came back, walking slowly, Jimmy walking beside her. Henry looked up. "What did he say?"

For what seemed half-a-minute she didn't answer. At last she said with a despairing look, "If they did it, he forgives them."

"The boys?" Henry waited.

She said, "Love thine enemies, bless them that curse

you, do good to them that hate you. Thus saith Simon Bale."

Henry snorted. "He'll change his mind when he sees them."

She shook her head, "I don't think so."

"The fire killed his wife," Henry said.

"It won't make any difference," she said. "I'm telling you, Henry. He's strange, really *strange*."

Her prediction turned out to be right, but Simon's behavior was, as Simon would have said, of no importance. The law was still the law.

10

The nightmares were nothing to worry about, Doc Cathey said. All children had occasional spells of that sort, some children longer spells than others; in any case, he'd grow out of them. He made them a list of foods they shouldn't give him within two hours of bedtime, and he warned them of scolding him too severely. Aside from that, there was nothing to do but wait. There was no question of there being any deep psychological disturbance, he said. He was sunny-dispositioned, placid, in a word, healthy.

They were relieved. Nevertheless it was a terrible moment when that scream would come, jerking them out of their sleep like a wire. It happened every two, three nights, sometimes twice in a single night. Henry would bound to Jimmy's bedside and scoop him up and say, "What's the matter? Bad dream?" They would never get out of him what it was he was dreaming about. It was hard enough to get the most ordinary information out of a two-year-old. Jimmy could talk well enough when he wanted to—in long, fairly complicated sentences, his eyes large and watchful, scrutinizing Henry's face for the first sign that the sentence had gone wrong. But it wasn't easy to make him advance information. He preferred to copy sentences he'd heard (in the morning they'd hear him practicing for half an hour at a time in his room, new expressions, new tones of voice). So what it was he was dreaming they never learned. Perhaps he forgot it all instantly, the minute he awakened. That was Henry's theory, because often Jimmy would go back to sleep at once, the minute Henry scooped him up, and sometimes he'd be asleep again even when Henry reached his bedside. At the end of the second week the spell seemed to be over. He went five nights in a row without crying out (it was Callie who kept track), and they began to breathe more easily.

They had another reason, too, for beginning to feel hopeful. On the Monday night a month and three days after Simon's first coming, Simon packed himself a lunch and drove down the mountain to the Grant Hotel. Henry and Callie had no idea when or how he'd gotten in touch with the man who owned the place to tell him he was coming back; in fact, until Simon got home, at seven-thirty the following morning, they had no idea where he'd gone. He left again the next night, and Henry said to Callie's mother, when they were standing in the diner with nothing to do (it was ten-thirty, always the slackest time of day), "Well, Ellie, Simon's started working again. He'll be on his feet in no time now. We'll soon see the last of him."

"I imagine Callie's pleased about that," she said. Henry smiled at her restraint. But she could not help adding, "I wonder how they feel about it at the Grant."

And when George Loomis came in that night, Henry said, "Well, he's gone back down to work, George. Must mean it won't be much longer."

"Maybe," George said.

Henry laughed at George's skepticism. He went on

chuckling, wiping off the counter; but something unpleasant began to nag at the back of his mind, and he could neither shake it nor make out what it was.

Again, Wednesday night, Simon went down to the hotel.

Doc Cathey said, "He's a different man when he's working. And you're a different man too, I'll say that."

"Different how?" Henry said. "Simon, I mean."

Doc Cathey shrugged, then tipped his head and thought about it, chewing the inside of his cheek. "Oh, tougher, I guess. More sure what he's about. I've noticed it before. You take a man that's different from everybody else around him and when he's holding down a job he'll do things he'd never even think of some other time."

Henry considered it. "It may be," he said. "I hadn't noticed it. Maybe so. I'm glad to see him pulling his life back together, just the same. You have to hand it to him, man fifty-four years old that's gone through what Simon has."

Doc Cathey went on chewing his cheek. Henry went over to clean the booth where Nick Blue had had his supper, and as he stacked the dishes he began to whistle under his breath. But it wasn't good spirits pure and simple.

Again on Thursday night Simon Bale went down to the Grant. He returned at seven-thirty the next morning, and Callie fixed him toast and eggs. When he'd eaten he went into his room and shaved with his electric razor, then took off all but his dirty underwear and went to bed. He got up around two in the afternoon and went out to sit in the garden, reading his Bible. (It had rained that morning. The garden was muddy and the bench soaking wet, but Simon seemed not to notice.) Jimmy wandered around looking for him, as soon as he discovered that Simon wasn't in bed, and finally, smiling, shaking her head at the thought of the mess she would have to clean up when the mud got him, Callie led him out the back door. He ran-slid along between the glittering lettuce and beets to the rose bushes and between the bushes to the bench where Simon sat. Callie smiled again, thinking how hard they'd all been on Simon, after all: However crazy he might be, some ways, there was something good in him or Jimmy wouldn't hang on him that way. After that she called into the diner to Henry to ask him if he'd remembered to bring in the mail, and when he said no, he was sorry, he'd forgotten, she went around to the mailbox out in front. There was nothing much—something from Farmers' Insurance, one of those Occupant circulars, the monthly statement from the bank. She opened the statement, without much interest, as she started back to the house.

He saw the canceled check to Wiegerts' lying alone in the middle of the kitchen table, and his breath went out of him. He got the bottle of pills in the pocket of his shirt. Callie wasn't in the house, and she wasn't in the diner either. *I'm sorry,* he thought. *It was all I could do.* But that was no good and he didn't want it. He'd done it and he would take whatever fury or grief was coming, because though it was all he could do he'd nevertheless chosen to do it, and it was as though the act were not his fate's but his own. It came to him then where she would be, out on the highway crying and walking off her rage or, no, fear—that sensation like falling through endless space, the feeling she'd learned from sixteen years of living through the battles of her mother and father. He thought of driving out to hunt for her, but then he couldn't make out whether he ought to or not: Maybe she was better off getting through it on her own. She knew he was not her father, or anyway that his foolishness was a different kind of foolishness (except that he was not going to admit for a minute that what he had done was foolishness, finally, and maybe Callie would make out even that, he didn't know). He decided to see if she was back in half-an-hour, and if not, to go look for her.

It came to him that she wouldn't have taken Jimmy with her. No doubt he'd be in the garden with Simon, if Simon hadn't left yet, but he'd better go make sure. He went down the steps and around the corner of the house. Simon was asleep on the bench, and he was alone. Henry went back into the house and through the downstairs rooms, calling. He called up the stairs, but there was still no answer. He went up the stairs, pulling himself up on the railing and puffing like an old woman. He'd just reached the top when Jimmy screamed. Henry's heart banged in his chest as if to split it. When he got to the door and looked in, Jimmy was crouching on the floor by his crib, clinging to to the railing and staring into the shadows in the corner of the room.

"What's the matter?" Henry roared.

"It's the devil!" Jimmy screamed, coming across to him now on all fours, as if he'd forgotten how to run, "Daddy! Daddy! *It's the devil!*"

And then Simon Bale was standing there too, behind him in the hallway, panting from his sprint from where he'd heard the screams in the garden. When he saw Henry's face he went back two steps, smiling as if in horror, ducking his head quickly down and to the left and whispering, "Forgive—"

"You!" Henry yelled, and it came out as much like awe as like rage. His rage came slowly—or so it seemed to Henry's suddenly racing mind—but when it hit it was like a mountain falling. He might have killed him if he could have done it (so Henry Soames would say later, dead calm, at the coroner's inquiry), but he couldn't even hit him because he was holding Jimmy in his arms; he could only advance on him, howling in his fury, feeling his neck puffing up and throbbing. The room around him was red and his lips felt thick. Simon was whispering, "Forgive, forgive," again and again and smiling as if his brain had stopped running (which perhaps it had, recalling like motionless, final judgments when Time was over and what was was—pictures standing out from the newsprint around them—his son Bradley Bale with a sign NIGGERS and something more that was out of sight, his daughter Sarah looking out with a thousand centuries of icy, prophetic eyes) and suddenly he turned and bolted toward the stairs. Henry shrieked, driving, as the man reached the top. He did not seem to step down but to leap, looking over his shoulder with a fierce grin, as though he thought he could fly, and Henry rushed toward him in alarm and hate or was rushing toward him already by that time. (He would wonder later which came first, the scene rising up in his mind undiminished; and he would wring his hands). He saw him hit halfway down and tumble and fly out in all directions, reaching. At the bottom he lay still a minute, upside down, his arms flung out and one knee bent, the light from the kitchen door like a halo on his murderous face, and then his body jerked, and quickly Henry turned his back so that Jimmy wouldn't see.

He sat on the toybox in the child's room, holding him, shaking his head and groaning, seeing it again and knowing Simon was still lying there staring toward heaven, waiting. It began to get dark—he could feel the mountains closing in. He wished Callie would come home and tell him what to do.

VI

NIMROD'S
TOWER

1

After the death of Simon Bale, Henry Soames took a turn for the worse. Doc Cathey said, wiping his forehead with the sleeve of his suitcoat, wholeheartedly meaning every word of it, at least for that moment (in the muggy, baking heat of August more impatient than ever with the mere humanity that always finally eluded his craft), "The hell with you."

Now, perhaps partly because of the heat—weather unheard of in the Catskills, a sure sign of witchcraft at work, or miracles brooding—the nervous eating that had troubled Henry Soames all his life slipped out of control, became a mindless external power against which it was impossible for him even to struggle, a consuming passion in the old sense, a devil (but blind, indifferent as a spider) in his guts. When he talked with customers in the diner he seemed on the surface as cheerful as ever; too cheerful, if anything, shouting over the drone of the fans in that high, thin voice of his like a goat's, banging the counter-top, whinnying with laughter; and he seemed at least relatively cheerful, considering, when he drove out on still, hot Sunday afternoons to look at the hills, the green-brown river, the corn going yellow for want of rain. He'd sit sweating behind the steering wheel, pulled over beside the triangular white concrete posts at the edge of the highway, looking down at the valley that gasped away toward brown-blue mountains as if he owned it, for what it was worth, owned all the Catskills as far as the eye could see. Because of his fat he sat tipped back like a medieval baron, and he surveyed the world over his heavy shoulders as if with imperatorial disdain. Sometimes if the heat was unusually bad he would get out of the car and open the door for his wife and child—the dog would be back at the house, asleep—and lead them over to the shade of a pine grove. They were fair-skinned, Callie and the boy, and the heat made both of them nauseous and lightheaded. Henry would lower himself onto a large, dusty surface root (the grass beside it bristly brown) and would fan himself with his hat. His hair was dark with sweat where the hat had been, and the folds of his neck were gritty. At last he would say like a king pronouncing judgment, "Hot." Both his son and his wife would nod, solemn. The pine needles over their heads were whitish from the heat and drought. But wherever he walked or stood or lay, Henry Soames had food with him, and he ate. He ate steadily, calmly, his small teeth grinding on and on, like Time setting out to fill all the void with Space.

("Like an elephant," Old Man Judkins said, with more insight than any of them guessed, though even in his own mind the idea was obscure. He was thinking, vaguely, being old and tired, of the time he'd stood for an hour-and-a-half at the Coliseum in Buffalo— that sick-sweet chemical stench in the air—looking through the bars at a gigantic lean old African bull whose left hind leg was chained to the floor: he would lift the leg a little and find the chain still there, and he would be—as it seemed to Old Man Judkins, who knew about elephants only what he saw—so enraged that he couldn't even trumpet, could merely set down his foot again and stand there hopeless, like an Indian waiting to die. After an hour or more of this he'd begun to walk around and around in a circle, sideways, each step a great, slow shifting of unspeakable weight. Old Man Judkins thought of Henry Soames' father walking by the roadside, enormous and placid as a saint, singing in his reedy voice, *Every time it rains it rains . . . pennies from heaven.* "Terrible," Old Man Judkins said, but no one paid attention.)

Henry Soames' wife would say, more cross than usual, in this weather, "What's the *matter* with you, Henry?"

"I'm sorry," he would say, and he would seem to mean it, rolling his eyes up toward her; but he would go on eating, taking it in like a combine, or like a cutting-box, or a silo. She watched the weight he had lost coming back, pound by pound. He began to need his little white pills more often; he seemed to her to eat them like candy. It was not frightening to her but acutely annoying, one more irritation among a thousand—the movement of clothes on chafing skin, the piercing pinpricks of the bell on the diner door in front, the dust that lay over everything, no matter what you did to get rid of it—on the piano keys, on every flange of the old carved picture frames on the walls, on the soup cans and tops of boxes in the diner. One night she exploded, "Henry, you act like a *crazy* person." As the words came out (she had said them many times before), she saw the truth. It was no matter of locked attics, burning churches, ice-cold hands around one's throat—the kinds of madness she'd heard stories about and seen in movies at Athensville. That kind of madness she hardly believed in, accepted merely as she accepted technicolor movies of, say, San Francisco; but this was real, not a matter of poetry but a study for her country rules—the rules that a child should have a father, that a wife should have a husband, and that a man trying to kill himself should be stopped.

She must act, she saw (wearily and angrily, flushed and spent, past all endurance), but how she must act would not come clear. With a part of her mind she wished him dead, the whole world dead; the heat coming up to her from the grill and flooding out into the heat of the room made her want to break free into violence. And yet even now, though abstractly, now, she "loved" him, for lack of a better word. She could think about her love—still there, she knew perfectly well, but dormant, an emotion locked up, waiting for September—as she might think about a pain she'd felt long ago and would one day feel again. It was the most vital emotion she had ever felt, on one hand, but, on the other, an emotion partly revolting to her: She had not seen much sign of it in her mother and father; it was an emotion they shrank from, lashed out against as they might at something obscene. She understood. But Henry, like her cousin Bill, or like Cousin Mary Lou, had accepted that feeling, had in a way made it into his identity, hugging her in his great loose arms, womanishly patting some truck driver's shoulder, bending down to kiss the forehead of their child as he slept. He *was* obscene to her, to tell the truth. His whole gross being, the very possibility of his existence at the height of a weedy, rainless summer was obscene. When he stood at the kitchen door watching her with eyes like an infinitely gentle pig's, his face thrown forward, leaning against the warm (she imagined) edge of the door, he would smooth the paint with absentminded fingers; and sometimes he would turn his face and touch the wood with his lips, this, too, absentmindedly, trying the texture with his mouth as a child would, and Callie would look down, revolted. Once she had said, "Henry, you're *kissing* that door!" and he had looked ashamed. Instantly she'd thought she shouldn't have said it, though she wasn't sorry. She'd never caught him doing it again, and, almost below thought, in the dark of her mind, she'd been annoyed at her pettiness—and his, for paying attention.

"Crazy," she thought, coming suddenly awake, toying with the word's dull echo in her head, standing over the hissing grill and staring through the grill's blackness at the pitch-dark center of things. She thought of

George Loomis, sitting alone in his unlighted, funereal old brick house on Crow Mountain, watching television in the kitchen, his eyes like a murderer's. Henry respected George, and George had a kind of sense: He could talk to Henry if anyone could, and George could do it without making them all feel like worms. She set her lips and, as though someone had suggested it, she nodded.

And so George Loomis sat down grinning in the armchair facing the davenport late one night and stretched out his legs, his left hand over his belly, relaxed, the empty right sleeve pinned up to the shoulder of his shirt. He smelled of whiskey. It gave her a turn, but she said nothing. She thought of her father, the car parked down in the creek below the DL&W bridge where he'd pulled to sleep it off. When he brought in the smell of whiskey with him, her mother would sometimes cry. "You never think of anybody but yourself," she would say, "that's truly all you think about." And he would nod, scowling, not offended by what she said but outraged by the maudlin vulgarity of her saying anything at all. Once, long ago, he'd hit her. When Callie was little, she too would cry, and her father would wince, looking at her, and then he'd shut his eyes with disgust and sit down and cover his face with his hands and wait for them to go. His verdict was right, she knew, and she knew that all women were evil. When they were loading hay he would lift her in his arms, laughing, and would throw her up onto the load. She was terrified—the load was high and round, and she was sure she'd roll off on the other side from the force of his throw—yet she would wish he would do it again and again, hoist her up in his arms and laugh, looking at her face for just a second, and throw her up at the white clouds and the deep blue glodes between. Her mother would say, "She'll be hit by dry lightning up there, Frank Wells. You know what happened to Covert's boy." "Crap," he would say. He would lift his arms and say, "Ok, scout," and Callie would half-slide half-jump and he would catch her. Her mother said someday he would break her leg, and Callie thought, *Evil, evil!* Once he had turned his back and let her fall. She was fourteen. He and the two hired men had laughed, leaning on their forks, showing their dark yellow teeth. That night she had run away, intending to drown herself, but beside the creek—Prince running up and down joyfully, yipping at shadows—she'd found herself too cowardly and base for even that; there was no hope left for her but forgiveness. It was the troopers that had found her, and when she got home her father was asleep in his chair, snoring like a horse.

George Loomis said, "How things going, boy?"

"Oh, so-so," Henry said.

Still no relief from the heat had come. Her head ached, and their voices sounded hollow, like voices in a dream.

George Loomis looked down for perhaps a minute, then cleared his throat and looked over at little Jimmy, playing with a truck on the davenport arm. George's hair was going prematurely gray, but across from Henry he looked like a high school boy. He had a boy's face, a boy's way of sitting—except for the one boot locked rigid in its iron brace. He had a look of innocence like a boy's, too, vaguely associated in Callie's mind with virginity.

"Sure dry," George said.

Henry nodded. "Things burning right up." His voice was mechanical, like his words. Even his eating looked mechanical, and George was doing nothing to help.

Callie looked toward heaven in despair.

(The Preacher would come to see Callie's father and would go out to the barn where he was milking, and Callie would go with him to show him the way. He'd step gingerly, behind the cows, worrying about getting manure on his pointed black shoes—good hon-

est shit, her father called it—and when her father saw
him he would nod politely. In front of her mother, her
father would mock religious people, but he was always
polite to them otherwise. He was not a cruel man—
she had learned that only lately, from Henry, or
rather had only lately discovered by way of Henry
that that was what she'd always known. He too was
like a boy, her father—in a different way from George
Loomis, though. Her father was easygoing, open, free
with his money, a storyteller people would listen to
for hours. He didn't believe or disbelieve in God, he
said; he just didn't like churches. He didn't like hearing what he had to believe and what he mustn't believe
—the very word *believe* made him curl his lip as he
would when he listened to tear-jerking poetry or talk
about flowers or songs about faraway places—and
above all, he said, he didn't like grown men standing
up and confessing in front of everybody, like drunks
or like young lovers. But that was not what he said
to the Preacher. He said, "Evening, Reverend," and
nodded, and when the Preacher talked about what a
fine herd of cows he had (it had chronic mastitis and
there wasn't a cow in the barn that gave more than a
gallon) he would agree. Rightly, Henry said. (That
too she had always known but had realized only when
he said it.) If you told the Preacher the truth he would
soon have control of you, would milk you dry. The
Preacher would say, "We've missed you lately in
church, Frank," and her father would say only, "I
haven't been going very regular, that's true." He hadn't
darkened those doors in fifteen years. The Preacher
would talk to him sadly, man to man, high-tone Bib-
lical language that embarrassed Callie, and after her
father had heard him out he'd look thoughtful and
say, "There's a lot to what you say, Reverend." She
would want to laugh, and only later had she come to
see that she'd wanted to laugh with fury. There was
something vile in her father's arrogant detachment.

She wondered what her father would say if someone smarter than he was had come to talk about religion to him. Henry's father, for instance, when he was alive, who'd read hundreds and hundreds of books. But she knew what her father would have done, of course. How could even arguments have touched him?)

All of that came back to her clearly, in the old vagueness that had captured her mind—those nights in the barn with the milkers chugging and the Preacher straddling a spatter of manure, huge gray moths batting at the whitewash-caked bulbs, the cool sound of pigeons in the mow overhead. She stood in the living room doorway listening as if in a trance to Henry and George Loomis, and when her mind came alive again her heart sank. They were equals, they would be honest with each other; and there was nothing George could do. (*I loved him though*, she thought, giving way again, seeing her father in her mind as before, his eyes cocked up at the sharply protruding hipbone of the cow. She'd been older than her father all her life, and even as she'd struggled to be the boy he wished she was, because the idea of her being his daughter was for both of them unmanageable, she had known the futility of it and had forgiven him. For an instant that seemed timeless but which nevertheless passed, she did not care whether George succeeded or not.)

For an instant she knew with a part of her mind that behind the house, motionless, oblivious to the deadly heat, Simon Bale's ghost sat listening in the dark, solid as granite, hearing all they said and thought and hearing the noise still miles away of something (wind?) bearing vengeance toward them: some change, subtle and terrible. They were caught. She concentrated. It was gone.

2

George Loomis knew well enough that he'd come for nothing. When he looked up at Callie in the doorway —pretty, in a tough-jawed, persecuted-looking way, her face flushed, prepared for wrath—he had a feeling that in Henry's position he might do the same damn thing.

Henry sat unmoving—as still as the enormous old sleeping dog by the door—huge, like the dog, and spent—huge and dark as the centuries-old pile of boulders and shale and crumbling mortar looking down Crow Mountain at the bottom of the shadow-filled glen. (It was a lookout tower from before the Revolutionary War, his grandfather said, and it was built by one of his ancestors, a Loomis. "Nimrod's Tower," his grandfather said. "So much for the pride of man!" And he, ten years old, had looked up at the tower, baffled between pride and inexplicable shame at the pride he felt—like his grandfather.) Henry Soames' forearm stood straight up, resting on the arm of the davenport, holding the box of gingersnaps, and his arm was so thick (it seemed for that moment) that if the boy were to pass behind it he would vanish from sight as though passing behind a tree. Callie gave George a meaningful look, something she'd learned from TV, he thought, and dropped back into the kitchen, out of sight. There were only two dim bulbs that worked in the gilt, Max Pies Furniture chandelier that hung by a chain from the middle of the ceiling. (That was Callie's work, he knew. Henry would never have chosen the thing.) He could see one of the bulbs reflected in the picture directly across from him, high on the wall over Henry's head, above the clock on the mantel, a brownish picture (a gift from Callie's mother, one of them had told him) of Jesus praying. The Soames' TV was on, over in what Callie called the music corner—radio, record player, television, sagging homemade shelves of records and old *TV Guides*—but the sound was turned off and the picture was flipping. It gave you a feeling of endless falling in space.

He said, "What's eating you, Henry?"

Henry smiled, gloomy. "Oh, I'm all right, George." He put a gingersnap in his mouth whole and let it dissolve there. "How things with you? Seems like we don't see you much any more."

George got out his cigarettes with two fingers, slipped one from the pack, and fitted it between his lips. He got out his matches. "Now don't change the subject, Henry." He looked at the matches, considering, and decided on directness. "You quit eating all the time or you'll kill yourself. You know it."

The little boy was down on all fours on the rug, running a black and yellow dump truck along the dark outlines of the faded flowers in the pattern. His face was unhealthily red, as his mother's had been. The line he was on led to his father's foot and he ran the truck up over his father's shoe and down again. He looked up at his father, half-smiling, sly. He looked like an elf, the way his bushy blond eyebrows tipped up. Still Henry said nothing.

"How you think Jimmy's going to feel?" George said.

Henry shook his head and let out a little heave of breath. He sat now with his hands limp in his lap, what there was of his lap—three, four inches, then his knees. His shirt was unbuttoned in two places, showing clammy gray skin and curly gray and black hairs. There were sweat rings under his armpits.

"Damn it all, Henry. I came here to talk with you, and I mean for you to talk. I asked you a question."

Henry looked anxious. He always looked anxious, because of the way the rolls of fat fell away like the wake of a rowboat from his nose, but now he looked more so. He said, "I'm sorry, George, I'm afraid I've forgot what you asked me."

"I said," George began grimly, hard-jawed—but by now he had forgotten too, and he had to think a minute. "I said, 'How do you think Jimmy's going to feel when you've killed yourself?'"

It sounded in his own ears like something out of Loretta Young. As if out of kindness, Henry said, "I don't know, George."

"Well, you're a damn fool then," George said, doing his best with a bad start, looking just over Henry's head. "I mean it. Listen. All you do is stop that blame eating all the time."

Henry studied the floor, politely not eating the gingersnap he had now in his hand. George listened to the clock. Outside the open window it was very quiet, bright with moonlight. Nothing moved. At last Henry said, "Maybe that's the answer, George."

"Oh, hell," George said. He felt the way he had felt long ago when his father would ask him, "Where have you been till this hour, young man?" knowing he had been nowhere, as always, had done nothing, as always, had driven his motorcycle around on the mountain roads in the vague hope that something new might happen, that the world might stand suddenly transfigured, transformed to a movie—a gangster picture, a love picture, anything but the tedious ruin it was, a worn-out country (not worn-out enough to be morbidly interesting), worn-out farmers, a worn-out sixteen-year-old boy partly too shy and partly too righteous (all things foul to his dry-rotted mind) even to look through car windows at lovers. He sometimes believed he had known all his life that he'd end up maimed, a brace on one boot, no arm in one sleeve, and no doubt worse yet to come. Once, lately, it had occurred to him that maybe he'd given up his foot and arm voluntarily, sacrificing up pieces of his body like an old-time Delaware to ward off destructions more terrible. It had seemed an interesting idea at first, but thinking about it an instant later he'd seen it for the paltry ruse it was, mere poetry, and, like all poetry, so irrelevant and boring he wanted to smash things.

He came partly awake. A movement of the drape, then stillness. A line from a tedious movie: *Maybe that's the answer, George.* Not even patronizing: pure filler. Or it was like the chatter at one of his mother's old-fashioned teas. *Exquisite,* they were always saying. Everything was *exquisite.* (He'd buried his mother in the way she'd wanted to be buried, in an iron casket with a window looking in at her now incorruptible face.) Because Henry knew perfectly well he had come because Callie had asked him, and knew there was nothing to talk about, that either he'd work it out alone or he wouldn't, and that all the sympathy on earth wouldn't change it by a hair, because Henry was no moron, after all. He would know without George's being here that George was pulling for him. (No meaning even in that, really: the prejudice of people who by accidents of place and time were friends.) What more? You had friends, and that was useful to remember, and Henry Soames was not a self-pitying fool who'd forget it, and there it was.

He lit the match, surprised that it worked, since the matchbook cover was soft from the dampness inside his shirt pocket, and raised the match to his cigarette, thinking about cancer. When he'd put the matches away he said, "It'd be easier if you were stupider. Even stupider than you are, I mean." And now he really did feel a twinge of anger, at nothing specific.

Henry smiled and for a second he was himself

again, not working automatically like an old man playing checkers at the GLF.

George said, "I'd be very serious. Grim, you know what I mean? I'd get a glint in my eye, and I'd say—" He became still grimmer, theatrically. "Listen, Henry Soames, you're feeling guilty, right? You're saying it was your fault he fell, you might as well killed him outright, and it was wrong. Well, listen, I've been through all that myself. Truth. Over in Korea I used to think, 'Some poor bastard comes at me, he no more wants this war than I do, they took his name from some crumby file and that made him a soljer and here we are.' But I'll tell you something. One day there was a Korean sergeant—South Korean, one of ours—tore off the fender from one of our staff cars with his jeep. That afternoon—this is the truth, now—that afternoon a couple of Korean lieutenants and this sergeant drive off with a shovel in the back of their jeep, and when they come back to the base, no sergeant. That's what they think of human beings. Maybe they're right and maybe they're wrong, but when one of them comes after you, you shoot.

"Now you take Simon Bale. Screw, I'd say—" He remembered that the boy was there, but Jimmy didn't seem to have heard it. He sat leaning his head from side to side, forming motor sounds with his lips, barely letting them out, vrooming the motor as he pushed the toy truck up his legs to his knees and over them and down in a rush to the rug once more to careen along the labyrinth of roads to the higher mountains, the elephantine legs of his father. (That was how Henry had driven in the old days, George remembered—before he'd married Callie.) Henry ran his forearm across the stubby underside of his chin. The gingersnap that had been in his hand was gone. George leaned forward.

"I'd say, full of righteousness—because I would be right and you would be wrong—'Simon Bale was the same as one of them Koreans, not civilized. You took him in out of the cold when his house burned and he scared your kid with his talk about the devil and you yelled at him, and out of his own stupidity he fell down the fucking stairs. You ought to have buried him like a cat and forgot it!' And there we'd be: I'd have you."

Henry smiled, only his lips, his eyes unfocused. "And what would I say to that if I was smart?" He spoke with his mouth full, and George puffed at the cigarette a minute, uncomfortable and yet half-enjoying the senseless game.

"You'd wipe your forehead and say, 'Sure is hot.' " He made his voice high and thin, mimicking Henry's.

Henry nodded, pleased.

George said, "I'd say, 'Pay attention, damn it. It wasn't your fault. Face up to it. It's just the way things came out.' 'Oh, it was my fault all right,' you'd say. 'Well all right, your fault then,' I'd say, 'but you couldn't help it.' 'Oh, I know I couldn't help it,' you'd say."

There was no movement out in the kitchen. Callie would be standing by the sink, listening, hopeless, feeling betrayed—not by George Loomis, exactly. Or by the open door, pressing her forehead to the screen. Betrayed merely by the nature of things, or the nature of men. He looked up at the clock. Five-to-twelve. Henry sat looking out the window, his head tilted, the gingersnap box standing upright in his hand like something up a tree. His nose and mouth and eyes were small in that wide, shiny face. His hair looked thinned by age, like the mohair on an old, old couch, or the hair of a dog with mange.

George said, "You'd say, 'Now *you* listen a while.' You'd tell me, 'I'd been waiting to kill him a long time—him or somebody or something. People don't know what they've got inside them. Except that Simon Bale did, or he wouldn't have gone around handing out pamphlets and preaching doom. All right. I'd been waiting all my life like a loaded gun and he'd been waiting to drive me to it, and neither of us is to blame for that; a lion's a lion and a cow's a cow. But people aren't only animals. When it's over, a man gets to judge. After he's found out, he can say *Yes* to it, or *No.* He can say *Yes, it was right*—no matter who it happened to or where or when—or *No, it was wrong.*' And you'd sit there like a grieved hippopotamus." He realized abruptly where the queer play was taking him and leaned forward farther, feeling sweat prickle on his back as he shifted position. "At last it would hit me, and I'd say: 'You think you're God!' And you'd say, 'Yes.' I'd be stopped. Cold. What can you say to a man that's decided to be God?" His voice crackled. He laughed suddenly, furious.

Henry squinted, thinking about it, or put off by that laugh. Callie stood now in the doorway to his right, the yellow kitchen walls shiny behind her, making her face very dark. Jimmy stood watching the television picture flip. He stood perfectly still now, spent. His face too was dark red, the eyebrows white.

"It would have taken me longer to say," Henry said. He smiled to show he meant it as a compliment. He was as far away as ever.

George ground out his cigarette in the ash tray from Watkins Glen on the table beside him. "What I can't understand is how a man with ideas as crazy as that can just set there, chewing away like a cow."

"Why, they're *your* ideas, George," Henry said.

It startled him. "That's not true," he said. He looked at Callie and saw that she too believed it. "Well, shit!" he said. He hit the chair arm with his fist. "They're not! That just isn't true!"

The clock began striking, a whir of gears, then twelve sharp, tinny notes. To Callie the strokes of the clock sounded like a voice, bored and scornful. After the last stroke the whir of gears stopped with a click and the room was unnaturally hushed. She waited, but George said nothing more. He went into a new, even queerer act, and Callie suddenly knew as she watched him precisely what George was going to be like when he was old. He cocked his head as if straining for the exactly right word, drew back the corners of his mouth and raised his hand, half-closed as if around an invisible rock. He held that position for a moment, tensely, then smiled, grim, with his head tipped as if to duck something; then, as if realizing there were no words for what he wanted to say, he lowered his hand again, letting the invisible rock roll out between his thumb and index finger. She knew (standing remote as the clock) that there *was* something he'd been trying to say, something that both she and Henry had missed. And she knew with equal certainty that he had no intention of hunting for a way of saying it now. They'd demanded of him already more than was decent. He was standing up, smiling, shaking his head, saying he had to leave.

"I'm sorry you can't stay longer," she said.

He shrugged as if sadly and said good-night to Henry. At the door Prince opened his eyes but didn't move. George stepped over him.

Outside it was even hotter than inside. The air was lifeless, heavy as dust. She felt faint. "Surely is dry," she said softly. Something nagged at her thought but refused to come clear.

George Loomis nodded politely. "Keeps on like this it'll burn up all the corn."

She looked at his face. He had his head bent now, trying to see his watch in the dark of the porch. The tilt of his head made her think of a raven. Beyond the porch, the moonlight made everything it touched unnaturally sharp: the lines of the diner, the garage, the burdocks, Henry's old black Ford up on blocks in the high brittle weeds. The mountains seemed very close, right over your head, stifling. She thought as she had thought before, at the kitchen window, looking out and listening to their talk in the living room, *Something is coming*. Nothing was, she knew. She felt tense, as if walking on a high ledge above dark, fast water. She was sorry for George Loomis, annoyed as she was at his senseless retreat. She should have expected it, of of course. Maybe she had.

"Well, sooner or later it's bound to rain," she said. "It always does." She laughed.

"Aeyuh," he said. He was thinking about something else.

"Thanks ever so much for coming by," she said.

"Don't mention it," he said, "it's been my pleasure."

They shook hands, and he went down the steps and limped over the moonlit path to his truck. His hair needed cutting—dark shadow against the bone-white of his ears. Dust rose from the path and hovered like granary sift behind him.

"Good-night, George," she said.

He half turned, smiling again, nodding, almost bowing.

She thought of her father, then of Henry's father as he stood in the picture they had upstairs, huge and placid, with a cardigan sweater that was buttoned wrong and under his arm an absurdly small violin. With a part of her mind she heard George Loomis's truck start up, saw the lights go on, and saw him backing away. Something flew soundlessly past, between the garage and where she stood. She knew what it was, but she couldn't remember for a moment what it was called.

At last, looking over at the gray-white bench in the garden, she saw the ghost of Simon Bale. He was staring mildly, patiently, at the house. He was bent forward slightly, his knees together, the Bible closed in his lap. One of the bookmark ribbons hung over his knee. When he saw that she was looking at him, he gave a start and reached toward his hat-brim, perhaps about to stand up. But then he vanished, leaving only the shadows of tamaracks on the empty, moonlit bench.

3

It was the next morning, at the crack of dawn, that the Goat Lady—otherwise known as "Mother"—reached New Carthage. You could tell where she was by the smell from a half-mile away, and if your nose wasn't working you could tell by the noise. She had home-made tin-can bells all over her homemade pink and purple cart, fixed on the sides with fencepost staples and baling wire, and her goats bleated like the seven angels of death. She had a shaggy, dun-colored billy-goat and a square, black, six-year-old nanny up in front, pulling as though the rig had no wheels, and there were four more nannies behind, dragging along Indian-file on braided binder twine. Alongside the last of the four was a six-months' kid. The four nannies in back were the milkers. One of them had tits so big she'd have stepped on them if the Goat Lady hadn't had them up in a kind of sling made out of some kindly farm-woman's bedsheet. On top of the cart she had a sign like a housetop—which in fact it was, the cart being the Goat Lady's house, the rear wall an old tarpaulin—and on the sign, in lettering that looked like a joke from some children's cartoon book that no child would think funny: MOTHERS GOTS MILK.

The Goat Lady sat up in front like a midget stage-coach driver or a burlesque of the fiery charioteer, her legs splayed out like an elderly madam's, her skirt hiked up over her dust-specked, yellow-gray thighs,

on her head a dusty black bonnet like an Amish woman's. She had on, despite the muggy heat, every
stitch of clothing she owned—a couple of coats, a
sweater, three or four dresses, a dark red shawl. She
had iron-toed shoes. People that passed her on the
highway would run off onto the far shoulder from
staring, and when she pulled up onto some farmer's
front lawn to eat her dinner or strip out her goats or
try to peddle her goat's milk and cheese, women would
call in their children from outdoors. She had a face
that caught the eye and held it, amazing and revolting,
flatly inhuman: yellow teeth like an old sick dog's,
eyebrows like a badger's, an enormous wide-bridged
nose very much like—a goat's. She looked about sixty
but she had said she was thirty-six, and no doubt it
was true. It was unthinkable that the Goat Lady should
lie, as unthinkable as that she should cheat or steal or
plan. Most people thought she was part Indian; the
Indians said she was a Gypsy. If people took her in,
nights, fed her, clothed her, provided her with orange
pop or root beer, it was not so much out of charity as
out of impotence in the face of her boundless gall. The
first place she stopped when she reached New Carthage, the Bill Kelsey place, they called the troopers;
but there was nothing the troopers could arrest her for.
In her old black purse inside the cart (the troopers
said after she'd gone for good), she had three hundred
dollars and a gun that was missing a firing pin. People
were surprised that the Goat Lady had three hundred
dollars, but how she came by her savings was no great
mystery. She could no more make change than fly, or
if she could she didn't; she would merely pocket whatever you gave her, accepting it as a mother's right, up
to and including a twenty-dollar bill, and if you had
nerve enough to ask for change she'd merely hold out
her money, with magnificent disgust—wadded-up bills
and dimes and quarters and three or four brand-new
galvanized nails—and you could take whatever you

wanted, including the nails. No doubt people gypped her from time to time—and perhaps worse. When a pack of small boys came close to her cart her eyes would awake like a chipmunk's, and she'd begin to squeeze her hands together in an agitated, fierce-looking way. But finally she was ungyppable and untormentable: charmed. She seemed not really to understand the value of whatever money she lost, though she could count when she absolutely had to, and her fear of small boys was manifestly impersonal, like other people's fear of snakes. She had more pack rat than human in her: She collected and jealously guarded her utterly meaningless treasure, and if in the end she lost all she'd saved, she lost it as pack rats lose their bits of bright cloth, old bobby pins, and tinfoil to large, inscrutable movements in space. At the same time, she was herself a large, inscrutable movement—as George Loomis said, though he knew her only by report, he said. She'd started out twenty-four days ago (this she had counted, marking off the days with a nail on the plywood wagon seat) from Erie, Pennsylvania, in quest of a son who'd left home in July to find work where the drought hadn't hit so hard, and who had loyally sent for her at last, telling her to come to a place she had never heard of, didn't know where to find and no longer remembered the name of. (It sounded like *Fair*.) She'd set out in an arbitrary direction, taking the only highway out of town that she knew (so that for her it was not arbitrary), and she'd been helped and hustled along (not even really knowing she was helped or hustled) in a generally north-eastward direction to the heart of the Catskills—through coal country and oil country and timber country—heading on in full confidence, saying only, when people tried in vain to break down the walls of her faith, "It's a small world." Now she was back in farming country, and she knew—though in fact her son may have been in, say, Blair, Wisconsin—she was getting there.

It was two in the afternoon when she reached the diner. The sun was a white ball of fire, and across from it the moon hung clear as could be. Callie Soames stared at the woman's rig as people had been doing now for twenty-four days, watching the woman pull up to the pumps, bells clattering, as if to gas up her goats, then on second thought turn short and pull her pink and purple wagon over to the door, blocking it neatly, as if by plan. Starlings careened in the baked sky. In the dust below there were sparrows and cowbirds by the hundreds, picking up grain truck spill. The Goat Lady got down and came over to the window and pressed her face to the screen, shielding both sides of her face with hands as gritty as a miner's. Then she came to the door and peered through the screen as she'd peered through the window. Finally she came in. Prince lifted one ear, then drifted back into sleep. There was oat chaff on the woman's hat and shoulders from fields where combines were at work. "Hi," she said. She stood four-feet-tall, with her big square brown fists on her hips—legs wide apart, mouth widely grinning, her nose like an elbow coming out of her face—so pleased to be here that for a moment Callie was sure the woman was someone she ought to recognize and struggled in her mind to place her.

"Honey," the woman said, "I was wondering if you happened to sell ice cream."

"Oh," Callie said. As if the words hadn't sunk in, she looked over at Henry where he sat in the corner booth picking at a piece of apple pie. (Jimmy was back in the house, taking his nap.) The woman turned, following Callie's glance, and Callie looked back at her quickly. The woman was still smiling. She was fat, in an unhealthy, poor woman's way, especially below the belt. It was possible that she was pregnant.

Henry said very solemnly, like a minister, "We do have ice cream. Yes'm."

"Why, that's your hubby," the woman said, delighted —even proud, one would have thought, as if she'd mistaken Callie for one of her own. When she laughed, her mouth seemed to slip right up behind her nose. "He's sure nice and plump!"

Henry scowled.

The goat smell and the stench of her sweat were everywhere, and Callie had to concentrate to keep from being sick.

"Apple pie!" The woman rolled her eyes at Callie, suddenly coy as a schoolgirl. "I ain't et apple pie in years. When I was six years old I was out in the orchid one time where my daddy was picking—my true daddy: he was a deputy sheriff—and you'll never guess!"

Callie waited.

She leaned far toward Callie, leering. "I set down on a bushel crate and wee-weed all over 'em!" She wrung her hands and drew her tan, flat face back and sideways, giggling, and above the motionless, patient-looking layers of clothing the fat, cracked and shiny flesh of her throat rippled. Tears washed down her cheeks, and into the curls sticking out in front of her bonnet and then, when she threw her head forward in her ecstasy, rolled down her nose and hung in a great gray drop at the end, like a pearl. Henry leaned his forehead onto the heel of his hand.

"What kind of ice cream did you want?" Callie said.

The woman climbed up on the counter stool, still giggling, turning again, after she was settled, to look over at Henry as before. She got herself into control and looked up at the ice cream flavors sign hungrily, wiping the tears from her eyes with the backs of both hands, then went off on a giggling fit worse than the last. "I wish you could of seen his face," she said. She turned again to giggle at Henry. Again she got herself in control. "I'll have choc'late," she said. The decision appeared to surprise and please her. Callie turned away.

"Honey," the woman said behind her, coy again now, "did you ever hear the name of Buddy Blatt?" She was lighting a cigarette.

Callie hesitated, the goat smell and cigarette smell mingling unpleasantly with the ice cream smell in the freezer.

"Buddy Blatt's my boy," the woman said. "I been looking for him."

Callie put the scoop back carefully, as though it might blow up in her hand if she jarred it, and covered the freezer again. She slid the dish of ice cream onto the counter-top, along with a napkin and spoon, then remembered to fill a water glass. "I don't think I've heard that name," she said, and after a minute, "Henry?"

Henry shook his head and looked out the window.

"He sent for me," she said. She coughed, and smashed out the cigarette almost untouched. She dipped her spoon into the ice cream and lifted her lips away from her teeth, then sucked a little off the spoon and let the rest slide back for the next bite. *"Mmmm!!"* she said. She reached down inside her collar and half-scratched, half-rubbed. Callie listened to the fans. No air stirred.

Then for the hundredth time, because like everyone she met they were the kind of people that would understand a mother's feelings, she told her story. Old Man Judkins came in in time to hear the last of it. It was the second time around for him. He'd heard it secondhand from Bill Llewellyn in New Carthage less than an hour ago. But it was only this time, hearing it from her own mouth, that he believed it.

"They all been real kind," she said. She tucked her chin in and giggled. "Down in Olean the police helped me strip out my goats."

"The police?" Henry said. It was the first sign he'd shown that he was listening.

"They was a green place right in the middle of the

city, it was just as green as anything, with flowers in the middle, and I pulled up there. It was milking time. And the p'lice come over and talked awhile and then helped me."

Henry looked out the window again, and Old Man Judkins picked his teeth.

"I got the cart fixed up so I can sleep in it, but I ain't had to yet," she said. "Every night but one I've slept in somebody's house, and the one night I didn't was because down in Endicott they let me sleep in the jail. They been very kind."

Callie said matter-of-factly, "And you really think you'll find him." She wondered whether the woman would pay for her ice cream.

The Goat Lady smiled, her upper lip vanishing again, her few teeth jagged and yellow in her black mouth. "It's a small world," she said. Perhaps the question made her nervous, or perhaps it merely reminded her of her business. She got down off the stool and gave a grotesquely formal little bow, smiling again. "I surely appreciate your kindness." Then, to Henry: "It's been real nice talking to you."

Henry turned, covering his mouth with his hand, studying her. At last he nodded. He said, "Good luck." It was as if for him she was gone already.

Callie stood at the door with Old Man Judkins, watching her climb up into her seat and start up the goats. *She didn't pay,* she realized at last. The cart was halfway up the hill by now, the clank of the bells far away enough to be pleasant.

Old Man Judkins said solemnly, tipping his head to one side, "It's like a pilgrimage. A mother in search of her son." He pulled at his ear.

Callie said, "I better go see if Jimmy's awake from his nap."

4

That was the last Henry Soames ever saw of the Goat Lady, though it wasn't by any means the last he heard. She was gone from the county the following day: some people said she'd moved on north; some said they'd seen her heading east, toward the resorts where the Jews were. Wherever she'd gone, she'd gone completely; it was as if she'd been swallowed up by a mountain, like any other gnome. Lou Millet wondered if maybe she hadn't run into foul play, and they speculated on that for a time; but after a week certain word came, by way of a letter George Loomis said he'd gotten from a relative, that she'd been given money by the Methodist Church in Remsen.

For a week more people swapped stories about her when they came to the diner. But gradually the talk died out.

Henry Soames was the first. He would go whole days without saying a word about the Goat Lady or anything else to anyone, even Callie. Often he wouldn't bother to get up in the morning. Doc Cathey would find him propped up on six pillows, in his undershirt, his eyes shut behind the steel-rimmed glasses, and his hair, what there was left of it, pasted to his scalp with sweat. If his mouth was closed and he wasn't snoring, it was hard to tell at first glance if he was living or dead. On the spindly table between his bed and the glass-knobbed dresser he had a red plastic glass of water and his little white pills. Beside him on the bed he had Oreo cookies.

"Are you *trying to die?*" Doc Cathey said. (Despite the weather he wore the black suit he always wore, his neck and head rising out of his collar like a brown, withered stalk.)

"No," Henry said. He was grumpy as a bear these days. It was pretty near worth your hide to ask him the time, Doc Cathey said. Henry said, "Something's wrong, that's all. I'm all right. Just leave me alone."

Doc said, staring fiercely down into the clutter of his medical bag, "My advice to you is, see a psychiatrist." He'd said it twenty times before, after Callie's mother had nagged him into believing that was the only hope, and once he'd shoved a pamphlet at Henry about mental illness; but mostly Doc kept off the subject for fear of starting an attack.

"I know what's wrong with me," Henry said. "I just need to work it out."

Callie said another time, unnaturally sweet, putting her hand on Henry's forehead, "Doc says it might be something chemical, Henry: He says there might be some pill you could take."

"No," Henry said. He sat forward to say it, as if trying to drive it through Callie's skull by physical force, and she looked at the curtains and drew her hand away.

It wasn't that he wanted to be contrary or that his sickness had made him a different man—irascible and spiteful—and certainly, despite their settled opinion, it wasn't that he was afraid of hospitals, doctors, pills— or afraid, even, of whatever more severe treatments the pills might give way to. He didn't like hospitals, true enough, but he would do more for the sake of his wife and son than any of them guessed. It was one of the few things he knew about himself for certain. He'd be willing to shoot himself for them if he had to. But this was something else. Neither was it that he didn't believe what Doc Cathey said. It was probably true that something went wrong with your chemistry and if you took some pill you'd be able to work the thing out calmly, the problem still there but not white-hot in your mind: manageable. But true or not, he had to do it his own way. He couldn't explain it because there *was* no explanation. About this, though, he was wrong. George Loomis could explain it.

Henry was sitting in the chair he had out by the gas pumps islands for hot summer nights, and George was sitting down on the curb of the island, smoking cigarettes, as always, one after another. There were rainclouds in the sky and the leaves had their backs turned and the wind was coming from the south gently, but the thermometer stood at ninety-four and they knew there would be no rain. Callie was leaning on the ethyl pump watching the drab, quiet sunset, not seeming to listen to their talk. The dog lay across the doorway to the diner, asleep.

Henry said:

"I keep seeing it over and over, George. I see it clearer even than it was, slowed down, like a movie. I see that look on his face, and me moving toward him, shouting at him, and it seems to me I have a choice, whether to keep on shouting or not, and I choose, I keep shouting, and then all at once he falls." The muscles in Henry's face were all out of control, and again, as before, his arm was rising uncontrollably to hide his eyes and he was twisting away a little in his chair to block the vision that stood before him closing out the hard reality of highway, trees, blue mountains in the distance. But George Loomis was looking at the asphalt not noticing his face.

Henry said:

"I hear his head crack, George. And then I see him lying there jerking like a chicken. Jimmy didn't see it, I don't think, but *I* saw it. I sit up in bed and try to think of something else, but right away it comes back, the whole thing over again. You double up against it and go through all the movements as if your whole body was thinking it, and you see that choice coming and you can't change it, and then there's that movement of his feet toward the stairs, no way to stop it under heaven, like the movement of a train." He felt tense all over, as if for a long time now he'd been holding his breath. "It's like drowning," he said. "I feel as if anybody comes into the room it will be just too much, I feel like I need to be somewhere out in the middle of a field, in the dark." He was quiet a moment, sweating big drops. Suddenly he said: "We're riding in the car on a narrow road and it comes to me in a sort of daydream I could reach out and slam my head against the truck we're meeting, or I could reach out my hand, and then all at once there it is again, Simon Bale and me at the top of the stairs, and I'm shouting at him, and my hands tighten up on the steering wheel—it's like a wound in your soul." Again the memory was upon him, and he clamped his eyes shut, concentrating on thinking nothing, but it was useless and he waited for the memory to be over. When he opened his eyes again George was looking at him, distant. Henry fumbled for the cheese crackers he'd brought with him, somewhere down under his chair.

George Loomis said, "You need some kind of a pill."

"Hell!" It came out like the bellow of a bull. "I *know* I need a pill."

Still Callie pretended to be paying no attention, vaguely watching the sparrows on the highway, but she stiffened, making the others be still. Jimmy came around the corner of the diner on his tricycle, red-faced, vrooming the motor quietly. He glanced at them shyly, as if conscious of the dividing line between himself and them, then looked back at his handlebars. He came over toward the gas island and at the last moment veered away and headed back where he'd come from. Where the asphalt ended the dirt was cracked in small squares and as hard as cement.

"But pills are beneath your dignity," George said.

"No," Henry said, quietly this time, not expecting

them to believe it, not asking even George Loomis to understand how he felt. Callie looked at the birds.

But George said, "Yes, they are." He was nodding to himself as if he not only saw how it was but partly agreed. "The trouble with taking a pill is, you might feel better. That would be the worst thing could happen. You wouldn't be human any more."

"Crap!" Callie said fiercely.

It was the first time Henry had ever heard her say it, and when he looked up, he saw that her lips were shaking.

George reached over, not even looking up, and put his hand on her shoe. "No, wait," he said. "It's true. He says he made a choice, the choice to go on yelling, which makes him to blame for Simon Bale's dying. But he knows that's only word games. He didn't know Simon would fall downstairs, and even if he did, it's one time in a thousand you kill yourself that way. It was an accident. Henry was the accidental instrument, a pawn, a robot labeled *Property of Chance*. That's intolerable, a man should be more than that; and that's what Henry's suffering from—not guilt. However painful it may be, in fact even if it kills him, horror's the only dignity he's got."

"That's stupid," Callie said vehemently. But Henry saw she'd understood.

"Right," George said. He looked at her, expressionless, and for a long moment they watched each other. Callie looked away first. She scowled at the woods across the road (the starlings were settling in the trees now) and she fiddled with her belt buckle, tightening it. She said:

"Why do men think they *have* to have dignity?"

"A word, an empty word," George agreed.

Henry said: "Why can't we just be like the Goat Lady?" He laughed.

He wasn't prepared for the way it shocked George. Callie looked disgusted, but George Loomis blushed dark red. Henry looked down, away from George, at once. After a minute he said, "I didn't know you even saw her, George."

"I didn't," George said. "I only heard about her."

Callie too saw that something was wrong. She said, "I'd better get Jimmy inside. It'll be dark soon." She left them quickly.

Henry and George sat there by the island for another ten minutes, but neither of them said a word. After-chores customers began to arrive. In the gray of dusk the figures of Henry and George grew less substantial, it seemed to Callie, watching from the diner. At last Henry pushed up out of his chair slowly and came in.

5

They came to the diner night after night when the chores were done, and sometimes they talked about the drought and the heat, sometimes they merely sat, quiet, preoccupied-looking, like men listening for something in the back of their minds: some voice out of dried-up hills, a sound of water moving down under the ground. Sometimes they played cards; other times they did nothing at all. Ben Worthington, Jr., would stand by the counter drinking his beer and studying the punch-board for hours at a time, as if the whole secret of the universe lay under one of those dots. Once as Callie was passing him with a tray he caught her arm and said, as if continuing an old conversation, "There's got to be a way to figure it." He pointed at the punchboard with the top of his bottle. "There's a way to figure everything."

Callie pulled away. "You tell me when you figure it out," she said.

Old Man Judkins said, "All the same, I can tell you where the clock is."

"The hell," Ben Worthington, Jr., said.

Old Man Judkins tipped his head back, so he could look through his glasses, and pointed at one of the dots without a moment's hesitation. It was as if he could see through the paper.

"Here's what," Ben said. "I'll give you five-to-one the clock ain't there."

Judkins shook his head. "No, sir. You pay for the punch and the clock's half yours, half mine, because I showed you where it is."

Ben looked at him, and slowly he reached in his pocket for change and paid for the punch. The clock wasn't there. Old Man Judkins stood with his head back, holding his old straw hat in his hand, looking surprised, and when he was sure the clock was really not there he shrugged. "Hunch was wrong," he said.

Days went by and it still didn't rain, and all of them grew more edgy. Old Man Judkins said, as though Callie Soames had not lived in farm country all her life (and yet she listened, remembering hand-loaded wagons of hay, thrashing crews, wheat standing on the hillsides in shocks): "It never changes. They bring in all them new machines, put all them chemicals into the ground, get dairies with a hundred cows, but they still got to wait on the land. Progress, they say. But th' earth don't know about progress. No rain, that means no corn and no hay, no feed in the winter. The old days, they might have trucked it in, but not now. Fifty cows was a real big barn in the old days, and two men could clean the gutters in half an hour. Now they got gutter cleaners—seven thousand dollars they cost, and you got to pay for it month by month, summer or winter, whether or not you got hay in the barn, because banks don't care about hay. We used to make it, in the old days, no matter how long the rain held off. But the way things are now, you can't compete without gutter cleaners and diesel tractors, combines, balers, crimpers, blowers, grain silos, motor-run unloading machines, hammermills, sorters, all the rest. Lou Millet bought that farm of his for four thousand dollars, house included. You know how deep he's in right now? A hundred thousand. Fact. Can't even sell it."

She shook her head.

"No chance any more of winning," he said. "They just try and survive." Old Man Judkins looked at her with his head cocked; then down at his hands. They were gnarled and liver-spotted and scarred, and she remembered suddenly what Jim Millet had said, the day of George Loomis's accident: "The goddamn cylinder was going around and around. You could see slivers of bone—I never see nothin' like it—red with blood and then redder in half-a-second, and the blade chewing away."

She said quickly, "I guess the oldtimers had their troubles too."

Old Man Judkins looked at her, and after a minute he smiled again. "You talk about the old days and everybody gets impatient. Things are getting better and better, that's what people have got to believe. Say it ain't so and they know for sure you're an old codger, not right in the head. Prophet of doom, they say."

Callie said, "You have to have faith."

The old man bent his head, drawing a square with one finger on the counter-top, moving the finger around and around the square. She said it again, as though it were important, louder this time, to penetrate what she knew was not mere deafness. "You have to have faith, Mr. Judkins." She glanced at the sleeping dog, and her heart caught.

Fred Judkins' finger stopped moving, and after a

238

long time he looked up again, lips puckered. "No," he said. "You have to have the nerve to ride it down."

But at least about this much Old Man Judkins was right: If it didn't rain soon every one of them would be finished. Henry said so, Doc Cathey said so, even Jim Millet said so. One night—Henry wasn't there at the time—Jim Millet said, joking, the tobacco cud bulging in his whiskered cheek, "You want the truth, it's all Nick Blue's fault. He could've done a rain dance for us a month ago if he'd wanted to, but you think he'll do it? Hell, no!"

They all laughed except Nick Blue, sitting straight-backed and solemn-faced, smoke going up from his nostrils past his small sharp eyes, and Ben Worthington, Jr., said, as if fiercely, "He's trying to get his land back, that's what it is."

Jim Millet slapped the counter. "You hit it on the head! That goddam redskin's got it in his mind he'll break us all and get back his heritage." He chewed fast, like a rabbit.

"Now, Jim," Callie said.

But they liked the joke too well to leave it.

"Nick Blue's a smart man," Ben Worthington, Jr., said. "He don't talk a whole lot, but he thinks." He tapped his temple.

The two truckers at the counter grinned without turning.

Lou Millet said, "Ah, you're too hard on him, Ben." He smiled, though. Even Lou was capable, these days, of going further than he'd dream of going some other time.

Jim said, "I bet you couldn't *get* him to dance. I bet he wouldn't do it for *nobody!*"

The truckers glanced at Nick and smiled. Nick sat as still as ever, as if made out of wood, moving only his cheeks when he puffed at the cigarette.

Then all at once they were standing up, Jim Millet

and Ben Worthington, Jr., and Emery Jones' albino hired man, and the trucker by the cash register was watching them, smiling, as if half-thinking of getting up too.

Callie pursed her lips.

Nick sat quietly smoking as though he were deaf, and when they were standing behind him, leering like monkeys, he put the cigarette down and squared his shoulders more.

"Now, that's enough," Lou Millet said.

Old Man Judkins watched calmly, as if he'd seen it all many times.

"Come on now, Nick," Ben Worthington, Jr., said, "have some mercy, eh?"

Nick turned his head like a man bothered by a fly on his shoulder, his yellow-brown forehead wide and smooth, slanted like an ape's, and for a long moment everything was still, as if even the wind had suddenly stopped to listen. Then, for no reason, it was over. They laughed—even Nick Blue was smiling—and they slapped his shoulders and told him, by God, he could take a joke, and then they went back to their counter stools, still laughing. Callie leaned on the counter. She said suddenly, as if to all the room, "What ever became of the Goat Lady?"

They seemed to think about it. Nobody knew.

"Do you think she ever found him, heading off blind like that?"

Nobody knew.

Late that night, in the kitchen (Jimmy not asleep, as they thought, but standing on the stairs, in the dark), Callie said: "Henry, I saw Simon Bale."

"What?" he said.

She frowned, realizing for an instant that perhaps it had not really happened.

"There's no such thing as ghosts," he said. "What if Jimmy was to hear you, talking like that."

She felt sick, and the absurd conviction came over her that if she let herself turn to the window Simon would be there, his face yellowish-gray against the dark of the mountains. But she knew he wasn't there, and to prove to herself that she knew, she kept from turning.

"He wants to tell us something," she said. It came to her that that was not so. He had nothing to say to them.

Henry said, "He spoke to you?" His eyes were slits, and she knew what he was thinking. He said, "Callie, you dreamed it."

She thought about it.

After a long time, as if by accident, as if not having meant to say it aloud, he said, "What does he want to tell us?"

"You've seen him, then?"

"No. Of course not."

The round white pain came under her collarbone.

"What did you *think* he wanted to tell us?"

"I don't know."

After that they were silent again for a long time. When Callie finally spoke, her words came out in a rush. "It's simple. He was an evil man and now he's tormented. He lived with us all those weeks passing out his pamphlets to people in the diner and scaring Jimmy with his talk of the devil, and now he *knows*. He's afraid he poisoned us. It wasn't true."

"You need to get more rest," Henry said. "You've been worried lately. And this heat." He looked at the table-top, biting his upper lip and squinting. He got one of the little white pills out of the bottle in his shirt pocket. He was remembering how he would sit in his car up on Nickel Mountain, in the old days, and the fog would be there all around him like a sea, and strange thoughts would come into his mind. He would think strange thoughts, knowing they were not true, strange, and knowing he could suspend the knowledge that what came into his mind was unreal, and he would savor that queer freedom the way he savored the smell of Catskill air at night or savored the obscure, continually shifting patterns in the fog around his headlights. When the night was clear he would push the old rattletrap Ford as hard as it knew how to go, and turning into a curve he would know exactly where the line lay between making it and not, and he would ride that line as he rode the line down the center of the highway, conscious every second of the choices on either side. He'd gone to stock car races once with George Loomis, and he'd been surprised: George Loomis wanted them to hit, wanted somebody killed, and he'd said, "Admit it, Henry, so do you." "No," he'd said. They'd looked at each other and they'd understood—as though everything had suddenly snapped into focus, past, present, future: They profoundly disagreed.

"He'll destroy us," Callie said, wildly now, no longer knowing what she was saying.

She thought of the Preacher, carefully avoiding the spatters of manure, her father carefully avoiding the Preacher, the milking machines chugging regularly, and she remembered: "You never think of anybody but yourself, that's truly all you thing about," her mother struggling against him futilely, stupidly, as once, wrongly, he too had struggled, hitting her for it, forgetting the truth that you had to ride it down. She remembered the day No. 6 died. They had to saw the stanchion off to get out the corpse, and they dragged it out of the cowbarn with a log-chain that peeled the dead hide off the leg; they tipped it over the bluff with crowbars, and when it rolled down over the tin cans, boxes, buggy-wheels, bedsprings, rusted fencewire, kettles, crocks—the corrupting record of seven generations—her father and the two hired men had yelled like Indians, with glee. It was natural that cows die, and fitting. One had no need for faith in what was reasonable, because they would survive. Faith was for what made no sense. She said again, with conviction: "He'll destroy us."

But Henry shook his head, squinting at her, "No, he'll save us."

And instantly Callie knew, in the mind-fogging heat, that he was right.

He got up early, the following morning, and most of the day he helped her in the diner. But he went on eating, and nothing she did was any use.

6

All Old Man Judkins knew was this: that in George Loomis's barn, among spinning wheels and casques and antique farm tools, half-hidden under an old tarpaulin, there stood a pink and purple goatcart, the rear end shaken or smashed to bits, the spokes of the left rear wheel broken. Maybe someone had run into it, maybe it had gone over a cliff; he couldn't tell. And he knew, too, that whenever anyone asked him about her, George Loomis said he'd never seen the Goat Lady—which sounded reasonable enough, except for that goatcart he had in the barn. For what would even the Goat Lady want on Crow Mountain? She'd have had to pull off the main highway and travel two miles up steep, winding gravel road, beechwoods on either side of her, an occasional sharply sloping haylot, ahead of her nothing but more steep road, beechwoods, haylots, one or two abandoned-looking houses and, off in the woods, out of sight from the road but marked by a blue and white state historical marker, a crumbling pre-Revolutionary lookout tower.

He'd stumbled on the cart by accident. The odds

against anybody else's stumbling onto it, or knowing what it was in that barnful of junk—especially since nobody ever came here—were a thousand-to-one. He'd been out walking one morning, as usual, because of a theory he had about arthritis—a theory he'd picked up from Albertus Magnus's *Egyptian Secret* years ago—and, as he did sometimes, he'd decided to turn up Old Joseph Napoleon Road, for the red raspberries and the view of the valley and to see how the tower was holding up. He was thirsty when he got to George Loomis's place, partly thirsty for ginger water, partly for talk, so he went up to George's door. There was nobody home. He went out to the cowbarn but that was empty too, the stables swept clean and powdered with lime, the rear doors wide open to let in the sun and air, and so he went on through the cowbarn and over to the old horsebarn, now storage-shed, and there he saw the goatcart. He was tired from walking, every blamed bone in his body aching, and he sat down on the flat rock by the door and pulled a timothy shoot and chewed the end. When the timothy shoot got stringy he took out his pipe, stoked it, and lit it. On principle, he did not speculate, merely looked around him at the farm.

It looked like a nigger's place. The fences were bad, the barbwire strung loosely, toggled to the fenceposts with baling wire—because, no doubt, you couldn't both nail and stretch with just one arm—and the weeds along the fencelines hadn't been cut in at least three years. The hayfield dropping away from where he sat was eroded and pitted, too rough to get over with a tractor by now, and the hay in it was brown, with bright patches of mustard weed, and long past prime, no good even for pasture, even if he somehow got a fence around it. The beehives at the foot of the hill looked abandoned. And the place was dry, of course. To the right of where Old Man Judkins sat, up the slope to the cowbarn from the tractor-shed, the barnyard was so dry it was powdery, like a hogpen that hasn't been used in years, or like ashes. Birds had overrun the place, both good and bad, pigeons, sparrows, woodpeckers, starlings, chippies, swallows, finches, robins. The beanloft would be caked with their droppings, the granary thick with nests, even down in the oats. There was no water at all in the big iron tub, and no gutting of the ground below from spillover, which meant George Loomis was taking it easy on the watering these days, maybe because his well was low, maybe because it was dry already and he was hauling his water in in milkcans, paying money for it, or promising to pay with labor—if he had that much nerve.

He waited for the pipe to grow cool in his hand, then got up, stiff from sitting so long, his rear end numb, and went over to the burdocks growing by the side of the tractor-shed. He picked four leaves and laid them out inside his hat, with excessive care, then he put on the hat and started home.

That night he went up to George Loomis's place again, not walking this time but driving his truck. He wore the same clothes he always wore, bib overalls, frock, the disintegrating straw hat, his pipe in his teeth. The lights were all out, as usual, but in the high, rounded kitchen windows he could see the flicker of the television. Old Man Judkins knocked, then leaned one hand on the cool brick of the wall and waited. The air around him was breathless and muggy, and the music from the TV sounded unnaturally loud, like water rushing down a gorge. "You'd better sit down for this," a man's voice said, and then a woman's voice: "Something's happened to Walter! Oh, please! You've got to tell me!" Old Man Judkins knocked again and, abruptly, the sound went off but not the picture.

George Loomis called from the middle of the room, "Who is it?"

"Fred Judkins," he said. He took his pipe from between his teeth in case he should need to say it again, more clearly. But he heard the clump of George Loomis's bootbrace coming. The door opened.

" 'Mon in," George said.

Old Man Judkins took off his hat.

For maybe fifteen seconds they looked at each other in the near darkness as if George had been expecting him; then Old Man Judkins went past him and over to the table. There was only one chair that looked safe to sit on, the wired-up, straight-backed chair facing the television, and George went into the living room for another, one of his mother's antiques, spindly and black, with flowers and birds painted on it. When he came back he said, "Whiskey?" He had a glass of his own on the table.

"No thanks," Old Man Judkins said. "Milk, mebby, if you got it."

George went over to the icebox, carried the pewter milkpitcher over to the sink and took a peanut butter glass from the drain-rack. He brought over cottage cheese and jam and two china dishes and two paper-thin, tarnished spoons. Then, formally, they both sat down.

"Long time since you come up here," George said.

"Yes it is."

They looked at the table between them. They'd traded work in the old days—not George and Fred Judkins but Fred Judkins and George's father. Old Man Judkins could remember when George Loomis was no bigger than Henry's boy was now—and exactly as much like an elf or an angel or any other natural thing—crawling around on the floor while his mother worked bread dough right here at this table. Long time, he thought, and nodded. In the corner of the living room that he could see from where he sat, he could make out the shiny arm of an elephantine, old-fashioned couch, a table with a bird cage on it, and a lamp with Tiffany glass.

"How have you been?" George said.

"I still get around," he said.

Their faces were white, with no light but the flicker of the television. They looked like dead men returned after a long time to an empty house to say some trifling, insignificant thing they'd forgotten to say in time. But they didn't say it. Old Man Judkins relit his pipe, and George Loomis said, "Still living there with your daughter, Jud?"

"No, didn't work out. Got a room over Bill Llewellyn's now. Better all 'round."

"I bet you miss the old farm, eh?" He lifted his glass and waited, respectful.

Old Man Judkins nodded. " 'Deed I do."

George grinned. "You give me about three dollars and you can have this place." He drank.

"Ain't worth it, George."

"That's the truth."

The pipe had gone out again and Old Man Judkins lit another match, but he forgot to hold it over the bowl; he was watching the silent television—a man in a cavalry uniform looking through field glasses at a hill. George looked over too.

The quiet made Old Man Judkins remember something, but for a long time he couldn't think what it was. Then at last it came to him. Steam. The old black steam tractor made no sound at all, sitting there opposite the thrashing machine, headed up. When they threw in the pulley the thrashing machine would begin to move, slowly at first, like something alive just beginning to wake up, the feeders rising and falling in a kind of sawing motion, utterly soundless, and then the team would bring the wagon over, that too almost soundless—the click of harness buckles, the creak of a wheel—and by now the feeders would be moving fast, a kind of whir like a ball on a string, and the crew would start working, a man on the bagger and one on the platform, two more men up on the wagon, pitching, a couple of boys hauling the grain off and bringing up new bags, no sound but from time to time the not-loud shouts of the men telling stories, joking while they worked, and the steady whir and the feeders catching the unthrashed wheat with a *chig-uff, chig-uff, chig-uff*.

"I ought to come see you sooner," Old Man Judkins said. "Folks get out of touch."

"My fault as much as yours," George said.

Not speculating, on principle, raising no questions, making no suggestions, Old Man Judkins watched the picture on the television, wondered vaguely what was happening, and finished his glass of milk. Out of a clean, cool waterfall came a pack of cigarettes. At last he stood up. "Long time, George," he said.

"Too long," George said. He stretched out his hand and the old man took it.

Then Fred Judkins went home.

In his room, sitting down in front of his turned-off coal-oil heater, the window-fan roaring, Old Man Judkins got out his pipe, cleaned it, stoked it. He knew that from time to time he would wonder again why the Goat Lady's cart was up in George's shed; he knew that despite his principles he'd be molested from time to time by doubts. Maybe the answer would come up some time in a conversation, or maybe someone else would stumble onto it, some loudmouth gossip or righteous fool from town, and he would find out. But probably not. No matter.

After a time he said, pointing his pipe at the reflection of himself looking in, dubious, through the nearer window, "Maybe there's such a thing as a heaven and hell. If there is, a man has a right to go where he's contracted for. I wouldn't mind going to hell if I thought I'd earned it. Better than getting a last-minute pardon, as if everything you did was no account, any more than a joke."

He glanced over his shoulder as if thinking he might

have been overheard. The room was empty. "There is no heaven or hell," he said. "That's a scientific fact, and there's the end of it."

He set his teeth down firmly on the pipe stem.

7

He lay in bed on his back in the muggy night heat, his hand under his head, smoking without ever touching the cigarette except to change it for a new one, the radio on the commode playing the American Airlines all-night concert, far away and tinny, interrupted once every hour for news, the same news over and over, the same voice: *Albany. Tonight eight counties have been officially declared disaster areas. In his press conference this evening, Governor Harriman said—*

There were flies in the room, the screens all shot. Beside the radio, a stack of paperback books, the loaded ash tray.

George Loomis lay perfectly still, as if tranquil. He was clean-shaven and combed, and the sheet was drawn over his bad foot, the good foot lying in the open, as though in this isolated mountain house he expected some visitor. But his mind was in a turmoil, struggling against thought.

"There are no disasters," his grandfather had said, "God moves in strange ways." But his mother was dying, so he'd gotten home from Korea on leave, shocked to find himself moved by her dying. He'd been young then, a romantic. Her face was sunken, and she drooled now, an effect of the stroke, and her ugliness made him see that she had been beautiful once and that he'd loved her. When she died his father said, "What shall we do?" and he had said nothing. *Bury the dead.* When she was embalmed, though, her face filled out and she wasn't as bad as she'd been before, almost beautiful in the casket with its ridiculous window for the worms to look through. *In carne corruptible incorruptionem.* He had not wept or wanted to, even at the graveside, but afterward he had gotten drunk, or rather sick, and had stood on a table at the Silver Slipper intoning Ovid:

Exitus auspicio gravior: nam nupta per herbas. . . .

For in those days there was still poetry. Still music, too. You would listen all night to the music your friendly American Airlines brought to you for your listening pleasure, and you would be pleased. Yet it was sound, even now; more comforting than silence. *God bless you, friendly American Airlines. Into your hands I commend myself.*

Then the memory flushed through him again, his headlights dipping over the crest of the hill as they'd done without harm ten thousand times, the incredible circus cart there in his road, straddling the crown, and again in his mind he hit the brakes with all his might and yanked at the wheel and heard the noise resounding like thunder through the glens. When that memory was over he saw Fred Judkins at his door again, nodding, sucking on the pipe, and after a minute the old man took off his hat. (But too late now to tell anyone, and no doubt too late from the beginning. An accident, one in an infinite chain.)

The American Airlines had chosen *Scheherazade* for him. He tried to listen, or rather he pretended to try to listen, consciously playing an empty role . . . no emptier, he thought, than others.

He ground out the last of his cigarettes and snapped out the light. In the darkness the music, like the heat, drew nearer, coming from all parts of the room at once. He rolled over on his stomach, the side of his head on his hand now, and closed his eyes. There had been birds circling above the back ravine. He'd been alarmed by the knock of the Watkins Man. But all this would pass.

(At the Dairy Queen in Slater there had been two young girls, strangers to him. One of them had smiled. She had long hair—both of them had long hair, one blonde, one dark, and they wore no lipstick. They were pretty, poised between child and woman, so pretty his heartbeat had quickened a little, and he'd imagined how they would look in those pictures you could buy in Japan, coarse rope cutting their wrists and breasts and thighs. The instant he thought it, his stomach went sour. They were young, pure: beautiful with innocence, yet corruptible. The one who smiled invited it. She was hungry for it. *Serpentis dente*.)

He twisted onto his back suddenly and sat up, soaking in sweat. "Please us," he whispered. He could feel the memory of the accident coming over him, and he got up to look for a smokable butt in an ash tray, and some bourbon.

8

They'd all heard somehow (this was three nights later) of Nick Blue's prediction. There was no more sign of rain now than there'd been all day: The clouds were piled up like tumbling mountains, blocking out the stars, but the dry breeze still blew, light. If the crickets were still it meant only that all signs fail. They talked though about how Nick Blue had a kind of sense (Nick Blue wasn't there), and about how he'd known three weeks beforehand when the blizzard was coming, the year before last. If he'd said the rain would come tonight, then it was coming. Eight-thirty passed, and then nine-thirty, and the talk went on, more tense now—sharp against the dull moan of the fans—as though they were talking to keep themselves from noticing. Around ten-thirty George Loomis came in, and as he came over to the counter, the brace clumping on the wooden floor, the empty sleeve hanging free, they said, "Well, what you think, George?" "I didn't throw on no raincoat," he said. "That ought to bring it," Jim Millet said. George said, "I'll tell you one thing for certain: if it comes it'll hit every farm in this country but mine." They laughed—howled like wolves—though each of them had said the same thing in one way or another, taking pride in his singular bad luck—and they went back to their talk of Nick Blue and the blizzard two years ago and then to the time when it didn't rain till the middle of September, in 1937. The talk got louder and at eleven-thirty the breeze was still blowing. Then Lou Millet said, "Henry, you old devil."

Callie looked up. He was standing in the doorway, filling it, able to pass through it all, it seemed, only by a trick of her vision. Jimmy came out from behind his father's right leg and around the counter, and she picked him up and put him on the stool by the cash register. "What are you doing up this time of night?" she said. But she kissed his cheek, holding his head to keep from pulling away.

"Daddy let me," he said.

"Henry, you ought to be ashamed," she said. But she dropped it. He was looking out into the darkness, and she knew why he was here. Nick Blue had been wrong, and they'd all believed him, and when the disappointment, embarrassment came, Henry wanted to be here. Because they're neighbors, she thought. All at once she knew how it was going to be when they realized what fools they'd been. She understood for the first time (but wordlessly) Henry's rage: It was not a little thing they'd come here expecting, and not something unduly fine, either ("No chance any more of winning," Old Man Judkins had said. "They just try and survive"). That much, surely, they had a right to expect. And so they'd come here with high spirits, expecting not salvation but merely rain to recover the corn and a little of the hay; but they were going to see they'd made fools of themselves, that any dignity they thought they had was a word, empty air, and to act on the assumption that they had any rights in this world whatever, even the rights of a spider, to survive, was to turn themselves into circus clowns, creatures stuffed with old rags and straw who absurdly struggled to behave like human beings and who, whether or not they succeeded, were ridiculous. All this Callie knew, not in words but in the lines of Henry's face, and she wanted to leave so she wouldn't have to watch it when it happened.

It was quarter-to-twelve. Emery Jones' hired man lit up, his buck-teeth gleaming, and he said. "Nick said it would come today. That means it's going to be here in fifteen minutes." He seemed to have no inkling of what a crazy thing it was to say. But they did. Old Man Judkins looked at his empty cup as though he'd just noticed a bug in it, and Jim Millet put his hat on and stood up. Ben Worthington, Jr., laid down the punchkey he was playing with and calmly, thoughtfully, pushed his fist through the board, then drew out his wallet. It was bulging with the money he'd gotten for his wheat and would be needing all this winter. "I'd like to buy that clock," he said.

"Ben, that's crazy," Callie said. "Forget it. We'll tell them it was an accident. Please."

But he shook his head. He threw the coat he had no need for over his shoulder and went to the register. Callie stood helpless a minute, then pulled the square, green checkpad from her belt and leaned on the counter to figure how much it came to, and then Henry was standing at her elbow. "Let it go, Callie," he said. Then, with a grim laugh, "It's on the house, Ben."

Ben glared as though it wasn't August he hated after all, but Henry Soames, as if Henry had denied him the vote.

Henry was saying, "The same for all of you. Tonight it's all on me."

"Some other time, Henry," Lou Millet said.

But Henry was possessed, dangerous. "I mean it," he said. "Tonight we're not taking a dime." He hit his chest three times with his thumb, his face incredibly serious; none of them laughed. "I mean it," he said again. "Today's my birthday." He yelled it as though he were angry. "Truth. Callie, give everybody cake."

"Here, O Israel," George Loomis said, "today is the day he takes upon himself. . . ." But Henry's face was dark red, and George shut up.

"We're going to sing 'Happy Birthday, Dear Henry'," Henry roared, not smiling at all, forgetting to smile, his fat fists clenched, and Callie was saying in a whisper that cut through Henry's roar, "Henry, stop it!"

"All together," he yelled, putting a cookie in his mouth, raising his arms.

And all at once, probably out of pure shock at first, they were doing it, cold sober as they were. And then a vast and meaningless grief replaced the shock. Tears streamed down Lou Millet's face, and he was choked up so badly he couldn't bring out more than every fourth word. In the beginning there was only three voices—Henry's, Old Man Judkins', Jim Millet's—then more: Emery Jones' hired man singing tenor, almost soprano but in harmony; Ben Worthington, Jr., whining out baritone, sweat running down his throat; even George Loomis more or less singing, with a pained expression, droning like the bad note on a banjo. Lou Millet stood up. They were singing it through again, but it seemed to have come to him that he had to get home, it was foolishness sitting here half the night, his wife at home alone with the kids. He left, hurrying, and after a minute Ben Worthington, Jr., picked up his wallet and followed him out. Old Man Judkins stood up after that, and then Jesse Behmer. Henry stood in the middle of the floor like a giant, slowly bobbed up and down too, quickly and lightly, waving shone and the belly of his shirt was pasted to his skin.

Behind him, his face as solemn as his father's—but solemn without weight, like a serious toy—Jimmy bobbed up and down too, quickly and lightly, waving his arms.

When midnight came, only George Loomis was still there. Henry sat down, panting, sucking air in and out through his mouth. Callie brought him a pill. "Well!" he said. He tried to laugh, but he couldn't get his breath.

For a long time after that nobody spoke. Finally George Loomis said solemnly, "Whooey."

"What's that supposed to mean?" Henry said.

Then George said: "But I'll tell you something. I'm beginning to believe in the Goat Lady." He said it lightly, but a hint of uneasiness came over him as soon as it was out.

"You saw her, didn't you," Callie said at once, knowing the direct accusation would shock him but suddenly not caring.

George went white.

"What happened?" Callie said.

They sat like people precariously balanced over a chasm, and everything depended on what George decided. Henry sat blankly, pulling at the fat below his chin, not eating the cookie he held in his left hand. George Loomis stared at his cigarette. He could tell them and be free (she saw what he was thinking) but then he would never be free again, because then there would be somebody who knew his guilt, shame, embarrassment, whatever it was. Except that maybe that was what it was to be free: to abandon all shame, all dignity, real or imagined. She remembered the funeral for George's mother, how they'd lowered the coffin carefully as if to preserve even in death her decorous, more than bodily virginity, and how they'd put the dirt in gently to avoid cracking the window through which the blind earth stared at her face.

At last George said, "No. I never saw her." He stood up.

Henry looked at him, pitying him, George Loomis no more free than a river or a wind, and, as if unaware that he was doing it, Henry broke the cookie in his hand and let the pieces fall. She realized with a start that it was final: George had saved them after all. She felt herself going weightless, as though she were fainting. And something said in her mind, as though someone stood behind her, whispering hurriedly in her ear: *Nevertheless, all shall be saved.* She thought: *What?* And again: *All. Everything. Even the stocks and stones. Nothing is lost.* She thought: *How? Why should sticks and stones be saved?* But the walking dream was passing quickly, a thing so fragile that she would not even remember tomorrow that she'd had it. The room was suddenly filled with ghosts, not only Simon, but Henry's father, huge as a mountain and gentle as a flower, and Callie's great-great-grandfather, with his arm suspenders, an almanac closed over one finger, and Old Man Kuzitski, drunk as a lord, and Mrs. Stamp, irascible and pretty, with a blue-black umbrella, and arthritic, bushy-browed old Uncle John, and there were more, a hundred more she didn't know, solemn and full of triumphant joy; and the space in front of the diner was filled, from the door to the highway to the edge of the woods, and the woods were full, an enormous multitude solemn and triumphant, and she saw in the great crowd the pink and purple (transformed, magnificent, regally solemn) of the Goat Lady's cart. They vanished. Henry stood out by the gas pumps now, gray-looking and old in the pinkish glow of the neon. She saw the lights of George Loomis's truck go on and watched him back down toward the road, then pull forward, turning. She watched his taillights move up the hill and, dipping over the top, snap out. Henry came back.

"What *did* happen?" she asked in the amazing stillness.

"I don't know," he said.

"Do you think the Goat Lady—?"

"I don't know."

Jimmy lay asleep below the cash register, like something (a bag of potatoes) turned in as a trade. Henry lifted him gently, without waking him, while Callie locked the door and turned out the lights.

Sometime during the night, while they all slept, missing it, or missing anyway the spectacular beginning that they'd surely earned the right to see (*but the dog saw it, rising slowly to his feet and tilting his gray, giant head*), thunder cracked, shaking the mountains, and it rained.

VII

THE
MEETING

1

It wasn't until he was already aboard and looking around him in the twilight of the coach that Willard Freund realized he'd forgotten to wire ahead to tell them which train he'd be on. The ticket had taken almost all the money he'd had, all but two dollars. If he had to spend the night in Utica it would have to be on one of the wooden benches at the station. But there was nothing he could do about it now. He took a seat near the rear of the half-empty car and settled himself for the trip. A red-headed old Welshman in a thin, threadbare coat with the collar turned up watched him with dim, angry eyes from across the aisle. One of the two middle-aged women talking about the blizzard and the lateness of the train, a few seats ahead of him, craned her neck around the side, like a chicken, to look at him. He pretended to stare through her.

His legs were cold already. By the time he got there he'd be frozen half to death. He pushed his hands into his overcoat pockets and remembered he'd brought the book, *Attack on Christendom.* He drew it out. He tried to read, but the shuffling and bumping of passengers moving down the aisle or settling themselves in the seats nearby distracted him. Worse yet, however hard he concentrated—now on the page, now on the strangers closing in on him, casual, determined, like a dog pack gradually encircling a sheep, his stomach churned with uneasy thoughts of home. At times it was a dull sorrow, at times a feeling of excitement mingled with anxiety, so intense he could hardly catch his breath. *Hypocrites,* he thought fiercely. It was a word that came more and more often to his mind, or rather, came between his mind and what threatened him: his mother and father living together all these years with no love between them, his father faithful to his mother out of cowardice, or habitual indifference, the way he was faithful to the Lutheran Church. And the neighbors were no better, however highly they thought of themselves. Philistines, brainless conformists. Sick.

He closed his eyes. None of that was true.

Now the train started up, so smoothly that, as always, it seemed at first the station that was moving. And still he was unable to read. He couldn't stop hearing the mumble of the wheels, steady and endless as banjo music, or watching the snow hitting the window to his right and sticking to the pane. He watched the gray buildings of Albany flitting past beyond the snow, then smaller houses with Christmas trees, then hills, luminous in the twilight, then the houses and crossings of small towns. The train stopped often, and passengers got on or got off, the same thing again and again, as in a nightmare: the murmur of voices, the glimpses of waiting or hurrying figures, the woman from the Salvation Army with her bell, the snow beating endlessly at the window. At last, entering the mountains—the train seemingly hanging suspended in darkness, then jolting suddenly, swaying on a curve—the churning in his stomach settled a little. He read for thirty minutes, then dozed and dreamed he was a child riding beside his father on the bobsled, hauling in wood. The dream was pleasant at first, but little by little it changed until at last, looking up at his father, he realized that though he sat erect, his hat seemingly brushing the stars, he was dead. He awakened with a start and for an instant thought the train was falling into some wide, deep gorge. When the brief panic subsided, he pressed his face to the window, raising his hands to the sides of his forehead like blinders, and saw snow and dead-looking trees standing in a desolate lake. He leaned back in his seat, his stomach churning so badly now that he thought he might have to vomit.

Except for the flickering red globes over the doors, the car was dark. As he looked, the conductor opened the door, letting in the suddenly loud rumble of the wheels, and called, "Utica, twenty minutes." He came through the car, swaying, light blanking out the lenses of his glasses, and when he reached Willard's seat he leaned toward him, his face chalk-white, and said again mechanically, "Utica in twenty minutes." Willard nodded with a jerk, as though he had not registered at first. He thought again, "All I have is two dollars," and sat rigid, shivering in the cold, his lips pressed together tightly, until he saw the lighted tar paper and asbestos fake-brick shacks at the outskirts of the city. He got up then, reached his suitcase down from the rack, and worked his way to the door. He felt the others watching him, and hurried.

As he stepped down between the two cars the wind snatched at him as if to tear him away from earth and bear him off into the void, but he caught hold of the cold doorpost and, clinging to it, pressing down the skirt of his overcoat with the side of his suitcase, stepped onto the platform and into the shelter of the building. On the train steps the wind had been fierce, but under the overhang there was a lull. He put down the suitcase and drew a deep breath of the cold, snowy air, and standing not far from the door he looked around the platform and the lighted station. The storm whistled between the wheels of the car, through the metal scaffolding, and around the corner of the building. A mail wagon creaked past him, barely missing the corner of his suitcase, and men moved back and forth, laughing and talking, in snowy coats and hats. Beyond the corner of the station men and women piled suitcases into waiting cars, shouting through the snowy darkness. The big doors behind him swung open and shut continually, and muffled figures darted by covered with snow. An angry voice shouted, "Which car for Batavia?" and he caught a brief glimpse of a bearded, scarred face. Then steam hissed, billowing around the wheels of the train, and the cars began to move. He glimpsed faces in the windows. Then suddenly he was looking at the tracks beyond and covered walks and signal scaffolds and darkness. When the swaying red light of the last car was swallowed up by the night, he turned to go in.

In the huge vaulted room there was no one he knew. People sat solemn-faced and bored on the pew-like benches, not talking, bundled in their coats and scarves. There was a two- or three-year-old boy in a snowsuit lying asleep beside a fat woman, and for an instant Willard's chest went light.

He was thinking of his illegitimate child, whom he'd never seen. He wondered uneasily whether he would see him this time. He looked away. Across the room there was a green metal rack of newspapers. He hurried over to it, running from one painful thought to another—from the child to the Bomb. Willard Freund inclined more and more to believe—though at times he knew it was foolishness—that the stupidity of mankind, and maybe especially the stupidity of American democracy, was going to destroy the world—and soon. Though normally he was shy, not talkative, more times than once he had gotten a little drunk and had talked about it with fraternity brothers at Albany, sitting in the dimly lit lounge with a stack of 45's on the changer—Tchaikovsky's *Pathétique*, Stan Kenton's *Innovations*—a cigarette hanging unlighted between his lips, head and shoulders thrown forward (image from some movie, Marlon Brando, maybe)—had teased the thought toward probability, half-aware as he spoke that his loss was more personal than he was telling them. His father's barn was the largest in the county, vaulted above like an airplane hanger, the cowbarn, below, as long and wide as a gymnasium. His father's hired men moved in and out between cows like factory workers, shifting milking machines, throwing open the chutes that brought down hay, or moving the milk-cans on stainless steel wagons to the cooler. He had told his father the girl was pregnant, he intended to marry her. His father had laughed, then looked at him hard, and then, without warning, had slapped his face. "Don't mix up pussy and business," he'd said, and Willard Freund had been filled with rage and shame—because it was true, he did not love her, though the sight of the Stop-Off made him ache with desire till Henry Soames' filthy shanty and diner, once for him a haven against the mechanized, cold-blooded, money-grubbing evil of *W. D. Freund and Sons Dairy Farms,* had become what it looked like to the casual eye, a seedy, run-down dingle of temptation and witchcraft. Stinging with rage, he'd snatched off the nearest milk-can cover and had thrown the can on its side so the milk came gushing out, thick and steaming. His father had bellowed and backed away a step, afraid of him, and Willard, crying now, had fled from the barn. He might have won, if he'd pushed, exactly as, later, he'd won the right to quit Ag school and become an English major. But he'd gone back to Cornell, had gone on getting letters from her, and, sick with indecision, had done nothing. Though he profoundly hated his father for it, his father was right: The God-spouting, hymn-singing, ne'er-do-well Welsh were not his kind of people. So he was ashamed of himself, yes; shocked at himself. But he talked drunkenly of politicians, kings of self-interest, and businessmen, shallowest, coarsest of men. And as he talked—he who had been all his life so quiet—he had thought, in horror, of his friend or once-friend Henry Soames, eccentric hermit, how Henry would sometimes get carried away and start babbling like a madman or drunkard. People smiled, made a circle in the air beside their heads, said: "Bonkers." Suddenly, remembering Henry Soames, Willard would stop talking, would pull at his upper lip (that too he'd gotten from Henry), and would bite his lips together and squint. "Freund, what's really eating you?" some fraternity brothers would occasionally ask. Though they talked day and night about their sexual conquests, he couldn't tell them. He'd told at Cornell, when he was there, and it was horrible. *I want to be a child again,* he thought.

He read the headlines on the papers in the rack and the lead articles down as far as the fold in the paper, his face squeezed shut, pouting. There was no news. There was never any news, merely the palaver those in power released to the fat, happy masses: a new artificial lake for their motorboats, a new skirt length from the change-mongers. His eyes filled with tears. From somewhere behind him came Christmas music.

He went into the men's room and looked in the mirror, then, after thinking about it first, washed his face and parted his hair with his fingers. They could have known what train he'd be on if they'd thought, or if they knew their own son at all; they could have known even that he'd forget to wire ahead. It was all very well to say, "Never mind, no harm done." None had been done: He could phone from here and wait for them to come in the morning (his father driving king-like through the darkness, holding the big gray Cadillac to the center of the road, and let anybody approaching from the other direction watch out). Or he could hitchhike. No harm. It sounded calm and grown-up. But there *was* harm. *Hypocrites,* he thought again, more angrily, more defensively (he knew) than before. All the same. . . . His father had bought every decent milker from Ben Wolters' barn, getting them dirt cheap because Ben was hard up, and when they were driving the loaded cattle truck home he'd laughed and said, "That poor devil don't even know I cleaned him out!" Willard had said, "*I* do, though, don't I," squinting like Roy Rogers. He'd been fourteen then. His father had looked at him and grinned, then looked back at the road. A little farther on he'd said, "It was him or me, Willard." Willard thought now, six years too late to say it: *Never. From the minute the two of you were born it was never you, only him.* Then he thought: *And me. Nicked in the balls from the beginning.*

And now again (meeting his eyes in the mirror) he was thinking sadly of his own son, nicked too, from before he was born, as though the old man had thought it out beforehand and set it all up. But too late now to worry about the child. Too late to worry about the mother either, not that she needed it. He swallowed and blinked hard, angry that tears had ambushed him. She'd done fine for herself, Callie had. Had somehow talked fat old Henry Soames, bad heart and all, into marrying her—by crying, maybe, or by walking into his bedroom naked, or maybe by telling her father old Henry was the one. He'd never have believed she was capable of it, three years ago; which showed how incredibly innocent he'd been. He'd thought he himself was the calculating one: He'd been tortured, lying in his bed at night, each time he left her, thinking simultaneously how beautifully innocent and good she was and what a bastard he was himself, teasing her on little by little, unable to stop himself, vile but at least *knowing* he was vile, believing in the goodness that was out of his reach—except that that wasn't true; all lies; all he ever told himself, he thought, was lies. He'd never known, right to the last minute, whether what he wanted was just to make her or to marry her. She was the third, but the only virgin, the first one there'd been any question about. A question he'd never really answered, in fact, until after he'd heard she was marrying Henry Soames. He'd had to leave for school, which gave him a chance to put off deciding, and pretty soon the thing was decided for him and he saw how lucky he'd been —for once in his life. It shouldn't have surprised him that Callie Wells had turned calculating. That happened, the minute a girl got pregnant. It was instinct, maybe. But was it possible Callie had been calculating all along? (Norma Denitz had said, "You fool, Willard, she planned the whole thing! She took you because she was chasing a bigger fish. A sick old man with money." "I don't believe it," he'd said; but he did believe it, or anyway believed it for that brief moment Norma had laughed. "Hah! Male ego. If men believed the truth about women it would be the end of cohabitation." She was wrong about that, though. He knew the truth about Norma Denitz. He meant nothing to her—"a good lay," she said, "ships smashing in the night." But he stayed with her. He might even marry her someday, if she got her neuroses straightened out.)

And yet Henry was no fool. Was his part, too, calculation? Was it possible that Henry himself had set it all up, hiring her at the diner when he didn't need help—maybe even knowing she was making it with Willard?—keeping her working there late sometimes, watching every minute with his little pig's eyes, pecker itching, as Norma claimed? He'd gone up to Henry's place almost every night, once. To work on the jitney or to sit in the lean-to room in back and talk. His mother had distrusted it, had felt, vaguely, disgusted by it, and when Willard understood what she had in mind he was furious. "He's a *good* man," he'd said fiercely. "He wants someone to talk to, and argue with. Nothing but that." She'd pretended to be convinced, but never again could Willard be thoroughly convinced himself "No one over thirty is seriously concerned with ideas," one of his instructors had said. "Ideas are either toys or tools—ways of passing the time, or ways of getting things." Surely *that* was a lie.

It came to him what it was that made his stomach churn as he drew closer to home. He was going back to the land of his innocence, the sunlit garden where all those years he had believed, in spite of everything, in parental love, the goodness and innocent virtue of girls, or at any rate of certain girls, the possibility of unselfish friendship. He was going back knowing it was perhaps all bullshit, and, for all his fear that it might be bullshit, he was going back expecting to find it still there, and holy.

He decided to hitchhike. He would give the old man no advantage, no chance to speak of how he'd driven half the night through ice and snow et cetera, like a postman, no chance to whine about Willard's forgetting to wire. Cold as it was, nobody would bother to stop for him but the drunks and fairies. Because hitchhikers could be dangerous, like any stranger. The drunks would stop because they were stupid, the fairies because they had an angle. All right.

He took a bus to the city limits and waited.

2

When Willard woke up the car was warm, moving very slowly. The radio was playing softly, Christmas music by an orchestra. The odd scent was still there, like a funeral. The man was bent forward, gripping the steering wheel with both hands tightly. There was light, curly hair on the backs of his fists. They were passing through a town. The streets were deserted and white, and the snow streaking toward the windshield made it impossible to see from one block to the next. Willard hugged himself, his legs clamped together, and watched streetlamps and dimly lighted store windows loom into sight one after another. From time to time the car floated for an instant, as it seemed, coming onto ice. Wreaths hanging over the middle of the street came into sight overhead and then vanished behind the car roof, unlighted and morose. Here and there there were parked cars along the curb, drifted-in, half-buried. Then they were out in the country again, passing unlighted farms and high, blowing drifts.

The man said, "Get any sleep?"

"A little," he said. He got out his cigarettes and lit one. Reflected in the windshield, he looked like Humphrey Bogart or James Cagney or someone, and the recognition simultaneously pleased and disgusted him. *Fake*, he thought; *sucker*. And that too was from some movie. Even his self-hatred was second hand, cheap show. He blew out smoke and took a deep breath of air but seemed to get none, like Fortunato in the basement.

"Storm's getting worse and worse," the man said.

"So I see." He studied the bright red reflection of his cigarette in the windshield, wondering how far they'd come. After a moment he glanced over at the man. He was medium-sized, chubby, well-off-looking. A brown, heavy coat that might be English. Brown hair under the jaunty hat brim; probably bald on top. A flabby, effeminate face. He looked pleased with himself, pleased to be driving an Olds 98, helping some poor damn hitchhiker home to its mother.

"Going home for college vacation?" the man said.

Willard nodded, thinking: *No. To visit my bastard son and my former whore.* (But he wasn't. Would dodge them, escape them.) He took another deep breath and closed his eyes, briefly.

"I thought so," the man said, pleased. "I'm visiting my daughter. We always spend Christmas together."

"That's nice," he said, all trace of irony suppressed. He drew on the cigarette and kept the smoke inside for a moment. "A family should keep in touch."

The man glanced at him. After a moment, he smiled. "I always visit her at Christmas."

Bringing presents, yes. Why, Daddy, how thoughtful of you to remember!

Sir, your daughter is pregnant. By a bicycle with the seat off. She's afraid to mention it, for fear you might disapprove. I speak as your friend, sir. It's only natural that a father would want to be informed. Panic rose in him, or claustrophobia. He remembered swimming in Lake George, driving up, up, up toward air unbelievably far from where it should be.

"Where are you in school?" the man asked.

"Albany."

The man nodded as though that, too, pleased him, but he said, "I meant, what grade are you in?"

"I went to Cornell, the first year," Willard said, "but I transferred."

The man thought about it. "I see."

"For the better living conditions."

To live with a slut, sir. Luckily, your daughter is not a slut. Although she is going to deliver a bicycle. Part Roadmaster

"The living conditions are better in Albany, you think?" He was torn between watching the virtually invisible road and squinting at Willard; he twisted his head from one to the other.

"Much better. Softer, if you know what I mean." After a minute, he added, "There are two main conditions of living, hard and softer."

The man laughed and nodded, then seemed to think about this, too, his head inclined to one side, face screwed up as if he'd bitten his tongue. Willard said, "What line are you in, exactly?"

"Actually," the man said, "I'm in flowers." After a second he explained, "*J. E. Jones' Flowers*, in Utica. You may have heard of it. Jones has been dead for years. I bought the business. My name's Taylor. Actually, most people call me Jones." He laughed. "I have a bank account under the name of Jones and another one under my other name. For personal checks. Saves confusion."

"How about that," Willard said. He added without thinking, meaning nothing, "I have two names too."

"Oh?" The man was squinting at him again, suspicious.

But he was remembering Norma Denitz's father. A psychoanalyst. He had curly brown hair parted down the middle, droopy eyes, a face as soft and pale as ass, fingers obscenely warm. He talked about patients, some man who'd put lye in his wife's douche bag, knowing (for certain reasons, Norma's father said) that she would never actually use it. He sat with a double martini in his pink, soft hand, wearing even in his own living room his obscene brown suit and vest, bow tie. Norma's stepmother was wearing a shiny white dress cut so low you could see her ample and only virtues whenever she bent over. She was forty-eight, but she'd had her face lifted. They believed in The New Morality, but when Norma had stood up and stretched, holding the martini out to the side, as if for a toast, signaling him to come up with her—screw right under their noses —he could feel their anger like electric shock reverberating through the room, smile as they might. *Hypocrites*. He said abruptly:

"I imagine it takes a sharp man to make it with flowers."

"Well," the man said tentatively, "you have to be cut out for it, that's true."

The snowfall was as heavy as ever. The hills and trees blocked the wind and the snow dumped down as if from a giant shovel.

"That's not what I mean. You have to know exactly what to buy, otherwise the whole mess would rot. You have to have enough but not too much, and then you have to talk people into taking it."

"Well, yes," the man said. "But actually—"

"And then, too, you've got to act interested in people. They graduate from grammar school and you've got to act like it's really something, or Uncle

Elmer dies and you've got to look sad, or some girl gets married—"

The man was looking hard at him, the car nosing toward the guard rail. He said, "I *am* interested in people. As I say, some people are cut out for it and some aren't. It takes all kinds."

"Oh sure, sure," Willard said. He lit a new cigarette from the old one. "It's a kick to talk to people sometimes—gives the ego a boost. But day after day, the same old. . . ." He stopped, looking at the guard rail in alarm. The man jerked the wheel and the car slid for a second, then straightened out again. It gave them both a scare, and for a while they were quiet. The radio played on, tinny, mechanically sentimental. The man sat back farther in his seat, driving still more slowly. They came to a town. There were no lights except, here and there, the snow-filtered light of a Christmas tree or an outline of colored lights around a porch. The big car moved through the town quickly, riding down the center of the deserted street. They jounced over a railroad crossing, then came into the open again, the highway a tunnel between snowplow drifts.

(It was right around Christmas the baby had come, three years ago. He'd been home, even had a vacation job at the Purina place; but he'd only stayed two days. After he'd gotten back to school, he'd gotten drunk and told them the whole thing, at the dorm. As soon as it was out he saw what he'd done. She was just some country slut to them, and what he'd done was of no importance. Only his misery was important. They turned it over and over, like a dead turtle, some of them laughing, some of them sympathizing, some sitting glum and embarrassed at his talking too much. After that he could hardly stand meeting them in the dorm halls. But it was all right. He'd transferred, and he'd never repeated his idiot mistake. He knew them now, all their talk about girls they'd laid, all their jabber about what buddies they'd always be.)

At last Willard said, "This must be a pretty heavy season for you. How come you can take off and visit your daughter?"

"Oh, I've got assistants," the man said.

"You trust them?"

Again the man was looking at him, ignoring the road. He was beginning to be alarmed. "Certainly," he said.

"Maybe you're right," Willard said. He could feel the nausea creeping back. "Crime does not pay. The easiest way to get ahead is to be honest. And we all want to get ahead, of course. Especially at Christmas."

The man didn't answer, and after half-a-mile Willard asked, his stomach churning badly now, "You *do* want to get ahead, don't you, Mr. Jones?"

A second too late, having stopped to think about it first, the man laughed. "It takes all kinds," he said. "That's America."

Willard Freund scrunched down in the seat, pushing his hands down into his pockets. The book was gone. He'd left it on the train. The smoke from the cigarette made him want to sneeze and burned his eyes like sulphur. Then suddenly, in a cloud of snow ahead of them, there were yellow lights. The man was squinting through the windshield, but he didn't seem to be seeing. *Snowplow,* Willard thought. *The danger is not where you think, Mr. Jones. I'm not going to knife you like a Commie rat, you're going to get flattened against a mountain by a snowplow. That's America.* But even as he thought it, he was shouting, "Look out!" The man jerked the wheel in terror. The car slid sideways and the plowblade came flying down toward them like a wolf's-head. The inside of the car was full of rushing light. He threw his hands up, trying to protect his head as they went into the collision.

3

He woke up lying on his back on the highway, some kind of blanket thrown over him. The car stood on one corner, wheels up, leaning against the snowbank, one headlight shooting up into the sky, every detail of the car unnaturally sharp under the blinding headlights of the plow. The radio was still playing. All around the car there were bits of glass, glittering like diamonds. In his head there was a steady mumble, like the mumble of the train wheels, and a suggestion of voices. Six feet away from him, in the middle of the road, a man in thick goggles and a cap that hid all but his goggles and chin was bending over a body, looking at papers from a wallet. Willard closed his eyes again, concentrating on the hardness of the ice beneath him, the pleasant cold coming through his clothes, the sharp wet-wool smell of the blanket. He could feel snowflakes landing on his eyebrows and lashes. He couldn't remember having felt delicate sensations with such force since his early childhood: It was as if his body had grown very large, as large as the night, and calm. He could still hear the murmuring voices. They were more insistent now, carrying intelligible words and phrases, stubbornly assaulting his pleasant calm as if from somewhere outside it. At last, realizing what really he had known for some time—that there were people standing over him—he opened his eyes again. His vision was not as clear this time as it had been before. Dust of snow blew along the road, rising out of the road like fire, obscuring the figures of the two men. There was another car now, bright lights facing the lights of the snowplow, closing him in. The men were troopers.

One of them was bending down to him, more like a machine than like a man, no feature showing but the flat impersonal mouth and the courthouse chin. "This one's waking up," he said. His voice was metallic, like the voice of Superman on the radio. He said, "Are you hurt?"

"I think I'm all right," he said. "A little headache." When he sat up the headache was suddenly ferocious, and his stomach was full of a flat gray pain. He thought of lying down again but decided not to. He leaned on his arms.

"Take your time," the trooper said.

The body on the road was wrapped in a thick gray cover. He was dead, then. *It's too bad,* he thought. *She's going to have a painful delivery. The front wheel's turned sideways, and there are always the pedals.* He stopped himself, frightened.

The trooper said, "You knew him?" His sheepskin glove pointed.

Willard nodded, then shook hs head. "He was giving me a lift. He said his name was Taylor."

"Where'd he pick you up?"

"Utica. I was coming home from school. I came to Utica by train."

Behind the goggles he was taking it down, maybe to write up later, inside his warm car. "Where were you heading?"

"New Carthage. That's where my parents live." He thought of asking how far they'd gotten.

The trooper said, "Can you make it to the car?"

He got up, the trooper helping him, and found that his legs still worked. Inside the car it was so hot he could hardly breathe, or so it seemed at first. The radio was going. The two troopers stood outside the door, talking, and then after a while they carried something past the window and put it in the trunk. They got into the car and the one who was driving lifted the radio receiver. "We're bringing back the body," he said. "No

point sending them out in this." Then he nosed the
car around between the snowbanks to head back the
way he'd come. The snowplow came behind him.
Willard closed his eyes and instantly the plow was
bearing down on them again, the lights swift and blinding. In the front seat, one of the troópers said something and the other one laughed.

The State Police Post was a converted farmhouse,
set back from the road, with sheds like chicken houses
behind, for the cars. (Most of this he saw later, after
the sun had come up and the storm was over: white
drifts stretching away toward the mountains and
mounded up on the shed roofs and the branches of
trees, so bright you could only glance at it. Icicles hung
from the eaves of the shed and beside the window
where he stood, the remains of some earlier storm.
The world was hushed and beautiful, and also terrible
in its emptiness, that morning; but that was later.
While it was still dark he saw only the room where
they put him to wait.) The room was dim, vaguely
like the waiting room of a smalltown dentist's office at
night. A desk, a calendar, a couple of lamps, nothing
much more. Over the window on the outside there was
a kind of grate—not bars, exactly, more like a heavy-
duty cyclone fence. Beyond the closed door he could
hear them talking from time to time, now and then a
voice on the radio, the click of a typewriter. He lay
on the cool green leather couch sometimes dozing,
sometimes listening. He went through the conversation
with the florist, the storm, the accident again and again,
as though his mind could not get free of it. There was
a doctor coming to check him, they said. That was
strange. He'd have thought they'd have taken him
directly to a hospital somewhere, if they thought there
might really be anything wrong. But no use thinking.
For the moment he was caught in the enormous web
of their inscrutable efficiency. Police system hung in
the air all around him, neither friendly nor unfriendly,

merely systematic: The radio in the next room barked and sputtered from time to time—the whole state on a party line, the sheafs of papers in the shabby gray files available in seconds to a trooper sitting at Niagara. Still he was seeing the snowplow bearing down on them, the body in the road, the troopers' muffled figures passing the car window, carrying something. One of them came in and asked him if he wanted coffee—his face not unfriendly (weak-chinned, dull-eyed) but as impersonal as the goggled faces on the highway—and after a long time he brought it to him in a thick, cheap restaurant cup. "I lost my billfold," Willard said. The man looked at him for what seemed two full seconds, and for the first time Willard wondered how he could have lost the billfold from his hip pocket, with his overcoat on over it. He said, "Am I being held for something?" The man said, "I guess they want a doctor to look you over."

It was hours later (the sky light now and the wind finished) that the doctor came. With him there was a huge, red-headed man with tiny, somewhat slanted eyes, wearing an overcoat. The red-headed man sat down at the desk and smoked a coal-black pipe while the doctor thumped Willard's chest and pressed his fingers into his abdomen. The two of them left ten minutes later, hardly having said three words, and twenty minutes after that the red-headed man came back. He sat down and heaved one foot up on the desk. "So you're a student," he said. When he smiled his eyes and teeth made him look like a fox. He relit the pipe.

Willard nodded.

"You're lucky to be alive," the man said.

"I guess that's right."

He shook his head, blowing smoke past the pipe bowl, picking up a sheaf of papers. "It must be because of your falling against him. His body was a kind of cushion. It wouldn't be so surprising if you'd been asleep."

Willard looked at him, but he was reading, paying no attention. "What do you mean?"

"Surprising you didn't get killed," he said. "When you're asleep your body's relaxed." He turned the page. He said then, "Strange neither of you saw it."

He nodded. "It's like I told the man who's here at night," he began. His blood went cold. He'd told the other one he was asleep when it happened.

The red-headed man was poking at his pipe with an unbent paper clip, scowling into the dark of the bowl as if paying no attention to what Willard was saying. But he said, "The sergeant with the crew cut?" He looked up to catch Willard's frightened nod. He too nodded, immensely satisfied with himself. "That's Tom Widdley." He stuffed the pipe again and got it going, and for a long time he just sat smoking, looking with pleasure at the smoke as it went up.

Willard said, "Is it all right if I leave? I've been up most of the night, and I've told you all I can."

"About all, yes," the man said, only his tone odd, his face as casual as ever. Then he said, "Certainly, certainly." He made a move to get up but paused, as if intending to hold him only a moment longer, and this merely from curiosity. "How come there was no one at the station to meet you in Utica?"

"I forgot to wire ahead."

He looked surprised. "Really?"

"I'm absentminded. I do things like that a lot."

Again the man took the pipe from between his teeth and poked it with the paper clip. He asked abruptly, "Where do you live?"

For an instant he couldn't remember. He said then, "My dad's place, you mean? A little ways outside New Carthage. Rockwater Road."

The man did get up, this time. "Well, I'll have one

of the boys drive you over. It's not all that far, and we've held you up long enough."

At the desk in front they had his billfold. He glanced in automatically to see that the money was there. It was. Everything else was there too—the bookstore credit card, social security card, Norma's picture. The credit card was in the wrong plastic window.

He said, surprising himself, feeling his neck going red as he spoke, "You found the money wasn't stolen?"

The red-headed man looked at him quizzically.

"When you checked the serial numbers, I mean."

The man laughed, harmlessly foxy. "Everything ship-shape." He put his hand sociably on Willard's shoulder. "Beware of those headshrinkers' daughters."

It wasn't until he was out in the car, waiting while the trooper checked out from the office, that Willard began to sweat.

4

No CREDIT, the sign at Llewellyn's said; and on the cash register a smaller sign: CASH IS KING. On the radio in the living quarters behind the store there was more Christmas music playing, a chorus this time. Children. He stood at the counter waiting for old man Llewellyn to come limping in. He'd be here pretty soon, he'd heard the bell over the door. He'd still be able to hear that bell when he was a hundred and four and deaf as a post.

The store smelled of malt and oiled wooden floor. The old man stocked everything a Catskills farmer could need—groceries and kitchen utensils and liquor in front; in back coal oil, nails, binder twine, Surge milking-machine parts, spark-plugs, lead and spun-glass pipe, rope, harness leather, three-legged stools; a few odds and ends for tourists, too—fishing rods, salmon eggs, shotguns. Willard Freund's memories were sharper here even than in his father's house. It was where they would come after swimming or after they'd bicycled to Slater for a show, he and Junior Rich and Billy Cooper, when they were kids.

He listened absently to the music. *Deck the Halls.* His mother had said, "We're so glad we could have snow for you, Willard. Christmas is always so nice when there's snow." His father had spent the morning digging out the tractor where it had slipped off the driveway into the lawn and gone in above the tires. "Eleanor, where's that coffee?" he'd said, and at once her hands had started shaking and her mouth had gone into the tic. The old man was furious that Willard had made it home alone, without any help from him. Willard had been furious in return, and yet, well as he knew what was happening, he had found himself slipping into the old sense of unatoneable guilt, the same crazy guilt he would feel as a child when his father made him work on the farm for nothing, when he might have earned good money in Slater, and his farmwork wasn't up to the old man's mark. *Nicked in the balls,* he'd thought again, and he'd clenched his fists; and when his mother looked grieved he felt guilty for hating his father too. And then after his father had gone, heading out for chores where Willard too should go, his mother had said, "Willard, why don't you drop in on Henry and Callie? You were always so fond of Henry, before. They've got the sweetest little boy." He'd said, "Mother, I just don't feel like it. Quit asking." "I've never seen you so upset," she said. "It's that accident. You just need to stop thinking about it, Son."

And so as soon as he could he'd gotten out of there. He'd walked the three miles into town—the macadam thawed now, the weather warm as April, the smell of melting snow an excitement in his chest. And all the way he'd been remembering things—the day he and his father had pulled down the chicken house, hooking onto the corner of it with the log-chain and driving away on the Caterpillar tractor. When the chicken house wall came down, towering over their heads a minute and then smashing to the dirt six feet behind them, dry chicken shit flying, his father had yelled out, "*There* you go!" He'd been as proud as hell that he'd thought of doing it with the tractor and chain, and Willard had been proud for him. Another time his father had rebuilt an old Case combine, welding on wheels six feet to each side: They were the only people in the county that could combine the fields on the mountainsides, and the whole job, combine included, had only cost two hundred dollars because his father had picked up the stuff from people who didn't know how to make use of it. When old Fred Covert saw what they'd done with the combine he'd sold them, he could hardly hide his fury. (Maybe it was true that the dead man had really been interested in flowers, had really liked talking to mothers of people who were graduating from the sixth grade.) Out by the big gray barn his father had two young Dobermans on chains. When dark came he would let them loose, and if a stranger came close to that barn they would tear out his windpipe.

He heard the bell over the door clink behind him, and he glanced around his shoulder. Instantly he felt blood rushing into his head. She stood in the doorway, bending over the child, encouraging him to come in. She had a farmer's red handkerchief tied around her hair and a sheepskin coat much too large for her. *Henry's*, he thought. "Come *on*, Jimmy," she was saying, and her voice was beautiful and painful to him. He'd forgotten she had that country whine, a voice no more musical than the rasp of a saw but, for all that, shockingly sweet, at least to him. She'd gotten fatter, and in a single motion of his mind he knew her ugly and beautiful. Her legs were winter-raw and muscular, her arms as hard as the arms of a man; her skirt had been washed too many times, and the slip showed gray. He thought fleetingly, absurdly, of hiding. And then her head came up and she was perfectly still, looking at him. As if without knowing she was doing it, she stepped in front of the child.

"Hi," Willard said.

"Hello, Willard." Her voice was cool, countryish, polite, and he knew in a surge of panic that she hated him.

He looked at the child peeking from behind her legs. He was beautiful—blond and dirty-faced, in patched and faded jeans that buttoned between the legs. Tears filled Willard's eyes, blurring his vision so badly he could only make out the outlines of their figures.

He said, "I'm glad to see you, Callie."

She could hear the catch in his voice; she knew well enough how it was for him, seeing his own son. She said nothing, merely looking at him. Then, amazingly, she smiled. "It's nice to see you, too, Willard."

"Candy!" the child said, rather sternly, fists doubled.

Callie laughed, threw Willard a helpless look. Then she bent down to the child again. "Come on, Jimmy," she said, "Mommy's in a hurry."

Then old man Llewellyn was there, shouting at them, red-faced and white-haired as a Millerite prophet. "Beautiful morning! Step right up, there! What'll it be this beautiful morning? Satisfaction guaranteed!"

Callie and the child disappeared behind the middle grocery shelf.

"Pack of Old Golds," he said. "Regular." His knees were shaky.

When he went out on the porch he saw Henry Soames sitting in his car, the flesh sagging from around his eyes, his skin unhealthy gray. He was huge and old as the mountains, and as patient. Their eyes met, but Henry Soames showed no sign of recognition, merely looked puzzled, reminded of something.

We were friends, Willard thought. *We used to talk half the night sometimes. I worked on my goddam jitney in your garage.*

He thought of the red-headed policeman, smiling, pretending to listen to nothing he said, and a chill went down his back. He thought of waving, as if noticing Henry only now. But it was too late. He went down the steps and walked across the road, opening the cigarettes as he walked. He could feel the old man's puzzled eyes on him, watching.

Shit passing in the night, he thought. He lit a cigarette, and it tasted worse than most.

Then, behind him, Henry called, *"Willard?"*

He froze, scared sick, his knees shaky. As soon as he was able, he dropped the cigarette and turned around. Henry was half out of the car, grinning, calling *"Willard, you devil!"* Callie and James were on Llewellyn's porch, watching like small, gentle statues from a church.

With more self-control than he'd have thought he could muster, Willard raised his arm and waved and then, without thinking, smiled at them. And then—who knows why?—he turned his back and began to run, ashamed of doing it even as he did it but also full of crazy joy. They'd forgiven him. Of course! Why shouldn't they? Wouldn't even he—even Norma, in fact—have done the same? He kept running, bringing his feet down hard on the road's packed-tight snow. When he was over the hill and around the bend, protected from Henry Soames' eyes by trees, he slowed down to a walk and thought, still smiling, "How absurd, all these years! A foolish nightmare, a sad, shoddy dream out of Plato's cave!" The day was bright, surprisingly warm, and the three-mile walk ahead of him seemed nothing. He crossed the bridge, hardly noticing, hurrying. "I was insane," he thought, startled. "It's as simple as that! I must remember, from now on. Whatever happens, I must remember." It came to him that he'd promised his mother he'd pick up something if he stopped at Llewellyn's. Was it baking soda?

And now, behind him, he heard Henry Soames' car coming noisily after him. They'd insist on giving him a ride, of course. There was no escape, nowhere to hide —if he ran for the woods they'd see him and think he was crazy. Willard laughed, blushing till his cheeks were like a girl's, then turned and flung up his arms in submission. The Ford came beside him, clanking and growling like the hound of heaven.

"Willard, you old son-of-a-*gun*," said Henry Soames.

VIII

THE
GRAVE

1

All morning there had been a gray truck parked in the cemetery on the mountainside across and a little down from where they hunted, and fifteen feet this side of the truck two men were digging a grave. Henry Soames wondered about it from time to time, when he sat resting for a minute on a rock or when he stood helping his boy with the rifle. They were burying someone he knew, most likely—only people from close around used the cemetery—but he couldn't think who it would be. Henry was always one of the first to hear about births and deaths, partly because of his running the diner (as he still sometimes called it, though the big sign in front of the new building said RESTAURANT, and it was no longer the Stop-Off but The Maples, which was more elegant, Callie said), but mainly because Henry Soames was the kind of man he was, interested as a spinster aunt in the life of the whole county and a partisan. Maybe it was Charley Benson's mother, it came to him after a while, and, not realizing he was doing it, he took off his cap and held it over his stomach a minute, thinking and looking at the ground. She was ninety-seven, and likely to go at any time. But it was odd that he hadn't heard. Maybe on the way back home he and Jimmy would cross over to where they were digging and find out for sure.

They were regular, hired grave-diggers, not relatives or friends of the family: They had a shade-canvas up, and they worked slowly and steadily. Over their heads the sky was bright blue, like the middle of summer, with a long, pale mare's-tail off to the west, and the maples, exploding to red now, were as motionless as trees in a dream. The shade under the trees looked cool and comfortable (here in the open it was hot as a day in the middle of August) and he thought of the creek over there, out of sight from where he stood, and the thought made him thirsty. The tombstones would be smooth and comfortable, some of them, for sitting on.

Jimmy seemed not to have noticed the truck, or at any rate he hadn't grown curious yet. A boy's curiosity took time to move out from wherever he happened to be standing, if where he was was unfamiliar. He wanted to know why the old barbwire fence was here, where as far as a four-year-old boy could see there had never been anything but stiff gray weeds and berry bushes and big rounded rocks. (There'd been a house here, years ago, a place where three old-maid sisters had lived, named Riddle. You could still find the chimney, down under the woodbine and burdocks, if you looked, and you could see where the road had been, and three of the stone supports of the smokehouse. There was one old pear tree, dead and white and brittle as bone, standing all by itself in the brambles like a stubborn old Baptist waiting for the Judgment.) The boy wanted to turn over every old stick or flat stone they found crawling things underneath. Henry would stand patiently or would sit, if there was a stump handy, giving his son his way. It was good for a boy to look things over. And then, too, Henry could use the rests. As it was he was farther from home than Doc Cathey approved of his going. He could look behind him and see his house and restaurant a half-mile down, way to the right of the cemetery, over by the highway: the house a little white box in the shade of maples and three pine trees scraggly with age, no grass around it to speak of, cinders instead for the trucks to park on—in front of the house and off to the left the red walls and the black roof of the restaurant. There was only one car there now, a Volkswagen; no one he knew.

He looked over at the grave-diggers again and shook his head.

Then Henry forgot about the cemetery for a while. In spite of the noise they'd been making shooting at cans and sticks, earlier, a rabbit walked right out in front of them, and Henry fired at it. The rabbit flipped when the bullet hit and flopped around in a half-circle, dead already, and lay still. They went to pick it up.

2

Any other time he might have picked it up at once, almost without looking at it, and might have stuffed it into his canvas bag and might have forgotten about it. But the boy hadn't seen a dead rabbit before—hadn't seen anything dead, in fact, as far as Henry Soames knew, except maybe flies—and so Henry stood with the rifle clamped tightly under his right elbow, barrel out, pointing off to the right, away from the boy, and held the rabbit on his open left hand for the boy to see and touch. He watched the boy's face and for an instant he felt himself slipping away again into that sense that he stood outside time, involved and yet dispassionate, like a man looking at far-off mountains, or like Henry Soames' father sitting motionless and huge on a broad stump, watching chipmunks or listening to the brook move down through the glen, rattling away forever, down and down. Or as Henry himself sat nowadays, more and more, thinking thoughts that had never before occurred to him, surprised and bemused at the way things fit together. He saw the boy's face as though it had nothing to do with himself, a face in an old, old photograph. His hair was the color of clean old straw, white almost, but with yellow glints and dust-gray shadows. It needed cutting; that was the way his mother liked it. His blue eyes had a pink cast, as they always did when the light was strong, and his eyebrows, white against the flush of his face, lifted up and out like wings. He stood bent forward, his trousers halfway down his hips, his hands behind his back in one of those old-man poses he was always getting into, and he looked at the rabbit with curiosity and no distaste. For him, too, the sun had momentarily paused, if it ever noticeably moved in a four-year-old's world. At last, tentatively, he touched the soft, short fur on the back, gray-brown fur speckled with a pure white (the rabbit was young), and stroked from the tips of the ears to the turned-down tail. The bullet had bit in the neck, snapping it clean, and the head lay now at an angle not natural in life, as though the back of the head rose straight from the shoulders, as if in ecstasy. There was very little blood: a stain around what seemed the insignificant wound on the side of the neck.

"He's killed, isn't he?" Jimmy said.

Henry nodded.

"Are you going to shoot him again?" Now a hint of distaste did come, but mainly the boy was curious.

"No point in shooting things after they're dead," Henry said.

The boy continued to move his hand very gently on the fur, his question not fully answered, Henry knew, because really it had nothing to do with shooting: a question about what death was, how a thing so unreasonable could be tamed, made to fit in a world of waterbugs, trees, mountains, customers at the restaurant. He said, "Why?"

"A thing can only die once," Henry said. "Things live and then they die."

He looked past the boy at the pine woods that began some fifty feet up the slope from where they stood, beyond where the Riddle place used to stand before it burned. It was utterly still in there and dark as a church. Needles on the ground kept out all growth, and wherever one entered, long, gloomy aisles radiated out straight and clean. The CCC boys had planted the trees in 1935 or so. He could remember coming here with his father to watch them work. The Riddles' place had been gone even then. His father would sit on a rock biting the sweet white tips off timothy shoots and he would chirp at sparrows or meadowlarks as though he were one of them and fond of gossip. Henry had come here two, three times when he'd first found out he was going to die. Self-consciously, sentimentally (as he'd come to see), he would slip into his father's poses: He would lean his gun against a stump and lower his great, loose body down beside the gun, plant his elbows on his knees, tip his cap back and stare in at the gloomy aisles that led away to the darkness farther in. But he'd gone on living, taking his pills when he needed them, and gradually he'd gotten used to it, and it had come to him that it wasn't the same. The gloomy aisles weren't there yet when his father had come, it was spindly new trees he'd looked at, and blowing grasses and birds. If he looked he could see the cemetery, across from here, the narrow gray stones in the shade of the maples and beeches there, but it wasn't that that had drawn his attention. If he ever looked there, he saw it with the same calm, like a man who'd been married to all that for fifty years. Though Henry couldn't have predicted it—you had to get to that point yourself to know that somebody else had been there—he saw now that that was inevitable. Everything passes, the carved-out rocks by the brook proved it, and the excitement of fear was no more enduring than anything else. A bad heart was the beginning of wisdom.

"Look at his eyes," Jimmy said.

He nodded.

"They sort of squint, don't they? Why do they squint?"

"Because he's dead," he said.

(Callie's mother had said, "What do you *get* out of it, shooting defenseless rabbits?"

He'd shrugged, and Callie had said, "Now, Mother, don't you go butting into Henry's business."

"It keeps him from shooting Baptists," Callie's father had said. "He, he, he!" And Henry had said, a little righteously, as it seemed to him later, "I don't want to shoot Baptists. It's not that at all."

"Well, then you're a goddamn fool," Callie's father had said. He kept beer in the refrigerator, purely as an affront to her, and he could swear like a trooper. He was her cross, she said. But he'd prayed, the time Jimmy had gone into convulsions, and Henry had understood it, whether Callie could or not. There'd been nothing they could do, once they got him to the hospital. Jimmy had been not quite two. At first he'd had a crazy look in his eyes, a clouded look, like the look of an animal dying. Henry had reached into the crib for him, Callie's father looking over his shoulder (it was up at their place it had happened), and there'd been that look in Jimmy's eyes, his face white in the dark room, and Jimmy had drawn back in terror, not knowing his own father; and then when Henry had him in his arms, Jimmy's eyes had rolled up and he'd gone stiff all over, and Callie's father had said "Holy God!" and on the way to the hospital he'd started to pray, with Callie's mother sitting stiff as a board beside him, holding the baby, keeping his teeth apart with her bare fingers, and Callie was glaring through the windshield like a madwoman, almost more furious at her father than scared for Jimmy—and that too was natural, it seemed to Henry, even good; yes. He'd driven like hell was after them and it was a wonder they'd any of them made it.)

But now the boy had lost all interest in the rabbit, and Henry thought, *Well, all right, then; everything in its time*. He dropped the rabbit in the bag.

The boy said, "What are they doing over there?"

Henry looked over where the boy was pointing. There was a car parked in back of the truck now, and a woman stood watching the grave-diggers. They were strangers, city people from their looks. The man had on a suit and hat, and the woman had on a gray coat and a hat with flowers in it. Both of them were old.

"They're digging a grave," Henry said, taking off his cap again, as if absentmindedly.

"No they're not," Jimmy said, "they're digging somebody up."

"Mmm," Henry said. Hardly noticing, he pulled up Jimmy's trousers and tightened the belt. After a minute he took the boy's hand and they started down.

"There's four of them," Jimmy said. "One, two, three, four."

"Mmm," Henry said. He stopped a minute to rest, then began again.

3

The world had changed for Henry Soames because little by little he had come to see it less as a yarn told after dinner, with all the relatives sitting around, and more as a kind of church service—communion, say, or a wedding. The change had in a way begun when they'd built The Maples. He'd felt a kind of awe, watching the place go up: not only awe at the looks of it (a gabled building like an old-fashioned Catskills barn, twice the size of Henry's old diner, with planter-boxes inside and out, and twelve tables, and a fireplace at one end), but awe, too, at what his wife had done to him, scooping up his old life like wet clay and making it over into her own image, and awe at how easily she managed it all and how easily, even gladly, he had accepted it, in the end. It was as if it was something he'd been thinking all along and had never quite dared —though God knew it wasn't. Her ideas had given him the willies, set in his ways as he'd been by then, and they'd probably have given him the willies even if she'd caught him younger; but he'd found there was no stopping her: She was hard as nails and mean as her mother when there was something she had to have. So he'd given in, and when he'd done it, not just in words but totally, freely choosing what he couldn't prevent, he'd felt a sudden joy, as though the room had grown wider all at once (which by that time as a matter of fact it had), or as if he'd finally shoved in the clutch on the way down a long straight hill it was no use resisting. He'd stood out by the road with Jimmy, watching the carpenters work and after that the nurserymen and the painters (all this a year ago now), and he'd given up all thought of the mortgage and whether the truckers would still pull in, and he'd mused like a man only half-awake on how it had all come about, the long train of trivial accidents, affirmed one by one, that made a man's life what it happened to become. It was a good life, he had to admit it, now that he could look at it, with nothing to do from morning to night but keep an eye on little Jimmy and from time to time catch up their books. (Callie was no good at the bookkeeping. The figures had a will as stubborn as her own: Twos, fours, sixes were as intransigently twos, fours, and sixes as stones were stones. She could no more juggle the bills than juggle dead tamaracks, and she would cry, and Henry would take over, and he'd have it all straightened out—as well as it could be—in no time.) He'd grown mystical, or, as Callie said, odd. He had no words for his thoughts; the very separateness of words was contrary to what he seemed to know. It began, perhaps, with his thought of what marrying Callie had done to him; if she'd made him into her own image it was nevertheless her own image discovered—for the first time to her as well as to him —in *him*: Henry Soames as he might, through her, become. Once he had fairly tested it, he knew beyond any shadow of doubt that the new life she had shaped was his own, it fit him the way his father's old coat had one day, to his surprise, fit him, and from that moment on he didn't just wear the new life, he owned it. He felt like a man who'd been born again, made into something entirely new, and the idea that such a thing could happen had startled him, and he'd seized on it, turning it over and over in his mind the way you turn over a hundred-dollar bill. But the new life he'd found in himself had no settled meaning yet: It was all a-shimmer and vague, like a dream. It lacked the solid reality that would come when he'd lived it long enough to know it had something in common with the old— long tedious hours in the middle of winter when no one came in, days when Callie was short-tempered and Jimmy had a devil in him.

With the passing of time he became in reality what he was, his vision not something apart from the world but the world itself transmuted. He'd hired Billy Hartman by this time, so he could rest himself more, at Doc Cathey's insistence, and he never served customers himself now except on special occasions—a birthday, say, or a wedding. His new detachment encouraged the mystical drift of his thoughts. He would sit with Jimmy eating supper and watching Callie at the cash register, everything around her a-glitter—the glass on the counter, the green and silver mint wrappers, the cellophane on the twenty-five-cent cigars, the glossy knotty pine wall behind her, with the picture of the pheasant on it—and Callie there in the center of it all like a candle—and he would be so moved, all at once, his eyes would fill. He was proud of her, and had a right to be proud, because she too had been changed. She would have been beautiful in any case, one way or another,

Henry knew, but marrying him she had found out possibilities not only in him but in herself as well that she might never have found some other way. She never spoke of loving him but sometimes when they locked up the restaurant together she would hold his hand, or when he sat holding Jimmy, reading to him, she would pat the bald spot on his head. And so like a man half-asleep he thought about marriage, which was the same thing as love or magic or anything else he could think of (he could no more distinguish between what was happening from day to day between Callie and himself and what happened between himself and his son than he could tell the difference, except in degrees, between those and the way the restaurant changed him and he, in turn, the restaurant), and he knew, not in words, that it was true, as Emmet Slocum had said once, that people sometimes killed themselves because of the weather but nevertheless they killed themselves by choice.

So it was that Henry Soames had discovered the holiness of things (his father's phrase), the idea of magical change. And listening to Callie's mother talk he began to see, he thought, why people were religious. She seemed to know nothing of holiness, Callie's mother, no more than the preacher at Salem Baptist seemed to know; but listening to her it came to him that the words she bandied about made a kind of sense. She would sit at the piano, up at her place on a Sunday afternoon, and would sing old hymns in her shrill, hard voice, and Henry would sit over by the window in the corner, staring vaguely at the African violets by the lace curtains on the window seat, patting the knee of the child in his lap, and it would come to him that the whole thing might be true. *In whisp'ring grass I hear him pass.* Maybe he'd been wrong; maybe they'd discovered the same thing he'd discovered and differed from him only in trying to talk about it: a vision of dust succinct with spirit, God inside wasps, oak trees, people, chickens walking in the yard. Maybe like him they had come to feel kindly toward old clothes, farm-women's wrinkled elbows, the foolishness of young people, expensive suits, even the endless political talk at the GLF down in Slater. And if he was wrong, he was wrong too to keep himself apart from them: What religion was was a kind of formal acting-out of what every human being felt, vague fears over things he could do nothing about, vague joys over things only partly his doing—the idea of holiness. So one day he had taken Jimmy to the Presbyterian Church in Slater.

It was the church where Henry had gone with his mother as a child. He'd sent Jimmy up to the Sunday School and then had walked around to the front and started in himself to listen to the service. There were people on the steps, not a soul he knew, mostly young or middle-aged, one old, old man—all beautiful as lovers, as it seemed to him, in their Sunday clothes, and all happy-looking, laughing, talking—so happy he thought they must really know what he'd guessed they knew, or not knew, felt: And he had felt humble, ashamed of his monstrous bulk and remoteness, and had crossed the street to look at the washing machines in the Salway Store window until they'd gone in. Then, steeling himself, he crossed again quickly. When he went from the sunlit street to the foyer it was so dark at first he could barely see, but even so he noticed at once a frail, coy-looking elderly woman in a dark blue dress, white hat, white gloves, and he knew by instinct that the woman was there to greet him. His heart leaped, and he snapped his fingers as if he'd just remembered something and turned on his heel and fled back into the light.

For maybe fifteen minutes he walked up and down on the sidewalk, sometimes looking at the maple trees on the church lawn, the gray stone walls, the arched windows, sometimes studying the washing machines, his blood all the while in such agitation he was afraid he might have an attack. When he got up his courage to try it again the woman was gone and the foyer was empty except for the ushers. He could hear the minister praying inside. The ushers left him to himself, and he went to the table where pamphlets were laid out. He picked up the first one that caught his eye, *Predestination?* in bright red on yellow, and carried it over to the door to leaf through it. It upset him. According to the pamphlet all Christians believed in Predestination, works were of no account whatever (What is human righteousness beside the perfect righteousness of God? it said), and the whole secret was to renounce the arrogant wish for free will and joyfully accept God's Plan. When he finished reading his hands were shaking. It wasn't so much that he disagreed; he couldn't tell whether he agreed or not. He minded the fact that they'd spelled it out: It was not what he wanted, what he wanted was—God knew. "Idealists," his father would have said: ministers, or the New York State troopers, or Welshmen who ran their families like the army. And then a new thought had come to him. Surely there weren't ten people in there who knew Predestination from a turnip. They accepted whatever the minister said, and forgot about it, and carried away a vague feeling that it was better to be good than bad, unselfish than selfish, if a man could keep his mind on it, and that somehow things made sense—like the hymn they were singing now, "Faith of our Fathers," whatever that was, not that it mattered, finally, in the least. And he felt unworthy to go where they were worshipping, and he left again to go stand humbly by the washing machines, waiting for Jimmy.

That afternoon he'd gone hunting again, his fat hands loving on the shotgun, and had shot three squirrels that seemed to him to dance like fire on the limbs. He became what he was, with a gun in his hands: doom and doomed and serene.

They reached the bottom of the slope and rested

awhile. Henry took one of his pills, and Jimmy held the gun for him, making a show of holding it very carefully, the way Henry had taught him, the barrel aimed away and toward the ground. The earth was softer here and the grass less brittle, thick and rich yellow-green, shaded by beeches. There was a horse's skull here somewhere, but he couldn't think where. Hunting through the grass with his foot, he found a pair of ladies' underpants, and he covered them up again quickly, embarrassed. They started up the hill. Above them, among the tombstones, the old man and the old woman stood solemn and silent, watching them come near.

4

They were digging up the body of their son. He'd died at fourteen, fifty years ago, and at that time they'd lived around these parts. Now they lived in Rochester, and since they were getting on in years, coming to the time when they had to take some thought about their final rest, they'd decided to move him to where they were going, a plot in a very nice cemetery on a hillside overlooking the Genesee. The woman was ninety-two, the man eighty-seven; their clothes hung on them like clothes on hangers. Inside his hat, and hanging down over his ears, the man had burdock leaves, and under the burdock leaves thick white hair. He had a brown, unadorned cane with a rubber tip. His skin was white as paper, with splotches on it, and he had white-blue eyes that bulged in his head like the eyes of a skittish horse. He made you think of a preacher, one of the old-timers, not the kind that cowered when he came to your door. The woman looked like a small, addled witch—sharp features, tiny black eyes that glinted like needles, a hundred thousand dirty-looking wrinkles from her collarbone to her hairline. She looked as if she had no water left in all her body, but the rims of her eyes were red. Jimmy clung with one hand to Henry's belt and watched them.

"I tell Walt it don't much matter where he lays," the woman said, "his soul's in Glory." She stood sideways to Henry, her big-knuckled hands folded two inches or so below her chin, and she spoke out of the side of her mouth, her eyes fixed, as if intently, on the ground.

"Mmm," Henry said, nodding, thinking about it.

The old man waved at her as if to hit her. "Oh, shut up," he said. Then, to Henry: "She's crazy. Always has been."

"Walt don't believe in God," the old woman said. She smiled, sly, still looking at the ground.

Jimmy leaned forward to look around Henry at the grave-diggers. Henry put his hand on the boy's head, glad to have an excuse to make no comment.

"He's dead and rotten," the old man said. He jerked his arm, with his cane dangling from the end of it, in the general direction of the grave. Again, however incongruously, he had the look of a hell-fire preacher. He said, "Now, you shut up."

Henry cleared his throat, preparing to leave. "Well —" he said. He glanced over at the grave-diggers. One of the two men was down in the hole, throwing the dirt up—all you could see of him now was his hat. The other man stood at one corner, poking with a crowbar. Beyond them the hillside sloped away in sunlight and shadow, from thick glossy headstones to the taller, narrower markers over in the older section past the statue of the Kunzmuller girl and the Kendall crypt with pine trees around it, and down to the creek, where the woods began. The shadow of a crow swept over the grass and out of sight in the trees, incredibly swift.

Jimmy left Henry's side now and walked a few feet toward the grave. He stood with his hands behind his back and watched.

"Fine boy you got there," the old man yelled.

"Yes, he is," Henry said, grinning.

"The Lord giveth and the Lord taketh away," the old woman said. She separated her hands for a minute, and the fingers shook.

Henry rubbed his nose and said nothing.

"She's crazy," the old man said.

"I believe in the resurrected Lord," she said.

Henry looked away, over in the direction of the old people's car. It was an old green Hudson, as big and square as a truck. It had a stubborn look, a kind of solid inflexibility that was vaguely impressive. He wondered how people as old as they were could get it to go around corners. He said, "I guess we'd better be getting on home." He took a step toward Jimmy, but the old man raised his arm.

"My boy," he said, then hesitated a moment. "—was fourteen."

"It's a shame," Henry said—the only thing he could think of to say, since any of the usual things one said might set the old man off. He looked at the ground, embarrassed, shaking his head and vaguely reaching for his cap.

"Just fourteen years old," the old man said. He raised his arms again. "I loved that boy—" Again he hesitated, hunting for words, or maybe hunting for some lost emotion, but whatever he was after it wouldn't come and he dropped his arm and said, "Hmph." The old woman was weeping. The old man patted her arm, but absently, staring past her, still hunting.

"We kept his room just like it was," the old woman said. She nodded as if someone else had said it, and rubbed her eyes with her coatsleeve, her fingers shaking.

The old man nodded too. "But then we moved."

"Life goes on," Henry said sadly, and the words filled him with a pleasant sense of grief. He thought of his own approaching death, how Callie and Jimmy would be heartbroken for a while, as he'd been heartbroken when his father died, but would after a while forget a little, turn back to the world of the living, as was right. And if it were Callie that died? or Jimmy? The question startled him, as if someone standing behind him had asked it, and instantly he put it from his mind. He glanced a little nervously at Jimmy, who'd moved closer to watch the digging.

"You never forget," the old man said.

"Never!" the old woman said sharply, suddenly meeting Henry's eyes. "When we meet him in Glory—"

The old man said, "Shut up."

For a full minute nobody spoke, there was only the rhythmical scrape of the shovel and the thump of the dirt as it fell beside the grave. Far away there was a tractor plowing for winter wheat. The motor would dig in for a minute, then whir a second while the man slipped the clutch in, and then the motor would dig in again. It reminded him of something, vaguely.

"Love—" Henry began at last, philosophically, but he couldn't think how to finish. The old man was still patting the old woman's arm, and, noticing it, Henry Soames half-frowned, thinking something more that he couldn't quite get hold of. Tears were still running down the cracks in her face, and her hands were clenched together.

One of the grave-diggers said, "There she is." He said it as if to himself, but they all heard it, and the old man jumped, as if frightened, and touched his hat. A limp burdock leaf slipped down farther over one ear and he slapped at it, not knowing what it was. The old woman rolled her eyes toward the grave, her eyelids batting, and turned very slowly, reaching out for her husband's arm with one hand, tugging up the front of her coat with the other, her black mouth open. After a second Henry went to her other side to help her over the grass. Jimmy was right at the edge of the grave now, on hands and knees, looking down.

"You keep back, Jimmy," Henry called, but Jimmy pretended not to hear, and Henry let it go. They inched over the grass, the two old people bent forward stiffly, clinging to each other, both their mouths open now, sucking in air. The old man's head was shaking as the woman's hands had before, and at every step he ran his tongue over his lower lip. He leaned heavily on his cane, and the cane's rubber tip pushed down in the ground, interfering with the progress he couldn't have made without it. When they were within five or six feet of the place, the man with the crowbar said, "We've hit the box. She'll still be a while yet." They stopped, and the old man stood leaning on his cane with both hands, breathing hard and rolling his head.

"You ought to sit down," the old woman said.

He looked at her angrily but said nothing, still laboring for breath.

The old woman said, "We ought to left him lay."

"A family should keep together," the old man said. As soon as the words were out, a coughing fit came over him. Henry watched helplessly, the old woman leaning on his arm.

"Our Bobby was struck by lightning," the old woman said, meeting Henry's eyes again. "It was God's hand."

The old man was furious, but he went on coughing.

"I believe in the resurrected Lord," the old woman said again now, taking advantage of her husband's inability to speak. "Walt don't believe." She smiled. Then she said: "He was only fourteen."

"He's dead and rotten," the old man yelled, "it's the Law of Nature! Consider the lilies—" He coughed again, a thick, racking cough that threatened to turn him inside out.

"God forgive this poor sinner," the old woman said, grim, and the old man swung his cane at her but missed and jabbed it back in the ground just in time, thrown off balance.

"Here now," Henry said. He glanced over at Jimmy but he hadn't seen it, he was still looking down in the hole. He was lying on the ground now, his trousers low and his skin very white between his belt and the bottom of his T-shirt.

"Our only child," the old woman said, and all at once she was crying again. The old man reached out toward her and made a patting motion in the air. She said, "But we've never forgot him."

"Never!" the old man said.

She pressed her lips tight together, weeping, and the old man struggled painfully to her side, swearing at the cane as he came. They stood there leaning on each other, and Henry, free to move now, went over to stand beside where Jimmy lay at the head of the grave. Most of the top of the box was clear, and they'd dug out a two-inch slit of dirt around the sides to about halfway down the walls. The man down in the hole looked up at the man on top and nodded, and the man on top went over to the truck. He ground on the starter and got the truck going and backed it around to the side of the grave, and they unhooked the chains hanging down from the winch and lowered them into the hole. There was a rod that went between the two chain ends, just above the hooks, so when the hooks were clamped to the ends of the box the loops at each end of the rod held them tight, like tongs. When the man down in the hole had the rig on and the man on top had the winch turned so the chain was taut, the man below climbed out, helping himself up with the chain. Henry moved back a little, drawing Jimmy up on his knees and back with him.

The old woman said as if angrily, "We kept his room just like it was the day he died."

"But we had to move," the old man said. "The farm was played out, and I had to get some kind of work, so we moved to Rochester."

"We had relatives here," the old woman said.

The winch creaked, beginning to turn, and Jimmy kneeled with his hands on his knees, in the shadow of Henry's leg. The chains pulled tighter and the rear end of the truck went down a little, and one of the grave-diggers wet his lips and shouted something and the other one laughed and nodded. Then the box came out with a sucking sound and tilted, free of the grave sides now, threatening to roll sideways and spill the dead boy out, but it righted and kept coming till it hung a little above the level of Henry Soames' belt. The taller of the grave-diggers, the red-headed one, went around front and moved the truck a few feet forward, and when he came back they swung the box into the truckbed. The old man waved his arm. "Well, there it is," he said. He was excited and pleased as if he'd managed the whole thing himself. "See how easy they done it, Hessie?"

"Praise the Lord," she said, weeping. Immediately the old man scowled and flapped his arm at her, waving her off.

The men slid the long, dirt-caked box to the front of the truckbed and chained it in place and got down and went back to their shovels. They began filling the grave. The two old people went over, very slowly, to look at the box.

Jimmy said, "Is there a dead man inside?"

Henry nodded.

The old man was patting the side of the truck. "I loved that boy more—" he began, but he seemed to lose track.

"Can we see him?" Jimmy said.

Henry shook his head.

"Are *they* going to see him?"

"I don't know."

The old woman was crying, wringing her hands. "We've always loved you, Bobby."

The old man said, confused, "Shut up." Then, finally, as if with relief, he too was crying. He began to pat the old woman's arm.

Suddenly Jimmy laughed. "They're funny," he said.

Henry turned to look at him, frowning anxiously, and said quickly, "No they're not, Jimmy. When you grow up——"

The grave-digger with the red hair said, with a look of disgust, "Just pitiful, sonny." He hardly glanced up as he said it.

"That's not true," Henry said. He chewed his lip and stopped himself from saying more.

The grave-digger smiled to himself, wry, but Henry pretended not to see.

They went back to the tombstone near the front fender of the old peoples' car, where Henry had left the rifle and the canvas bag that held the rabbit. It was after noon and Callie would be worried. *I lost track of the time,* he thought. *I'm sorry.*

"Please, why can't I see?" Jimmy said.

"No," Henry said. "I already told you once."

"You never let me see anything." A whine this time.

The old people were crossing the grass again, leaning on each other, as always, seeming to make no progress.

"You don't like me," Jimmy said. He started to cry.

Henry clenched his jaws; but looking at the boy's face, seeing beyond any possible doubt that however trivial the cause, however ridiculous the words, the child's grief was perfectly real, the injustice terrible and never-to-be-forgotten, he bent down to him and said, "Now listen, Jimmy. I love you and you know it. Now quit that crying."

"Well *I* don't love *you*," Jimmy said, not looking at him, seeing what would happen.

Henry smiled sadly, reaching out to touch Jimmy's shoulder. "Poor dreamer," he said.

He was tired and it was a long way back. He thought how good it would be to lie down, only for a little while, and rest.